How had they c ...
together on the ...

Embarrassment and confusion coursed through Caitlin, causing her to shift her gaze hurriedly from Nick's passion-glazed eyes.

He gently took her hands in his as he stood, drawing her up to meet his tall frame. He kept his eyes on their joined hands, unable to relinquish her completely. He understood why she wouldn't raise her head and look at him, why her hands lay stiffly in his. He had overstepped the boundary, and she had every right to be angry.

Glancing up, Caitlin read guilt and remorse, along with an emotion she couldn't name, shadowed in Nick's eyes. Was he feeling as flustered as she was, or was he sorry that this had ever happened at all? His face displayed such intense emotions that she wondered if they had anything to do with his past, his life before she met him. Had he finally remembered something – or someone?

Dear Reader:

We at Silhouette are very excited to bring you a NEW reading Sensation. Look out for the six books which will appear in our new Silhouette Sensation series every month. These stories will have the high quality you have come to expect from Silhouette, and their varied and provocative plots will encourage you to explore the wonder of falling in love – again and again!

Emotions run high in these drama-filled novels. Greater sensual detail and an extra edge of realism intensify the hero and heroine's relationship so that you cannot help but be caught up in their every change of mood.

We hope you enjoy this new Sensation – and will go on to enjoy many more.

We would love to hear your comments about our new line and encourage you to write to us:

Jane Nicholls
Silhouette Books
PO Box 236
Thornton Road
Croydon
Surrey
CR9 3RU

ANN WILLIAMS
Devil in Disguise

Silhouette Sensation

First published in Great Britain in 1991 by Silhouette Books, Eton House, 18-24 Paradise Road, Richmond, Surrey TW9 1SR

© Peggy A. Myers 1989

Silhouette, Silhouette Sensation and Colophon are Trade Marks of Harlequin Enterprises B.V.

ISBN 0 373 58027 4

18 – 9101

Made and printed in Great Britain

ANN WILLIAMS

gave up her career as a nurse, then as the owner and proprietor of a bookstore, in order to pursue her writing on a full-time basis. *Devil in Disguise* is her first book, although she began writing for fun when she was only nine.

Ann was born and married in Indiana, but she now lives in Texas with her husband of twenty-three years and their four children. They consider themselves native Texans.

Reading, writing, crocheting, classical music and a good romantic movie are among her diverse loves. Her dream is to one day move to a cabin in the Carolina mountains with her husband and "write to my heart's content".

Chapter 1

God, it was hot! Though it was only late spring, she couldn't remember when it had last rained. It looked as though it was going to be one of *those* Texas summers.

Caitlin was working in her vegetable garden. It wouldn't be long before she'd have to get in touch with the agriculture teacher in town and find out how many summer helpers she could expect back this year. If not for them, she wouldn't be able to keep the ranch going.

Sitting back on her heels, rubbing at the sweat drenching her forehead and temples with the back of one grubby hand and only adding streaks of dirt to those already present, she looked hopelessly at the clear blue sky. Not a cloud in sight. The thought of the much-needed rain made her realize how parched her throat felt.

"Water."

Caitlin jumped, twisting around in surprise, one knee going down against the hard soil she'd been tilling.

Her first impression as she looked at him was that he bordered on the ludicrous: he looked like an out-of-date hippy. Dark, overlong hair, badly in need of washing, hung from a side part into his eyes. The lines of mouth and jaw were hidden by several days' growth of beard.

A filthy shirt of unbleached cotton hung over a pair of holey jeans—jeans with less color than the shirt, and far dirtier. A hole in the right knee extended from one seam to the other, exposing a large expanse of one hairy leg and a bony knee covered with a nasty, painful-looking scab.

Eyes continuing down, she noted dirty, mismatched, once-white sneakers, minus shoestrings, with several toes poking through. Her startled glance returned to his face as he spoke again.

"Water," he croaked, eyes sidestepping direct contact with hers. He waited motionlessly, shoulders slumped, head down, hands dangling at his sides.

"You want a drink?" she asked carefully. Though not a particularly nervous person, she was alone on the ranch, with her nearest neighbor a couple miles away, and he presented a less than reassuring picture, so she kept a cautious eye trained on him.

"Drink," he repeated, nodding slowly.

Caitlin stood and dusted off her jeans, eyeing him from beneath long lashes. He wouldn't meet her glance, but stood silently with his eyes trained on the ground at his feet. She wasn't afraid of him, but something about him bothered her. He appeared to be both more, and less, than the usual run-of-the mill drifter who occasionally found his way to the ranch looking for a few days' work or a handout.

After standing for a moment longer, scrutinizing him closely, then mentally shrugging, she moved toward the house. But she stopped after only a few steps and turned back.

"Are you hungry? Would you like something to eat, a sandwich, maybe?"

For a brief instant his glance lifted, and his black eyes gazed back at her. One eye was partially hidden by a swath of hair, but the other observed her clearly, sharply, then darted away.

Caitlin shivered, a sudden feeling of foreboding making her want to run into the house and lock the door behind her until this strange man was gone. The feeling faded as quickly as it had come, leaving her feeling somewhat foolish. He was just a poor unfortunate looking for a handout, not Jack the Ripper.

"Hungry, yes." He spoke slowly, awkwardly.

Smiling slightly, Caitlin offered, "You're welcome to sit on the porch in the shade. It's mighty hot today."

Rounding the corner of the house, she glanced back over her shoulder. Instead of following her, he was standing where she had left him, looking down at the garden. Pausing, she waited to see what he would do, but he only stood, head angled down, hands motionless at his sides. Perhaps he wasn't very bright, she thought. Retarded, maybe? That would be too bad, she found herself thinking with a bit of surprise, because underneath all that grime, she thought she saw the potential for a good-looking man.

In the house, feeling suddenly a bit guilty for her momentary fear, and also sorry for him, Caitlin made thick ham sandwiches with slices of pickle and tomato and poured glasses of freshly squeezed lemonade. After placing everything on a tray, she carried it outside.

The porch was empty. Caitlin set the tray on the white patio table and followed the porch around to the front of the house in search of him. He wasn't there, either. After stepping down off the porch and checking the other side of the house, she returned to the garden at the back.

She found him there, kneeling in the soil, apparently deep in concentration. Coming up silently behind him, she observed what he was doing. After digging a hole with strong, well-made hands, he lifted a plant carefully and inserted it into the hole, covered it over with soil, then patted the ground smooth. He paused to scrutinize it carefully, then continued the procedure.

He was planting tomato plants, exactly as she had been doing when he found her. She wondered how long he had observed her before making his presence known.

"I've set the food on the porch. Are you ready to eat?" She spoke softly, not wanting to startle him. He jumped, anyway, and whirled around, the small garden shovel clutched tightly in one powerful-looking fist.

After a moment the defensive posture relaxed, and he sat back on his knees, shoulders hunched, eyes on the ground. His whole attitude bespoke fear and uncertainty.

In an attempt to reassure him, Caitlin said mildly, "It looks as if you did a fine job planting that row of tomato plants. Thank you. If you'll follow me, I'll show you where you can wash your hands before we eat."

He complied slowly, reacting automatically to the gentle tone of her voice. Laying the shovel down, he stumbled awkwardly to his feet and followed her across the yard to the well-house.

A spigot on the side of the small building enabled him to remove most of the dirt from his hands. Before she could offer the towel she had carried with her, he wiped his hands down the sides of his dirty, faded jeans.

Oh, well, she thought wryly, he's the one eating with them, and they did match the rest of him.

When he had finished washing, she led him around the house to the porch. Ignoring the seat she offered at the patio table, he dropped down onto the top step of the porch. Hands hanging between his knees, eyes lowered, he waited silently, patiently, for her to hand him the food.

"Here," she said, offering him a glass. "I brought a glass of water for you to drink first, and a glass of lemonade to go with your sandwiches. I hope you like ham."

He gazed at the glass solemnly before taking it and gulping the water down, wiping his mouth with the back of one hand and handing the empty glass back to her.

"Thank you." She smiled and offered him a plate with sandwiches, along with a cold glass of lemonade.

"Thank you," he repeated precisely, without the accompanying smile. The first sandwich she could swear he ate in two bites, the next one, maybe three.

"Would you like another sandwich?" she asked, indicating the one remaining on her plate. "I'm not as hungry as I thought."

He eyed it hungrily before finally reaching for it and cramming it into his mouth. Mouth full, he looked at the glass sitting beside his plate.

"Thank you," he mumbled around the food.

Tilting the lemonade to his lips, he drank thirstily, emptying it in one long swallow. Glancing at her from the corner of his eyes, he hesitated, watching as she patted the moisture from her lips with a napkin after taking a drink from her glass.

Picking up the napkin she had handed him with his plate, he imitated her actions, then wadded it into a ball and dropped it onto the porch beside him. Leaning back against the rail in satisfaction, eyes on the ground at his feet, he absently fingered the hole in the knee of his jeans.

"Are you from around here?" Caitlin asked. She was feeling at a loss now that his attention was no longer focused on food. What did you talk about with someone who didn't seem to be quite all there?

It was a long time coming, but finally he answered. "Don't know."

"You don't know where you're from?"

"No," he answered, shifting on the step.

"Where do you live?"

He shrugged, pushing at the hair hanging in his eyes and scratching his knee. Because he hadn't been restless before, Caitlin decided her questions were making him uncomfortable. As a matter of fact, he had amazed her with his capacity for stillness.

"Do you have a job?" she asked as she laid her uneaten sandwich on the plate. He shrugged again, making no verbal response. She suspected it was a defense mechanism he used when he didn't want to answer, and tried again. "What kind of work do you do?"

"I sweep." He concentrated on relieving an itch at the tip of one ear, pushing again at the black hair lying across his forehead and reaching into his large dark eyes.

"You sweep," she repeated softly. An idea was forming in the back of her mind, but she wasn't sure it was a wise one. "Are you planning to stay around this area long?"

Rubbing at his right thigh, his face turned away, he ignored her question.

"Have you got a place to stay?" she persisted.

"No." He looked around uneasily and slid to the edge of the step. "No," he repeated nervously, climbing awkwardly to his feet. "I gotta go now."

Backing away, he missed his footing and narrowly saved himself from a nasty fall. His face screwed up with pain, he grabbed at his right leg, rubbing at an area just below his hip.

Caitlin jumped to her feet, one hand extended, ready to go to his aid. He was clearly in pain, and compassion and sympathy warred with her former apprehension. She wanted to help him, but something held her back. Innate good sense, her father would have said, if he were alive.

"Are you all right?" she asked anxiously. Her voice sounded harsher than she'd intended because of the battle being waged within.

"I got to go," he muttered, backing farther away, still rubbing at his leg. Turning, stumbling now and again, he limped down the lane, getting smaller and smaller as he passed out of sight.

"Wait…" Caitlin let the word trail off. No, she couldn't ask him to stay. What was she thinking? She wouldn't be able to sleep at night with him on the property for fear he would murder her in her bed.

Did she really believe that? Granted, something about him bothered her, but she didn't think he was dangerous. A few times she had even thought she'd seen a spark—a look in his eyes—of understanding? Well, it didn't matter now, anyway; he was gone.

A loud rumbling from overhead jerked her attention to the sky. Dark clouds were rolling across the sun. In the distance, jagged streaks of lightning danced from cloud to cloud. It was going to rain! Caitlin looked toward the lane with regret; then another, louder, growl from above sent her scurrying toward the garden and the rows of newly planted tomato plants. All thought of her unexpected visitor was forgotten in her haste to reach the plants before the rain did. A heavy downpour could drown the new plants, break off limbs, or just wash them completely away if she didn't protect them.

Many people, mostly friends and business acquaintances of her father, hadn't thought she would last this long on her own. But she stuck to her guns and refused to listen to their repeated urgings to sell the ranch and move into town.

Her father, and his father before him, had been born in the old stone ranch house across the creek, farther back on the property. Growing their own food and raising cattle had been the way of life for the Barratt family for over a hundred years.

There was a time when drilling for oil had been a part of it, too, but the oil wells had been pumped dry long ago. And though the cattle were few now, Caitlin prevailed.

The ranch had changed greatly in the last two years. In her father's day, cattle had roamed the range and the land close to the house had been farmed. But that had been too much for her to handle alone.

She had reduced the herd to twenty head, built a chicken house and fenced in a small area for the chickens to run around in, enlarged her yearly vegetable garden and started cultivating the orchard so she could sell the fruit. The remainder of the land she leased.

Occasionally she gave riding lessons to town children, to help maintain the two horses she kept purely for her love of riding. Those lessons helped pay for their food.

The old saying that everything in Texas is larger than life proved once again to be true. After no measurable rain for weeks, it proceeded to rain the proverbial cats and dogs for the next seventy-two hours. Instead of fearing her garden would burn to a crisp, she was afraid it would end up washed into the next county. It was the end of the week before she could manage a necessary trip into town for feed and household supplies.

Arriving in town, her first stop was Shay O'Malley's boardinghouse, where she had four dozen eggs to deliver.

Caitlin knocked, trying to put her worries behind her and planning to enjoy a few minutes' visit with an old school friend. "Hi," she greeted Shay smilingly. "It's the egg lady."

Caitlin spent the better part of an hour visiting with her friend, then promised as she left to see her again the following week.

The next stop on her agenda was the town library. Megan Jones, the librarian, was Caitlin's best friend. Caitlin dumped an armload of library books onto the wooden counter and turned to watch her friend introduce a large colorful storybook to a squirming preschooler.

Catching sight of her, Megan waved, settled her small charge with his book and made her way across the room.

"Hi, I didn't expect you today."

"I got caught playing Noah and the Ark and couldn't get away until now."

"Got time for coffee?" Megan asked with a gesture toward the small office behind her.

"Thanks, but I had some with Shay. You know," Caitlin gestured toward the child held spellbound by the large colorful pictures, "as much as you love them, you should have two or three by now."

"Hey, you need a husband for that, remember? Can you imagine the town's reaction if I had one without a husband? Mabel Henderson would be in seventh heaven for months talking about it."

"What about Logan?"

"Come on." Megan grabbed her arm. "Come back here while I, at least, have a cup of coffee, and we'll compare notes on what's been happening around town. Logan Carrington is a closed subject—for now."

The two chatted gaily, catching up on what they'd been doing since their last visit. Though they were neighbors, both led busy lives with few opportunities to get together for plain old girl talk. After a while, and more coffee, which she didn't really want, Caitlin told Megan she had to run.

"Listen, kid, can I leave my truck parked here for a couple hours while I make my rounds? It's nice and cool today, and I need to soak up as much of this weather as possible while I can. It won't be long before it's sun, sun and more sun." Caitlin laughed.

Megan agreed, smiling, but threatened to run across the street to the Sheriff's office if the truck remained past five o'clock.

"I can't have all and sundry abandoning their vehicles in the library parking lot, now can I?" she asked pseudo-severely. Drawing herself up to her full five-foot-two-inch height, she looked down her snub nose at Caitlin. She couldn't hold the pose for long, and they both burst out laughing, covering their mouths as they glanced at the Quiet Please sign posted on the wall behind the book return desk.

With a wave of her hand, Caitlin started down the concrete steps toward her pickup. Two dozen eggs that had yet to be delivered rested on the seat. After crossing the narrow street from the library parking lot, she passed the big square window labeled Sheriff's Office.

Bart Raymond, the sheriff and a longtime friend of hers and of her late father's, raised a hand and waved, and Caitlin waved back.

It was nearly noon by the time Caitlin completed all of her errands, except for a trip to the feed store and one to buy groceries. Noticing a distinct hollow feeling in the pit of her stomach, she crossed to the north side of the square and turned down the main street to the small luncheonette on the corner, across from the bandstand.

Sliding into a booth next to a window, she relaxed back against red vinyl with a tired sigh. After running her eyes down the items listed on the blackboard behind the Formica countertop, she settled for what she always ordered, a hamburger with everything, and a bowl of chili.

While glancing at the newspaper she'd picked up at her last stop, she became aware of the conversation going on around her.

"Well, I think it's just disgraceful, letting someone like that hang around town. Why he could be a thief—or a rapist," a voice whispered loudly. "Sheriff Raymond ought to run him out of town."

"Oh, Mabel, I feel sorry for the poor thing," another, more strident voice put in. Caitlin recognized it as that of Mrs. Watson, owner of the luncheonette. "He's not quite right in the head—you know, a dummy. Anybody can tell that just by looking at him. How can you be so uncharitable, wanting to lock the poor boy up?"

"Humph!" Mabel snorted. "You mark my words, there won't no good come from letting such as that roam free in this here town."

"Look." Another voice joined in the conversation. "There he is now."

Curious, Caitlin turned to gaze out the window across the road to where several wooden picnic tables sat under tall live-oak trees near the bandstand.

It was him! The man who had showed up at her ranch asking for a drink of water. Caitlin watched him as he loped over to one of the benches and sat down, unwrapping something.

"What's he doin'?" Mabel asked. "What's he got?"

"Can't tell from here," someone answered slowly.

"Well, whatever it is, he's eating it," Sarah Watson stated matter-of-factly.

"Lord! What do you suppose it is? He sure ain't got no money to buy nothin'," Mabel speculated avidly.

"Don't know," someone answered. "And don't want to."

Caitlin was so angry at their callous talk that she wanted to throw something at the old biddies. Where was their Christian charity now? It wasn't Sunday morning, and they obviously felt safe in being spiteful and insensitive. Wanting to spike their guns, she called out, "Make that two orders of everything, Mrs. Watson. Add two Cokes, and make it to go, please."

When the order was ready she paid for it, accepting the sacks, knowing what would occur when they saw where she was headed. Holding her head high, she marched from the shop. The bell on the door clanged loudly as she swept regally through.

"Well, really," Mabel Henderson snorted as she watched Caitlin make her way across the street, heading directly for the lone figure sitting at the picnic table, head down, hands dangling between his knees.

"Hello, do you remember me?" Caitlin asked softly, careful not to startle him. He looked up swiftly; he'd been unaware of her approach until she spoke, and his dark eyes were wide with alarm. Then a light of recognition sparked in their depths, and a tentative smile curved the corners of his beautiful mouth.

My Lord, there was a dimple in his chin, nearly hidden in the growth of dark stubble. Despite his generally scuffy—no, downright dirty—appearance, she could again see the promise of a powerfully good-looking male. It was such a pity he appeared to have some sort of learning disability.

What was the matter with her? she wondered. She sounded exactly like those old cats in the luncheonette. He was as God made him, and he should be accepted as such. Not degraded or pitied, but accepted with understanding and helped to maintain the dignity everyone deserved to have.

"I brought something to eat. Are you hungry?" Smiling, she nodded to the sacks she had placed on the table between them.

"Yes," he answered solemnly, waiting, as before, for her to open the sacks and sort out the food.

While they ate, Caitlin wondered how to broach the subject of his working for her. How much, she wondered, would he understand? He didn't appear to be severely handicapped, perhaps just a bit slow.

Her eyes alighted on the wrapper from a candy bar on the ground at his feet. She smiled to herself. The old cats in the luncheonette, no doubt watching at this very moment, would be greatly disappointed to learn he had eaten nothing more disgusting than a chocolate bar.

Clearing her throat, she watched him gobble down his hamburger and wondered how much, or how little, he'd had to eat since that day on the ranch. Then again, perhaps he always ate in this manner.

"Do you have a name?" she asked abruptly.

He stopped chewing to look at her blankly, but only for a brief moment, then continued to eat.

"I guess that means no," she answered herself wryly. "Listen, do you have any identification?"

He continued to chew, his eyes on her face, without a hint of understanding marking the strong lines of his brow.

Laying her sandwich on the table, she sorted through her purse, searching for her wallet. "Look," she said as she turned to her driver's license and showed him the picture. "Do you have anything like this?"

He glanced down at what she held, then back to her face. Laying his sandwich carefully beside hers and patting his pockets, he came up empty-handed. Palms up, he looked from his hands to her face and then bent over, as if searching the ground around them, glancing up at her from the corners of his eyes. Straightening, he lifted her purse, looked beneath it, laid it down, then shrugged and shook his head negatively, picked up his food and resumed eating.

Caitlin watched his antics with a frown. Was he being facetious? Was that a glint of humor she saw in the depths of those dark eyes? Shaking her head, clearing it of such fanciful notions, she realized she was being foolish. He wouldn't begin to know how to be facetious.

"Okay. You don't have a wallet and therefore no I.D. and apparently no name. So, with your permission, I'll just have to come up with a name. Is that all right with you?"

His answer was to continue eating, ignoring both her and her question. Taking that as permission, Caitlin frowned in concentration.

"How about..." She eyed the dark, finely arched brows over black, black eyes and decided he bore a striking resemblance to descriptions she had read of the dark angel. Satan. As a matter of fact, dressed differently and better groomed, he could have posed for the picture she'd seen in a magazine advertising a new book called *Lucifer, the Dark Angel*. Old Nick.

"How about Nick? I think that name fits you admirably."

He glanced up from the chili he was consuming. "Okay." He shrugged. His answer seemed to please her, he noticed, because she smiled widely and nodded her head. He paused for an instant to bask in the warm light shining from her green eyes. He wasn't used to people smiling at him; it made him feel strange inside. His eyes darting quickly away, he resumed eating.

Touching his arm, she said, "My name is Caitlin."

His hand stilled, his spoon suspended halfway to his mouth, chili dripping unnoticed back into the white cup. His eyes were arrested by the sight of her hand lying, so pale and delicate, on his bronzed arm.

As he slowly raised his eyes to her face, she searched their depths and found herself wondering again if he understood more than he let show.

"Nick, do you remember coming by my ranch a few days ago? You asked me for a drink of water. Do you remember?"

He nodded, watching her closely, a slight frown wrinkling his winged brows.

"You told me that when you work, you sweep. Well, I need someone to do things like that. There are other things, too, but we can discuss that at the ranch—if you're interested in working for me.

"I couldn't pay much, but you would have a place to stay. You know, a home, and all the food you could eat." Her rush of words halted while she looked at him, waiting, expecting some kind of reaction, something besides the solemn look he gave her.

"Would you like that? To work for me?" she prodded.

"Okay," he answered finally, because she seemed to expect that answer. And he liked her smile and the way she touched his arm.

They finished the meal in silence, and Caitlin led Nick to where she had parked the truck. The next stop was the feed store run by Joseph Eagle, the town's one and only native American resident.

Caitlin made the introduction, deciding they had a lot in common. Both were short on words and long on silence.

Joseph took her keys and, with Nick in tow, went out to move the truck around back, where the large sacks of feed could be loaded. Caitlin was glancing through a brochure on meat processing when the buzzer over the door heralded the arrival of another customer.

"Joseph is out back, but he'll be back soon—" she called over her shoulder, then stopped when she saw who had entered.

"Well, hi, Bart. I didn't know you fed the prisoners from the town feed and grain store," she quipped with a small smile.

Sheriff Raymond smiled back obligingly, strolling casually over to where she stood. Picking out a colorful brochure, he glanced at it idly, his attention centered on the attractive woman, not the booklet he held in his hamlike fist.

"How you doin', Caitlin? I saw you pass by the office earlier."

"Fine. I've been running errands all morning and delivering eggs. That rain we had earlier in the week put me way behind."

Bart folded and unfolded the booklet in his large hands, his mind on what he had to say, not the damage he was doing to the brochure. He was well acquainted with Caitlin's independent nature and fiery temper, and he wanted to pick his words carefully. Must be the red hair, he guessed silently, giving it a quick glance. Just like her daddy's.

He didn't know where to start, because, after all, he had no official reason for interfering. She would be perfectly within her rights to tell him to go to hell. And knowing her, she was more likely to do just that than to listen to his advice.

Caitlin sensed his unease and wondered what was on his mind. Tired of his towering over her like a huge monolith, she crossed her arms over her breasts and turned to face him.

"Okay, out with it. I take it you didn't come here to get food for your dogs, either."

Bart cleared his throat, shifting his big body back and forth uncertainly. He would rather face an armed and desperate criminal than confront a woman and tell her something she didn't want to hear in the first place.

"I, ah, you still needing help out at the ranch?" Puzzled, Caitlin nodded. Bart cleared his throat noisily. "Found anyone yet?"

"What exactly are you getting at, Sheriff?"

"I don't want you to do anything foolish, that's all."

"Foolish? What are you talking about?"

"Your daddy and I were good friends, and I feel a certain responsibility to see that no harm comes to you...."

A light of dawning comprehension flooded her green eyes, turning them to ice green. Her arms tight at her sides, her hands balled into fists, her stance told him she was ready to do battle.

"Which one called you? That old cat Mabel Henderson, I'll bet."

"Oh, now look, honey, she was only looking out for you—"

"Hah! Don't make me laugh! That old busybody doesn't look out for anybody but herself."

"Anyone would be right to be concerned. You don't know the man, do you?" His golden eyes watched her closely. Caitlin shook her head, a stubborn look on her angry face. "He appears to be a bit—" he made a circular motion at the side of his head with one finger. "He could be dangerous."

"Have you checked him out? Are there any warrants out on him?"

"It's nearly impossible to find information about someone who can't even tell you his own name. It just isn't safe to have him out there alone on the ranch with you. You don't even have a neighbor close by in case there's trouble."

"What do you call the Joneses, then?" she asked, knowing they were hardly what you could call close by.

"Megan is in town until late every day of the week except Sunday. And that damned brother of hers—" He made a disgusted sound deep in his throat. "You'd be more likely to get trouble from him instead of help."

"Are you telling me I can't hire this man if I want to?" Her voice belligerent, her cold eyes challenged him. He could almost swear that red hair of hers had caught fire from her temper.

"You know I can't do that, not officially. But I sure hate to see you do something you might live to regret."

Despite her anger, Caitlin read the very real concern in his homely face, and some of her anger dissipated.

"I know you're only thinking of what's best for me—in your opinion," she stressed, touching his shoulder lightly. "But I think you're worrying needlessly. The man's a little slow, not crazy, and he's not violent. Honestly, he's as docile as a lamb. I promise you, if I have the slightest bit of trouble from him, he's gone." She snapped her fingers. "Just like that. All right?"

It wasn't all right, but what was he going to say? Besides, there was something about the man. He couldn't put his finger on it, but something nagged at his memory. He'd seen him around town for a few days now; there had even been a few complaints. Maybe he should have run him off the way they had wanted him to do, but he hadn't. Something about the man had caught his attention; he couldn't figure out what it was that bothered him, though, and that was one reason he would let him stay—as long as he didn't pester anyone.

Scratching his chin thoughtfully, he eyed the stubborn set of her jaw. "I can't talk you out of it?"

Her answer was to lift her chin higher, and that dangerous glint came back into her eyes. He hadn't a hope in hell of changing her mind. Giving in to the inevitable, he said, "You have one iota of trouble from him, you call me, you hear? I'll take care of gettin' rid of him for you."

Caitlin nodded, smiling. "Sure. Thanks, Bart."

The sheriff nodded absently, heading for the door. Maybe it wouldn't be such a bad idea, having the man hang around town, out of trouble, while he figured out what it was about the fella that bothered him.

Chapter 2

Nick sat with hands folded in his lap, his gaze directed out the window at the passing scenery as the truck picked up speed and headed out of town. The muscles in his arms and upper torso ached from the strain of lifting fifty-and hundred-pound feed sacks. But it felt good, not like the almost constant ache in his right leg. That was a burning pain that at times made it difficult to walk and kept him awake at night. Those were the nights when the dream came to him. No, he didn't want to think about the dream.

He wished he understood what was happening to him. Why he was frightened all the time. Why he thought everyone wanted to hurt him. If only he could know things, things everyone else seemed to know. What was it about him that made him different from other people?

How was he different? Why did some people say they liked him when he sensed they really didn't? They had a *look* in their eyes. They made him feel bad, worse than the ones who yelled ugly words at him.

Sometimes he didn't see the look right off; some people could hide it for a while, but sooner or later they got it—and he left.

Some of them said they liked him and would give him food and a place to sleep, but they treated him like their dogs. Only, he sensed they liked their dogs better.

It was all so confusing, and trying to figure things out always made his head hurt.

Turning his head just a fraction, he watched the woman from the corner of his eye. What did she really want from him?

She said he could work for her, and she would give him food and a place to stay. Did she mean it? Or was she just another one of *them*? She thought he didn't understand the things she said, but he did—most of them.

He watched from the corner of his eyes as the wind from the open window swept the fine red hair back from her forehead and face, revealing the delicate lines of her cheek and jaw. Soft curls blew onto her forehead and into her sparkling green eyes. Was she different? Or was she like that other one? The one with the long blond hair?

Her name was Marcie. She had found him on the street and taken him home with her. She fed him, bought him clothes, even bathed and shaved him. She, too, said he could work for her. He thought she was good, different from the others—but he was wrong.

At first she made him feel good, made him almost believe he was like everyone else. But she only wanted to use him. Hands tightening on his lap, he remembered, one night in particular—the night he had left her.

He might be different from most, but there were some things he just *knew*. Well, he'd fixed her—he'd left without telling her.

He saw the woman glance over at him, studying him for a moment before looking back at the road. If she was like that other one, or if she ever got that *look* in her eyes, he would leave her, too.

Caitlin pulled the truck up the narrow gravel drive and stopped beside the porch. With Nick's help, she unloaded the groceries and carried them into the house. Getting back into the truck, she drove around to the back entrance of the red wooden barn and climbed out.

"This is where I store the feed. Come on." She led the way. "I'll help you unload."

Watching his tall, rangy body as he bent over a fifty-pound sack of feed, she saw that he looked as though he hadn't had regular meals for quite some time. The long-fingered hands narrowed to bony wrists, and there was a hollow look to his face beneath the hair and grime. The clothes he wore hung on his frame like old clothes on a scarecrow.

Taken by surprise at the sudden rush of maternal feelings at the thought of his being homeless and hungry, she scolded herself harshly. He's a full-grown man, probably a few years older than you are, she insisted silently. He doesn't need a mother.

When the feed had been unloaded, Caitlin took him to the stalls that housed Flame and Caesar. Flame, a beautiful mahogany-colored mare, was as gentle a creature as ever walked the earth, Caitlin assured a nervous-looking Nick.

"She won't bite. Here, look." Taking a handful of oats, Caitlin held them out between the bars of the stall. Flame nickered softly, moving a step closer. She recognized the woman, but was shy of the man.

"Come on, my pretty, see what I have for you," Caitlin crooned softly, a look of love on her face.

Nick stared at her, not at the horse, captivated by the warmth in her smile, the gentle tone of her voice. He couldn't remember anyone ever looking or smiling at him like that. A strange feeling he didn't recognize as jealousy spread through him, filling him with anger toward the horse and a yearning he couldn't identify toward the woman. He wanted her to smile for him, not the horse, because it made him feel warm and safe inside, and just a little bit uncomfortable.

When they had first entered the barn, he'd been wary of the unfamiliar animal and had stayed back and to the side of the woman as they neared the mare's stall. Now, when the horse moved closer and raised her head to nicker a welcome, he saw the large teeth exposed, Caitlin's hand extended toward them. Nick darted an alarmed glance from the woman's hand to the horse's teeth.

Grabbing Caitlin's hand, he jerked it back between the wooden slats, spilling the oats and catching the tender flesh of her wrist on the rough wood surface.

Startled, she yelled angrily, "What are you doing?"

"It will bite you," he answered anxiously.

"She," Caitlin stressed. "She was only going to take the oats from my hand. You did that."

Jerking her arm from his grasp, she turned it over, exposing the angry red scratch that now marred its smooth pale surface from wrist to elbow.

At a loss, Nick looked from the scratch on her arm to the restless horse and back to her anger-flushed face.

Something was different about him. Even through her anger, she recognized the difference. He stood taller, shoulders back, and there was expression on his face—yes, that was a large part of the difference. The blank look was gone. Alarm, determination, confusion and, lastly, contrition appeared on his dark countenance.

Wiping a hand across his face, Nick sighed heavily. He had done it again. Stepping away from the woman, head lowered, shoulders returning to their former slump, he turned away. He'd better go before she yelled at him like the others.

"Sorry," he mumbled.

"Just where do you think you're going?" Caitlin called in strident tones. "You get right back here and meet both these horses, because it's going to be your job to look after them."

He hesitated before turning back. "You don't want me to go?"

Was that relief she saw in the far depths of his eyes, heard in the deep rough tones? Questions nagged at her. Was this man more, or less, than he appeared?

Observing him carefully for the next hour, she introduced him to both horses, explaining his duties in feeding and grooming them. He showed no further sign of the intelligence she had briefly glimpsed earlier. But the question persisted: Didn't it take some intelligence to show emotion?

After another hour of having to explain over and over, step by step, what was required of him, Caitlin was prepared to throw up her hands and dismiss the idea out of hand. As long as he remained on the ranch, she would have to take him at face value and not jump to unwarranted conclusions.

It was late by the time they left the barn, and a chill wind had sprung up. Hugging her arms across her chest, Caitlin hurried across the yard to the side door of the house. Pausing there, she looked back. Nick was following slowly, hands in his pockets, shoulders hunched against the wind. He looked like the most disreputable bum she had ever seen.

Fool that she was, she hadn't even considered what he would wear, or where he would sleep. Glancing up at the sun hanging low in the sky, she gave the matter careful consideration. Was the sheriff right? Was she making a big mistake having him here, virtually isolated as she was?

By now Nick had reached the porch and was standing by the steps, waiting, staring into the distance with that peculiar ability he had for stillness. Now and again he gave a violent, convulsive shiver. He looked tired, and even in the waning light, she could see the dark circles around his red-rimmed eyes. The growth of beard hardly masked the pale, haggard cast to his cheeks.

"How about a cup of hot chocolate and a little rest?"

There was still a great deal of work to be done, due to her having spent the day in town, but he needed a break. Obviously he wasn't used to this kind of work, and there were his knee and the limp to consider, the pain of both more evident with each passing moment.

When she caught his glance, she could almost have sworn there was gratitude in the look he bestowed on her.

"After that," she continued, "we'll feed and water the chickens and lock them up for the night."

Nick's eyes dulled at her words, shoulders seeming to slump a little lower, but he nodded and bent to sit on the wide lower step of the porch.

"Inside. Come on, it's warm inside. We need to discuss where you're going to sleep and so on," she added briskly, denying the small lurch she felt as his dark gaze met and held hers for a brief span.

Caitlin wished she could have interpreted the strange expression she glimpsed for a bare instant before, eyes going blank, he looked quickly—warily?—away.

The sacks of groceries were sitting in haphazard fashion along the counter, where Caitlin had left them in her hurry to get on with the chores. Nick stood in the doorway between foyer and kitchen, gazing without expression at the chaos.

Caitlin began emptying sacks, stacking everything in a pile with complete disregard for any sort of order, dropping the brown paper bags on the floor as they emptied.

Stopping abruptly, she turned to the man looking uncomfortably out of place, still hesitating in the doorway.

"Come with me. I'm going to show you where to wash your hands. Then you can help empty sacks, while I start putting this stuff away. After that we'll have our hot chocolate."

Caitlin led the way across the hall to a small bathroom containing a sink and toilet. Flipping a switch on the wall, she flooded the room with bright light. Then, pulling a fluffy towel from the pile stacked on a shelf in the corner above the toilet, she turned around.

She'd been unaware of how close he was in the small confines of the room, and her face made abrupt contact with a dirty, smelly, solid obstacle.

Her first instinct was to wrinkle her nose at the strong sour smell of unwashed masculinity and say, ''Yuck!'' Instead, she jerked back, swallowing against a sudden upsurge of nausea, and cracked the top of her head against the underside of his chin, causing his head to snap up and back.

''Oh!'' She saw stars.

''Umph!'' He bit his tongue.

Feeling dizzy and at the same time foolish, Caitlin put up a hand to rub at the throbbing ache above her forehead. Leaning back against the sink, she took a moment to focus her bleary eyes. Finally she looked up, his height surprising her, and caught his own slightly glazed look.

''I'm sorry.'' She spoke too loudly, unaccountably breathless. How could she have been so clumsy? He would think her a complete idiot. No he wouldn't, because he was—hurt?

A small trickle of bright red blood seeped slowly from the corner of his mouth, down his face, disappearing into the thick black bristles on his chin. Guilt all out of proportion to the accident overwhelmed her. It was like hurting a child, or a small, defenseless animal.

Without conscious thought, she reached out to touch the side of his lean jaw. Her fingers were instantly buried in the surprisingly soft hair of his beard. Her thumb moved of its own volition against the hard-looking mouth, registering the dry cracked skin, before gliding across to the warm wet stickiness of blood.

Fascinated, she watched the bright red disappear beneath the whiteness of her thumb, her eyes momentarily mesmerized by the sight.

A strange new feeling fought its way through to her consciousness, but, frightened by it, she wouldn't allow it to surface. Jerking her hand from his face, she sagged back, reality coming to the fore.

Here she stood, alone in the bathroom with a dirty, smelly stranger, touching him—touching him in a manner that could be misconstrued as provocative. She felt suddenly ashamed of what she had done. If her thoughtless action had evoked a sexual awareness in the man, she would have had no one to blame but herself.

She didn't see the astonished light of response that sprang into the dark eyes above her, or the hand that hovered close to her soft bright hair. She couldn't know that he didn't mind that she had touched him; it hadn't made him want to run, as other such gestures had in the past.

And then he saw her face. He'd seen that look many times before. It was the look he had feared seeing. His hand clenched as he dropped it to his side. The light died from his eyes, leaving them dull and opaque once more. It was the look that always made him want to run, but for some reason his feet refused to move. He wanted to stay.

What if he hadn't seen it? He chanced a glance at her face. It was gone. She looked funny, but the *look* wasn't there. Should he stay? If he kept away from her—didn't do anything to make her look at him like that again—would she let him stay?

Shoving the towel into his hands, with her eyes turned away, Caitlin explained in a small, tight voice about the bar of hand soap. After instructing him to turn off the light when he finished, she left him to it. She couldn't get out of the room fast enough.

Wishing she'd had the good sense to feed him and leave him in town where she'd found him, she stomped into the kitchen.

Never had she suspected that there was a side of her that could respond to a man as debilitated as this one appeared to be. The idea repelled her, leaving her feeling lost and unsure of who, or what, she was. Afraid to delve too deeply into herself, fearing what unpalatable truths she might learn, she cut her thoughts off right there.

Could she have made a bad mistake in bringing him here? She needed time to rethink the idea of his staying with her alone on the ranch.

Caitlin adopted a busy air when Nick rejoined her a short time later. From the corner of her eye she noted that he had not only scrubbed his hands but the blood was gone from the corner of his mouth and beard. The short hair curling at his sideburns and the lock of hair stuck damply to his forehead showed signs of a recent wetting. Angry at the small ball of warmth forming inside her at his obvious attempt to please her, she spoke very little, and then only to show him where to put the groceries.

She was well aware of the looks of entreaty he threw in her direction. And later, when the atmosphere became more strained, he couldn't hide the hurt expression darkening his eyes, though he tried.

Fear battled with compassion. Could she in good conscience put him out, send him back to the street where she'd found him? Wouldn't that make her as bad as the women she had scorned in town? Was it fair to make him pay for her perverse thoughts and emotions?

Leaving him alone in the kitchen to drink his hot chocolate, Caitlin slowly climbed the stairs. On this floor there were two bedrooms with a bathroom separating them. One of the bedrooms had been hers as she grew to adulthood and the other a guest room. After her father's death, she had placed his things, the things she couldn't part with, in the guest room. Her decision was made before she entered the room. Nick could stay; her response to him was her own problem, and she could handle it. Her father had taught her many things, and one of them was to be strong.

Handling her father's belongings brought his memory poignantly into focus. Sitting on the bed, she carefully selected items of clothing she imagined would fit the man downstairs. She knew her father would approve of their being put to good use. Brushing a stray tear from one eye, she piled the items together and returned to the kitchen.

"I'm not certain how many of these things will fit. You're a bit taller than Dad was, though not quite as broad," she told him uncertainly, laying the clothing on the edge of the table.

"Dad?"

"Yes, my father. He passed away nearly three years ago. I kept most of his things. They aren't doing anyone any good hanging in a closet upstairs, and I know he would want you to have them."

When he made no move to look at or touch the clothing, she reached out as if to touch him in reassurance, but drew back at the last moment.

"I want you to have them—really."

A short while later they left the house, the clothing still piled neatly on the table. The cup of chocolate at his place remained untouched, Caitlin noted in passing. And for some reason that made her chest feel tight and uncomfortable.

Nick proved more adept at caring for the chickens than he had the horses. In fact, he seemed to enjoy feeding them and gathering the eggs.

The sun was gone by the time they trooped back to the house, a basket of eggs hanging from Caitlin's arm. She was exhausted, and with the lines of pain around his mouth and his dragging gait, she didn't need to ask how Nick felt.

While she did the dishes, she left Nick in her old bedroom upstairs, the clothing lying on the bed and an assortment of necessities for his personal grooming in the adjoining bathroom.

Originally she'd had the vague notion of putting him up in the office-like area of the barn. But looking across the table at him as they ate the meal she had prepared, seeing the wan, pinched look on his face, she didn't have the heart to tell him he would be staying in the barn with only the horses for company. She had a feeling he'd had a surfeit of spending the night in such places.

Some people, the sheriff for one, would call it idiocy, having him to stay in the same house with her at night. But the large master bedroom downstairs, where she slept, had a good sturdy lock if she felt the need to use it.

Perhaps it might seem strange to some, but she had no fear of him. Whatever else he might be, she didn't feel he was a threat to her safety.

Before retiring, Caitlin climbed the stairs to make sure he had everything he needed for the night. At first there was no answer to her knock. Finally, after she'd called him several times, he responded in a stiff voice, asking what she wanted.

She told him that there was a pot of coffee on the stove downstairs, if he wanted some before going to sleep, and asked if he had everything he needed for the night. He told her that he had, thanked her briefly, and almost as soon as she'd left, she heard the bathroom door open and close.

She was on the point of turning away, but something made her turn back and try the doorknob. Cautiously, she twisted the brass handle. The door was locked from the inside.

With a wry smile and a slight shake of her head, wondering just who was afraid of whom, she descended the stairs and headed for her long-awaited soak in a hot tub and bed.

The next morning, Caitlin went upstairs at first light to rouse Nick. She found his door standing open and the bed neatly made. Surprised, she looked around inside the bathroom. It was unaccountably neat. Though there were obvious signs of recent use—the wet towel folded neatly across the rack, a razor with the plastic protector removed, and a comb with a few dark strands caught in its teeth—there was no sign of the man.

Feeling a bit apprehensive, she took the stairs two at a time, passed through the living room and barreled into the kitchen, only to come up short. It, too, was empty.

Where was he? Could he have left in the middle of the night? The bed didn't look as though it had been slept in. Maybe he'd only used the bathroom and waited long enough for her to get settled before taking off. But why? What possible motive could he have had for leaving like a thief in the middle of the night? She had nothing of value to steal.

For a moment she considered going outside and making a thorough search of the grounds, to see if he'd started work. But somehow she couldn't picture him having the initiative to do anything on his own.

Feeling disappointed—and, she had to admit, a bit relieved, as well—she began to prepare her breakfast. The world went on, and she had plenty of work to do, whether he was there to help or not.

Flicking on the radio perched on a shelf beside the refrigerator, Caitlin listened to a local station while she made a fresh pot of coffee. She was turning from the refrigerator with a bowl of large brown eggs in her hands, thinking how good the first pot of coffee smelled in the morning, when she glanced up into a pair of shy dark eyes.

Her hands juggled the bowl, and she managed to save all but the top two eggs. And even those were saved thanks to a pair of quick tanned hands.

"Thank you," she breathed in a strangled voice, knowing she was staring, but unable to look away.

God, he was beautiful! What had happened to the derelict from the night before?

Jet-black hair, clean and shining this morning, was parted on the side and swept back from a high forehead, revealing the beauty of large dark-lashed eyes set below finely arched brows.

Freshly shaved, the smooth pale skin stretched tautly over high cheekbones and a square jaw. Even the dimple in his chin looked smooth, and she wondered idly how he managed to shave the narrow depths without cutting himself. She wouldn't have thought him capable of such an exacting feat.

Her eyes moved up to sensually full lips parted to show a dazzling display of straight white teeth. He smiled innocently at her, seemingly unaffected by her close scrutiny, arms stretched outward, holding an egg in each hand.

"I got them." He sounded as though he'd just won a million dollars.

"Yes," she managed in a small suffocated voice. "I see you did."

Her hands were shaking as she set the bowl on the stove and took the eggs from his long tapered fingers, being careful not to touch his skin.

When she was close to him, the tantalizing smell of lime-scented shaving cream mixed with the heavier musky scent of his body and made her knees go weak in a very disconcerting manner.

She wished now that he *had* left in the middle of the night. She wished *she'd* had the good sense to listen to the sheriff and leave him in town where she'd found him. She wished he were still dirty and smelly, not clean and neatly dressed in one of her father's familiar blue plaid work shirts and worn jeans. And she *hoped* that every time she looked at him from now on, she wouldn't forget that he was not like other men.

Forcing back the irrational desire to order him out of her kitchen *and* her life, she asked instead if he would like scrambled eggs and bacon for breakfast. He agreed and sat down at the table, hands folded neatly before him, to watch her.

"As soon as we eat, we'll need to see to the chickens—" she began nervously.

"I did." He broke across her speech quietly, a smile beaming on his face. He'd been up for hours, working, trying to do a good job; he didn't ever want to see that *look* on her face again.

"You did?" She turned to face him inquiringly, her nervous awareness forgotten for the moment. "You did what?"

"The chickens." He nodded to a collection of brown eggs sitting clean and shining on a towel beside the sink. She hadn't noticed them, hadn't noticed much of anything since he'd entered the room.

Her eyes on the eggs, she asked, "You fed and watered them? And remembered to put the medicine in the water?"

He nodded once. "Six drops, like you said." When she made no immediate response, only kept staring at the eggs, he frowned, asking, "That right?"

"Yes," she answered finally. "That's exactly right."

Wasn't his taking the initiative this way a bit strange? She would have to think about that later. Her voice sounding odd even to her own ears, she turned to look at him and asked half-fearfully, "What else have you done this morning?"

"Put stuff in the dirt—" he began, stopping short when she bolted past him and out the door in a mad dash for the garden at the back of the house.

He had planted rows and rows of onion sets, and every one she uncovered had been planted upside down. They would all have to be dug up and replanted.

Clenching her teeth, taking a deep breath, steeling herself not to yell at him, she kept telling herself that he had only been trying to help.

A long shadow fell over her.

"I did it wrong," he stated hollowly.

"Afraid so. We'll have to dig them up and replant them—I'll show you how," she added slowly.

"You mad?"

Caitlin would never know what it cost him to voice those two little words. By voicing them, he opened himself once more to the possibility of more pain and humiliation.

Some part of him desperately wanted her to like him, wanted to share in the warmth and caring he'd seen her show her animals, while another, darker side of him feared her and the hold she already had on him.

Keeping her eyes on the ground, she heard the timid, yet earnest, need in his voice to hear her answer.

"No," she answered finally, and, strangely enough, as she answered, she realized that she wasn't mad. Despite the time that would be involved in having to replant, she was pleased, because he had shown himself capable of and willing to do the work.

"Come on." Climbing to her feet, dusting off the knees of her jeans, she led the way to the house. "The bacon must be burned to a crisp by now. Let's eat first, and then we can get started putting this to rights."

Nick followed so closely behind her that he bumped into her when she stopped suddenly and turned to face him. Her finger under his nose, she instructed firmly, "No more working on your own unless I've approved what you do beforehand. Got that?"

He looked startled and backed away from her threatening finger. Then he grinned, nodding in agreement.

Caitlin swallowed with difficulty, feeling an achy tightness somewhere in her chest at the innocent beauty of his smile. She hoped he wouldn't flash it around too often.

For the next few days she was kept too busy teaching him the ropes to worry about any unwarranted attraction she might feel toward him. They worked from sunup to sundown.

There were times during that period when she found herself forgetting who and what he was and talking to him as though he were any normal man working alongside her. He grasped the rudiments of ranching with amazing speed, and a small voice in the back of her brain began to question the true state of his capabilities.

She tried asking him questions about where he had lived before coming here to Fate, Texas, but he became quiet and morose when she did. And if she persisted, he would just walk away, refusing to hear her when she called him back. Something told her that he wasn't what he seemed, but, lacking any logical explanation for why someone would want to be thought retarded when he really wasn't, she let matters rest—for the time being.

In the evenings they watched TV, and Caitlin read. They didn't talk much, but were content to share these quiet periods of relaxation together.

Eventually she began to notice that he seemed interested in the books she read. She also noticed that he listened carefully when she spoke to him, and sometimes she wondered if he were mimicking her speech patterns.

His sentences became longer and better constructed. He was learning to express himself more clearly. Or was he only becoming relaxed in her company and inadvertently allowing her to see how much he was really capable of understanding?

Just when she'd thought she had accepted him for what he was, he had begun to change before her very eyes.

Unfortunately for her peace of mind, his way of speaking and thinking weren't the only changes she began to notice.

The sun had tanned his skin to a dark golden honey, a shade that appeared devastating against his dark coloring. The regular meals and exercise toned his muscles to mouth-watering proportions. The sight of him working shirtless, the play of muscles gliding under sweat-slickened skin, had Caitlin feeling the need to avoid him in earnest.

Her eyes strayed too often in his direction when they were together. She found herself wandering over to whatever on the ranch where he happened to be working, with the flimsiest of excuses. It would have to stop.

Now, at night, she pretended an interest in the TV and books that she didn't feel, forcing herself to ignore the puzzled, hangdog looks he threw her way if their glances chanced to meet. She began to feel hunted. It was getting harder to think of him as someone beyond her reach.

Only once in all that time did she come close to revealing the true nature of the feelings she was trying so desperately to deny.

It happened the day the baby chicks arrived. They were kept penned separately from the older, larger chickens for safety's sake. The roosters and hens would trample the little ones, and if one became injured, the others would peck it to death.

Always worried when there were chicks to consider, Caitlin checked on them frequently. That evening, when dinner was over, Nick disappeared, as he seemed to do more frequently of late, and she made her way to the chicken house across from the barn.

Nick was there. In the light from the small warming lamps, she saw him on his knees in the midst of the little fuzzy yellow creatures, looking like a giant Gulliver among the Lilliputians. The chicks were all around him, peeping loudly, chasing each other around the pen. A few, braver than the others, hopped onto his lap. One, bolder than even those few, sat perched atop his shoulder.

His face in shadow, his hair falling over the side toward her, he held one tiny chick cupped gently in both large hands. And while she watched from the darkness, he leaned over and set it carefully on its feet amidst the others. In so doing, he dislodged the one perched on his shoulder. With a soft, deep laugh and a deft move, he caught it, touched his lips to the soft downy body and bent to place it beside the other. His face, now revealed to her, held such a look of tenderness that it stole the breath from her lungs.

Eyes misting over, she smiled. A slight sound must have escaped her trembling lips, because his eyes lifted to find hers, a remnant of that tenderness still caught in their dark, glowing depths.

Caitlin was unable to move as his gaze found and held hers while he stood and let himself out of the chicken coop. His movements sure and quick, he stopped before her, mere inches separating them, and still she couldn't move, or speak, held captive by the light of tenderness shining from his eyes.

Hard thighs brushed against her softness. Work-roughened hands lifted to touch the delicate skin of her face, his trembling fingers separating the fine strands of her hair with worshipful delicacy.

Her eyes drifted shut as she felt his breath blow soft and warm against the cool skin of her face. She wanted to raise her arms, run her fingers through the thick hair at the back of his head, down the strong corded neck, across the hard muscles sheathed beneath the warm, smooth skin of his back.

But her hands remained empty, her arms leaden weights dangling at her sides, a small voice of reason cautioning her to stop this situation before it got out of hand. She had fought her growing awareness of this man for too long to give in to it now.

Nick's heart pounded violently in his chest, just as he'd felt the rapid thumping of the baby chicks' hearts when he'd held them in his hands.

He fought the dizzy feeling causing his knees to go weak. He was confused about the way she made him feel, but, more and more, he liked it. He knew he should stay away from her or he might have to leave, but she drew him with her warm smiles, her trust, her aura of femininity.

For a while after he'd first started work on the ranch he had thought she really liked him. But then she'd begun to avoid him, hardly talking to him, even at mealtimes. He felt hurt, and wondered what he'd done to make her mad at him. Tonight was the first time she'd smiled at him for days, and it went to his head.

Closing his eyes, acting on instinct, he stepped closer, molding her body against his hard length. The conflicting emotions

coming from some untapped source deep inside, emotions he
was only now becoming aware of, confused him. He was
frightened by the feel of her softness under his hands. A part
of him felt panic, the need to run from both the woman and the
way she made him feel. But the sweet scent emanating from her
skin made his senses spin. He couldn't stop his head from dipping toward hers and—she was gone!

Wrenching herself from his arms, Caitlin rushed blindly from
the building.

Nick hung his head in shame, clenched his fists at his sides
and fought for control. He could hear the breath rasping in his
throat, and the sound shook him. He must really have frightened her for her to have run from him that way. He knew about
fear; it was his constant companion.

Following her outside, the words "I'm sorry" on his lips, he
was in time to glimpse her figure, barely discernible in the
moonlight, disappearing into the house. He wasn't fit to touch
her boots. He knew that, not a—*dummy* like him.

But he was getting better, wasn't he? Sometimes he thought
things, seemed to *know* things, that surprised him. And Caitlin had appeared to like and trust him, except in the last few
days. She didn't stand around and watch him while he worked
anymore, telling him how to do things he already knew how to
do. She wasn't at all like the people he remembered working for
in the past.

And now, because of tonight, she was scared of him. He
rammed his fist against the building in self-loathing, but he
didn't feel the pain.

She would want him to leave now for sure.

He would miss seeing the baby chicks grow feathers, never
see the seeds he'd helped plant sprout above the ground. He
would even miss the horses now that he no longer feared them.

But worse, the thing that hurt the most, he would miss the
woman, strong, hardworking and independent—gentle and
caring.

He moved through the quiet shadows, his footsteps faltering the closer he came to the dark, silent house. He didn't want
to go inside, because he knew she would have shut herself up in
her room by now, the closed door a final barrier between his
world and hers.

As he leaned against the porch his hand absently massaged
his right thigh. He didn't want to leave this place. He felt dif-

ferent here. Though he didn't understand what was happening
to him, and sometimes he was afraid, he knew he was changing,
growing, feeling things he didn't remember feeling before.

There were nights when he couldn't sleep. He would come
suddenly awake, a distant echo of another place, other sights
and sounds, ringing in his head. Memories, or dreams, came to
him in those dark hours, causing him to worry that he might
actually be as crazy as others had told him he was.

Some nights the dream came, knotting his insides with fear,
wracking him with pain, drenching him in cold sweat. The
dream eventually faded, but the fear remained long after. Those
were the nights when he couldn't return to sleep and dragged
himself from his bed to begin work while the sky was still black.

Work pushed the terror from his mind. He could pretend for
a little while longer that everything was good. As long as he had
the work, the fresh air and the woman, his life had meaning.

Throwing his head back, he gazed at the stars, millions of
bright lights looking so close that he felt as though he could
reach out and catch them in his hands. A shooting star hurtled
across the heavens. His eyes followed it until it disappeared
from sight.

Another soul had gone to heaven. Where had he heard that?
What did it matter?

Wouldn't Caitlin be surprised if he suddenly burst into her
room and laid a handful of stars beside her on the bed? Maybe
then she wouldn't be afraid of him, and she would smile at him
again the way she had, for just a moment, tonight.

Chapter 3

Caitlin left her bed later than usual the next morning. She'd spent a restless night worrying about her growing attraction to Nick and his own unconcealed reactions to it. Despite repeated reminders of the futility of such an attraction, her senses reacted strongly whenever he was near, and a small niggling voice whispered to her, reminding her of the developing changes in him, changes that were evident with each passing day.

His personal grooming was meticulous—had been since that first day—which caused her to wonder if the state he'd been in had been due to circumstances and had nothing to do with choice. For another thing, he made decisions—minor ones, granted, about what he wanted to eat and drink and what to wear—but they were his choices.

He asked intelligent questions about why she did things a certain way. He worked hard, never pausing until a task was completed. And he never asked for help until he'd tried every way he could think of to do something on his own.

Less and less did she find him staring morosely, blankly, into space, that lost, lonely look on his face.

Now, not surprisingly, he was outside taking care of the numerous chores he performed every morning. Sitting down with a cup of coffee, she gazed with unseeing eyes at the blue-and-white checked tablecloth.

What was she going to do about him? Should she ask him to leave before things got out of hand? She didn't want to. For one thing, he was a great help to her, but mostly because she couldn't bear the thought of his returning to the hell his life must have been before.

Not that she saw herself as some kind of savior—far from it—but she had given him a job and a home, given him an opportunity to prove he could work and take care of himself with dignity. With the stability of work and a home, he was gaining self-respect. Could she take that away from him?

In fact, the changes were becoming so great that if she hadn't met him previously, she wouldn't have believed he was the same person. So why was she fighting the growing awareness between them? Was it because she couldn't forget the man he'd been?

No, it was more complicated than that. He was different, yes, but she still sensed something not quite right about him. He appeared more and more like a person who had been shut away from the world for years, rather than one who lacked the capacity to learn and understand. Every day he appeared to look at the world with new eyes, discovering and delighting in things that everyone else, including herself, took for granted. He both intrigued and frightened her.

Nick, too, felt the growing awareness between them, and that was a large part of her problem. How could she tell herself to ignore what was happening between them, to deny that it existed, when she could feel and see it growing daily with a mere look into his soulful dark eyes?

She could never really be sure of exactly what he felt, of course, because he wouldn't or couldn't open up to her. They didn't communicate the way any other two people living in the same house would. They didn't sit and talk, discuss likes and dislikes, or the past—his past.

Because he had no past? The ridiculous thought pushed itself into her conscious mind. How could anyone have no past? He certainly hadn't sprung full grown from out of nowhere a few short weeks ago. Or had he?

Sipping at the too-hot coffee, she began to formulate a plan. Perhaps she could discover more about him, maybe look into the possibility that he wasn't retarded after all. Depending on what she learned, it might make a difference to their situation.

And what if she discovered something she didn't want to know? What if, by some stroke of fate, he was suffering from amnesia? What if he were married and had a house full of kids? But the possibility of restoring Nick to a full and productive life had to take precedence over any fledgling hopes or needs she might have developed.

"Someone's here." Nick stood framed in the doorway.

Caitlin looked up, but only as far as his waist. She wasn't ready to meet his eyes. The hand holding her father's battered Stetson looked bruised, the knuckles red, raw and swollen. The sight caused her to glance quickly away, and when she glanced back, that hand was buried inside the stained crown of the hat.

"Someone's here," he repeated.

"Invite them in. I'll start breakfast."

"Not hungry," he muttered, moving through the door, ramming the hat back on his head as he went.

Caitlin leaned weakly against the table, trying to forget the bleak sound of his deep voice. She hadn't heard that particular despairing note since his first days on the ranch. And she knew with certainty that she was to blame for it. Their relationship had been strained since the night in the chicken house.

Her visitor turned out to be a very puzzled-looking sheriff. He greeted her at the door with, "Who's the cowboy?"

Caitlin invited him in for coffee before satisfying his curiosity. "Don't you recognize him??"

"Should I—" he began, then hesitated as comprehension slowly spread across his ruddy face. "No—you don't mean that's the vagrant?" Caitlin poured the coffee, smiling at him over the rim of her cup. "Well I'll be damned—ah, pardon me," he murmured absently.

"Quite a change, don't you think, Sheriff?"

"Where's he stayin'?" he asked abruptly.

Caitlin looked everywhere but at him, feeling a bit too warm under his close scrutiny.

"Upstairs—" she began, but he cut her off.

"In the house?"

"It's been chilly at night—I couldn't very well put him in with the chickens, or, for that matter, with the horses, either."

Jumping to her feet, she moved to the stove, her back to him. "I was just getting ready to fix some breakfast, Sheriff. Have you eaten—'' She didn't hear him move, but suddenly he was behind her, his hamlike hands turning her around.

"Caitlin, honey, don't get mixed up with him. I've known you all your life, and I don't want to see you hurt." She started to speak, but he silenced her with a slight shake of the head. "There's something not quite right about him—and I don't mean his head. I can't put my finger on it. It's just a feeling I have. Let me find him a job on another ranch, with a—'' He broke off, seeing her green eyes darken with anger.

"A man!" she spat at him, jerking from his grasp. "You're as big a chauvinist as the rest of Dad's friends. Just because I'm a woman, you think I don't have the brains to take care of myself."

She was as mad as a hornet. He knew he'd lost any chance of getting her to listen to him now.

"Well, let me tell you something, Sheriff. I've kept this place together since Dad's death, and I did it without the help of any man!"

The sheriff picked his hat up off the table and moved to the door. Nick stood there, eyeing the two combatants silently.

"Just what do you call *him*?" Bart nodded toward Nick, but his eyes remained on her startled face. He didn't wait for an answer, merely shouldered his way past the silent man and strode out the door.

"Yes, what do you call me?" Nick asked softly after a long, strained silence, his eyes locked on hers.

Caitlin opened her mouth, but no words came out. Closing it firmly, she tore her gaze from his. When she glanced back, the door was empty. Grabbing the first thing that came to hand, she hurled it across the room.

It took the better part of the morning to get all the egg off the walls and floor. Later, she slipped and almost fell in a puddle she had missed in the hallway outside the kitchen door. Muttering dark curses about men in general, and a certain sheriff in particular, she cleaned that mess up, too.

Sheriff Raymond slid into the chair behind his desk and reached for the phone. After consulting a list of names in a small pocket directory, he punched out a set of numbers.

In a moment he had Robert Jamison on the line. The man was a state's attorney in Austin and had a "you scratch my back and I'll scratch yours" kind of relationship with the sheriff.

A few minutes later the sheriff replaced the receiver and stared thoughtfully down at it. If anyone could come up with information about Caitlin's mysterious stranger, it would be Jamison. Maybe Jamison could even discover what the paper he'd found in his files that morning meant. He would bet everything he owned that there was something fishy about the stranger.

"Dr. Shepherd's office, Hildy Crane speaking. May I help you?"

"Hildy, this is Caitlin Barratt."

"Well, hi there, Caity, how you doin'?"

Caitlin smiled, picturing the large, dusky-skinned woman who had been with Dr. Shepherd since he'd taken over old Doc Spencer's practice nearly ten years earlier. He had inherited Hildy along with the practice when the old doctor retired.

"I'm fine," Caitlin answered, "but I need to talk to the doctor. Is he available?"

"No, sugar, I'm afraid not. He's at the hospital all day today."

"Oh." She couldn't keep the disappointment from her voice.

"He's got some time on Friday. Want me to make you an appointment?"

"Well . . ." She hesitated. She had envisioned asking him a few pertinent questions on the phone, but maybe a visit would be better.

"Is there anything I can help you with?" Hildy asked when Caitlin made no immediate answer.

"No—I guess you'd better go ahead and make me an appointment with the doctor."

"How about ten, that suit you okay?"

"Ten, yes, that's great. Thanks, Hildy. See you Friday."

"Bye-bye, sugar, you take care now."

Caitlin put the phone down and gave a start when it immediately rang. "Hello."

"Hi, it's me. What are you doing tomorrow? Can we have lunch?"

"Hi, Meg. Sorry, not tomorrow. But I have to come into town for a doctor's appointment at ten on Friday. How about I drop by the library afterward?"

"Doctor's appointment? Are you sick?" Megan asked anxiously.

"No, nothing like that—I just need to talk to him, that's all," Caitlin reassured her.

"Is something wrong?"

"I'll tell you Friday, promise." Caitlin didn't want to discuss it over the phone.

"Oh, all right. I kind of need to talk to you, too."

"Problems?"

"Sort of—oh, not really—I don't know," Megan answered uncertainly.

"You want to talk now?" Caitlin asked.

"No," Megan answered after a slight pause. "It'll keep till Friday. How are things on the ranch?" she asked on a brighter note.

"Oh, pretty good—I have a new hired hand."

"Hired hand! You didn't tell me! When did that happen? Who is it—do I know him? It is a him, isn't it?"

"Whoa, girl, one question at a time. I, ah, hired him a couple of weeks ago. No, you don't know him, and yes, it is a him. I've been so busy, I haven't had time to stop and talk when I delivered the eggs."

Sensing more in what she wasn't saying, Megan asked, "Is he giving you any trouble?"

"Not the kind you mean." Caitlin hesitated. "Not exactly."

"Then what kind, exactly? Hey, you want my big brother to come knock him on his can?"

Caitlin laughed. "No, you idiot. Listen, I need to go. We'll talk Friday, all right?"

"All right," Megan agreed reluctantly. "Friday it is. So long."

For the next couple of days Nick worked as far from the house, and Caitlin, as possible. He left before she was up and came home after he knew she'd be in bed. His meals were left warming in the oven and sometimes she left instructions for something she wanted him to do the next day. The days rolled slowly by, with hardly a word, or a glance, passing between them.

Caitlin had been surprised to learn early on that Nick could read and write, though some words appeared to have no meaning for him. This, too, gave added strength to her amnesia theory.

One day, shortly after he'd come to the ranch, they'd been grooming the horses, and Caitlin had needed a certain medication to put on a sore spot Flame had developed on the inside of her ear. She'd looked high and low, but had been unable to locate what she needed. Muttering beneath her breath, she'd begun randomly shoving things around the shelves, the air around her static with her temper.

"What did you call it?" Nick asked uncertainly.

Caitlin paused to glare impatiently in his direction. What difference did it make to him? He couldn't read. Guilt followed immediately on the heels of the unkind thought. Lowering her eyes, she told him the brand name.

A moment later a hard brown hand shoved the bottle at her, and, back stiff, he stalked from the barn. Caitlin realized unhappily that he must have read her thoughts in her expressive face.

It was only much later that he returned and, picking up a currycomb, began to work alongside her in affronted silence. Caitlin glanced at him several times, wanting to apologize, curious as to how much he could read and understand. But the uncompromising set of his jaw kept her silent.

Later that evening, over dinner, he blurted, "I can read—some."

After that Caitlin never assumed anything in regard to his limitations. In the brief conversations they shared about work, if she wanted to know whether he understood something or not, she asked. She encouraged him to ask questions, allowing him to decide what he wanted to know, and noted that he listened carefully to her answers. And if her explanations went over his head, he asked her to repeat them until he grasped their meaning.

One evening about three weeks after Nick's arrival, Caitlin sat at home, waiting for him. She was feeling lonely and wanted the comfort of another's presence, even that of the man she'd been avoiding.

She still felt a bit embarrassed over the incident with the sheriff, but the pull she felt toward Nick, along with her desire for company, outweighed her feelings of guilt.

It was nearly nine when he came trudging tiredly into the house, pausing at the sight of her sitting fully dressed at the kitchen table.

He was dirt from head to toe, the sweat-stained Stetson riding low on his forehead. Caitlin took in his appearance with one sweeping glance. From the dark blue bandanna, twisted and tied around his sweaty neck, her eyes traveled over the threadbare brown shirt stained with dark circles under both arms. Opened down the front, it revealed a path of bloody welts visible in the pelt of dark hair arrowing down toward his trim waist.

"What happened to you?" she asked in mounting alarm.

"Barbed wire," he answered shortly, then shrugged, wincing at the sudden pain. With dirty, bloody fingers, he reluctantly removed his hat, hearing her gasp, audible clear cross the room.

He hadn't actually seen the scratch himself, beginning at the corner of his right eye and extending across the cheekbone, barely missing the edge of his mouth and ending in the center of his chin. Though it stung like hell, it hadn't bled much, and he couldn't understand why she was looking at him in such an odd fashion.

He hadn't expected her to be waiting for him. Usually by this time she was in her room. He planned it that way. If he'd known she would still be up, he would have washed up in the horse trough before coming in from the barn. He was doing his best to follow her lead and stay away from her. He didn't want her to make him leave.

"Come on." She bit her lip anxiously. "Let's see what the damage is." She moved swiftly across the room, her steps slowing when she realized he wasn't following. "Well, are you coming?" she asked impatiently.

"I'm okay."

"Don't be an idiot—"

His head came up, smoldering black eyes locking with hers. The room was fraught with a sudden tension. The ticking of the antique windup clock sitting on the china hutch was the only sound in the silent kitchen.

"I'm sorry." She kept her voice carefully low and without expression. She had once again spoken without thinking. He was very touchy about certain words, idiot being one of them.

"If you'll allow me, I'd like to make certain none of your wounds needs stitching."

He followed her unwillingly through her bedroom to the large bathroom where she kept the first-aid supplies. She saw him glance around curiously at her things.

"Sit here." She practically shoved him onto the toilet seat, realizing almost too late that the lid was raised. Turning hastily to the medicine cabinet, she left him to deal with the lid.

"Take off your shirt," she murmured as she turned to face him. "Let me see how bad it is."

Nick pulled his shirt slowly from his jeans—jeans that had grown indecently tight, she couldn't help but notice. Movement was so obviously painful for him that she reached around behind him, tugging at the shirt, helping him to free it.

This close, she could smell the not unpleasant odor of mingled horse and male sweat. Fighting the light-headed feeling his nearness brought, she jerked urgently at the material, needing suddenly to put some distance between them. He cried out when the shirt stuck to him, and Caitlin dropped the material as if suddenly burned, hands flying in alarmed contrition to her reddened cheeks.

"I'm sorry, I didn't mean to hurt you."

"It's okay," he muttered, not looking at her.

He was embarrassed to be in her bathroom with his shirt off. He felt really naked, not like when he worked shirtless outside. And, too, he felt stupid for getting caught in the wire in the first place. She had been right earlier when she'd called him an idiot, no matter how much it had hurt. Worse than anything, he was embarrassed to have her touch him when he knew how much she hated it. He wished he could have gotten to his room without her seeing him.

"I'm going to need to wash all the dirt from the scratches before putting antiseptic on them. I don't think there are any deep enough to require stitching, but you may need a bandage or two."

Caitlin kept her back to him as long as possible, arranging cotton, antiseptic and bandages before wetting and soaping a clean wash cloth. The bathroom was large by any standard, but his presence seemed to fill it, dwarfing its roomy proportions.

She decided to begin with his face. Though the scratch looked wicked, on closer inspection it appeared less damaging than it had at first glance. There were only a few small spots across his cheekbone where blood dotted the surface.

Feeling awkward, wanting to touch him, yet fearing the contact, Caitlin bent slightly at the waist, catching his firm chin in one unsteady hand. She turned and tilted his head to the light, feeling the sharp bristles of his beard bite into the sensitive skin of her fingers and palm. Her heart skipped a beat.

Nick closed his eyes at the first stinging touch of the soapy cloth, and a tight knot formed in the pit of her stomach as she watched the thick black lines of his lashes fan over his tanned cheeks. After pausing for a second to note the tiny lines at the corner of his eyes, she swept the cloth downward.

At the edge of his mouth her unsteady progress slowed; her heart thumping madly, her eyes lingered on his sensuously full lips. Guiltily she wondered how they would feel molded to her own.

Sensing her disquiet, Nick turned his head slightly, and Caitlin met his eyes, struggling to hide her heightened awareness of his masculine beauty.

Their glances locked, and something flickered far back in the depths of his dark eyes. Disconcerted, unable to read the unspoken message, Caitlin took a deep steadying breath, jerked her hands from his face and turned away.

Masking her inner turmoil with a deceptive calm, she silently soaked a cotton ball with antiseptic and applied it to the scratch. Even when he caught his breath and gazed up at her with watery, reproachful eyes, she kept determinedly quiet.

In short, clipped words she told him to turn until his back was facing her. Then she gazed unhappily at one nasty-looking laceration starting beneath one shoulder blade and running diagonally across his back to the other side. The edges looked raw and puckered, and her own flesh tingled in sympathy. Thankfully, the remaining scratches appeared to be superficial.

Nick remained stoically silent while she worked, sitting slightly hunched over, elbows on knees, head bent forward.

Once, as she cleaned the deeper gash, the muscles across his lean back tightened, quivering. When she hesitated, he turned slightly to look at her, his lean jaw rigid, a white line showing around his tightly drawn mouth. After a brief glance from pain-darkened eyes he turned quickly away. It was a moment before she could continue her ministrations.

At last, feeling like a wrung out dishrag, Caitlin directed him to slide around to face her. Contemplating the broad muscled expanse of hair-roughened chest in sudden panic, she came instantly to the decision that there was no way. Licking her lips nervously, she almost shook her head. She could *not* do this.

Standing at arm's length, she bent over to him, only to discover that, though she wasn't particularly tall, the toilet seat was too low. Against her better judgment, she found herself on her knees stationed between his long muscular thighs.

With one all-encompassing glance she took in the dirt-stained ridges of muscle covered with black springy hair. She swallowed once, tightly, before touching the cloth to his chest.

Never having bathed a man until now, she had no way of knowing how the soap would foam in the matted chest hair. To her total embarrassment, she needed to rinse the cloth three times, and still white bubbles clung stubbornly to the dark wiry curls.

Disconcerted by her rampaging senses, she attempted to put her awareness aside and concentrate with detachment on the task at hand, a feat she found nearly impossible to perform.

Though numerous, the cuts on his chest also appeared to be superficial. But it was agonizingly slow work, sifting through the unyielding hair with ultrasensitive fingertips in order to thoroughly search out and cleanse each small abrasion.

Perspiration popped out across her upper lip and along the back of her neck, slipped down the narrow valley between her breasts. Her blouse stuck damply across her shoulders and chest.

One small, nasty-looking scratch lay beneath the swirls of hair just above his right nipple. Working slowly, her clumsy fingers parted the intractable strands and in the process grazed the sensitive bud, causing it to pucker tightly.

Caitlin pretended not to hear his startled sound of surprise, or see the accelerated beat of his heart, evident in the pulse kicking at the hollow juncture between his neck and chest.

Despite her continued pretense of calm, a tense silence filled the room. She felt as though a tight band had closed around her chest. The hand holding the cloth pressed to the rigid muscles tightened involuntarily, sending a stream of liquid spiraling down his chest and stomach. Without conscious thought, her hand flew out, fingers gliding along the same path, along the dark hair arrowing beneath the waistband of his jeans.

Nick sucked his stomach muscles in with a soft gasp, suppressing a groan. His long tanned fingers closed firmly over her pale questing hand, halting its dangerous descent. Breath suspended, he pressed tightly, holding her hand captive against the heated flesh of his abdomen.

Caitlin's eyes grew wide at the sight of her fingers clasped intimately against the taut line of his virile body. Feeling weak and dizzy, able only to breathe in short, shallow gasps, she closed her eyes to momentarily block out the disturbing sight.

Almost instantly, against her will, her eyes opened and were drawn upward, caught by his unsettling gaze. Like a fly in a spider's web, she was caught and held, unable to tear her glance from his. But though he held her with the burning gaze of his midnight eyes, his face remained perfectly expressionless.

As though compelled by an unspoken command, Caitlin's free hand began a slow climb toward the rigid planes of his stern face. Gentle fingers threaded through the thick black silk tumbled across his forehead, smoothing it back from his eyes.

One finger traced, oh, so lightly, the path of destruction the wire had taken from eye to chin. Head tilted, driven by a force she couldn't resist, Caitlin leaned forward. Her soft breath whispered warmly across his supersensitive flesh an instant before she touched him with gentle lips.

Lightly, she caressed the indentation in his chin before moving slowly upward, leaving a trail of feather-light kisses along the uncompromising line of his jaw.

Nick's heart pounded, then jerked to a standstill. Her touch triggered primitive feelings, created desires that confused him. The air rushed from his lungs in one wild gasp. Senses reeling, he tasted her heady perfume. She smelled of spring flowers and the medicine she had used on his cuts. Her scent, the tingling effect of her touch, spread through him like wildfire.

He allowed himself the brief thrill of touching unsteady lips to the short curls at her forehead and temples. He remembered what had happened the last time he had touched her, though. It took all his strength, but he kept his left hand clenched tightly on his thigh.

He would gladly have given anything to be able to press his lips to her soft cheek and chin as she had his. To be able to touch the creamy expanse of her neck, tilt her head and press hungry lips to hers, take her sweetness onto his tongue.

But he didn't do it. He felt the changes taking place in his lower body with alarmed embarrassment. Releasing her hand abruptly from its prison against his body, he pressed it, and her, resolutely away. She would be angry, afraid, if she learned his guilty secret. He didn't know how he knew, but he did.

Caitlin dimly registered his lack of response, the rigidity of his body. And when he removed his hand to shove hers away, it was like a slap in the face. Her senses returned sharply to normal; eyelids flying open, she found herself eye-to-eye with him, her hand still clasping his shoulder. Disoriented, disconcerted, her first thought was a desire to disappear—sink through the floor and never face him again, ever.

Here she was throwing herself at him, crawling all over him, while he held himself aloof. As she registered the stern, set cast of his features, her second thought was to get as far from him as she could, as quickly as possible.

Easing to her feet, bile rising rapidly in her throat, she looked everywhere but at him.

Keeping her voice even, though at great cost, she said, "I think you can finish by yourself. I have something to do in the laundry room. Just use whatever you need." Edging toward the door, she whirled from the room.

Once outside, she leaned back against the wall, closing her eyes in despair, willing her unsteady legs to support her. Dear God, she felt like such a wanton fool. How could she have done that? How could she have touched him? Her fingers tingled even now at the memory of rock hard muscles, sheathed in satiny smooth skin. His taste lingered on her tongue, his scent on her skin. She wished she never had to face him again, or speak to him, or have him remember...

She moved quickly to the door. "Have you had a tetanus shot?"

His head whipped toward her, a look of soul-wrenching dejection in his dark eyes. At her sudden reappearance, the look vanished instantly, his features becoming impassive.

"I don't know," he answered flatly. There was too much he didn't know.

Caitlin's glance swerved over his head. "You'd better come into town with me tomorrow. I should have thought of this before. There are certain shots you need to have, especially working around horses and cows."

"Shots?" A note of fearful curiosity entered his voice. He didn't recognize the word.

"Yes, like with a needle—" She stuck a fingernail sharply against the skin of the opposite arm.

"I don't want—" He started to shake his head.

"You get the shots, or you don't work," she stated uncompromisingly.

His glance darkened. "When?"

"We leave at nine."

"Okay."

Caitlin left the doorway, leaving him alone once more with his unhappy thoughts. Was she going to let him stay? he wondered. Was that why he had to have those shots she said he needed? A part of him stood back, amazed at the things he was coming to understand. So many things he had to learn, so many thoughts and feelings to deal with.

Before coming to the ranch, he had lived...in the dark. That was the only way he could describe it with meaning to himself. Since he'd met Caitlin, he'd found the sunlight.

Chapter 4

Dr. James Shepherd folded his hands neatly on the desk top and looked expectantly toward the attractive young woman sitting across from him.

"Well, Caitlin, you appear to me to be in good health."

"That isn't why I'm here."

"Does it have anything to do with the man in the outer office? The one Hildy had cornered with a wicked-looking needle?" he asked, grinning.

"As a matter of fact, it does. I would like to ask you some questions about mental retardation—and amnesia. I hope you won't think I'm crazy..."

He made a quick gesture of denial, settling more comfortably in the brown leather chair.

"Here goes." She licked her lips nervously. "Could a person appear to be retarded, even if he really wasn't?"

James Shepherd raised one quizzical blond brow and asked, "Let me see if I've got this right. You want to know if someone, your friend out there, for instance, could pretend well enough to fool a medical man?"

"Well, anyone, I guess." She shrugged, on unfamiliar ground. "Can someone appear, you know, that way—and not really be that way?" She faltered, out of her depth.

Dr. Shepherd eyed her consideringly before replying. "It's possible. As a matter of fact, there are some well-documented cases where it has occurred. But why do you think he would want to appear retarded?"

"I don't," she answered quickly. "It's just so strange. The man, I call him Nick, sometimes acts as though he's retarded. As a matter of fact, until a short while ago, I thought he was. But there have been instances lately when I've seen him respond with understanding and intelligence.

"I finally began to wonder if there was an alternative to his being retarded. Sometimes, when I show him how to do something on the ranch, or talk to him about something I read in a magazine, it's almost as though he knows about it beforehand, without my telling him.

"I don't know why, maybe for that reason, along with a couple dozen others, I got this amnesia idea into my head and couldn't get it out. That's why I decided to come see you. I wanted you to tell me if it was more likely to be amnesia Nick is suffering from rather than retardation."

"Without a thorough examination, there's really no way I can give you an answer."

"Can't it be done—" she interrupted herself, gesturing with her hands "—without a lot of that kind of thing? I don't think he'd let you examine him."

He shook his head. "I'm afraid not. In certain kinds of amnesia, well..." He paused, as though searching for the right words. "You could almost call it a form of retardation of the memory process, though that's a simplification of a very complicated illness."

Caitlin fiddled with the clasp of her handbag, avoiding his eyes. She wanted very much to believe in the amnesia theory. "What would cause such a thing?"

"Oh, any number of things—an accident, for instance, or a serious illness, maybe a severe shock. There are many situations that can bring about a loss of memory, and to varying degrees, as well.

"Say you started out to a party for instance, and the next thing you know, you found yourself there without any idea of how you got there."

"Really, something as simple as that?" she asked amazed.

"Amnesia is more common than most people suspect, but it's the traumatic kind that makes the news."

"Um, do people ever remember all the things they've forgotten?" Caitlin stared intently at the curtains behind the doctor's curly blond head.

"No, not always, and those who do usually don't remember the interval in-between."

"But what if it's years? Or what if they've made a new life, have come to care about other people—people they met while suffering from the amnesia?"

Dr. Shepherd shook his head. "I'm afraid that doesn't seem to matter." Caitlin looked so upset that he felt compelled to add, "I'm sorry. And that isn't necessarily conclusive. When dealing with the human mind, it's nearly impossible to predict the outcome." Glancing down at his gold watch, he asked, "Is there anything else I can tell you?"

"N-no thanks." She knew she sounded disturbed. At the door she turned back. "What would bring back a lost memory?"

He spread his hands on the desk top. "That's hard to say— a familiar face—or a place—a shock—an accident. Sometimes a memory will manifest itself in a dream."

He rose from the chair, walked around to lean against the corner of the desk and crossed his arms over his chest. "You see, Caitlin, the subconscious never gives up. It constantly strives to force those blocked memories to the surface. And eventually, maybe not everything, but part will be restored—a little at a time. In most cases," he qualified.

"Thank you again, doctor." She opened the door, then hesitated. "One thing more, if you don't mind," she said over her shoulder. "How can you help someone with amnesia, the kind where they don't remember much of anything?"

"Retrograde," he murmured. Catching her inquiring glance, he repeated, "Retrograde amnesia—it's a severe form involving much more than one's personal identity."

"Is there any way to help the person to remember?"

"All you can do is try to give them a stress-free environment, establish a regular routine and help them by answering any questions they may have. If any other problems develop, by all means consult a physician.

"Caitlin," he spoke suddenly, moving away from the desk, shedding his relaxed pose. "Would you like me to try to persuade this Nick to let me examine him? I don't guarantee I can diagnose that it's amnesia you're dealing with here, but I can give it a try.

"You know, there is the possibility that he's really retarded and those flashes of intelligence you think you're seeing are mostly in your own mind."

She opened her mouth, closed it, then shook her head. "No." She found her voice at last. "That is, I'd like to know, so I can help him. But he's so skittish. It was all I could do to get him here for the shots he needs. I'm afraid if I force the issue, he might just up and run off. He was in such a state when he came to work for me—I don't want to do anything that might scare him off.

"And besides, if it is amnesia, from what you just told me, there's no way to force his memory. And if he's retarded . . ." Her voice died out, and she gazed helplessly at the doctor.

"If he is retarded," the man took up the sentence, "giving him work and a place to stay, teaching him farming or ranching, some useful type of occupation, is more, unfortunately, than most handicapped people are offered during their lifetime."

"Yes," Caitlin agreed slowly, while her mind was busy assimilating the facts he'd told her about amnesia. Despite his reminder that Nick could be mentally retarded, she was sure that wasn't the case. She prayed it wasn't so. She was determined to keep working with Nick, delving beneath the surface of his reluctant friendship to discover for herself what his real problem stemmed from.

Caitlin thanked the doctor once more and left the room quickly, expelling a long breath. She had a whole lot to think about.

"Child, am I glad to see you." Hildy stood, her hands on her broad hips, a fierce scowl marring her usually placid features.

"What is it?" Caitlin asked anxiously, searching for a sign of Nick.

"What it is—is that man of yours. First he won't give me any background information, then he flat refuses to let me give him the shots. I hope you have better luck convincing him he needs them."

"Where is he? Is he all right?"

"Calm yourself, sugar. He's fine, jes' fine. I got him layin' down the hall there." She nodded toward a closed door.

"I'm sorry he gave you so much trouble, Hildy."

"Never you mind, honey." The older woman gave her a knowing look. "Go on now an' see about him. He was askin' for you," she added softly. Her features returned to their usual good-natured expression. "And convince him I'm not the bad guy, okay?"

Caitlin threw a smile over her shoulder and headed for the door.

"By the way," Hildy's voice stopped her in her tracks, "what happened to that boy?"

"H-happened?"

"Yeah, he looks like he tangled with a wildcat—an' lost." She chuckled.

"Oh." Caitlin relaxed, smiling, too. "Barbed wire—he tangled with barbed wire."

Hildy clicked her tongue. "Well, it looks worse than it is. You did a mighty fine first-aid job, sugar. I put on a little salve an' a couple new plasters." She shrugged her massive shoulders and chuckled. "He's one stubborn dude."

"Thanks again, Hildy. I'll be out in a minute with his permission for you to give him the shots, I hope."

Hildy nodded and, humming beneath her breath, good humor restored, waddled into the outer office.

"Nick," Caitlin called softly as she entered the small examining room. The lights were turned off and the curtains open, making the room appear dim, not dark. Nick lay on his stomach, on a brown vinyl examining couch, with his shirt off. Two new white strips of bandage had been applied to his back.

"Nick," she called again, moving closer. He stirred, raised his head and turned it in her direction.

"Hi, how are you feeling?"

"You alone?" he inquired apprehensively, trying to see around her slender figure.

"Yes, why?"

"That woman, that—nurse," he spluttered, making it sound like a four-letter word. "You know what she wanted me to do?"

"What?" she asked innocently, hiding a smile, recalling the part of her anatomy where she'd been given her own tetanus shot.

His face, pale before, flushed pink to the tips of his well-shaped ears. "Nothing," he answered, shaking his head slightly. He looked so pitiful that Caitlin found herself smoothing the damp hair from his flushed brow, receiving a look of surprised wariness from beneath narrowed lids for her trouble.

She dropped her hand hastily, asking, "Do you feel ready to let her give you the shots?" Once again his reactions appeared so *normal* that she forgot herself.

"No," he muttered stubbornly.

"That's too bad," she answered softly. "Then I guess we might as well leave."

As easy as that? She was going to let him get out of it as easy as that?

"You mad?"

"No, I'm not mad. But I'm disappointed. I'd hoped you'd be around for some time to come. I've gotten use to your help on the ranch."

"I have to leave?"

"I told you, no shots, no job. It's as simple as that. They're for my protection as well as yours. I can't afford a big hospital bill if you get really sick. And I certainly can't afford the cost of a funeral," she added as an afterthought, then wondered if that were too much.

He wasn't sure what a funeral was, but apparently it wasn't something Caitlin wanted to buy. And it cost a lost of money. He knew about money. If you didn't have any, you couldn't eat, or sleep in a bed. Unless you worked for someone who did have money, like Caitlin. But maybe she didn't have much. He wouldn't want her to have to live like he had before she took him in. And he didn't want to have to leave the ranch—or Caitlin.

"Okay." Turning over onto his side, he fiddled with his belt buckle. "I'll do it."

As they passed through the outer office a short while later on their way out, Hildy called to them.

"I need a name here, Caity, for the insurance." She indicated the forms in her pudgy hands. "Nick?" she prompted.

"Rivers," Nick responded automatically.

"Rivers?" Caitlin questioned.

"Rivers." Hildy repeated with satisfaction.

On the sidewalk out front, Caitlin turned on him. "Why did you tell her that?"

"I don't know." He looked mystified.

"W-where did you come up with it?"

"I don't know," he repeated uncomfortably. "It just—came to me. Did I say something wrong?" He really didn't know where the name had come from. When the other woman asked for a name, suddenly it was just there in his head, and he said it. Now he worried that maybe he shouldn't have.

"No," she answered slowly. "You didn't do anything wrong. But when we met in town the day you came to work for me, I asked your name. You remember?"

He didn't answer, just stood looking at the sidewalk at their feet.

"You didn't answer, and when I suggested Nick, you agreed. Do you have a name? Something other than Nick?"

Nick shrugged, unconsciously flexing the fingers on his sore hand. "I like Nick."

"But why did you act so odd that first day, when I asked you who you were?" she persisted.

"People leave me alone when I do that." She had to lean close to hear his muttered admission.

People left him alone? He had determined what put others off and contrived to act that way to be left alone? In other words, it was all a clever charade. That was definitely not the reasoning of someone of less than normal intelligence. She began to feel excitement bubble up from inside. Perhaps now was the time to propose the idea of an examination by Dr. Shepherd.

In the excitement of this new discovery, she grasped his arm urgently. "Do you remember anything about where you lived before you came here?" She'd asked this question before and had always been met with hostile silence.

When he only stood looking at her hand on his arm without answering, she pulled at him, even in her agitation aware of the powerful attraction he held for her, and forced him to meet her gaze.

"Nick, what happened to your knee? When I first saw you it was all banged up, and you limp sometimes. What happened to it?"

"I hurt it. Can we go home now? Let go of me, please." Fighting the embarrassing reaction his body always had to her, he pulled his arm from her hold. "Can we go now?" he asked again stiffly, not meeting her eyes.

"Excuse me." A bony elbow jabbed Caitlin in the back. "Oh, is that you, Caitlin?" The birdlike woman peered keenly over the tops of her glasses.

"Yes, Miz Henderson, it's me," Caitlin acknowledged in resignation. The last person on earth she wanted to see at this moment was standing before her, sepia-colored eyes darting curiously back and forth between her and Nick.

"Well, ain't this nice. It's been such a long time, dearie, since we've had the chance for a heart-to-heart chat."

A long time? Try an eternity. They had never had a heart-to-heart anything.

"The ranch keeps me pretty busy, especially this time of year," Caitlin answered, moving a step farther along the sidewalk, making her desire to get away obvious.

"I was real sorry to hear about your daddy, such a good man—and so hardworking—a real pity to be snatched away like that, in the prime of life."

Her father had been gone nearly three years now, and the old hypocrite had never had a good thing to say about him while he was alive. Eyes like hard bits of green glass, Caitlin took Nick's arm, preparing to turn away.

"I don't believe I've had the pleasure." Mabel ignored the girl's reluctance to stop and pass the time of day. Preening like a peacock before the darkly handsome young man standing silently at Caitlin's side, she introduced herself and asked his name.

"Why, I'm surprised you don't recognize him, Miz Henderson. You surely must have seen him before now." The light of battle was clearly flashing in Caitlin's stormy green eyes. "Spending as much time in town as you do, you must have seen him hanging about." Caitlin gestured toward the picnic tables, near the bandstand, where Nick had sat that first day, eating a candy bar.

Caitlin didn't see Nick's eyes cloud with uneasiness, his face flush in shame, as dawning recognition rounded the older woman's sharp, beady little eyes and caused her mouth to drop open. Disbelief was followed by disdain. Drawing her narrow shoulders tight, she stepped aside, as if fearing contamination from breathing the same tainted air.

"If you all will excuse me," she said haughtily, "I really must go." Back stiff, on spindly legs, she hurried away, eager to impart the news around town of the goings-on at the Barratt ranch. And wouldn't poor Mr. Barratt just turn over in his grave if he knew.

Caitlin fumed under her breath, only now becoming aware of the silent reproach emanating from the man at her side. Looking at his closed face, she bit her lip in contrition, guilt gnawing at her.

She had shamed him by bringing up his earlier appearance to the town's most notorious gossip, and all for the sake of getting back at the woman. She deserved whatever bad thoughts were lurking beneath those cold black eyes staring down at her.

"I'm sorry." She spoke in a thin voice. "There is no excuse for that." Smiling sadly, she added, "When I was growing up my father cautioned me—frequently—to stop and think before I spoke." Her glance shifted away, a slight dampness at the corner of one eye. "I never listened then, either."

He gently captured the moisture at the corner of her eye and rubbed it between his thumb and forefinger, a look of wonder replacing the coldness in his eyes. "For me?" he whispered on a deep note.

Their eyes met and, despite intentions to the contrary, clung, then darted away self-consciously, the air around them charged with an undeniable vibrancy.

Caitlin's heart fluttered wildly in her breast, her senses alive to the tangible bond that seemed to be growing between them. Feelings they weren't ready to deal with, unable even to rationalize, coursed through them, leaving them both confused and uneasy. Too much had happened to them in a short period of time for either to be able to take it all in.

Caitlin was more encouraged than ever about the amnesia theory. And though she felt she needed to take things slowly, she was convinced that, working together, they could jog his memory back into focus.

She conveniently ignored the little voice reminding her of what the doctor had said about the possibility of his intelligence being all in her mind. It was *not* just wishful thinking on her part—was it?

They moved a little apart; then both took a deep steadying breath and spoke at the same time.

"I need to go to the library for a few minutes."

"Can we go home now?" he repeated for the third time.

Caitlin explained about needing to talk to her friend Megan as they crossed the town square to the library. They passed several people who spoke in friendly tones to Caitlin, while throwing curious looks at the man striding along at her side.

"I could go on back to the ranch," Nick offered tentatively, uneasy about meeting someone new. People made him nervous—Caitlin was one of the few he remembered who didn't, except at the beginning.

"How? Walk?"

"Oh." He looked sheepish. "I can thumb." He held up one thumb and grinned.

"Nick, can you drive?" A week ago, even a few days ago, she wouldn't even have considered asking the question. Today it seemed possible.

He shook his head. "No."

Caitlin stopped him with a hand on one shoulder. "We need to talk. I did something a little while ago that I want to discuss with you."

"What?" he asked shortly, distrust filling his eyes with reserve.

Caitlin shifted uneasily under his stare. "Let's talk about it later," she answered awkwardly. They resumed their walk, maintaining an aloof attitude belied by the jolt of physical awareness generated each time their swinging hands brushed against each other.

"Don't tell me that gorgeous hunk is the new hired hand!"

Caitlin had left Nick in the main reading room, looking through books while she went in search of her friend. Opening the door to the office at Caitlin's knock, Megan caught a glimpse of Nick's profile, just enough to make her eye her friend in surprised speculation.

Seating herself at the small round table, giving herself time to deal with the unexpected stab of jealousy that left her wanting to clutch at her middle, Caitlin nodded silently.

"So what's the story?"

Pulling at the hem of her cinnamon-colored skirt, very nearly the exact shade of her hair, Caitlin cleared her throat and met her friend's worried brown eyes. "I'm very confused, Meg."

"What's wrong?"

"That's just it—I'm not sure what's wrong. I think I need to think about things for a while longer before we discuss it. Okay?"

"Drink your coffee," Megan told her with a small grin.

Smiling, Caitlin did as she was told. "You always were bossy. It's only because you're so small and you think no one will hit you." They both laughed at the familiar childhood taunt and sipped from their cups in companionable silence for a moment.

"So what's his name?" Megan asked, wondering at the strange smile on her friend's face as she lifted her cup.

"Nick, Nick Rivers. He just showed up at the ranch one day, asking for a drink of water. The next thing I knew," she shortened the actual chain of events, "I'd hired him to work for me."

They talked companionably for a while until Caitlin realized Megan was looking more tense and strained than usual.

"You haven't mentioned what you wanted to talk to me about," Caitlin said. "Is it David?"

Biting her lip, Megan nodded. "He's getting worse, Caity. I'm afraid to leave him alone any more than I have to. Sometimes..." Caitlin had to strain to hear the soft admission. "Sometimes I'm afraid of him."

"He'd never hurt you," Caitlin rushed to assure her friend.

"No, I don't suppose he would...." But she didn't sound one-hundred percent sure.

"You know darn good and well your brother would never harm a hair of your head. This is the guy who nearly broke Billy Needham's nose for calling you pizza-face at the school picnic. And Billy was a good twenty pounds heavier and a couple of years older than David. He'd kill anyone who hurt you."

Megan quickly glanced up. "That's what I'm afraid of. I know his behavior comes from his experiences as a POW in Vietnam. But when he goes around the house checking all the doors and windows, muttering to himself, and refuses to talk to me for days on end, or sneaks out at night with a gun and doesn't come home until dawn—it scares me."

"Tell me what's got you so upset this time."

"Logan called last week—to ask me out." She twisted the small gold ring on her right hand. The ring Logan had given her on her eighteenth birthday, in lieu of an engagement ring.

"What did you tell him?"

"I told him no."

"Meg," Caitlin protested softly.

"He called back the next day, and that time I said I'd let him know," she confessed unhappily.

"So what's the problem? Don't you want to go out with him?"

"Yes—and no." Megan spilled her coffee and reached for a paper towel. "I don't know."

"Is it David? Are you afraid he'll object?"

"Not really." She laughed dryly. "I already *know* he objects—he made that clear when Logan called the first time."

"Meg," Caitlin ventured, touching her friend's hand urgently, "I know you feel you owe David a lot for his taking care of you the way he did after your parents' deaths, and later, after Vietnam, when your aunt passed away. I know he's been through hell himself. He's hurt, angry and bitter because of his experiences in Vietnam and the reception he received when they came home. But you're a grown woman, and it is your life, after all."

"You think I should go out with Logan, no matter what David says, or thinks?"

"I didn't say that. I'm only saying it's your decision. You have to make it. I don't know what happened between you and Logan—" She shook her head as Megan opened her mouth. "I'm not asking. If you ever feel the need, I'm here." She echoed Megan's earlier words to her. "I'm just saying you have to make your own choices."

They were silent for a time, just looking at each other. The shadows lifted slowly from Megan's eyes, and a small tentative smile curled the edges of her wide mouth. "What do you charge an hour?"

Caitlin grinned self-consciously and patted her friend's hand. "For you, it's on the house. Now I think I've left Nick out there alone long enough. What say we join him, and I'll make the introductions?"

A few moments later Megan smiled her approval as Nick stood and was introduced to her. Sensing an undercurrent between her friend and the oddly reticent man, she did her best to put him at his ease. By the time Caitlin and Nick took their leave, she and Nick had established a tenuous rapport.

"You like her very much," Nick commented softly as the truck sped out of town.

Caitlin took her eyes off the road to glance at him, detecting an odd note in his deep voice. Could he be jealous?

"We're more like sisters than friends," she affirmed, past images flashing through her mind, bringing a reminiscent smile to her lips.

Nick shifted slightly so he could watch the fleeting expressions cross her mobile face. While her eyes were busy on the road, her attention focused on the past, he allowed his hungry eyes to probe her features.

Her features were delicately carved, her red lips full and ripe. Sunlight kissed her face, bringing out the golden undertones, showing the light dusting of freckles on the smooth satiny skin. Her short nose was slim and fine, the nostrils delicate.

He watched intently from beneath his lashes as Caitlin pulled at a tendril of hair, blown by the wind until it was caught against the moist softness of her parted lips.

His breathing quickened as a finger of sunlight picked out the burnished highlights amid the fiery tresses. He recalled the sensuous feel of her hair in his hands, clinging like silk to his roughened fingers. He imagined what it would feel like to bury his face in its lustrous bounty, nostrils filled with the flower-like scent that seemed always to cling to it.

"Wow!" Caitlin screwed up her face, flapping a hand in front of her nose.

Startled, Nick sat up straighter in the seat. "Something wrong?" he asked, trying to clear the disturbing pictures from his mind and noticing an acrid odor in the air.

"Skunk," she answered succinctly.

Braking lightly, she checked the rearview mirror, pushed in on the clutch, downshifted and pulled over to the side of the road, a mischievous smile playing around the corners of her mouth.

"Trouble?"

"Uh-uh. Remember in town, I asked if you could drive?"

"Oh, no!" He sounded panic-stricken as he caught her drift.

"Oh, yes," she insisted, shifting into neutral, then killing the engine.

"No!"

With her head back, her chin thrust forward with iron determination, her green eyes glinted at him. "Part of your job, Mr. Rivers, is to haul feed and hay to the cattle. So far I have been doing your job. You—" she poked at his chest—he hated it when she did that"—are not fulfilling your obligations, as outlined in your job description."

"Job description," he echoed blankly. "What's a job description?"

"Never you mind—just get your butt out and come around
here. I'll slide over the gearshift."

Which she proceeded to do, in the process exposing a long
expanse of silk-clad thigh.

Eyes riveted on the sight of so much luscious skin, he took
an unexpected header out the door and onto the hard shoulder
of the gravel road. Muttering imprecations only half-heard over
her anxious murmurs of sympathy, he dusted off the seat of his
jeans and limped to the front of the truck.

"Now don't be nervous," she cautioned as he took his place
behind the wheel, thereby filling him with a surge of mounting
anxiety.

"Okay." He gripped the steering wheel tightly with both
sweating hands. "I'm ready."

Caitlin helped him to adjust the seat and mirrors to suit his
extra height, then began to instruct him in the procedure for
clutching, shifting and accelerating. By the time she finished
explaining what to do, what not to do and what to be careful of,
he was thoroughly confused.

"Can't I wait till we get home?" He kept glancing worriedly
in the rearview mirror. On their way into town a large truck had
pulled up behind them, and he had been terrified to see it so
close to their bumpers.

"There isn't a soul around. Come on, don't be a chicken,
foot on the clutch." She watched him reluctantly comply.
"Right foot ready to give it gas."

"What's wrong?" His puzzled glance shot to her face.
"Nothing happened."

"Try turning the key—it helps."

A dark red tide crept up his neck. "Oh," was his only comment. After several false starts, Nick finally coordinated both
feet, managing to move the vehicle a few yards.

"What's wrong with it?" he asked nervously.

"The engine is trying to tell you something. You need to shift
again, into a higher gear."

The ride was not without incident. They narrowly missed a
couple mailboxes, as well as the turn into her lane. But, all in
all, Caitlin was satisfied with his performance. It wouldn't be
long, she was certain, before he was driving the truck as easily
as she did. And she suspected that, though the straight stick

appeared relatively unfamiliar to him, driving a vehicle was not. Watching the road carefully, hunched over the wheel he gripped in both hands, he missed the assessing glance Caitlin shot his way. What other unsuspected talents was he hiding?

"Why are you mad?" he asked abruptly. They were ready to climb from the truck, which was parked in front of the garage.

Caitlin blinked dumbly. "Mad?"

"Yeah, you been watching me like I did something really bad." After a moment he asked uncertainly, "Are you mad?"

"No, I'm not angry." But she didn't elaborate. "You did great on the drive home. It won't be long till you're handling the truck as easily as I do," she assured him.

"Oh." He swallowed, keeping his glance carefully trained on his hands, still tight on the wheel, while his pulse rioted at the gentle tone of her voice. He followed her out of the truck and went about the evening chores, basking in the remembered glow of her approval.

"You closin' early today, Megan?"

Megan gave a start and looked around at the big man standing at the bottom of the steps. She hadn't heard his quiet approach over her own tumultuous thoughts.

"It's Friday, Sheriff." She indicated the printed hours on the door. "I always close at this time."

Bart Raymond stepped onto the porch, his glance flicking from the sign to her bent head as she continued to turn the key in the lock.

"Bob Colter and Fred Taylor came by the office today."

Megan froze, head down, eyes on the wooden porch where her keys had just landed. Bending with surprising agility, despite his massive bulk, Bart retrieved them and silently held them out to her.

"He didn't hurt them, Sheriff," she whispered through stiff lips. "They were trespassing."

"Threatening somebody with a rifle can be a dangerous thing. It could have some real bad repercussions."

"I know." She looked at him beseechingly. "You aren't going to arrest him, are you?"

"Naw, I can't arrest him. Like you said, he was on his own property, and they were trespassing. But maybe I ought to have a little talk with him."

"No!" she protested quickly. "Please, let me do it. He's not at his best just now. My brother isn't a bad person, Sheriff—"

"I know that, honey." He felt like a hawk that had cornered a small animal when she looked up at him with those enormous liquid-brown eyes. "But he can't go around shoving a gun under people's noses just 'cause they innocently stumbled onto his property."

Though, knowing the men involved, he sincerely doubted the innocence of either one.

"Did Bob or Fred file a complaint?"

"Naw." He rubbed at his jaw, faintly registering the bristles. "They were pretty mad—scared, too, I'll bet."

A gleam of humor showed far back in his golden eyes. Bob and Fred were not exactly model citizens. The thought of a little fear penetrating their tough-guy exteriors pleased him. "They just wanted to let me know what happened."

They had wanted him to go out and haul Jones's butt to jail, but he had pointed out that they were trespassing and Jones could file charges against *them*. That had cooled their ardor somewhat.

"You talk to your brother, honey. Talk real hard. Make him listen and understand my position. The next time, he might not be so lucky. Someone might shoot back."

"I'll tell him, Sheriff, I promise. I'll make him understand." If only she could. "Thank you."

He nodded, shifted his glance and cleared his throat. "That Caitlin Barratt's pickup I saw parked here earlier?"

"Yes," she answered, eyeing him curiously.

"She alone?"

"No," she replied shortly. Why the sudden interest in Caitlin's comings and goings? "She had her new hired hand with her," she added.

"You meet him?"

"Yes." She wasn't going to give anything away. Caitlin was her best friend. If he wanted to know something, let him ask.

"How'd he seem to you?" His probing glance shot to her face, capturing her eyes. She got the uneasy feeling that the real purpose behind his visit had little to do with her brother.

"Nice, Sheriff. He seemed very nice."

"Say where he's from? What he's doin' here?"

"I didn't ask." Her chin tilted a fraction. She wasn't a snoop; she didn't gather information about her friends and carry tales to *anyone*.

The sheriff smiled suddenly, revealing an attractiveness that wasn't evident when his face was in repose. "I'd better let you go. I'll bet you have a list of things to do on your only day off early."

"As a matter of fact, I do." She was glad to see him leave; his inquisition had made her nervous.

Moving down the steps, he reminded her, "Don't forget to talk to that brother of yours, now."

"I won't forget," Megan assured his retreating back.

The smile was gone from the sheriff's face as he moved deliberately down the steps. It was all over town that Caitlin had that bum staying at her ranch. That, and his amazing transformation, had the gossips' tongues wagging.

He was determined to find out who the man really was, and why he couldn't get the idea out of his head that the man was dangerous. If he didn't hear from Jamison soon, he'd call him back and put the heat on. He didn't know why, but he was sure this was important.

Chapter 5

"How do you feel about him?"

Caitlin and Megan were talking over coffee after Sunday evening church services, sitting at a small café at the edge of town.

"That's a hard one," Caitlin answered, frowning down at her hands, which were busily shredding the napkin. "He's hardworking, gentle, thoughtful. He tries to do his share of work and mine, too. He gets up early every morning, long before I do, and has most of the chores done before breakfast. He never complains, never asks for anything—he makes me feel . . . special," she confessed.

Smiling self-consciously, her face turning a bright shade of pink, she added a pause. "I care about him."

"Are you falling in love with him?" They had known each other for so long that they had few secrets from each other.

"I don't know," she whispered, not ready to even consider such a possibility. "I'm attracted to him physically, but—you know me—I've never been serious about anyone for long. And there's so much about him I don't know. What if he *has* lost his memory, and there's someone else in his life? Or, worse, what if he really is retarded?"

"But that isn't what you think, is it?" Megan asked gently.

"No, but how can I be sure that isn't only because it's what I want to believe?" She was playing her own devil's advocate.

"What are you going to do?"

"Keep asking questions."

"Won't that be kind of hard, if he is suffering from amnesia? How can he tell you something he can't remember?"

"That's a good question. But since he's been working for me, he's changed so much. I didn't tell the doctor this, but I think he is remembering. Just little things, maybe, but he acts different.

"He used to defer to me about everything, including what to eat and how to eat it. Now he makes his own choices, small though they are so far. Can you see me leaving him at the ranch alone for the whole afternoon and evening, the way I did today, if I weren't confident he could handle things?"

Megan shook her head. She knew how much the ranch meant to Caitlin, and how hard she had worked for the last three years in order to make it pay for itself.

"You think I'm a fool for wanting to believe it's amnesia on such meager evidence?"

"I don't know," Megan answered truthfully. She had never seen Caitlin so involved in anything outside the ranch before.

"Me, either," Caitlin admitted glumly. "I guess I keep asking him questions, keep looking for the truth, and keep trying to win his confidence. Maybe eventually I can talk him into allowing Dr. Shepherd to examine him without spooking him so badly he'll run off.

"A few weeks ago my only worry was whether or not I'd have enough money to keep me out of the poorhouse, and now . . ." She shrugged helplessly.

"What if he turns out to be retarded?" Meg asked quietly.

It was a question Caitlin had asked herself since the first time she'd reacted so strongly to his masculine beauty and the sensual hold he had on her.

"I hope I don't ever have to make a decision about how I feel based on that fact," Caitlin answered softly with downcast eyes.

"If you really want to help him, really care about him, don't give up on him," Megan advised as they paid their check and left the restaurant.

* * *

Nick washed the last of the eggs and set them to dry on the sink. The chores were finished, and the whole evening stretched emptily before him. Leaning back against the sink, he pushed his hands deep into the pockets of his jeans and surveyed the room.

His eyes were drawn to a white ceramic mug with a big colorful rainbow slanted across its surface—Caitlin's mug. He could picture her, green eyes alight, smiling at him over the rim.

His eyes slid away and came to rest on the blue checked apron she never used, but kept folded neatly across a chair—just in case. Pulling his hands abruptly from his pockets, he strode impatiently from the room.

In the living room he checked to make sure there were plenty of logs for the fireplace. The evenings had been warm lately, and they hadn't used many. The stand was full.

Moving about the room, he touched a china figure on the mantle, picked up a framed photograph of Caitlin's parents and set it back down without really looking at it. Round and round the room he paced like a caged tiger. Finally he settled down to watch TV, only to blink a short time later and stare at the screen, knowing he had no idea what the program was about.

Jerking to his feet, he switched off the set and turned away. Glancing about, he moved toward the blue velvet rocker sitting in the farthest corner of the room—Caitlin's chair. Settling down against the deep blue cushions, he sighed heavily, leaned his head back and closed his eyes.

What was wrong with him? The work was done. This was the first time Caitlin had left him alone on the ranch, trusting him to take care of everything without her being there in case something went wrong. He should feel good about that, especially since he had handled everything without a hitch—so far. He'd even cooked his own dinner.

The house was so quiet—that must be it, the reason why he couldn't settle down. It gave him too much time to think, and his thoughts unsettled him. He didn't know what scared him the most, the dark fears—*memories?*—that haunted his dreams, or his growing feelings for Caitlin.

Caitlin. The name lingered around the edges of his unconsciousness, whispered across his mind. His eyes popped open, coming to rest on the small table beside the chair.

Everywhere he looked something reminded him of her, causing memories, like a roll of film, to unreel in his mind. He saw pictures of her smiling at him over an article she read in the newspaper; her swearing at him angrily because he'd left the gate to the chicken coop open and they'd had to chase down a dozen squawking chickens; her eyes drifting closed as she sat over a book or watching TV after a hard day's work.

His heartbeat quickened at the memory of her face all soft and rosy from her bath, the gleaming mass of auburn hair tied atop her head, wispy curls escaping to cling damply around her face and neck.

He swallowed, dry-mouthed, fighting the dull ache the pictures created inside him. Brows drawn together in a determined expression, mouth clamped tight, he forced the disquieting images from his mind.

There could never be anything between them. How many times would he have to repeat that to himself before his senses accepted the truth of it? He was a bum, a dummy, with nothing to offer any woman, least of all someone as special as Caitlin.

He recalled with shame the way his body tightened whenever she stood close to him, the irresistible pull that compelled his eyes to seek her whenever she came within sight.

He spent many nights in a fever of longing, imagining how it would feel to have her in his arms, her soft creamy breasts pressed against the hard muscles of his chest, her warm sweet breath mingling with his, filling his mouth....

Snapping to his feet, he patted his shirt in an absent, searching gesture and returned to his agitated pacing.

If she knew all about him, the things he'd done before finding his way to the ranch, she would want nothing more to do with him. And then the realization that he knew this stopped him dead in his tracks for a moment.

Most of the memories of the time before coming to the ranch were dim and hazy, half-remembered snatches of dreams—or nightmares. The time before that was empty.

Caitlin talked about her father; he had seen pictures of the man, and of the woman she called Mother—her parents. Nick had no recollection of two such people in his life. Why not? This was only one of the questions that had begun to bother him lately. What made him different?

If not for Caitlin, he felt sure he wouldn't be able to recognize the changes in himself, or understand as much as he did. Thanks to her guidance and belief in him, it was possible to see the changes, ask the questions. His thoughts were no longer a dark, empty wasteland but full of sights and sounds and the never-ending questions.

The dream had come again last night. But this time, unlike the past, the images had not faded upon awakening. With a thudding heart, he recalled how he had stuffed a corner of the sheet into his mouth to choke off his horrified cries.

Where did it come from? The horror of it made him fear himself. Crazy. The word made him cringe inside. He didn't know how, but he understood what it would mean to be crazy. And the thought was one more thing that stood between him and Caitlin.

Trembling, he asked himself—was he a madman?

Standing in the middle of the room, eyes darting nervously about, a hard fist of fear clutching at his insides, every nerve stretched to the limit, he felt the walls begin to close in around him. He had to get out of the house. He had to get out before Caitlin returned and found him like this.

As if propelled by an explosive force, he whirled and stumbled blindly from the room. Footsteps thundering, he erupted from the house.

He ran awkwardly, his right thigh protesting the strain, around the house and past the garden, through the orchard to the back pasture. His one and only purpose was flight from the memories, the nightmares, the fear.

The uneven terrain caused him to trip several times in his headlong flight, once nearly pitching him face first against a jutting root. The damaged muscles of his right thigh knotted, shooting pain up into his groin and down into his knee. A tortured groan swelled in his throat, the taut muscles standing out, working as he bit the sound back. Lungs burning, each rise and fall of his chest an agony, pulse hammering in his ears, he stumbled along the rocky path, dodging trees and brush.

At last, unable to go a step farther, he was forced to stop, coming to rest against the gnarled trunk of an oak. Head dropping, shoulders hunched, hands braced against his thighs, he tried to slow his breathing. Taking and holding each breath, letting it out slowly, eyes closed, he leaned his head back against the tree. Sweat soaked his shirt and dripped from the hair clinging to his forehead, burning his eyes. Gradually his physical equilibrium reasserted itself, and his emotions receded, as well. Once more he was in control.

After several long minutes he straightened, turned his right shoulder into the scabrous trunk of the tree and wiped at the perspiration on his forehead and cheeks, then pushed the hair from his stinging eyes. He had no idea how far he'd come from the house, and only a hazy idea in which direction. He wasn't even sure he was still on Barratt land.

The terrain looked unfamiliar. There were numerous stands of knotty oak, thorny mesquite and prickly pear dotting the Barratt property. This could be any one of them. In the weeks since starting work he had traversed most of it, keeping his bearings by picking out and memorizing one particular feature. Now, skimming his eyes keenly over every tree, bush and rock, he realized that nothing looked even vaguely familiar.

Moving away from the tree, he turned in a complete circle, searching for something familiar, anything, but dust and heat were his only companions. Then, from the corner of his right eye, he detected movement. Whirling immediately, he glimpsed a patch of brown quickly disappearing from sight through some scrub brush about ten yards away.

Remembering that Caitlin had her cattle grazing in the pasture at the back of the house, he suspected he was witnessing the disappearing tail end of a cow. It could lead him in the direction of the house. He lurched off in hopeful pursuit.

The stiffness in his leg slowed his progress, allowing him barely a glimpse now and then of his quarry as it disappeared around a rocky outcropping or thorny bush. He followed laboriously, sometimes cursing, sometimes pleading with it to slow down and let him catch up. Just when he was certain he'd lost it, a soft lowing would reach his ears, or he would glimpse a speck of brown and he'd be off once more, hot on the trail.

His feet slipped on sand-covered rock, and he fell jarringly onto his hands and knees, pain shooting through aching, abused bone and muscle. As he glanced up, the breath died in his chest, and the sweat froze in his pores. He was facing a six-foot rattler, paused as if listening, at what appeared to his frightened eyes to be a distance of mere inches but was in actual fact several yards. After a moment in which both man and snake were caught in watchful stillness, the reptile moved on, and the man breathed a heartfelt sigh of relief.

He stood up and looked around the narrow gully in which he found himself—alone—no sign of the animal he'd been following. To his left a small narrow trail led up the side of the wash and over the top before disappearing from sight.

The cow could, he supposed, have wandered up over the hill. Turning his head, he glanced down the arroyo as far as he could see. It could have gone that way, too, and be out of sight around a curve. Either way, it was a gamble.

The arroyo broadened, he discovered, and was dammed at one end to form a watering hole. Nick found his errant quarry drinking placidly at the cool water's edge.

Hot and dirty, he stumbled to the dry sandy bank alongside the cow. He lowered himself slowly to his knees and cupped shaky hands to the cool water, becoming suddenly motionless.

He was caught by the glare of the dying sun, its golden rays refracting off the surface of the water into his eyes, momentarily blinding him. Instinctively, overcome with a sudden gut-wrenching terror, he threw one arm over his face for protection.

His mind began to fill with blurred, distorted images. A face wavered in and out of focus, never clear enough to distinguish features, the mouth a black gaping hole. A hole that issued sounds, harsh rasping breaths and grunts, half-heard words echoing as though coming from the end of a long, dark tunnel.

Nick shivered. Cold was all around him, he was floating in a sea of ice, but inside he burned. Hot coils of fire stretched from deep within, reaching out to mind and limb. Mouth filled with a bitter, salty-copper taste, he choked. Chest heaving, he fought against the heavy pressure sucking the life from his agonized body.

"What the hell do you think you're doing?"

A cold, hard object rammed against the back of Nick's skull, causing his head to snap up with a jerk. Eyes wide, a glassy opaque look in their depths, he tensed. The voice registered as an extension of the nightmare-vision. Muscles bunched with the power of adrenaline surging through his veins, and suspended breath, he waited.

"I told your friends what I'd do the next time I caught one of you bastards on my land. You better lean over, grab your knees and kiss your butt goodbye—cause I'm fixin' to blow it away."

The intense silence that followed the stranger's words, broken only by the gentle rhythm of the animal lapping at the water, was shattered by the metallic click of a shell being loaded into the rifle's chamber, ready for firing.

Moving swiftly, Nick's right hand shot up, knocking the rifle barrel away. At the same time, gripping the barrel firmly with his left hand, he gave a mighty pull, jerking the man off balance. The rifle discharged harmlessly into the distance as Nick's right hand came up again, his body pivoted in a graceful arc and he landed a powerful right cross to the stranger's waiting chin.

It was over in the blink of an eye. The man lay flat on his back, with Nick's right knee braced across his chest. The rifle was clamped horizontally beneath his chin, biting into his Adam's apple and shutting off his air supply.

The man didn't struggle once his astonished glance met the cold threat in the black eyes above. One wrong move and he knew his larynx would be crushed. The man above him had moved with deadly precision, his actions choreographed with one purpose—to come out the victor.

At one time he, too, had been trained to move with such speed and accuracy. But that was another time, another life, before shrapnel from an exploding grenade ended his fighting days and very nearly his life.

Ears still ringing from the report of the rifle, Nick shook his head, the cold deadly glaze slowly fading from his eyes. Eyes that blinked in amazed compassion as they inspected the face of the man he held captive.

The right side of the man's face was in total ruin. From the eye to the corner of his hard mouth the flesh lay in one twisted, puckered whirl of scar tissue. Pink and purple angry-looking ridges drew the corner of the eye down and the edge of the mouth up in a grotesque parody of a smile.

"Who are you?" Nick spoke first.

"Who the hell are you?" a raspy voice countered.

"Why did you attack me?"

"Attack you! Who the hell's laying on the ground being strangled?" he choked out. Was this one of the crazies? He'd been getting their messages for weeks now.

The pressure against his windpipe eased abruptly, surprising him.

"I'm sorry if I hurt you," Nick said as he sat back, loosening the rifle from across the man's neck.

"Let's cut the crap—we both know who you are, what you are. Well, I'm tired of running and tired of hiding. You better shoot me with that gun while you got the chance, 'cause the next time I catch one of you on my land, you're dead."

Nick eyed the man in confusion. He didn't understand most of what he was talking about. But all at once, though he didn't know how, he knew all about guns.

Nick heaved the rifle one-handed into the brush. "Do you know me?" he asked with a puzzled frown.

The stranger searched Nick's face with narrowed eyes. There was something weird here. Was this guy for real? "I've never met you," he admitted. "But I've seen plenty of evidence of your handiwork. I don't take kindly to the killing of animals for sport," he ground out. "You can tell your boss I got the message with the dead animals—and you got my answer."

"I don't know what you're talking about." There was honest confusion in Nick's face and voice as he held the other man's steady gaze.

Sliding slowly to his feet, Nick held out a helping hand toward the man on the ground. The hand was observed and pointedly ignored. The other man labored unaided to his feet. They sized each other up, neither giving an inch, eyes doing silent battle.

"My name is Nick Rivers. I work for Caitlin Barratt," Nick said, conceding the fight.

"That doesn't explain what you're doing on my property. If you haven't been sent by who I thought sent you, then who are you?"

There was no concession in the man; though some of the hostility had left his battered features at the mention of Caitlin's name, his face remained tight with suspicion.

"I was out walking—" Nick's glance slid away; he couldn't tell the man about the state he'd been in at the time. "I must have lost my way. I saw the cow and decided to follow it—I thought it would lead me back the way I'd come."

"You say you work for Caitlin, huh? What at?"

He didn't trust this Nick. He was a trained combatant, and what in blazes did Caity need with the likes of him?

"I do ranch work, planting, feeding—" he shrugged "—whatever needs to be done."

"Well, you ain't on Barratt land now—you're on mine."

"You never did say who you are."

"Jones, if it matters. David Jones. I'm Caity's nearest neighbor."

"Jones? Then you must be Megan's brother."

"That's right. Where did you meet Megan?"

"I saw her in town last Friday. She's a very nice lady—your sister."

A bit more of the hardness left the twisted face. Megan was the only person left on earth David cared a damn about—except Caity Barratt. And he had his hands full trying to protect them both.

"So, you work for Caity—well, let me tell you something, fella. You damn well better be straight with her, 'cause if you ain't, I'll do worse than stick a gun to your head—next time I'll take it off."

If Rivers was one of the crazies, at least now he knew he'd been found out. There was no question the message would get back to his boss, David thought. Maybe his own life wouldn't be worth a plugged nickel now, but it hadn't been such a great one since Nam, anyway. He needed to tell someone about what was going on in the town. He'd tried it once, but there was no one he could trust.

Black ice had formed in Nick's eyes at the man's threat, his face all hard angles and planes. "You can try," he answered dangerously, not recognizing himself at all.

"Get off my land," Jones told him uncompromisingly. "And don't come back."

Nick backed slowly away, pivoted on his left heel and, with a powerful, angry set to his broad shoulders, limped away.

"Rivers!"

He halted and turned reluctantly. "Yeah?"

"You're going the wrong way." Jones pointed in the opposite direction, a nasty smile twisting an already twisted face.

The house stood dark and eerily silent as Caitlin sat gazing at it from the seat of the Jeep Comanche. A cloud passed over the moon, and she shivered, gooseflesh raising the fine hair on her arms.

She wondered in sudden trepidation what Nick had done while she'd been gone. Certainly nothing to warrant her feeling this sudden apprehension. He probably hadn't even left the house.

Megan had given her something she thought might help him, and Caitlin was excited about it. She hoped Nick would be, too.

She had missed him, she admitted to herself as she climbed out of the jeep, locked it and crossed the drive to the house.

She unlocked the door with her key, thinking how glad she was to be home. After passing silently down the hall and through the living room, she drew level with the open stairway leading to the loft-like upstairs.

Nick had left the small light at the bottom of the stairs turned on for her she noted, pleased by his thoughtfulness. Though it was rather dim, by its glow she could make out his door, and it appeared to be open a bit. Caitlin hesitated. Should she let him know she was home? He might already be sleeping.

The stairs creaked ominously despite the care she took to tread softly. If he was awake, he had surely heard her. Hand poised to knock, she hesitated. She hadn't been in the room since the day Nick arrived, though it had once been hers.

It hadn't been intentional, putting him in her old room. But now it made her feel deliciously risqué to think of him lying in the room above, on the same bed she had once used, staring at the same walls and ceiling. Seeing the same scenes from the window where, as a romantic teenager, she had sat dreaming on warm summer evenings.

"Nick," she called softly, rapping gently on the door panel. "Are you awake?" When there was no immediate response she couldn't resist pushing the door open, peering inside. It was only, she assured herself firmly, to make certain he was safely inside for the night.

The room lay in shadow, silver light from a full moon glittered from between gently billowing curtains, finding and capturing the still figure spread out over the sheets.

Lying on his back, Nick had one arm curved on the pillow above his dark head, the other resting at his hip. The sheet, folded down to his waist, revealed a bare expanse of muscular chest rising and falling softly with each breath. His face lay couched in shadow, hiding what expression the innocence of sleep might disclose.

Try as she might, she was unable to deny the small thrill she experienced at the sight of him, or to repress her imagination.

In her mind she crossed the small expanse of carpet from door to bed, slid beneath the sheet and lay close beside him.

She caught her breath softly on a moan. What ecstasy, to have the freedom to curl her fingers in the crisp springy hair beginning at the base of his strong throat and slowly trail them down over the tantalizing swell of muscle covering his chest and abdomen. Clenching an empty hand, her face hot with embarrassment, even with no one to witness it, the blood pulsing hot and heavy through her veins, Caitlin stepped back out the door.

"Who's there?" His voice, sounding deep and raspy from sleep, sent shivers down her spine.

"It's only me." She swallowed, forcing the words from between shaking lips. "I just got home. I thought I'd check and see if..." Her voice trailed off.

"I'm glad you're home," he said.

Caitlin held her breath.

"I need...to talk to you in the morning."

Caitlin sagged back against the door. What had she expected him to say? That he needed *her*?

"Y-yes, all right." Her voice barely audible, she nodded in the dark. "I'll see you in the morning, at breakfast."

The door closed behind her with a soft snap. Nick listened to the sound of her retreating footsteps, picturing how she had looked moments ago, an indistinct silhouette hovering in the doorway.

He'd been lying awake, listening for her return, sleepless until he knew she was safely home. He wished he was able to tell her how glad he was to see her, how he'd missed her, how empty the house felt without her presence—how empty *he* felt without her near.

What changes she had wrought in him in the short time he'd known her. She made him feel things, yearn for things, that until now he'd never suspected he had missed or wanted.

It was as though she were helping him to build a new identity, one more in tune with the world around him. The careful way she treated him, teaching him, helping him to understand those things that confused him, correcting him instead of laughing at him when he made a mistake, all those things made him want to please her. And when he pleased her, he pleased himself, too.

He wanted to tell her so many things, one of them the strange encounter he'd had that evening with her neighbor. But he couldn't trust himself alone with her in the intimacy of the night. Because while he was learning, building on new experiences around him, he was growing emotionally, as well.

Not a day went by that he didn't glance at her without feeling the strange new clenching at his insides. Just the sight of her was enough to make his mouth go dry and every thought fly out of his head. He hadn't wanted it, but it had become so.

But he couldn't tell her that any more than he could tell her how much he feared and desired the one thing he needed above all else. Her—he needed her.

Chapter 6

He was watching her from the doorway; she could feel him poised there long before he spoke. Her heart skipped a beat, her hands became suddenly clumsy and her face turned a bright shade of pink as she recalled her thoughts from the night before. Why didn't he speak, so she could acknowledge his presence? She was uncomfortable, knowing his eyes followed her every move.

"Good morning."

Caitlin continued transferring pancakes to a plate, giving herself time before she answered. "Morning. I hope you're hungry this morning, because I made sausage and pancakes."

"I'm starved," he admitted. After gathering utensils and napkins from the drawer, he placed them on the table.

"You didn't eat anything last night," she observed, eyeing him curiously. "The casserole was still in the oven this morning."

"No, ah, I wasn't hungry, so I took a walk. I thought it might make me hungry." Eyes on his plate, he talked while serving himself from the platter of sausage links and spreading butter and syrup over the hot golden-brown pancakes, his mouth watering at their aroma.

Caitlin sat across from him, pouring coffee from a ceramic server. After setting it on the trivet, she prepared her own food.

"You said you wanted to talk to me." She took a bite of pancake, syrup dripping from the fork, and her eyes met his across the table.

"Yeah." He swallowed, looked away and cleared his throat. He could see the golden flecks dotting the green irises of her eyes. Her eyes were one of the things he found most alluring about her. "I wanted to talk to you about your neighbor."

"You want to talk about Megan?" she asked, forgetting about her own breakfast.

"David."

"David?" she asked, surprised. "What about him?"

"I...saw him while you were gone. I went for a walk and got lost. He said people killed animals in his woods, and he thought it was me. Do you know what he means? Do people kill your animals, too?"

Screwing her face up in thought, she answered slowly, "I don't think so. I've been busy, but not too busy to notice something like that. I know Dad had the place posted because of the cattle. We ran a pretty big herd during his day." She smiled sadly. "I'm not much on hunting myself, but I've never run anyone off the ranch. People around here hunt wild game to eat—"

"No." He shook his head firmly. "That's not what he told me." Knowing David, she wondered what else he might have said; whatever it was, it seemed to have made an impression. "He said he didn't take kindly to animals being killed for sport."

"That's disgusting." She shuddered, looking down at the sausage grease congealing in a pool of syrup on her plate. The idea of eating meat, or wild game, didn't bother her. She was, after all, a rancher's daughter; cattle were raised for food. But the idea of killing anything solely for the sake of killing made her blood run cold. "Why would anyone want to kill for sport?"

"I don't know." He couldn't imagine wanting to harm any of the small creatures he'd seen since working on the ranch. In his mind's eye he saw the fuzzy yellow bodies of the baby chicks after someone had shot them. A fierce anger at the very idea darkened his face in a heavy scowl.

"Nick." She wasn't sure how to put this. "Sometimes David can—well, he has an explosive temper. He always did, even when we were kids, and since Vietnam, well..." Nick's black eyes found her face. "David was a POW for almost two years. He's never been the same."

"You mean he's crazy?" He voiced his own personal nightmare with difficulty, the word that had been yelled at him more than once.

"No!" Caitlin hastened to deny. "He just gets...excited, upset—damn!" she muttered.

"You think he kills the animals himself?"

"No!"

"You think he's lying?"

Biting her lip, she shrugged slightly. "It's not exactly lying. He could have found an animal someone had poached, and—" She spread her hands helplessly.

"I saw some dead animals, too, but I thought they just died."

"Maybe they did."

"Who else lives round here?"

"The Carringtons," she answered automatically. "Why do you ask?"

"You think somebody's killing their animals, too?"

"I sincerely doubt Logan Carrington knows, or would care if he did. He owns over two-thirds of this county and half the next."

"Maybe we should ask him. I don't like the idea of somebody killing animals."

Caitlin shuddered at the thought of wanton killing. "What can we do, even if it's true? There's no law that says someone can't hunt for sport. We have No Trespassing signs and No Hunting signs posted, and the fences are kept in good repair, but the place is too big to patrol."

"I don't know. I just think we should find out, that's all," he answered doggedly. "They might come here and kill the chickens, or the horses."

"All right, we'll look into it." She smiled tentatively, a bit taken aback by his vehemence.

Was this man sitting across from her with the determined expression and very masculine sense of outrage the same man she'd taken under her wing?

The idea that his true self might be showing through, perhaps bleeding into his personality, excited her. And in a way it frightened her, as well. It was hard to resist him now; what would it be like in a few more weeks if he continued to grow and change at this rate?

"Vietnam?" he asked curiously, as if only now assimilating the unfamiliar words.

"Oh, yes." She left his question unanswered for the moment. "That reminds me of something I want to discuss with you. Megan had a suggestion last night. I think it's a good one, and I hope you will, too. The library has a set of children's learning books—sort of encyclopedias. She offered to loan them to you, a few at a time—if you want." She held her breath in anxiety.

"Encyclopedias?"

"Yes," she began enthusiastically. "There are all kinds of things in them, and they have big colored pictures, so you can see what everything looks like as you read about it."

She waited tensely, hoping he would accept the idea. She and Megan were certain the books, with their simple but informative text and colorful pictures, would jog his memory. It was something she suspected was happening on its own a little more each day, anyway.

Though she'd been wanting to broach the subject of amnesia after the visit to the doctor's office, she couldn't find the courage to delve into the topic, not quite yet. Maybe the encyclopedias would force him to admit he had a problem, and then they could set about identifying it and its cause.

"Yes," he answered finally. "I'd like to try them."

"Good!" Caitlin stood, excitement bringing a becoming color to her cheeks. "I have some in my room." Her color deepened at his look. "We stopped by the library last night after church—I was hoping you would want to see them."

Together they pored over the books for over two hours, chores forgotten for the moment in their mutual excitement. But after a while they put the books aside until evening. The work of the ranch had to take precedence, after all.

The following week was like an anticlimax after the way Nick had spoken up against the poachers. Once more he retreated into morose silence. He spoke only when spoken to, did his work, and retired to his room as early as possible. And if he looked through the encyclopedias, it was while he was alone upstairs. Had they lost all the ground they had gained? What was going through his mind? She wished she could ask him.

The week ended without any further progress, leaving Caitlin feeling frustrated and unsure. Perhaps what Nick really needed was professional help, after all. Maybe just someone's caring wasn't enough.

Sheriff Raymond listened intently to the voice coming over the wire. "Okay, Clyde, I'll be out this afternoon to take a look. Yeah, right. So long."

Replacing the receiver, he sat back and turned his chair to face the big square window to stare blindly at the building across the street.

What the hell was going on? Old Fred Taylor had cattle missing, Jed Foster was complaining of strange lights on his property at night, and Ben Springfield's son had come home in the middle of the night from a camping trip, babbling about men from outer space landing in their pasture. Now Clyde Barker wanted him to come look at some strange things he'd found on his property.

Swiping a weary hand over his eyes and down across his broad jaw, he sighed heavily. He picked up his coffee cup and held it suspended, watching Megan Jones unlock the door to the library and go inside. Old Fred had also mentioned Jones's threat to young Fred. Bart hoped Megan had talked to her brother, put the fear of God into him. The boy had been acting mighty strange the last few months—boy, hell! He was six years older than Jones himself. But sometimes, like now, he felt like an old, old man.

Turning to face the desk, he gave a start as the phone rang. Lifting the receiver to his ear, he leaned an elbow on the desk and spoke into it.

"Fenton County Sheriff's Office. Sheriff Raymond speaking."

"Bart, this is Robert Jamison, in Austin. I told you I'd get back to you with that information you wanted."

So maybe something would finally go right today, after all. Bart's face lightened, then darkened, as he listened.

The voice continued, bringing a heavy frown to the sheriff's florid face. In a moment he was staring at the dead receiver clutched in his hand.

What the blazes had that been all about? Had the whole damned world suddenly gone crazy? Robert Jamison had just mouthed a bunch of poppycock in his ear, glibly told him to have a nice day and hung up.

Have a nice day—fighting words if ever he'd heard them.

From his vantage point the stranger watched the tall, heavily built man lumber out of the Sheriff's Office and move to the white Ford topped with the red and blue lights. His first impression veered close to the stereotyped southern sheriff learned from TV and Hollywood—fat, dumb and corrupt.

As the sheriff moved back into view, sunlight glinting on his dark gold head, the watcher had the uneasy feeling that there was a whole lot more to the man than the obvious. And it wouldn't pay for the sheriff to be too smart; things were complicated enough as it was.

By evening, in typical Texas style, the weather had changed from blue skies to clouds, from sunshine to rain. Caitlin stood for a moment watching the wind-driven rain lash the kitchen window. Then, after pouring hot chocolate into two mugs, she carried them to the table, setting one before Nick and one at her own place.

He was studying the books Megan had sent, and she was going over some material she had gotten in town, at the feed store. It felt good, sitting there, all warm and cozy, listening to the rain outside beat against the house.

He had surprised her that evening by coming downstairs after supper with a pile of the books Megan had loaned him and sitting down at the table to study.

There was a new strength in his face, and purpose in his step. His hair was neatly combed, and the lime-scented after-shave she hadn't been able to resist placing in his bathroom wafted from his freshly shaved cheeks. Apparently, he had come to terms with the devils that had plagued him for the past week.

But he still appeared more reticent than usual in her company, and no matter how many times she told herself that there was too much standing between them—even if her amnesia theory were correct, he could be married—his attitude still hurt.

She'd been watching him, under cover of her lashes for quite some time now. Watching as he meticulously studied each picture and read each page. His unconscious habit of moving his lips to form the words drew her gaze to his firm sensual mouth.

She watched the strong muscles of his jaw and throat flex beneath his sun-bronzed skin as he swallowed.

The overhead light cast a glow over his silky black hair, throwing the upper part of his face into shadow, making it impossible to read the expression in his eyes.

Caitlin's glance slid stealthily down the front of his worn brown workshirt. Opened at the throat, the material was stretched mouth-wateringly tight cross the breadth of his shoulders and chest.

Her eyes traveled down to where he'd rolled back the sleeves, revealing lean, muscular, deeply tanned arms, liberally covered with silky black hair.

Swallowing uneasily, she lowered her glance, afraid he'd look up and catch her watching him. She didn't notice the square jaw tense, or the long-fingered hands, knuckles showing white, grip the book tighter.

She was driving him out of his mind.

Glancing at the cup she'd placed before him, he felt a sudden powerful thirst, but he was afraid to reach for it. His hands were shaking, and if he spilled the contents he knew he'd feel so embarrassed he'd have to leave the table and go back to his lonely room. And he didn't want to. He wanted to be with Caitlin. Even if they didn't talk, as long as he could look up and see her across the table from him, that was enough.

He didn't know when it had happened—he'd fought against it—but somehow her kindness, her trust and her caring had gotten under his skin. Every time his eyes met hers, he looked for that special glow that would tell him she felt the same way. He wanted to see it, even though he knew he couldn't do anything about it; he needed to see that special look he'd begun to notice she reserved especially for him.

"What happened to David Jones's face?" he asked abruptly, his voice sounding loud in the quiet room.

Caitlin blinked, his words a half-heard buzz in her ears. "I'm sorry," she said, her voice sounding as though it were coming from a long way off.

Nick cleared his throat, afraid to risk meeting her emerald glance, feeling as he did at the moment.

"Jones, your neighbor, what happened to his face?"

By now Caitlin had herself firmly under control. She answered, ignoring the breathless quality her speech seemed to have acquired in the last few minutes. "Vietnam." She met his eyes squarely. "That's what happened to David—Vietnam."

"I don't understand." He frowned.

"A war, Nick—a war that wasn't a war." He studied her face with dark, intent eyes. "David was barely eighteen when he enlisted. It was the tail end of a conflict in southeast Asia—a place on the other side of the world called Vietnam. The year of his graduation from high school, he lost his parents in an accident and enlisted in the Marine Corps. They sent him to Nam.

"He was there less than a month when his Marine platoon was overrun by the Vietcong. A grenade exploded, and his division pulled back, leaving him there. I guess they thought he was dead." She tried to shrug fatalistically, but it didn't quite come off. "He was taken prisoner. They had him for two long years. When he came home, he was never the same."

Unable to sit still, she stood and moved about the room before finally settling with her arms folded across her breasts and her hip against the sink, staring out the small window into the stormy night.

The memories came back to her with surprising clarity despite the intervening years. She and Megan had been ten the summer David enlisted. The family had been close, and Caitlin had been an accepted part of it, until that fateful day when a storm much like this one had caused the death of John and Betty Jones.

After their deaths an unmarried aunt, their only living relative, came to stay with Megan and David. Caitlin remembered the woman as she had seemed that day fifteen years ago to a ten-year-old grieving the loss of loving friends. Tall, raw-boned, gray hair scraped back in a bun, a woman already well into her sixties. Never having been married, she had no experience with children.

Megan had cried herself to sleep that first night. Caitlin, barely holding her own grief in check, held her hand in the wide double bed down the hall from where the newly arrived relative slept.

The next day David had enlisted in the Marines. He left a boy and, three years later, returned a man, broken in body, mind and spirit. Caitlin related all this to Nick, her own pain and unhappiness brimming to the surface.

"What happened to the aunt?" His deep baritone whispered over her frayed nerves, causing her to shiver and hold herself tighter.

"Aunt Lucretia—Aunt Letty, we learned to call her. She made us love her—" She faltered, shaking her head. How could she explain the strong impact the woman, fiercely independent on the surface, but gentle and loving underneath, had had on two motherless girls not quite ready for puberty?

"We loved her," she said simply. "She made up for all that was missing in both our lives. My mother died when I was a toddler. I knew her only through pictures and the few remarks my father made. He didn't like to talk about her—it hurt too much, I guess.

"He was a great father, the best. We did everything we could together. But running a ranch the size this one was at that time..." She paused. "He didn't have a whole lot of free time. Aunt Letty stepped in without stepping on Dad's toes. She was . . . just there whenever Megan or I needed her.

"Maybe if David had waited, given her a chance, she could have helped rid him of some of his hurt and bitterness." Sighing, she blinked back the tears. "If she had lived long enough to see David come home, I know she would have been able to help heal his wounds."

"She died?"

"Yes. She had a bad heart. She lived long enough to know David had been found and was being sent to a hospital before coming home.

"She died in her sleep before he made it back. Meg and I found her the next morning. I had spent the night—we were celebrating because David would soon be with us." Her words slurred.

Hard arms came from behind, pulling her back against the warmth of a powerful chest.

"I don't seem to have much luck with the people I love." Voice thick with tears, she added, "I think I must be a jinx."

"No!" He swung her almost violently around in his arms, protesting his need of her as much as the word he didn't understand.

Gathering her against him, he held her snugly yet gently, rocking back and forth, her silent tears wetting the worn material of his shirtfront.

He couldn't believe he had her where he'd dreamed of having her, locked tightly in his arms. But not like this . . . closing his eyes, a kind of anguish on his face, he absorbed her pain with gentleness, the way his shirt absorbed her tears.

Lowering his rough cheek to her hair, he stood, hardly daring to breathe for fear she would realize where she was and move out of his embrace.

After a while her scent, an exotic blend of sweet-smelling hair and warm skin, befuddled his senses. His reasons for being this close to her blurred in his conscious mind and he pretended she was there because she wanted to be—and that it was all right for her to be there.

There had been no one, Caitlin realized, for her to lean on since her father's untimely death. And in the interval she had learned to rely on herself, as her father had taught her to do, taking pride in her self-sufficiency and independence. But now it felt so good, so right, to let her guard down and allow herself to be wrapped snugly in the invisible shield of Nick's protective caring. It felt remarkably like coming home.

Was she wrong to let him hold her this way? Should she give in to the feelings she'd been trying to deny for so long? What if she encouraged him this way and he belonged to someone else? What if he were another woman's husband? A child's father?

Would that hypothetical woman condemn her for what she was allowing? What she was feeling? In that woman's place, how would she feel? She hoped she would be understanding of the need Nick had for the warmth of human contact, the feel of someone's caring.

And if he weren't suffering from amnesia? That didn't make him any less a good man. That didn't take away the gentleness, the innate kindness, she'd seen in him as he worked around the ranch day after day.

If only she had something to go on, one small clue about who he was, where he was from. Something she could perhaps tell the sheriff; then maybe he could help her discover more about Nick. But if Nick had remembered anything about his past, he was keeping it to himself. And she was still apprehensive about being too insistent in asking questions. He didn't like being questioned, he reacted strangely.

The seconds ticked away, the quiet broken only by sounds of the storm, heard in the distance. The tears dried, leaving the skin over her cheeks feeling tight and itchy. She longed to rub her hands over them, but she didn't want to move away from the comforting contact with Nick's chest.

His embrace was meant to give comfort, so she tried to ignore the insistent yearning gradually taking over her body and senses, the growing awareness of firm muscles and taut limbs.

Tremblingly aware of the heat emanating from his body, the musky smell of his skin, the throbbing beat of his heart drumming beneath her cheek, she moved restlessly against him. Forcing herself to deny what was building, making the air crackle between them, she attempted to ignore the sharp pinpoints of friction dancing like tiny fingers over the skin of her face, her neck, her arms. At all costs, she must hold her emotions in check.

With an unexpected shock she felt the changes taking place in his lower body, heard the harsh uneven tempo of his breathing, and realized that he, too, was feeling the attraction.

Nick stepped suddenly back, drawing away from her body. She met the look in his smoldering black eyes with a lurch of her heart. Senses spinning, a tingling awareness in the pit of her stomach, she felt her lower limbs turning to water.

Liquid black eyes locking with hers, Nick took her face between unsteady hands. Holding it carefully, eyes gentle with understanding, he held her glance. But when she would have leaned into him, he held her away, their only point of contact his work-scarred fingers cupping her flushed cheeks. She closed her eyes, waiting....

Then he raised her face, and his lips descended slowly to meet hers. The kiss was not smooth, nor practiced, its very awkwardness making it all the more precious.

"Caitlin." He breathed her name like a benediction.

The sound whispered across her throbbing lips, and her eyes drifted open, slowly focusing on his face; the uncertainty written there wrenched at her tender heart.

Lifting an unsteady hand, she touched his cheek, traced the lean square jaw down to the sensual curve of his lips. She drew a delicate fingertip across their width, then dipped it into the moist depths, lightly touching the tip of his tongue, before moving it down over his full bottom lip to the shallow groove centered on his firm chin.

Bracing her hands against his chest, she leaned forward, standing on her toes, and placed a kiss at the corner of his mouth. His eyes closed tightly at her touch, his heart thudding wildly against his ribs. She could feel his body shaking against hers.

"I can't do this, Caitlin," he whispered abruptly in guilt.

"Shush," she breathed, her fingertips touching lips still damp from her kisses.

"But you don't know—"

"I know all I need to know—" Drawing his face down to her, she settled her mouth firmly onto his.

Nick resisted her. His hands gripping her shoulders tightly, he held his body stiffly away from hers. She was killing him inch by inch. He was trying to do the right thing, to keep her safe from something that could hurt her—himself. But, oh, how he wanted her, her softness, her warmth, her caring. The muscles in the arms holding her quivered. Even with his eyes closed against the sight of her beauty, her image stayed in his mind, indelibly printed on the undersides of his closed lids.

The storm outside raged closer, bringing the rumble of thunder echoing in the hot blood coursing through his veins. He fought the need to relax his straining arms and draw her fully against the length of his body.

At last his control snapped, and with a shuddering groan that rippled down the length of him, he let his mouth take hers in a soul-shattering kiss.

Moving his hands down her shoulders to her waist, he drew her into the cradle of his hips, letting her know the full extent of his need, a need that grew wilder as the storm grew closer.

Catching her breath, opening her lips to him, she taught him all there was to know about a kiss. Pressing against the rigid muscles of his thighs, her hands at his waist, she felt him surge against her, searing her with his heat.

Her breasts were aching almost painfully, crushed as they were against his chest, and she felt the buttons of his shirt dig into their softness. She wanted it all, the pain, the ache of breasts full and heavy, nipples drawn tight, straining against the confines of her clothing. Wanted to feel his hands rough against their softness, touching them as no other had.

His lips left her mouth to trail soft, wet kisses along the line of her jaw to the curve of her neck. Finding a sensitive spot just below her ear, he made her shiver in delight. Gasping, knees sagging, she held on to him, her own hands roaming the length and breadth of his shoulders and back.

Time had no meaning except that she wanted this moment to go on and on. She would be happy to spend eternity locked in his embrace, his roving hands and mouth sending tingling spirals of ecstasy wherever they touched.

Lifting the heavy fall of hair from her slender neck, he buried his face in the strands of fire. Touching reverent lips to their flame, he ignited the flame of his senses, feeding a blaze that was already out of control. Lips slipping from silken hair to silken skin, his tongue tasted and caressed the ultrasensitive area at the top of her spine.

The sultry air filled with the tortured sounds of their breathing. Nick's tormented groan, issued low in his throat, was an intoxicating invitation that Caitlin couldn't resist.

Her hands pulled the shirt from his jeans, slid up the naked skin of his back, kneading the hard muscles, tracing the ridge of his spine before moving down to the slight indentation above his hips.

Nick's questing lips left her neck to slide around to her mouth, leaving a trail of fire in their wake. His breath hot against her ear, he whispered to her, words whose meanings were lost against her velvety skin.

This time, when he took her mouth, passion overlaid tenderness, and he drew her response with long drugging kisses. Knees buckling, bodies tightly locked mouth to mouth, thigh to thigh, in perfect unison they dropped to the floor.

A repeatedly insistent sound penetrated the deep fog of their senses. On their knees, they drew reluctantly apart, staring at each other in confusion. The sound came again, this time followed by a loud voice.

"Caitlin! Caitlin! Are you in there?"

"Sheriff Raymond?" she whispered almost guiltily, embarrassment and confusion causing her to shift her glance hurriedly from Nick's passion-glazed eyes.

How had they come to be kneeling on the floor with their clothing in such a state, their bodies damp with sweat?

"I'd better see what he wants," she murmured, not knowing how to get up, how to move away from him.

He took the necessity out of her hands by climbing to his feet, taking her hands in his and drawing her up. Keeping his eyes on their joined hands, he rubbed a thumb slowly across the backs of her fingers, unable to relinquish her completely just yet.

He understood why she wouldn't meet his eyes, why her hands lay stiffly in his. He had overstepped the boundary, and she was beginning to realize what liberties she had allowed him to take. Easing his hands slowly from hers, he discerned her predicament. She had every right to feel angry, even disgusted with him.

Glancing up, Caitlin read his guilt and remorse, along with an emotion she couldn't identify far back in his eyes. Was he feeling as flustered as she was at the untimely interruption, or was he sorry this had happened at all?

She wanted to ask him why he felt guilty for kissing her. Did it have something to do with his past? His life before she had met him? Had he remembered something? If so, why couldn't he open up and tell her about it? She only wanted to help him; why couldn't he see that?

She had finally let someone past her guard, opened herself up to another human being, let herself care for someone—and who had she picked? A man who couldn't remember his own name—if he'd ever known it in the first place.

"I'd better let the sheriff in." Voice carefully devoid of expression, she drew her hands from his and turned away. She didn't see the hesitant step he took in her direction, or the hand he held out to her, only to drop it mutely at the sight of her rigid stance.

A moment later, shaking the rain from his hat, Bart Raymond stepped into the house, followed Caitlin into the kitchen and accepted a cup of coffee.

"That's a real gully washer out there. Your drive is knee-deep in mud. It's a good thing I had the foresight to get the jeep out. I couldn't have made it without four-wheel drive."

Placing his hat on the table, he sipped at the coffee, eyeing Caitlin and Nick's strained faces speculatively over the rim. He wasn't immune to the atmosphere. It was so thick, you could cut it with the proverbial knife. They watched him carefully, but avoided eye contact with each other. What had he walked into?

Caitlin pulled out a chair, moved the book she had been reading earlier out of the way, folded her hands on the table and waited for the sheriff to explain the reason for his unexpected visit.

"Did you come all the way out here to give us a weather report?" she asked finally, an edge to her voice.

"Not exactly." Taking another sip from his cup, he looked at the tall man standing with his gaze concentrated on the floor. "You seen David Jones the last couple days?" He addressed himself to Caitlin, while watching the other man from the corner of his eye.

Though surprised, Caitlin answered him steadily. "No, I haven't." When he didn't elaborate, only sat there, his unwavering gaze on her face, she asked, "Why, is he missing?"

"Yeah." He stunned her with his reply. "He is."

"What? What are you talking about? I was just over there yesterday. Meg didn't say anything about him being missing."

"Nope, don't suppose she did." Taking his own sweet time, he sipped again at the steamy coffee. Caitlin seemed genuinely surprised, even alarmed, but the man standing behind her hadn't batted an eyelid. "It seems Megan saw him last about 4:00 p.m., hasn't seen him since, nor has anybody else, if what I've been told is fact."

"Where can he be? He never goes anywhere, just stays on the ranch...." Her voice wavered to a halt. Yesterday? Nick had run across him yesterday. Why didn't he speak up?

"Yes? You remember something?" The sheriff pounced when she hesitated.

"N-no, I was just thinking, he could be hurt. He might have fallen down and broken a leg or something. Have you searched for him?"

He didn't believe her; her eyes wouldn't meet his squarely, looking instead somewhere above his right shoulder. He glanced down at her hands, which were twisted together on the table. She knew something, all right, something she wasn't telling.

"Caity, honey, if you know anything—anything at all— you'd better tell me," he coaxed. "It doesn't matter how small or unimportant it might seem. There have been too many unexplained things going on around here lately."

His gaze shifted to the man. His eyes, the sheriff noted, were on Caitlin, an unreadable expression on that somber face.

"I don't know anything." She sounded nervous, her voice high-pitched and unnatural.

"Caity—" Bart leaned toward her across the table.

"I saw him."

The sheriff set his cup carefully onto the table before training his contemplative gaze on the man. He heard Caitlin make a slight sound of protest.

"Did you, now?"

"That's right. I saw him yesterday evening just before sunset." Nick spoke in flat, even tones, neither his voice nor his face giving anything away.

"He was here?"

"No." A little uneasy now, he tensed. "I was out walking before sunset. Caitlin had left for town. I got lost and Jones . . . found me."

"Jones ain't a very sociable person. He seem glad to see you?"

"No—he stuck a rifle to the back of my head."

Caitlin gasped and whirled around to confront him. "You didn't tell me that."

Face softening, Nick met her wide, accusing eyes. "No, I didn't—I didn't want you to be mad. We parted . . . amicably."

"Friendly-like, you say, huh?" the sheriff asked skeptically, drawing Nick's gaze.

Neither man caught the look of surprise on Caitlin's face at Nick's casual use of the word 'amicably.' His vocabulary was improving by leaps and bounds, she observed silently, dryly.

"I didn't say that. I—he didn't shoot me." He shrugged broad shoulders. "So I guess it was—well, like I said, he didn't shoot me."

"Did you shoot him?"

"Sheriff!" Caitlin protested, facing him now, anger marring the delicate lines of her beauty. Her own niggling suspicion was buried in indignation.

"Did you?" Bart persisted, his penetrating gaze locked on the other man.

"No, I didn't," Nick answered coolly, his eyes holding the sheriff's.

A tense, waiting quality saturated the heavy air, fragile, breakable, as the three eyed each other in mistrust.

Caitlin stared from one man to the other. She wanted to scream Nick's innocence at the sheriff, to rage at Nick for not telling her about the encounter with David, and to beg him to deny the accusation she saw forming on the other man's lips.

"We need to find him." She broke hurriedly into speech, forestalling any further charges from the sheriff.

"I know." Bart shifted his gaze reluctantly from Nick. "Megan said she didn't realize until this morning that he wasn't home. He could have been gone all night long. She wanted to look for him, but she couldn't find a trace of where he might have gone.

"I'd like to keep this as quiet as possible for now. If he's gotten himself caught somewhere, with a broken leg, as you suggested, or just holed up to escape the weather, there's no need to spread it all over the countryside." He had his own reasons for not wanting to draw undue interest to the area.

Caitlin nodded her agreement. David had a reputation for being downright hostile and eccentric; he didn't need to have it embellished any more than necessary.

"Poor Megan, she's probably worried out of her mind. Unless there's anything else, Sheriff, I think I'll give her a call."

"You go right ahead, honey. I'll just wait here and drink a bit more of this good coffee. You make it just like your daddy used to. Besides, that brother of hers might have shown up by now.

"You settled in here right smart, I see," he commented to Nick when Caitlin had left the room. "Caity's a real nice girl. I knew her daddy real well. Knowed her since she was a baby, and I'd hate to see anybody take advantage of her. In fact, I'd be real upset, take it personal-like. Especially if I was to suspect anybody of tryin' to pull the wool over her eyes—take advantage of the fact she's all alone way out here since her daddy died." Could he be any plainer with his meaning? If the man was other than he appeared to be, now was his opportunity to speak up.

Except to lean his hips back against the sink and cross his arms over his chest, Nick made no sign of having heard the sheriff's oblique comments.

Caitlin reentered the room slowly, hands in the pockets of her faded jeans. Nick's glance lifted from his intent examination of the scarred boots he wore to her face. Stomach knotting, he gazed at her beauty; even with her red hair in a tangle and clouds of worry darkening her eyes, she took his breath away. His reaction was not lost on the sheriff.

"Is she all right?" Nick asked gently, drawing her glance.

"W-what?" Caitlin looked at him absently.

"Megan—is she okay, Caity?" The sheriff took up the inquiry, beetling his heavy brows over his gold-brown eyes in a deep frown.

"Oh, yes, she's fine. David is back. He got back about an hour ago."

"Say where he's been?" Bart asked, not appearing in the least surprised at the news.

"No, she didn't. Just that he was back and to tell you she was sorry she'd made such a fuss. She hopes you won't be angry because she called you out on a night like this."

"All part of the job," he commented, getting unhurriedly to his feet. "I guess I'll brave the storm and head on home. If you talk to Megan again tonight, tell her I'll be out in the mornin' to have a word with that brother of hers."

After the sheriff had taken his leave, Caitlin sat at the table, silent and remote, resting her chin on her hand, with eyes staring at the printed words on the page of the book opened before her. She hadn't turned a page in over five minutes.

"What's wrong?"

"I beg your pardon?" She glanced up in surprise.

"Is something wrong? You seem...worried." Dark eyes probed her pale face.

"No." She shook her head. "Nothing's wrong."

"Sure?"

"Yes, I'm sure." But she didn't sound it, and she knew it. She didn't feel it, either.

Suddenly she was uncomfortable sitting at the same table with this man. This man she didn't really know. In the past few weeks she had watched him struggle along as though he were an alien in an alien world. She had struggled right along with him, moving from pity to empathy to caring. And now she found herself uneasy and uncomfortable in his presence, though she couldn't account for the reason.

They had come close to making love before the sheriff's untimely arrival, yet she knew so little about him. She had no idea, even, if it would have been a new experience for him. A short while ago the thought of their making love had filled her with sweet anticipation. Now she felt only embarrassment at the thought, and relief that they hadn't, and—wariness.

She had caught the sheriff's words, his far from subtle accusation when they thought she was out of the room. Nick had made no reply, neither admitting nor denying what the sheriff had so obviously implied. At first she had been angry with Bart for his unwanted interference. But as she thought about it, she, too, became doubtful. For someone who had known so little a few short weeks ago, Nick had come a remarkably long way in a relatively short period of time.

One part of her had been thrilled when she suspected he returned her developing feelings. The other, more practical part of her stood back, observing, voicing distrust, urging caution. Things were moving too quickly. She had again lost control, control of her feelings, control of her life, control of . . . Nick?

Was that the real problem? Was she upset because he had begun to think for himself, reason for himself? Or had he always possessed that ability?

"Megan said David won't talk to her," she blurted. She didn't even know why she had told him that, unless it was to see what kind of response it would engender in the stranger sitting across from her wearing Nick's—her Nick's—face.

He looked startled, then concerned. If it was an act, he was very good.

"Did he say where he'd been?"

"No, she said he won't talk to her at all."

"She has no idea why?"

"No. When he first came home from the hospital he would get like that sometimes, especially at night. He was on medication for a long time. I think he might still be—but I'm not sure."

"Maybe it's the weather," he commented absently. "It rains like this in the jungles of Vietnam. Maybe it's bringing it all back to him."

Caitlin froze, her eyes staring unseeingly at the book. Jungle? What did he know about the weather in a jungle? How did he know Vietnam was covered in jungle? This morning he hadn't even known Vietnam existed. And now he was an expert on its weather and geography?

Cautiously, she raised her eyes to him. He was totally engrossed in the book he held, unaware of her scrutiny or his slip of the tongue. Had it been a slip? Or, as she first suspected, was he starting to remember. A slip? Or a memory?

Who was Nick Rivers really? And how had he become mixed up in her life? Was it by chance? Or design?

Chapter 7

Caitlin found a number of chores to occupy her over the next few days, nearly all of them as far from Nick as possible. Late one afternoon he found her in the garden on hands and knees, a pile of weeds behind her attesting to the fact that she had been industriously occupied for some time.

"I'll do that." He spoke without preamble from directly behind her, and she gave a little scream and jumped, breaking off a small branch of a tomato plant instead of the weed she had been after.

"Damn it!" She turned on him angrily, her face flushed from the heat and ill-temper. "Can't you make some kind of a noise—scrape your boots, snap your fingers or whistle—so I'll know you're around?"

The ready smile died on his lips. Glancing away, he cleared his throat unhappily. "Sorry, I didn't mean to scare you."

Dropping down onto his knees, close—too close—he reached for a weed—the same one Caitlin was reaching toward. Their fingers met, remained absolutely motionless for a moment, then, as if electrified, jerked apart.

"I'll do this," she gulped hastily, her voice coming out in a breathless rush.

"I'll help—"

"No!" she almost shouted. "Go curry the horses."

"But I—"

"Go!" She pointed toward the barn. "Go curry the damned horses!"

Looking at her rather oddly, he got to his feet, hesitating, his glance encompassing the angry glitter in her eyes, the stubborn twist of her rigid mouth, the agitated flutter of her hands. Shrugging, an unhappy look on his broodingly handsome face, he turned reluctantly toward the barn. Caitlin caught his barely discernible mutter as he loped out of sight.

"How many times a day am I supposed to curry the darn things?"

She opened her mouth, about to call out to him, then sat back on her heels instead and burst out laughing. And it felt good, so good, to laugh. Since the sheriff's last visit she'd been feeling as though she were living on the edge of a precipice with a stranger. One she had to watch diligently, in case he gave her a sharp nudge while her back was turned, hurling her over the edge.

He must have felt it, her suspicion, her hostility, but not once had he approached her to ask why. She didn't know whether it was because he feared the answer, or the question. Was he afraid to admit to her, to himself that all was not as it should be? If nothing was voiced, no questions asked, did he think he could continue with his pretense of normalcy?

She had caught him eyeing her several times in the last week, at first with uncertainty, but lately his expression had changed to a mixture of resigned acceptance and wary speculation in the face of her remoteness.

He once again took up the habit of working long after the dinner hour and retreating to the out-of-doors whenever possible.

This was the first time in days that he had actively sought her out. Now that she had actually allowed herself to look at him, she realized that he looked tired and drawn. There were lines around his mouth and shadows she hadn't noticed before under his eyes. For the first time she found herself wondering about his age. She reckoned he could be anywhere between twenty-five and forty, though she'd seen no strands of silver in that midnight-black hair.

Their conversations lately had consisted of what chores were to be done for the day, and "please" and "thank you" at the

table if they chanced to have a meal together. But every time he
entered a room, stood close to her, or spoke her name in that
deep smoky voice, she remembered the night of the storm. The
feel of his rough hands gentle on her face, his breath warm
against her skin, his lips ... Caitlin shook herself, pushing the
disturbing pictures from her mind. How, she asked herself,
conscious of the uneven thrum of her heart, could he make her
feel this way when she distrusted him so?

After piling the weeds in the wheelbarrow, Caitlin hauled
them to the trash barrel set back from the house. Dusting her
hands, she looked closely at one finger, where she had gotten a
thorn deeply embedded in the sensitive tip. She supposed she
should wear gloves, but she hated them. They were hot and
awkward to work with both indoors and out. She hadn't used
them for dishes since cracking a china plate that had belonged
to her mother.

She rubbed at the sweat on her brow, then looked at her
soiled fingers and shrugged. She had a fairly good memory of
how she had looked this morning, standing before the mirror
in her bedroom, with her hair pulled back from a face turned
pink by the relentless Texas sun, work-roughened hands with
short unpolished nails, dressed in a snug, faded work shirt and
jeans. Shaking her head, she muttered wryly, "Face it, old girl,
a femme fatale you're not."

The man eyeing her from the cover of the trees a few hundred
yards away, a pair of high-powered binoculars against his face,
wouldn't have agreed.

From the tip of her curly red head to her widely-spaced green
eyes, from the thrusting breasts discernible beneath the cotton
shirt to her nipped-in waist and enticingly curved hips, his eyes
traveled over her form, admiration and lust equally distrib-
uted in their icy gray depths.

So, he was at it again—he might have known. When he
hadn't showed up for their designated rendezvous, he should
have guessed what he'd find. His *old buddy* holed up with a
good-looking broad—but this time he'd gone too far.

Eyeing the woman as she climbed gracefully to her feet, he
pursed his lips and gave a soundless whistle. Damn! How did
the man do it time and time again? Whatever his secret, it never
failed. He wondered where this one fitted in as he watched her

cross the yard, an eye-riveting swing to her nicely rounded bottom.

"Damn!" he muttered again, licking his lips. "Damned lucky bastard!"

Nick saw Caitlin waiting for him when he left the barn. Leaning back, one foot propped against the corral railing, head bent, she was closely examining one finger. Apparently she hadn't heard his quiet approach. Mindful of her earlier anger and the results, he puckered his lips and gave a tuneless whistle.

Caitlin's head snapped up at the familiar sound of a wolf whistle. Eyeing him closely, she was once more puzzled by a familiar gesture she wouldn't have associated with him a few weeks earlier.

Face pink, she straightened from her relaxed pose and watched his slow, easy approach. How could anyone who was so obviously hot, tired and dirty be at the same time so sexy-looking? From his dusty, sweat-soaked hair falling into his eyes, to his broad, hair-roughened chest, laid bare with his shirt hanging open, to the tight, dirt-stained jeans, Caitlin couldn't help but stare.

What was it about a man in his grimy state that made a woman not curl up her nose and point out the nearest bath but instead have vivid visions of two naked bodies, limbs passionately entwined, lying on cool white sheets, beneath a brass and wood ceiling fan?

Nick's gaze, when he caught her eyes on him, darkened with some secret message she refused to understand. He knows, she realized nervously. Somehow he's looked into my mind and seen the same provocative images. How? How can he do this to me? Not so long ago he was a ragged, pathetic figure—for that matter, he wasn't the picture of a debonair man-about-town. The odor of horse, hay and manure clung to his long frame. But pathetic? No way.

As she swallowed tightly, her gaze shifted, becoming fixed on the hand moving slowly toward her face. Don't do this to me again, she begged silently.

As delicate as a butterfly's wing, hard fingertips smoothed a wisp of hair back from her hot face and behind a shell-pink ear.

Hardly daring to breathe, Caitlin closed her eyes against the bolt of electricity surging through her at the feather-light touch.

"You worked too long in the sun without a hat. The tip of your nose is sunburned."

The low, whiskey-mellow voice vibrated along her nerve endings as he tapped the object of his scrutiny with one long finger.

She was so lovely, standing there with the pure, delicate lines of her face turned so trustingly up to his. Unable to resist his need to touch her, he drew an unsteady finger across the long gold-tipped lashes shadowing the secrets in her cat-green eyes. Eyes the same color as those of the tabby cat she kept in the barn to scare the rats away. Rats the size of small dogs, she had assured him solemnly, the light of mischief in her eyes. As he traced a smudge of dirt across her forehead and down one cheek, his whole body began to shake.

There was no way he could put words to the emotions she awoke in him. Each time he caught sight of her a new one found its way into his heart. His need of her was becoming an all-consuming hunger that drove him night and day—drove everything from his mind including the nightmare dream that had haunted his sleep for as long as he could remember.

Now his dreams were filled with erotic fantasies. Fantasies that, in the light of day, made him cringe in embarrassment.

Swallowing a groan that had started in the depths of his soul, clenching his jaw, he stepped from Caitlin—away from temptation. He had to find himself, had to discover who—or what— he was before he could even consider giving in to the longings tearing him apart. He had to continue a conscious effort to keep away from her, the way he had for the last few days.

Sensitive to the sudden change in the atmosphere, Caitlin opened her eyes. Nick watched her broodingly, tempering the fires in his own dark eyes. She was right to avoid him, as he knew she'd been doing recently. It was impossible to be in her presence for even mere seconds at a time without hunting her with hungry eyes, touching her in his mind.

"I've finished with the horses. I need to haul feed to the cattle." His voice harsh, he tore his glance from the hurt bewilderment clouding her upturned face.

"Nick!" she croaked, then paused, before speaking more evenly. "Let the feed go until morning—please." As he hesitated, his back to her, she continued. "The cattle can graze tonight. I—it's—I'm fixing something special for dinner tonight. It's my—"

"The feed's already loaded. I'll be as quick as I can," he cut across her words.

Caitlin stared after his retreating back, eyes filled with pain, a slight quiver to her soft mouth. He'd done it again, lifted her to the stars, then shot her down. What was the matter with her? One moment she was telling herself that she didn't trust him and needed to keep her distance, and the next she was in an agony of torment because of his careless treatment of her.

He didn't pause or look back, just climbed into the truck, gunned the motor and drove toward the pasture.

She couldn't know how his hands trembled on the steering wheel, how his eyes were dark with pain as he watched her figure diminish in the side mirror.

"I'm sorry, little Cat," he whispered. "I'm sorry I hurt you."

It was after nine when Nick drove the truck across the cattle guard, down the short lane and around to the garage. His arms felt leaden, his back ached, and his right thigh was cramping agonizingly. He was so tired he could have dropped his head onto the steering wheel and fallen asleep instantly.

The work didn't need to have taken this long, but he had stayed clearing brush away from the creek after he'd finished taking care of the cattle, dulling his heightened senses with backbreaking labor. He'd worked until every muscle protested violently, until the disturbing thoughts of Caitlin were dulled by the burning ache filling his chest.

After climbing slowly from the truck, he crossed the yard, stumbling a little on the uneven ground. Stopping at the edge of the porch, he breathed deeply, identifying the sweet smell of apple blossoms from the orchard and the heavier scent of mimosa growing near the corner of the house. Their perfume filled his tortured soul with a kind of peace.

He entered the house cautiously, wondering if Caitlin would be waiting for him. Irrationally fighting disappointment, he saw by the light over the sink that the room was empty. He knew he'd find his meal warming in the oven, but suddenly he wasn't hungry. He only wanted the relief of a hot shower, the cool comfort of fresh sheets and the blessed oblivion of sleep.

He removed the meal from the oven, covered it and placed it in the refrigerator. Reaching for the light switch by the sink, he glanced down at the white box with a cellophane top sitting on the counter. Through the transparent window he read, Happy Birth-Cai—the rest had been cut away.

"Oh, no," he whispered despairingly. That was what she had been trying to tell him earlier. It was her birthday, and she had spent it alone. Because, dummy that he was, he had deliberately stayed away.

A snowy white envelope lay half-hidden by the cake box. Picking it up, he slid the card from inside it. The front was a colorful array of flowers and butterflies, and inside was a short message wishing her a happy birthday. It was signed David and Megan Jones.

After dragging his protesting muscles up the stairs, daring to cast only a brief glance at her closed door, he prepared for bed.

He tried to sleep; his body was willing—even eager—but his mind was not. After a time, fearing a recurrence of the dream because of his agitated state, he climbed from the bed to lean beside the open window and stare out into the night.

The night was velvety, a whisper of wind ruffled the leaves on the trees outside his window. A flicker of light in the distance caught his eye. Concentrating on where he thought he'd seen it, he strained for another glimpse, hardly blinking, but it was gone—if it had ever been there in the first place. Shrugging mentally, he glanced away.

There! There it was again. He caught a glimmer out of the corner of his eye. It appeared to be coming from the direction of the old farmhouse Caitlin had said her great-grandfather had built in the early 1900s. It flared for a few seconds, then was gone.

Or was it just his tired eyes playing tricks on him? Perhaps there was nothing there at all. He continued watching for a time without seeing the light again. Yawning hugely, his mind at last giving way to the fatigue of his body, he clambered back into bed. In the morning he would take a look at the old house. If anyone was messing around he'd know it, and he'd put a stop to it.

Maybe it was the same people who were so fond of killing helpless animals and leaving their carcasses nailed to trees. He hadn't told Caitlin about that. He didn't trust someone of that mentality anywhere near the ranch, or Caitlin.

When Nick returned to the house for breakfast the next morning it was waiting for him, along with a note. Caitlin had errands to run in town; she would see him later.

Disappointed, but also a bit relieved at the postponement of his apology, he ate quickly, cleaned his dishes and left the house. He was still determined to find time to check out the light he'd seen from his window the night before.

It was afternoon by the time he finished his work, grabbed a cold drink and a piece of fruit, and headed through the back pasture to the abandoned house.

The walk reminded him of the last time he had headed out alone like this—only not really like this. It wasn't fear driving him this time but curiosity.

As he walked along he thought about David Jones and their strange encounter. And the waking dream he'd had that day. What did it mean? Who was the person whose face he couldn't make out? Why did the dream frighten him? Puzzles. His life was one big puzzle, like the ones he and Caitlin occasionally worked on at night. Only some of the pieces were missing, the largest being his identity. Who was he?

Was he the lost, frightened dummy Caitlin had taken in, or someone—something—altogether and frighteningly different? Sometimes he felt as though all this—the ranch, the work, even Caitlin herself—was the dream—the charade—and that soon he would awaken to find himself, as before, all alone.

After pushing through a tangle of overgrown bushes and vines, he stopped. The house was in sight. At one time the lane from the road running past the ranch house had extended all the way back, crossing a small wooden bridge built over the creek. The bridge he had just crossed sagged now, missing boards making it unsafe for a vehicle to cross.

Moving closer, he saw that the house was a basically square structure made of whitish stone taken from the pasture in which it stood. The marks of the stonecutter were evident in straight lines gouged here and there on uneven, rocky surfaces. The stones were held in place by a porous, grainy mortar.

Two large stone steps led up to a wooden porch covered by a sloping roof that extended across the front of the structure. Two doors, side by side, approximately four feet apart, led into the house. The porch sagged a bit, and he could see holes in the screen doors and windows from where he stood. But all in all the place looked to be in fairly good condition. A veritable palace compared to most of the places where he had holed up before finding his way here to the ranch—and Caitlin.

A walkway pieced together with the same stone as the house, cracked and overgrown, led up to the steps. Mimosa, crepe myrtle and dogwood trees were scattered over the grounds. A trellis, with pieces of wood missing, flanked one side of the porch, and a rosebush filled with dark red blooms, badly in need of pruning, climbed its way to the top.

Nick made his way slowly around the house, searching, but with no idea of what he was searching for. There was nothing suspicious in warped boards, crumbling mortar, or sagging screens.

A small stone building about fifteen yards from the house proved, on closer inspection, to be an old outhouse. A grape arbor, built and grown as a cover for lawn chairs on warm summer evenings, sat between the main house and the outhouse. There were several flowering bushes he didn't recognize, and more of the crepe myrtle and mimosa.

Since there was no entrance to the house from the back, he walked around to the front, climbed the steps and tried the handle of the nearest door. It opened easily under his touch, and he found himself in an empty room that appeared to have been a kitchen.

Low wooden cabinets painted an aged cream color, the paint cracked and peeling, lined one whole wall. The wall to the right of the door was taken up by a huge stone fireplace, the blackened hearth showing no signs of recent use. The twelve-foot ceiling had large brown stains marring its surface. The walls were painted an echo of the cream cabinets. White curtains hung at the windows, looking limp and dirty. Spiders had made their webs in two of the corners, and cobwebs laced back and forth around cabinets, curtains and ceiling. Nick's footsteps echoed hollowly on cracked, faded linoleum. The air of desertion and neglect about the place made him feel unaccountably sad.

Making his way through each room, he discovered that the two rooms at the back appeared to have been bedrooms, and the room on the other side of the kitchen, sharing the fireplace, a living room. Except for the nest of mice he unearthed in an old mattress left in one of the bedrooms, he found nothing unusual.

Perhaps he had imagined the light, or maybe it had been a shooting star. No—not a shooting star.

Outside once more, he sat on the front porch, his knees drawn up under his chin, popped the top of his soft drink can and took a long satisfying swallow.

If he hadn't set the can on the uneven edge of a warped board, he would have missed the spent match. It could have been there a long time, but he didn't think so. Neither he nor Caitlin smoked; besides, the match looked dry, so it certainly hadn't been there before the rain a couple days before. He looked around carefully for a cigarette butt without finding one, but was convinced there had been one.

It was possible, he reasoned, that someone had only stayed the night and moved on in the morning. But where had they come from? There were a great many acres between the main road and this house. What business would a stranger have on Caitlin's land? Hunting? The land was posted, but that didn't necessarily rule out trespassers. Remembering the sheriff's talk of strange happenings around the area and the mutilated animals he himself had found, he decided to keep an eye out.

A slight sound alerted him seconds before a voice spoke mockingly from behind him.

"Well, well, alone at last."

Bills paid, errands run, Caitlin headed for the town library. She wanted to thank Megan for the cake and the present she'd brought by the night before.

"Whew! I think everyone in the county returned books this morning." Megan breezed into the undersized office, stopped and stared. "You look absolutely gorgeous, if I do say so myself." She grinned as she reached for the coffee pot.

Caitlin preened, drawing her shoulders back in an exaggerated model's pose. "Me, huh?" she drawled, batting her eyelashes. They both laughed while Megan joined her at the table. "Thanks, Meg, it's beautiful."

She ran her fingers lightly over the pale yellow sweater buttoned at the throat, with short cap sleeves and banded waist. The design molded her breasts lovingly.

Her friend shrugged, a half smile on her face as she gazed down into the depths of the coffee cup she held gripped tightly in both hands.

"How's David? Is he talking to you yet?" Caitlin asked gently, sensing the other woman's tension.

Megan worried her lip, shaking her head slightly before answering. "Not much. He isn't eating or sleeping, from what I can tell. And he's started going out at night like he used to do right after he got home from the VA hospital—he takes a rifle and shells with him. I'm scared to death. I don't know what to do. I'm afraid to talk to anyone. I almost called the sheriff, but I'm afraid he'll threaten to lock David up or something, and that will only make him worse."

"Have you considered calling a doctor, maybe one of those he had in the hospital?"

"God, if I even mention doctors or the hospital he gets wild."

"Do you think it would do any good for me—"

"Thanks," Megan interrupted, shaking her head, "but no, he won't talk to you. It might make him worse."

"I'm sorry, kid." Caitlin touched her shoulder in sympathy.

"Yeah, so am I," Megan whispered. "How about you?" She looked up. "How are you and Nick getting along?"

Now it was Caitlin's turn to shrug and look away. The hurt of the night before was still too fresh to discuss, even with her best friend.

"Hey, is anybody here?" a throaty voice called out, followed by the sound of heels tapping on the wood floor.

"Shay?" Megan whispered delightedly, then jumped to her feet and rounded the table, hurrying to the door. "We're in here," she said to the small voluptuous figure in red.

"Hi. For a minute there, I thought you'd deserted these hallowed rooms." Swinging her long black curls, teased, sprayed and held in place by combs with feathers, pearls and sequins, Shay O'Malley sauntered into the room. "Well, if it ain't the egg lady come to roost." She laughed in a deep, sultry voice, brown almond-shaped eyes alight in a face that could only be described as totally bewitching.

"Come join the party," Caitlin invited, scooting her chair over to make room at the tiny table.

"Coffee?" Megan inquired, admiring the way Shay seemed to float gracefully onto the seat.

"Only if it's strong, black and bitter."

"You're in luck." Caitlin grinned. "That's the only way Meg knows how to make it."

"So what's been happening with you all?" Shay asked above the jangle of the many colorful bracelets adorning one delicate wrist.

"Caity has a new hired hand," Megan whispered in a loud undertone. "And is he gor-r-geous," she said, drawing out the word.

"Oh?" Raising a finely arched brow, Shay turned a shrewd glance on the silent redhead. "Not a big gorgeous blonde, by any chance, with muscles out to here?" she gestured exaggeratedly.

"Blonde?" Megan and Caitlin looked blankly at each other and then at Shay. "No, he's dark. Why?" Caitlin asked.

"Oh . . ." Shay frowned, blew at the steaming coffee, then crossed one shapely leg over the other before answering. "A guy rented a room from me for a couple of days, said he was looking for farm work. He asked if I knew anyone in the area who would be looking for help. I told him several people, including Caity." She shrugged indolently.

Pulling a package of cigarettes from the purple clutch bag that matched her spiked heels, she ignored the No Smoking sign posted on the wall and slipped a long thin cigarette between garnet lips. Holding a silver and turquoise lighter to it, she drew deeply, a look of pleasure slowly spreading across her lovely features.

"Well, he didn't show up at my place," Caitlin said, watching her.

"Maybe the Carringtons or old Fred Taylor hired him on," Shay answered, after releasing the smoke from her lungs. She looked around for an ashtray and, finding none, flipped the ash into the wastebasket beside the table.

Megan eyed Caitlin in consternation, but made no comment. Caitlin, hiding a grin, raised her cup to her lips.

"So who is he? This gorgeous man you hired?" Shay turned thickly lashed eyes toward Caitlin.

"A . . . transient. He needed work, and I needed help."

Shay drowned the cigarette butt in her tepid coffee, then flipped it into the waste basket and rose sleekly from her chair. After rinsing her cup at the tiny sink, she turned back to the other two.

"Guess I'd better get going. I slipped out for a minute to take Bart a loaf of sourdough bread."

"You've already baked this morning?" Megan asked, chagrined.

"Yeah, today bread, tomorrow it's woodwork and walls." Sighing heavily, she grabbed her purse and headed for the door. "You know what they say about a woman's work . . ."

"It's never done," all three chanted, laughing.

Shay paused at the door to gaze back over her shoulder. "Bring the new man over for dinner one night. I'm dying to meet him. Thanks for the coffee." She waved a hand and, trailing a cloud of jasmine, drifted out the door.

"She is something else," Megan murmured, sitting back in her seat. "If I didn't know for a fact that she really did get down on her hands and knees to clean—well, would you believe it?"

"I know, she looks like she wouldn't know one end of a broom from the other. And her sourdough bread is the best I've ever eaten."

"Wonder what happened to the blonde she mentioned," Megan said thoughtfully.

"Who knows? Maybe he got fresh with her and she put him out."

"That's a distinct possibility." Megan nodded. "It's funny, as downright sexy as she is, I don't remember her ever dating in high school."

"Her father wouldn't let her."

"Oh."

"You know, I think the only man she's ever gone out with is Bart Raymond."

"Yeah, and who can figure that one out?"

"He's really a nice man, Meg. He's gruff and chauvinistic, but he's a good sheriff—a good man."

"I guess," Megan agreed reluctantly. "I just associate him with David—you know. About the only time I see him is when someone has made a complaint and he comes around to quiz me or David about it."

"He's only doing his job."

"I know, I know."

Caitlin searched the ranch when she returned from town, but Nick was nowhere to be found. Wandering beyond the garden and through the orchard, she recalled her disappointment the evening before and her reluctance to face him this morning. Yesterday had been her twenty-sixth birthday, and she had wanted to spend it with him. But he had deserted her.

Megan had once asked her if she loved Nick, and she hadn't known how to answer. Now she knew she was closer to loving him than any man she had ever been attracted to, and that scared her, maybe even more than the thought of being alone.

Her nature made it hard for her to open up to other people. Megan, David, Aunt Letty and her father had been the only exceptions. She had learned at an early age to rely on herself and not expect too much from others. People let you down. Sometimes it wasn't their fault—her mother, her father and Aunt Letty had died, and they couldn't help that—but surely it was better if you didn't let yourself in for all that unhappiness and pain.

Nick frightened her because of the hold he already had on her emotions after only a few short weeks, and by the very nature of the mystery surrounding his past. He could hurt her badly if she gave him the opportunity. Her fear was that the option was no longer hers to give.

While she pondered her dilemma, she had been walking, and now she found herself near the old stone house. It stood just over the hill. She hadn't really expected to find Nick here, but the walk had given her the opportunity to think over some of the problems facing her, and the exercise was helping to clear the cobwebs from her mind.

It was the murmur of voices that warned her she was no longer alone. Cautious, more curious than afraid, she peeked around the corner of the house. Nick stood facing her from perhaps two yards away, arguing with another man, whose bright cap of blond hair glistened in the sunlight.

The man was a stranger to her, and then her earlier conversation with Megan and Shay came to mind. Could this be the blond stranger who was looking for work? How did he know Nick? He certainly wasn't treating Nick as though he were retarded. What was going on here?

"Is this some kind of new game you're playing, Rivers? Because if so, you damned well better let me in on it." Built on massive lines, the unknown man, his back toward Caitlin, spoke in harsh tones.

"I don't know what you're talking about," Nick insisted stubbornly. But Caitlin caught a flicker of something deep in his dark eyes.

"Bull! We've been through this before. I know you like to play it close to the line, but damn it, I have a part in this deal, too." Anger was smoldering just below the surface of the words, barely held in check.

"Deal? What deal? There isn't any deal," Nick said.

"That's where you're wrong. I know how you work, but let's get one thing straight—I don't like this thing with the broad. You're taking a chance there, and it could be dangerous for one of you, maybe even fatal." Hands on his hips, he glared across the small space separating him from Nick.

"Fatal?" Nick repeated questioningly, frowning.

"Yeah, fatal—as in dead. I got to say one thing, the red-head is a real looker—just like they all are. How the hell you manage to find one every damned time is beyond me." In the middle of shaking his golden head, he jerked suddenly still. Head cocked in a listening attitude, he whirled abruptly, then darted toward a barely audible sound coming from around the corner of the porch.

Both men swore as they caught sight of bright red hair disappearing over the side of the hill.

"Oh, no! Caitlin!" Nick groaned.

"So that's her name. Well, like I said, she's a real looker. Listen, ole buddy, I'll let you take care of that yourself." He motioned with one huge hand. "And you'd better do it fast. Before she blows everything to hell and back."

Nick started after her at a dead run, his mind hardly heeding the raspy sound of the blond man's voice.

"Rivers!"

Something in the tone stopped him cold; impatiently, he turned back. "Yeah?"

"Tonight, ten o'clock—here—alone." Cold gray eyes bit into him. "Tonight," the man repeated succinctly. Then, not waiting for an answer, he rounded the corner of the house and disappeared from sight.

"Tonight," Nick repeated numbly. "Caitlin," he whispered suddenly, shaking his head to clear it. "Caitlin!" he called louder and, twisting around, dashed madly in her wake.

Chapter 8

Nick crashed through the underbrush, stumbling over rocks, tripping through tangled vines. His mind was a morass of confusion. He had to find Caitlin, had to find her and explain, had to keep her from calling the sheriff. Because the blond stranger had said her life might depend on her silence.

Silence? The word reverberated through his chaotic thoughts. Silence about what? He had no idea what the man had been referring to. Nothing he'd said in the short time they'd been speaking before Caitlin's untimely interruption had made any sense.

Only two things remained firmly fixed in his mind: he had to find Caitlin and keep her silent. Nothing, no matter what, was worth risking a hair on her head.

Where was she? Panting, he stopped as he crested the next hill and ran his eyes along the dry creek bed. Nothing. She was nowhere to be seen.

She had to be here somewhere. Breathing deeply, hands on hips, slightly bent at the waist, he turned once more to survey the immediate area.

"God, Caitlin, where are you? Please, let me find you—please," he whispered desperately over and over as he descended the hill, stymied as to where to look next.

* * *

Caitlin ran willy-nilly, without thought or direction, around trees, through bushes, over rocks, uphill and down, a voice screaming inside her head. Nick was a killer! He had stood there calmly listening as his *buddy* discussed killing her. What was she going to do?

Her mind whirled in a vortex of bewildering thoughts and conflicting ideas. The man she'd taken into her home, treated with kindness and respect, wanted to repay her—by killing her? No, it couldn't be. There had to be some other explanation. Had she misunderstood the strange man's words? Who was he? He talked as though he knew Nick—knew him intimately. Was this the clue she'd been looking for, someone from his past, someone who could help jog his memory?

But they had talked about killing her. Nick, a killer? No! Her mind rejected the idea. Not the gentle, thoughtful, kind man she'd come to know. Not the man who handled baby chicks as though they were fragile and precious. Not the man who vehemently protested the wanton killing of animals. Not the man she'd come to—love?

Caitlin stopped abruptly and looked dazedly around. Love? When had she come to love him? She cared about him, certainly, wanted to help him—was physically drawn to him, she readily admitted—but love? The idea terrified her. The people she loved had all left her. One way or another they had all left her—all except Megan and David. And part of the reason for them being drawn together was because they had all three lost everyone close to them who mattered.

No, she thought, climbing to the top of a hill, where she shook her head and stamped her feet. No! No! She did not love Nick! She didn't love him—she wouldn't love him.

If the uncertainty of his background and mental state weren't enough—though she had stopped believing he was retarded weeks ago—now there was the question of whether or not he was dangerous.

Panting, wiping the sheen of sweat from her brow, pushing at the tangle of hair falling into her eyes, she whimpered, "No, I don't love him—I don't. I can't, not now, not after what I just heard."

In her perturbed state of mind she misjudged her footing. One foot slid from beneath her and, as if in a specially-choreographed move, the rest of her body followed suit. Head over heels, she tumbled down the hillside, the cry, "Nick!" bursting involuntarily from her lips as she hurtled toward the bottom.

Nick found her lying, deathly pale and still, in a crumpled heap at the bottom of the hill. He'd almost given up hope of finding her and decided to head toward the house when he heard his name echo through the hills.

Kneeling beside her still form, his heart in his mouth, he smoothed the bright hair, bits of leaves and twigs caught in the strands, back from her ashen face. With a lurch of his heart he knew she meant more to him than his own life. A fierce protective feeling spread through him, and he vowed silently, that, no matter what it took, he would keep her safely out of his life. Whatever mess he was in, she had no part in it. And nothing— no one—would ever touch her, harm her, because of him.

Whispering her name, he bent over her, laid a cheek close to her face and, with heart-steadying relief, felt her breath feather his skin. Carefully he examined each limb for signs of injury and, finding none, looked for the cause of her unconsciousness.

With unsteady hands he sifted through the fine strands of her hair and found a large knot on the side of her head beneath one ear. The skin was unbroken, the area around the edges firm and dry. Laying two fingers on her neck, he felt for her pulse and was reassured by the steady rhythmic beat against his unsteady fingertips, which were instinctively adept at searching for signs of injury.

Sitting back on his heels he studied her. For the first time since they'd met, he had the freedom to let his eyes roam from feature to feature.

Gently, as if afraid of awakening her, he touched hesitant fingers to the smooth skin stretched taut over her delicately carved features. Hungry eyes devoured her face, memorizing every soft curve, every sweeping line.

His heart swelled, filling him with both joy and a strange sadness. Bending closer, one hand tangled in her dusty curls, unable to resist the temptation, he touched his lips to hers, bestowing a kiss as tender and light as a summer's breeze.

All at once he stilled, his lips a hairsbreadth from hers. Had she moved the slightest bit? Had he felt her beginning response, or, desiring one, had he only imagined it? Drawing slightly away, he gazed down into her open eyes.

"Again," she whispered throatily.

Without even a thought of resisting, he slowly lowered his head. His lips took hers in a whisper-light caress, then drew back a fraction and hovered for a breathtaking instant before returning to reclaim her lips as he crushed her to him, his control suddenly shattered by her passionate response.

Slipping an arm beneath her, he drew her up into the cradle of his arms. Easing back against the hillside, unmindful of the bite of rock or sharp prick of briars, he gathered her onto his lap, his mouth holding hers captive.

The warm lips on hers as she regained consciousness had sent wave after wave of shock coursing through her entire system. All thought had fled except for the realization of his kiss. Caitlin snuggled closer, one arm going around him as she hesitantly caressed the hard jutting bones of his hip through the rough material of his jeans.

Aroused by his touch as never before, her earlier fears blocked from her mind, she allowed her own passion to surmount caution. Too caught up by long suppressed needs, she felt no shock at her own eager response. With one hand gripping the back of his head, fingers entwined in the vibrant black hair, she pressed him closer, opening her lips, urging him on with a deep, compelling demand.

Gliding his hand down the back of her head, Nick loved her with gentle fingers, stroking her neck and shoulders while his lips roved her face, planting warm, moist kisses on her forehead, eyes and lips. Pulse hammering, senses heady, dizzy, exhilarated, he breathed her name against the soft curve below her chin. He wanted her so badly that his whole body shook with his need.

Closing her eyes, drowning in waves of sensation, Caitlin dropped her head back against his shoulder, allowing his caressing lips free rein. Shivering in delight at his touch, she moaned as he showered kisses from the edge of her mouth along the line of her jaw and back before taking her mouth once more with a savage intensity.

Her hands were all over him; she couldn't touch him enough. She wanted to feel every part of him, hardened muscle, hair and skin, against her softness. Pulling at his shirt, tearing it free of his jeans, sliding her hand over the smooth, firm expanse of his muscled back, she kissed and tasted his cheek and chin, then nibbled along the ridge of his collarbone to the springy hair at his throat.

"Touch me," she sighed. "I love the feel of your hands on me." Her fevered words ripped at what little self-imposed restraint he had left.

Their hands met, elbows collided, clumsy fingers fumbled at his shirt and her sweater. A cool breeze whispered across the naked flesh slowly becoming exposed. Goose bumps rose on her arms, his chest, fanning the flames of anticipation.

Taking one of his hands in both of hers, Caitlin guided it to her naked breast. She felt him tremble as his fingers gently outlined the circle at the center of one soft globe. Closing her eyes, gasping at such sweet agony, she felt her nipple harden against the heat of his palm.

"Caitlin, look at me."

His dark eyes locked with hers, a stunned look in their depths. She was so soft, her skin creamy smooth where the sun hadn't touched it, like satin beneath his touch. Breath suspended, a fire in his loins, he silently marveled at the difference in texture between her skin and his.

Lowering his head, he cupped one breast to his face, pressing a soft kiss against its fullness. He took the dusky nipple into his mouth, then drew it out slowly, his tongue rubbing gently against the ultrasensitive tip.

Caitlin felt the thrill all the way to her toes, a strange, never-before-felt sensation flooding her body with a yearning for something she couldn't identify.

Turning his head slightly, feeling the damp puckered bud against his cheek, he drew a moist line with the tip of his tongue to the edge of her chin, around the curve of her jaw, to below her ear. Stopping there, he nibbled delicately at the pink lobe and felt her shiver as his teeth nipped gently at the flesh of her neck.

Caitlin caught her breath on a moan at the touch of his tongue on the sensitive cord below her ear. Breasts full and heavy, insides tight with desire, she pressed her face against his head, feeling the coarse hair tickle her skin. She was all sensation, all feeling, all woman, aroused to fever pitch. Irresistibly drawn, her hands slid the length of his back to his buttocks, testing, kneading, gripping, pulling him to her. She wanted him—no, she needed him.

They sought each other's mouths, tongues dueling in a dance as old as time, while the world spun, careening on its axis. Incapable of withstanding such heart-wrenching ecstasy, Caitlin pulled her mouth from beneath his. With lips throbbing from his kisses she kissed his rough jaw, the dimple on his chin. The sound of his tortured whispers echoed loudly in her ear.

Nick pulled her tightly against him, her nipples like small blunt darts prodding his hair-roughened chest, bringing a groan almost of pain to his lips. He was fast losing what little control he still exerted over his baser desires.

Bodies slick with sweat, breaths coming in labored gasps, they drew slightly apart, taking long, steadying draughts of air in unison.

Nick closed his eyes against the sight of her loveliness in an agony of conflicting emotions. Then, with trembling hands, he drew her head against him, holding her still against his chest.

"Caitlin—Caity—Cat—" he gasped, dreading the words he was about to say. He didn't want to stop, he wanted her as badly as she wanted him, but . . . "Cat—we can't—I can't—"

"W-what?" Lifting her head, she looked at him dazedly. "W-what do you mean w-we can't?"

With passion misting her gold-flecked eyes, lips swollen from his kisses, she attempted to focus on what he was saying.

"You don't know what I am—what I was—you don't know anything about me. I have no right—"

His face worked as he struggled for the words to tell her that he had no right to touch her this way. He had no experience with women—none that he remembered, anyway. The only time he'd come this close to a woman had been with Marcie, and that experience had scared him so badly he'd run. Somehow he didn't feel inclined to run from Caitlin, but maybe he should.

Caitlin's fingers closed firmly over his lips as she at last comprehended his incoherent speech. Her eyes compelled his to meet her glance. "It doesn't matter."

"You don't understand . . ." His lips moved against her fingers, causing her to yearn for their more intimate touch.

"Nick, I understand." He shook his head violently. "Yes," she insisted, "I do. It doesn't matter if—"

"Oh, God—will you listen to me! It does matter." Gripping her shoulders fiercely, he shook her. "I don't know how—I don't know what to do—"

Shamefaced, he floundered. Their coming together each time before now had been purely by instinct, a need to feel her warmth, a need for contact with another human in an attempt at dispelling the void he felt inside. But now, hazy though the idea was in his mind, he knew something more was involved here, and he wanted it to be clear in his mind before he took this further step with Caitlin.

"Nick, look at me—look at me." Waiting until she held his unhappy gaze, she continued. "Would it matter to you if I told you I was a virgin?" She didn't stop to consider the fact that he might not understand the word. Taking his face in both hands, she forced him to meet her eyes.

"No," he answered, the reference to virgin going over his head. He was reacting as he always reacted to Caitlin, on a purely instinctive level. He had trusted her kindness in the beginning by instinct, and every advance their relationship had made since those days had developed by his following those same instincts.

"Then it doesn't matter," she repeated. But still he hesitated.

"You don't know it all." He sought the words to tell her about Marcie.

But though he resisted Caitlin mentally, he couldn't keep from rubbing his face gently against the soft hand cupping his cheek, couldn't stop his own fingers from moving rhythmically, caressingly, on her shoulders.

"I can't—I—" he began again, attempting to deny the sweet sensations generated by her hand moving slowly from his jaw to his throat. Caitlin pressed a thumb lightly against his larynx, feeling the movement as he spoke, swallowed. Nick shivered, his mind losing what little grasp it had on his actions.

Swallowing again, determined to bring his errant thoughts back into focus, he spoke doggedly once more.

"I ran—" He could tell from the expression on her face that she was paying no heed to his words.

"Yes," she whispered somnolently. "You ran." Her hands moved against him, learning him, absorbing the feel of him through sensitive fingertips.

It was too much. Emitting a low growl, he jerked her tight against him, his lips tasting the fragile hollow of her throat. Burying his face in the soft dewy skin, he crushed her naked breasts against the hardness of his bare chest. Caitlin squirmed closer. Nick groaned, his jeans an uncomfortable restriction to his throbbing desire.

Slipping a hand around his neck, Caitlin ruffled his hair, massaging the sensitized muscles at the base of his skull. Her other hand slipped between them, pressing flat against the thick, hard ridge beneath his jeans.

Finding her mouth, he took it eagerly, drawing the kisses from her lips. Closer, he needed to be closer. Smoothing his hands over her shoulders, he slipped them down her moist skin, catching his fingertips around her erect nipples, rubbing them gently as his tongue stroked hers in a parody of lovemaking.

His senses clamored for more. They ate each other's lips, melded sweat-slickened bodies, while his passion surged against her hand. He felt her fingers tugging at the waistband of his jeans. The snap popped suddenly open, sounding like a shot, freezing him instantly to stillness.

It took a while for his withdrawal to penetrate the fog of Caitlin's inflamed senses. Gradually, though, the controlled way he held his body stiffly away from hers seeped in.

Drawing back at last, she noted the incongruity in the rigid line of his kiss-swollen lips. A chill passed over her, cooling the fires that had been raging out of control, freezing the heat of passion into a thin sheet of ice over her skin.

"You don't want me," she stated dully.

He wanted her. Lord above, how he wanted her. His need was a fever in his blood and a pain deep in his belly. But too many things stood between them. Too many unanswered questions. Things she didn't know, wouldn't understand. Things he didn't know. Questions he was afraid to ask—afraid to answer.

For weeks he'd resisted his growing desire for her despite the fact that her every touch, every look, every word, fired him anew with longing. At night he lay awake imagining the feel of her delicate body beneath his. He might not remember what it was like in actual fact, but that didn't curtail his fevered imaginings. Such thoughts kept his emotions in a constant state of upheaval.

Yes, he wanted her all right, with an intensity that drove him to work eighteen-hour days to get the sight, sound and smell of her out of his system. But she was always there, in one way or another; her presence never left him.

When he returned to the house at night, ready to drop in his tracks, she was there waiting for him. And if she had retired, there were signs of her presence all about him. Her perfume lingering in the air, clean towels in the bathroom, his meal cooked and waiting.

He wanted her, but he couldn't take her, not now, not like this. Not when her safety, maybe her life, depended on him—not unless or until he knew more about himself and where he belonged in the scheme of things.

Finding her as he had, unconscious and vulnerable, had blown him away. His control gone, he had permitted her to get beneath his skin, find the places he kept secret, guarded. This situation was his fault. From the look of pain on her face to his own confused and uncomfortable state of arousal, the blame was all his. But this was where it stopped. He would protect her, even if that meant he had to protect her from himself.

"I'm sorry," he murmured, turning away.

Caitlin grabbed his arm, her nails biting into the hard muscle, every other emotion overshadowed by a deep, sinking feeling of rejection.

"Just one thing. Look at me—look at me, damn you!" She jerked him toward her, her nails breaking the skin. "Don't you ever do this to me again. Just stay away from me in the future, got that? Just stay the hell away from me."

Dropping his arm, her rage turning to humiliation at his total lack of reaction, she climbed awkwardly to her feet. Sensing rather than seeing the helping hand he held out to her, she jerked away from his touch. Tear-studded lashes shaded her eyes, making it impossible for her to read the despair in the opaque depths of his. Back straight, head high, she marched out of sight.

Arms hanging emptily at his sides, Nick stood helplessly by, watching her, dying a little inside with each step she took. One hand moving to his right thigh, spreading flat against it, he absently kneaded the bunched and aching muscle.

Caitlin glanced at the large clock on the mantel for perhaps the fifth time in the last five minutes, then glanced out the window at the blackness outside, watching a streak of lightning dart across the night sky. Crossing her arms over her breasts, she glanced again at the clock.

Where in the world was he? It was half past nine, and still he hadn't come home. She no longer suspected him of wanting to kill her. There must be another explanation for the conversation she'd overheard. In the beginning, in her humiliation, she had been so angry with him that she had wanted to strangle him. All the way back to the house she had prayed that she would never have to see him again. In her thoughts she fired him, told him to leave, never to show himself on her ranch again.

She had expected him to follow her, waited to enjoy ignoring him, making him feel small and mean and uncomfortable. When evening rolled around and he didn't show for the evening chores, she cursed him. When he didn't show for the evening meal she relented—a little. And now, almost eight hours since she'd last seen him, she alternated between anger and fear.

Where could he be? He didn't know anyone but her. What if he was hurt? Snake bitten? She shuddered at the thought. What if he had left and wasn't coming back? Maybe she should call someone—or go look for him. No! Her stubborn pride wouldn't allow her to confide her worries to anyone else, nor would it let her go off half-cocked, searching through the dark for him.

Going into the kitchen, she looked out the small window above the sink. The sky looked every bit as threatening as it had from the living-room window. The storm was moving closer.

Back in the living room once more, she plopped down into her favorite chair and rocked furiously. But the rocking failed to soothe her as it had in the past. Maybe she *should* go look for him. No, he was a full-grown man; he could take care of himself. Couldn't he? A picture of him as she had first seen him came to mind. He hadn't been doing such a great job of it then. But he was different now. She wouldn't let herself think just how different, of the ways in which he was different. Her senses couldn't take another onslaught of Nick Rivers, not again today.

Why had he frozen up? Why had he turned away from her? She couldn't leave it alone. Did it have something to do with what he had been attempting to tell her? Had he realized he was suffering from amnesia? Had he regained his memory—part of it? Was there someone else? Did he remember a sweetheart, fiancée, a wife?

All evening, since her return, she'd been pretending to forget, to put the whole afternoon out of her mind. But she was only fooling herself. It was all she could think about: Nick withdrawing from her; Nick going still in her arms; turning away from her; whispering, "I'm sorry," in that dead-sounding voice. What was the matter with her? One minute she avoided him for days because she was afraid of developing a deeper relationship with him, and the next she was blazingly angry because he had backed off from her.

Rocking harder, she picked up her needlework from the table, looked at it, then put it down again and glanced at the clock. Almost ten, she thought as she listened to the storm building. Where was he? Damn him for letting her worry this way!

Nick sat on the porch, his back against the rough stone, knees drawn up to his chin, arms locked around them, eyes on the rolling mass of clouds barely visible in the darkness overhead. Thunder rumbled in the distance.

He had returned to the abandoned house shortly after Caitlin had stalked off, leaving him near the creek. Somehow he couldn't stomach the idea of following her, watching the hurt in her eyes each time she looked his way. He didn't want to cause her pain, though he knew he had. The best thing he could do for her was to do as she had asked—no, demanded—leave her alone and hope time would take care of the damage he'd done to her self-esteem and their relationship. He didn't know what he would do if she made him leave now. He needed her in more ways than she could imagine.

He spent the afternoon becoming familiar with the old farmhouse and its grounds. Finally, mentally exhausted from too little sleep and their recent emotional encounter, he had fallen asleep. It was dusk when he awakened, too late for the evening chores, so, nauseated at the thought of food, he remained at the house.

Taking up a place on the porch, he watched the thunderheads gather and block out the sun. Night fell swiftly after that, and he spent the time watching lightning dart from one cloud to another. He felt the wind freshen and listened to the thunder growl in the distance, announcing the storm's imminent arrival.

His thoughts turned continuously to Caitlin. He wondered if her anger had cooled, if she was worried at his absence, and why she hadn't mentioned the man she had seen him with on the porch. The man whose arrival he was now awaiting. He didn't have a watch, but he guessed it must be close to ten.

He sensed he was no longer alone before the smell of the cigarette reached his nostrils. Turning his head, he saw the small red glow.

"Well, what do you know, you're on time for a change." The man spoke from the shadows, a deeper shadow at the end of the porch. Boards creaked with his weight as he moved closer. He appeared tall, over six foot, Nick guessed accurately.

"Nothing to say for yourself?" the big man asked.

Nick remained silent and watchful.

"That isn't like you. What the hell's happened to you, man? Where have you been? You just dropped out of sight without a word to anyone. I should have guessed you'd be playing the game by your own rules. But this time you've really done it. The old man thought you were dead. You'd better come up with a damned good reason for playing it so close to the vest, or he'll nail your hide to the wall."

"Who the hell are you—and who the hell do you think I am?"

"What the—"

"Do I know you?" Nick asked with a puzzled frown.

"Damn right you do."

"How?"

"Look here—"

"Tell me." He didn't raise his voice, but the big man beside him recognized the dangerously familiar command.

"You're Andrew Rivers."

"How do you know me? What do I do? Where am I from?"

Sounding as though he were humoring a particularly recalcitrant child, the stranger answered, "You're a special agent with the FBI. You come from Washington, D.C. You were sent to Texas on an undercover assignment, posing as an arms dealer. You were supposed to find and infiltrate a survivalist group known to be in this area and suspected of gunrunning, and trafficking in illegal drugs and smuggling them across the Mexican border."

"FBI agent?" He'd read a little about the FBI in one of the many books Caitlin had gotten from the library. The man might

Escape into a world where Romance and love mean so much more...

Free Books and Gifts claim

Yes Please send me my 4 FREE Silhouette Special Editions together with my FREE Gifts. Please also reserve a special Reader Service Subscription for me. If I decide to subscribe, I shall receive 6 superb new titles every month for just £9.90, post and packing FREE. If I decide not to subscribe I shall write to you within 10 days. The FREE books and Gifts will be mine to keep in any case. I understand that I am under no obligation whatsoever. I can cancel or suspend my subscription at any time simply by writing to you. I am over 18 years of age.

1S1SE

Mrs/Miss/Mr _____

Address _____

_____

_____ Postcode _____

Signature _____

NO STAMP NEEDED

Reader Service
FREEPOST
P.O. Box 236
Croydon
Surrey CR9 9EL

Send NO money now

as well have told him he was the President of the United States.
"Why me?" he murmured.

"You volunteered," the man beside him answered shortly.
"Now, you want to tell me what's going on?" Hunkering down
beside Nick, he pulled out a crumpled package of cigarettes and
offered Nick one.

Nick looked at the cellophane-wrapped packet and asked,
"Do I smoke?"

"Like a chimney," came the quick reply.

"Well, I quit—I guess."

"What? Come on, this is me, your ole buddy you're talking
to. You could no more quit smoking than settle down with one
woman." The man laughed. They'd both tried to quit smoking once, right after a mutual friend, a fellow agent, had
learned he had lung cancer—it hadn't worked. Taking a cigarette from the pack, he lit it from the tip of the one in his hand.

"I know a lot of women?" Nick asked curiously, making no
comment on the fact of his previous habit.

"That's an understatement. You've been working your way
through all the women in Washington since we first met, ten
years ago, in college. But no one has caught you, yet."

Settling more comfortably against the porch, he took a long
drag from the cigarette, blowing the smoke out through his
nostrils. "Okay, ole buddy, give. What's going on?"

"I don't know. I don't remember any of what you've been
saying." Too much information had already been thrown at
him. He was reeling from the knowledge that he was *someone*,
not a dummy, but a real person with an identity, and a life—one
he still knew too little about.

"Are you putting me on?" the man beside him asked skeptically.

Nick shook his head.

After a long moment of silence, the stranger sighed heavily
and asked, "What *do* you remember?"

Their glances met in the flare of a match, silent and watchful, each filled with wary curiosity about the other.

"Do you remember me?" the blond stranger asked at last,
already guessing the answer. It explained a lot.

For some reason Nick wished he could say yes. He wanted to
apologize to the man as he shook his head negatively. "No, I
don't."

"Damn!" His breath whistled out. Slumping back against the house he asked, "No joke?"

"Do I look as though I'm laughing?" Nick asked darkly.

"Some things don't change," the man beside him muttered. "So what do we do now? This was your operation. I'm only here as backup. I guess that explains the last communiqué from headquarters."

"Headquarters?"

"Yeah, someone is mighty interested in you and what you're doing here in Fate. Their questions got back to headquarters."

"What kind of questions? I thought you said you thought I was dead," Nick reminded him somewhat suspiciously, still having difficulty accepting his sudden new identity—despite his desperate desire to do so. "And who's been asking?"

The man beside him was having a few reservations himself about accepting his friend's amnesia story. This wouldn't be the first time Drew had acted out an unorthodox charade for the sake of his cover. Nevertheless, he went along with him and answered his question.

"I don't know for sure. I was only given the info that you might be here—somewhere around Fate. And since I'd been looking for you—hell, half the agents in Texas have been looking for you—I trotted on down here, pronto. As to the who—well, it seems the sheriff is mighty interested in you."

"I've met him. He doesn't like me much."

"I'm not surprised. He's a slick customer. From what I hear, not much goes on around here that he doesn't know about."

"Does that mean he's involved with the crooks?"

The man at his side eyed him for a moment without replying. "You sure you can't remember—" He broke off at Nick's impatient expletive. "Well, damn it, you sound just like you— I mean, you drop out of sight, and then you show up suddenly, telling me you don't remember anything . . ." He shook his head.

After a moment he continued with his explanations. "The sheriff appears to be clean. I checked him out as best I could without raising too many eyebrows around town. But there's a character here, name of Jones—what?" He broke off at the sound of Nick's half-smothered protest.

"Why do you suspect him?"

"The guy is a real nut case. He's a Vietnam vet, and he was a POW for about two years—sad to say, but you can never tell what they're gonna do after something like that. He's got a psychiatric profile you wouldn't believe.

"I checked him out with Washington after I heard some of his neighbors' comments about him. He had some pretty weird things to say about the government and the survival of the American people after he first got back from Nam. Don't know if he's changed his mind in the last few years. He keeps a pretty low profile, but the word around town is that he's looney and like a time bomb ready to blow."

"I've met him, too—he's pretty different, all right."

"Yeah, well, what are we going to do about you? It sounds as though your cover has been blown, and any information you managed to get, you can't remember."

"You have any proof of what you've been telling me?" Nick asked abruptly. He wanted to believe him—somehow, everything the man had told him about himself felt right. And besides, it meant he was normal, and he wanted desperately to be normal. Otherwise he knew he couldn't have Caitlin.

Lightning flared, throwing the man beside him into stark relief, a dumbstruck expression on his rough-hewn features. He hadn't considered the possibility that his friend might not believe *him*.

"You think I've been lying to you? Why? I've got proof of my identity, but I sure as hell can't give you any immediate proof of yours." Voice tight, he drew himself up angrily. "There's a number you can call—"

"Okay, okay. Look, what do I call you?"

"Frazier," the blond man answered stiffly. "Matthew Thaddeus Frazier."

"Damn!"

"That's exactly what you said the first time I told you my name." He grinned widely.

Suddenly they both laughed, dispelling some of the tension that had been standing between them since their meeting. Whether he knew it or not, Nick was falling into the old easy relationship they had shared since their first meeting in college. As far as Matt was concerned, his friend might have a slight lapse of memory, but the fundamental man remained unchanged.

"Okay, Matt, what do you suggest we do?" Thunder clapped, and wind howled around the building, and rain began to slap the ground.

"You have any memory at all about what happened to you after you got to Texas?"

Nick shook his head. "A few scars that may or may not be new, and a dream."

"Dream?"

"More of a nightmare—that's what I always thought it was." He didn't mention his fear, finally laid to rest, for his sanity. "But then I had it again a while back. Only this time it was broad daylight, and I was wide awake, and—I saw a face."

"You mean you can identify who—"

"No, the face isn't clear. I can't recognize any features. Besides, I don't know where the dream comes from. Now that you've told me I have a past I can't remember, it could be a dream from my childhood. Couldn't it?"

"Listen, Drew, I don't know a lot about amnesia, but couldn't that be a sign, a good sign, that your memory is trying to come back?"

"Maybe," he answered thoughtfully. "I never saw the face before—just that last time. Everything's hazy, sort of out of focus."

Looking contemplatively across the dark expanse of yard shimmering in the intermittent flashes of lightning, Matt nodded. Thinking of the long wet night ahead of him, he commented absently, "Like looking through glass or rain—"

"That's it!" Nick grabbed Matt's arm. "Damn it, Matt, that's it!" Sounding more like his old self to his friend's ears with each passing minute, he continued. "It's water. And the face—it's a man. I'm sure of it. The sound I hear could be a motor."

"The man, what's he doing?"

"Yelling. He's yelling something." Nick frowned in concentration, listening to some inner voice buried in the dark recesses of his memory. "I can't make it out above the noise." Staring almost hypnotized at the wall of driving rain, he was transported back in time into the midst of his nightmare.

His grip tightened on Matt's arm, a desperate tone entering his voice. "I'm in the water. It's dark, and so cold." He shivered in the clammy night air, eyes wide, the storm wild around them. "There's pain—my head, Lord, my head—and my chest—burning—" Suddenly he jerked his arms above his head, as if warding off a blow.

"Oh, God, he's hitting me—with the oar—my head—the
ain—" Jerking, bobbing, flinching, he moaned, his body re-
cting to each imaginary blow from the hard wooden paddle.

"Drew! Drew!" Matt grabbed him, shaking him, recalling
im with difficulty to the present. "It's over, buddy, it's over."

"Yeah," Nick answered finally, pulling away. Wiping a
aky hand over his damp face, he felt the moisture with a sick
read. "Yeah," he echoed, "it's over."

"Sounds like you had a pretty rough time," Matt com-
ented softly after a moment.

"I suppose," Nick answered tiredly and rested his head
gainst the rough stone wall. That wasn't the half of it. *Now he
new.* Someone had tried to kill him. His hand rested on his
ight thigh. Closing his eyes with a slight shudder, he pictured
gain the scene in the water. That explained the pain in his hip.
Everything was clear to him—except the man's face.

"You think we could pull this job off, find the bastard who
ried to kill you, without letting HQ know your situation?"
Matt asked hopefully. "No, maybe you *should* be in a hospital," he added anxiously.

"No hospital!" Nick sounded alarmed. Matt recalled that
Drew had never liked hospitals. "I don't know about continuing with the job. I don't know how much good I'll be. Some
things have come back—little things have been coming back for
a while. But I still don't have a full picture yet.

"I remember *things*, but I don't remember people. I think I
remember my job—but names..." He shook his head. "It's like
I remember everything but *me*. I still don't know me. I can't
recall friends, family, my taste in clothes—women...." His
voice trailed off as he stared out into the storm.

"Well, you're still single, if that helps."

"I don't know if I'd be any help to you on this case with only
half a memory," he continued, ignoring Matt's reference to his
marital status. Somehow he'd already known that.

"Listen, friend, I'd rather have you beside me in any situation I can name, on half throttle, than any other field agent I
know on full. We can fake it. We always did, anyway." He
laughed half-seriously.

"All right," Nick agreed after a long thoughtful hesitation.
"Lay it out for me. I want to know everything you know or
suspect about what's happened up to now." Straightening,
concentrating on the man beside him, he made his decision.

Maybe the best—the only—way to regain his memory was t₀
confront the cause of its loss.

"Our information was impeccable," Matt began. "The wor₀
was guns and drugs. All tied in with a survivalist group re
ported to be active in North Texas—"

"Survivalists?" Nick interrupted in confusion.

"Yeah, you know, nuts who believe the human race is boun₀
for World War Three. They don't care who starts it, or wh₀
wins—they just plan to be around afterward, to pick up th₀
pieces.

"Well, anyway, we'd been gathering information about them
for quite a while, but nothing on who the leader was, or why
they were involved in smuggling drugs and guns.

"You were sent in undercover, as a man selling guns, guns
the survivalists wanted to get their hands on pretty badly. The
last we knew, you were set to meet with our informant, the
person who had contacted the FBI with the information in the
first place.

"You dropped out of sight, but we expected that. We
expected you to resurface for our prearranged meeting, where
you would pass along the information you'd learned to me,
hopefully with the name of the leader of the group. That was
one thing our informant was very careful about—he wouldn't
give the name, except in person to one of our agents.

"You never made it to our rendezvous, and no one heard
from you again—until now.

"At first we all thought it was okay. We were used to you re-
vising the plan if a situation called for it. But as time passed and
no one heard anything..." He shrugged massive shoulders. "It
was assumed you'd been made and taken out." His voice
sounded a shade gruff.

"The operation was shelved. We'd been searching for you for
months without finding a trace, and I was on my way back to
Washington from Austin when I received word to get my butt
here, pronto. It seemed you had resurfaced—at last—playing
the game by your own set of rules."

"So, either somebody slipped up in Washington, or I was set
up," Nick reasoned, once again surprising his friend with his
quick grasp of the situation, considering the present circumstances. "But how did you know it was me when they told you
to come here?"

"I didn't. At least, I wasn't sure until I actually saw you. I've been staking out this ranch for a couple of days now. Ever since I heard in town about the new hired hand this female rancher had hired herself. I also heard you were kind of strange. But, knowing you, I figured it was part of your cover."

"I wish," Nick commented dully. "So, what do you think happened to me?"

"Well, the way I see it, someone talked. There were only four people who knew who you were." He ticked them off on his fingers. "You're looking at number one, our section chief was another, our informant—your contact here—and you."

"What happened to the contact? Anybody talk to him yet?"

"He disappeared right about the time you did."

"And?"

"Either he got cold feet or someone found out he talked. I go with the latter. I think they must have been waiting for you, and the only way that's possible is with prior knowledge."

"Sounds right. I still don't see how you found me."

"I told you, our section chief received inquiries."

"How?"

"A couple months after you disappeared, a discreet bulletin was sent to all law enforcement agencies in Texas. You know the routine—oh—" Matt stopped short for a moment, realizing Drew might not remember.

"We sent a kind of 'Have you see this man' sort of thing," he explained. "Along with a description. No warrants were issued, just an information query. Nobody picked up on it until a few weeks ago. It seems the town sheriff here has a sharp eye and one hell of a memory.

"Apparently, shortly after you showed up around town, he recalled the query and contacted a friend in Austin and—voila!—I appear as if by magic."

"Now if only my memory would," Nick put in wryly.

"Yeah," Matt agreed glumly.

"This friend of the sheriff's—what's his part in all this?"

"He doesn't have one. Apparently he called a few friends in Washington and was told very distinctly to mind his own business. He passed the information along to the sheriff. But it seems the friend had mentioned the sheriff's uneasiness about the man, and I was told to get out here and find out if it was you and reassure the sheriff you weren't a desperate criminal."

"Well, I think you should pay him a visit all right, but I don't think you should mention my lapse of memory. See what information you can get from him about Jones, and whether he has any idea about the survivalists—if they *are* in this area."

"You're the boss," Matt answered automatically.

"Right." Nick laughed ironically. What would Matt have to say about that if he'd seen him a few weeks ago? "Where are you staying?"

"I spent a couple days in town at the local boardinghouse getting the lay of the land and looking for you. The last few days I've been camping out around here.

"That broad that runs that place in town is one sexy babe. A lot like your usual number. That little redhead, now, she isn't your usual type at all. I see you haven't lost your touch."

"I have to leave the ranch. If I don't, I'm putting Caitlin's life in danger," Nick reflected worriedly.

"I think it's too late to worry about that. She's already in danger. If the people we're after are anywhere around here, by now they know you're back, and they can't be sure this Caitlin isn't helping you. So if you leave, that gives them a clear field to get her. I'd say she's safer with you close by."

"God." Running his hands through his hair, Nick leaned a shoulder against the house. "I've really messed this up, haven't I?"

"It isn't your fault, man. It's the chance we take when we play the game."

"Yeah, but Caitlin was never a player—until now."

Nick was surprised when the door opened easily under his hand. He had half expected it to be locked. After stepping into the short hall leading to the kitchen at one end and the living room at the other, he removed his boots and placed them in the corner by the door. Then he turned toward the small lavatory off the kitchen and quickly took care of his needs without turning on a light.

He didn't want to look into a mirror and find the same face staring back at him, giving the lie to this new feeling of self-respect generated by Matt Frazier's startling revelations. He'd left the house earlier searching for an obscure light and found instead his true identity. But he was still lost, lost somewhere inside himself, and he wavered between wanting, needing, to know that other person, and fear. Some of the things he'd learned about himself tonight he didn't much care for, though he didn't doubt Matt's word about who and what he was. Somehow it felt right. Whether he liked it or not, he knew he was the man named Andrew Rivers.

He felt torn in two—two totally different men inhabiting the same body. Which was the real man? Nick—ranch hand and dummy? Or Drew—hotdogging special agent for the FBI, and womanizer?

Which did he want to be? Could he ever see himself as a combination of the two? Matt Frazier had seemed to recognize him despite the changes, so did that mean Drew the FBI agent was the stronger personality of the two?

Who would Caitlin choose? Nick? Or Drew? Would the real Rivers please stand up?

Rubbing rain from his face and hair with a towel, Nick left the bathroom and moved into the kitchen, heading for the ever ready pot of hot coffee. But the pot was turned off, the coffee cold.

Lightning flashed in the window over his shoulder; thunder crashed and rolled overhead. The storm seemed to have turned and headed back for another assault. Nick tried the light switch, and, when nothing happened, he knew why the coffee was cold. Quietly he moved to the living-room door.

A single candle glowed on the table beside Caitlin's chair, the flickering light shimmering across her sleeping face. He almost walked right on past and climbed the stairs to his bed. He was halfway there when he suddenly turned back.

He couldn't leave her to sleep all night hunched over in the chair, to awaken in the morning with a stiff neck. Bending down, he reached for the candle. He didn't see the bottle his arm brushed against until it clinked into the glass.

Nick eyed her sleeping form speculatively before moistening a finger and thumb and dousing the flame. Then, after wiping his fingers on his damp jeans, he bent to lift the sleeping woman in unsteady arms.

She was heavier than he'd expected, and the muscles of his back and shoulders rippled under the strain. But it was pure heaven to feel her soft weight against his chest, her hair tickling his mouth and chin. Straightening, he simply stood, eyes closed, holding her tightly against him, breathing in her special scent, letting the tide of emotions rise up like a giant wave and crash over him.

If only he could awaken her and tell her who he was, that he was a person, someone with an identity. But he couldn't. He'd already put her life in danger just by being on the ranch, and if he told her who he was, and why he was in the area—if his murderer should learn where he was—her life wouldn't be worth a plugged nickel. As far as Caitlin and his relationship with her were concerned, nothing had changed. To her he must remain Nick, a strange man she'd felt sorry for and taken into her home—and into her heart?

Caitlin murmured unintelligibly and snuggled into him, pressing her face against his neck, her whiskey-scented breath blowing warm against his chin. His arms trembled, and the room, which had been chilly before, felt warm, close. His knees almost buckled. She unmanned him; even defenseless in sleep, she turned him into a quivering mass of jelly. That old familiar ache she caused in him whenever he was anywhere near her began to take over, and he knew he had better get her into bed while he still had the strength to resist her.

Breathing deeply, strengthening his resolve and his spine, he started toward her room. His only choice was to get her there as quickly as possible and make a strategic retreat.

It took some maneuvering, but he got the door open without wakening her. Turning sideways, he passed through without mishap, then missed the lurking corner of the vanity, though he barked his shin on the heavy chest sitting at the foot of her four-poster bed. Smothering a curse of pain, he rounded the bed, then stood, undecided about how to get her into it without rousing her from sleep.

Caitlin murmured again, her lips whispering across his throat, pressing against his Adam's apple. He swallowed nervously, chest contracting, loins on fire. He was becoming dangerously vulnerable. Where was Drew, the unsung expert on women, now?

As he leaned over, his right knee braced against the mattress, Caitlin curled her arms around his neck and shifted her weight, drawing him down onto the bed with her.

Quickly, in panic, he levered his weight from atop her and onto the mattress. What could he say in his defense if she were to awaken? He was trapped by his arm beneath her shoulders, her leg thrown over the top of his. And when he tried to move, she turned into him, face burrowed in the crook of his shoulder, her breasts, loose beneath the cotton gown and housecoat, swinging unrestrainedly against his suddenly heaving chest.

Nick found himself torn by conflicting needs. The need to slide his fingers through her hair and pull her mouth to his. The need to slip the nightclothes quickly from her body and make slow, passionate love with her. The need to get off the bed and out of the room as quickly as possible—while he still could.

Lifting her gently, he eased his arm from beneath her shoulders and slipped off the bed. In the flickering light from the storm, he stood looking down at her. The first three buttons of her nightgown had opened during his attempt to leave the bed, allowing a brief glimpse of the shadowy hollow between her creamy breasts. Her hair lay loose about her face, creating a fiery halo on the white pillowcase. She was so beautiful that he ached from looking at her. He pulled a blanket from the foot of the bed and covered her sleeping form, then left the room, closing the door softly behind him.

Upstairs in his own room, he shed his damp clothes quickly and, wearing only his undershorts, threw himself across the bed. He lay for a long while staring out the window, watching the play of light, listening to the furor created by nature, his thoughts mirroring the tempest outside.

After a time his clamoring senses quieted, his body relaxed, his mind found peace for the first time in a long while and he slept. His last conscious thought was a picture of Caitlin sleeping alone in the big bed below him—so near, yet so far, so very far away.

Outside, its fury spent at last, the storm, too, yielded to the night. But not everyone slept. Watchful eyes kept a close guard on the dark, silent house, while other eyes kept silent watch on the watchers.

Chapter 9

Caitlin pulled the pillow over her head and scooted farther down beneath the blanket. The lightning was really bad, almost a constant flare against the back of her sensitive eyelids. She tensed, holding her breath, waiting for the crash of thunder. Nothing happened. There was something, though, a sound her groggy mind didn't immediately identify. Poking her head out from under the pillow, she opened one eye cautiously, then closed it quickly with a loud groan and drew back like a turtle into its shell.

That wasn't lightning out there, it was light. Sunshine, bright sunshine, and the noise was the throbbing beat in her head. Calling herself seven kinds of a fool, she contemplated crawling from the bed and struggling to the bathroom before her imminent need became a sorry embarrassment. But the sun was so bright. Why had she never before noticed how bright the sun was? It was causing small pinwheels of light inside her head, even now, with her eyes closed beneath the safety of her pillow. And the pain, the pain separated itself from every point of light and flew in all directions, gathering force until it finally reached the center of her brain, leaving her feeling weak, nauseated, cold and sweating.

Why did she feel this way? Was she coming down with a virus? She had felt perfectly fine the night before while waiting for Nick. All afternoon and evening she'd waited for him. As she remembered, a sudden storm had blown up—storms made her nervous—so she'd had a small drink to steady her nerves, and then the lights had gone out. She hated it when the lights went out—it made her feel so helpless.

It seemed to her that with as much money as the electric companies collected each month, they should be able to develop a way to keep storms from interfering with the regular flow of things.

Oh! God, her head hurt! And if she didn't get to the bathroom soon...Walking hunched over, as if on eggshells, her eyes carefully turned from the window, she guided herself with a hand on each object she passed on her way to the bathroom.

Nick came looking for her a few minutes later. "Caitlin," he called softly, rapping on the door panel.

"What!" She jerked to attention, clasped her hands to her head and groaned. "Don't yell. I can hear you."

"Sorry." He smiled behind the door. "But I wasn't yelling." After a long silence he asked, "Are you okay?"

"Fine," she grumbled irritably. "Just fine."

"Headache?"

"How do you know—no! I don't have a headache." What was he, a mind reader? By now she was sitting on the floor, wishing she could be sick. There was silence from the other side of the door. Good. She hoped he'd gone, left the ranch. She never, ever, wanted to see him again. This was all his fault! His fault she had been upset and alone last night. His fault she had been at the Jack Daniels—probably his damn fault the storm had blown up and the electricity had gone off, too! She hated him—hated him!

"Here, try this." He was kneeling beside her, a glass of clear liquid held out toward her.

Caitlin eyed the glass suspiciously, wondering if she should trust him. What the heck? She couldn't feel any worse. The liquid tasted vaguely familiar, but that didn't stop her from gagging at the slightly bitter taste. She tried to hand him back the glass without finishing it, but he grasped the back of her neck firmly and held the glass tilted to her lips till she drank it all.

"Oh, God! What was that?" He opened his mouth, his lips only inches from hers. "No! I don't want to know." Closing her eyes against a sudden assault of dizziness brought on by nothing more than his nearness, she shook her head, felt her senses spin, her body go weak—and he was there.

Lifting her into hard arms, he carried her to the bed, laid her gently down on the colorful quilt and stood looking down at her.

"I have work to do," she protested halfheartedly. She couldn't possibly spend the day in bed.

"You rest. I'll take care of the work."

"B-but—oh—what was in that glass?" Caitlin asked faintly, her eyes opening and closing every few seconds, the room spinning.

"Nothing to harm you." It was only a couple of large white tablets mixed with water, something he'd seen her take when she suffered with a headache or upset stomach. It was only her unusual state of mind this morning that had kept her from recognizing the taste. "Do you feel any better?"

"A-a little. My stomach isn't quite so queasy but I feel so sleepy...." She yawned and closed her eyes. A peaceful expression stealthily rearranged her features.

Nick smiled and cupped a tender hand to her soft cheek. Already he felt like a different man—more like his old self? Would Caitlin see the difference? Would she like it?

"You still here?" Caitlin blinked open her eyes, caught her breath and stared. Even in her dazed state she recognized the naked emotion spreading across his unguarded face. Nick hastily withdrew his hand. Caitlin closed her eyes and took a steadying breath, and when she looked again, he was gone.

Glancing toward the closed door, she listened intently. The house was silent. Maybe she had only imagined the last few minutes? Lying back, eyes closed, she ran her tongue over dry lips. Her mind vaguely registered a slightly bitter taste as she drifted into sleep.

Nick stood outside the bedroom door with an inscrutable look in his dark eyes. Things were getting more complicated by the minute. His only intention in seeking her out had been to talk to her about moving out of the house. It would suit his purpose admirably to move into the old abandoned stone house. There he would be free to come and go as needed, help Matt clear this mess up and, in the process—he hoped—regain his full memory, without having to explain his unusual behavior to Caitlin.

But, after getting no response to his knock, he had peeked into her room, found her bed empty and panicked. Remembering Matt's words from the night before about his presence bringing danger to her, he had burst into her room, driven by fear for her safety. And then, as always, her nearness had blown all coherent thought from his head. What was he going to do?

Matt was waiting for him, his back against the rough stone house, a cigarette dangling from his lips.

"You look like hell. Didn't you get any sleep last night?" Nick asked, noting the dark circles under the other man's icy gray eyes, the pinched look to the wide mouth.

"It stormed last night—or didn't you notice?" Matt asked gruffly.

"Yeah," Nick answered, "I noticed. Look, why don't you get your things and move them here?"

"What about the redhead?"

Though the term annoyed him, Nick hid it. "She doesn't come out this way much. I don't think she'd find out."

Shrugging broad shoulders, every bone and joint in his massive frame aching, Matt agreed to the idea. The ground was rocky and hard, and last night it had been wet to boot. Hell, he was getting too old for this kind of work.

"Where do we start?" He straightened his body away from the house and dropped the cigarette butt, then ground it into the dirt with his heel.

"I think we visit Jones first," Nick answered.

Matt started to lope off, then stopped and turned back when he realized Nick wasn't following. "What are you waiting for?"

"I don't know where Jones's spread is." Nick grinned sheepishly. "I work around here—not visit with the neighbors."

Matt laughed. "Well, I work around here, too, but it just so happens I do know where he lives. Come on."

While they tramped along, Matt furtively eyed the man at his side, amazed at the differences evident in him. If in the beginning he hadn't believed the amnesia story, he sure as the devil believed it now. The transformation in Andrew Rivers—Nick— was too marked to ignore, astonishingly so.

The two men had met in college. Drew had been in his first year, after a stint in the military in Vietnam, and Matt had been a senior. Drew, young though he was, already a war hero and handsome as the devil, had the girls standing on their heads for his attention. The stigma that had seemed to go along with Vietnam, and the men who served there back then, had no part in Drew Rivers's scheme of things.

After they became friends, Drew told Matt that he had enlisted and asked to be sent to Vietnam. Not, he said, out of some idealistic political belief in his country, but because his father would have a flying fit when he learned about it. And anything his father was against, Drew was automatically for.

It wasn't until months later, after he'd fought alongside others, held the dying in his arms, watched the suffering of innocent villagers, men, women and children, caught by both sides in a war they didn't understand or want, that it all became real for him.

Those few times early in their friendship when Drew spoke about his experiences in Nam were the only times Matt was allowed to see beneath the younger man's carefree exterior to the real human being inside.

Later, when Matt, still undecided about his life's goals, was approached by the FBI, he willingly allowed them to seduce him into joining their numbers. Drew, because of their friendship and his desire to get as far from his father's corporate image as possible, followed suit.

In the ten years since then, Matt had known Drew to be dangerous, both in the field and out of it. His private life was strewn with bodies, the bodies of beautiful women, all of whom had been positive they could tame the wild beast.

Knowing what drove him, watching him volunteer for one dangerous assignment after another, jump from one woman to another, Matt unhappily concluded that the only thing that could stop Drew's headlong rush to destruction was a bullet. And when this assignment had first unfolded, when Drew failed to meet him, had left no word, made no further contact, Matt had feared the worst. He'd been sure that Drew's bullet had found him.

The man now walking pensively at his side, unaware of his close scrutiny, surprised him at every turn. And though he felt somewhat disloyal at the thought, Matt was becoming convinced that this was the man God, or nature, had always intended the boy would become.

They followed the creek down past the dry wash Nick recognized as the place where he'd first met Jones. It was perhaps forty-five minutes later when they left the creek, rounded a hill and stopped. Hidden in the sparse cover of some cottonwood trees, they gazed down at the Jones spread.

"You think he's in there?" Matt asked.

"Hard to say. Like you said, he's a strange one. But somehow I can't see him smuggling drugs, or as the head of a survivalist group. Caitlin said he doesn't leave the place much, sticks close to home."

"Uh-uh." Matt shook his head.

"What do you mean?"

"He wasn't there last night—or the night before."

"No?" Nick asked softly.

"No."

"Then where the hell was he?"

"I, uh, I'm not sure," Matt sort of mumbled. "He...slipped out his bedroom window—that one." He pointed toward the back of the house. "About midnight. I followed him—"

"Sounding like a bull elephant in a china shop." The raspy voice came from directly behind them. "I wouldn't do that if I were you," the voice cautioned. The bolt action of a rifle sounded loud in the sudden silence. Matt dropped his hand from his coat.

"Okay, turn around nice and slow, hands above your shoulders, both of you. Now ease your hand in—slow!" He motioned toward Matt with the rifle barrel. "Two fingers only—lift it out and drop it gently to the ground." He waited until the gun lay on the ground between them. "Now, kick it away—easy!" he cautioned. "That's right."

Bending down, eyes on the two men, David lifted the gun, slipped it into the waistband of his fatigues and smiled his lopsided smile, looking more than a little threatening. "Now, who the hell are you and what are you doing snooping around on my land?"

"You know who I am." Nick spoke cautiously, looking for an opening.

"I know who you say you are," David corrected.

Matt and Nick eyed each other furtively. David, intercepting the look, cautioned, "Don't try it. One of you is sure to get hurt."

"Show him your ID," Nick told Matt.

"W-what?" Matt protested. That would be giving the game away with a vengeance.

"Let's see it." David motioned with the rifle. "That's right—good for you," he approved sarcastically as Matt slipped the small black leather case from his pocket. Flipping it open, he held it where David could see it.

"Where did you get that?" He didn't sound impressed. "From a cereal box—or a dead man?" he asked obscurely.

Nick frowned, eyeing the man with narrowed eyes. "Matt, you said you followed Jones last night and the night before," he said, suddenly watching for Jones's reaction. "Where did he go?"

"Shut up!" Jones snarled, stepping closer, the rifle pointed at Nick's midsection.

"Where did he go?" Nick repeated, ignoring the implied threat.

"I don't know—not for certain—I lost him in the woods," Matt admitted reluctantly.

"Where?"

"I told you to shut up," David said, but his voice lacked the earlier aggression.

"Near the drinking hole we passed on the way here," Matt answered.

"In other words, he stayed close by. Was he armed?"

"Yeah, he was carrying a rifle—probably that one." Matt nodded toward the barrel now pointed in his direction.

"You were guarding Caitlin's house last night. Why?" Nick asked abruptly.

"I don't know what you're talking about," David denied.

"I found bootprints around the garage and the corral this morning."

"So? What's that prove? Everyone wears boots around here." They both glanced automatically to the size fifteen sneakers Matt wore.

"The damned pointed toes pinch my feet," he muttered defensively at the look the other two exchanged.

"Not everyone leaves a deeper print with their left boot because their right leg is just a bit shorter," Nick added quietly.

David's face tightened, and his fingers tensed on the rifle's trigger as their gazes locked. Watching, Matt wondered what it was that passed between the two men. For a moment the air was rife with unspoken tension, threats, and then suddenly they both relaxed.

"Okay, I was there," David admitted. He looked cautiously around before adding, "Let's go to the house. I wasn't the only one outside in the storm last night."

Matt and Nick led the way, David bringing up the rear, the rifle not exactly trained on their backs, but not really relaxed, either.

"Sit down," David said once they were inside. Taking a seat directly across from them in the living room, he placed the rifle across his knees. "Now, let's talk."

"Why were you watching Caitlin's house?" Nick asked.

"Caity is like a sister to me. I was only watching out for her."

"Protecting her? From who? What?" David's blue eyes gazed at him steadily. "From me?" Nick asked. He shook his head. "I don't buy that. I've been staying with Caitlin for a few weeks now. Why the sudden anxiety on her behalf?"

"I hadn't met you until a few days ago," David answered caustically.

"You think I'd harm her?"

David shrugged. "I hear things. I don't go to town much, but word gets around all the same. You're not what you appear to be."

"And you are?" Nick interjected softly.

The only sign David gave that the shaft had hit home was a slight twitch on the damaged side of his face. "I don't know what you mean. I'm Caity's neighbor, her friend. We grew up together. I won't let you—or anyone—hurt her."

"I don't want to hurt her. What reason would I, or anyone, for that matter, have to hurt her?"

"Who are you?"

"Just who I appear to be. A man working on the Barratt ranch. I spend my days doing what any other ranch hand would do." He shrugged.

"And the nights?" David asked insinuatingly. "How do you spend them?"

"That's none of your damn business!" Nick grated from between clenched teeth. Muscles bunched, he was ready to spring, to shove the insinuating words down the other man's throat. Matt touched his arm lightly, and he relaxed slowly back against the cushions.

David turned his attention to the man with the physique a wrestler would envy. "What's an FBI agent doing in a town like Fate? Somebody kidnap a steer and hold it for ransom?" he asked sarcastically.

"I'm conducting an investigation," Matt answered quietly.

"Into what?"

"I'm not at liberty to say," Matt replied in his best official voice.

"What has your investigation got to do with me?"

"I'm not at liberty to say," Matt repeated.

"Uh-huh. And him." He pointed to Nick. "What's he got to do with it? I know, I know," David forestalled him. "You're not at liberty to say." Pulling Matt's gun from his belt, he emptied the shells into his palm, snapped the gun together and flipped it into Matt's hands.

"I suggest the two of you get off my land. And don't come back." He escorted them to the door. "The next time I catch either one of you on my property, I'll shoot first and ask questions later. Oh, yeah, Mr. FBI agent—if you ever find yourself at liberty to say what the hell's going on, let me know."

After slamming the door behind them, David locked it and leaned back with closed eyes, sweat popping out all over his quaking body. Should he have believed them or not? It would relieve him of a burden of guilt if he could. But anyone could get a false ID made up these days.

"Well, what do you make of that?" Matt asked as they left the house behind.

"I'd say that's one scared man," Nick answered, having perceived the all-too-familiar look in the man's blue eyes. It was a look he had become used to seeing, staring back at him from the mirror each day. "I'd give a lot to know what he's scared of—or who," he added thoughtfully.

Caitlin was surprised at Nick's prompt arrival for dinner that evening. She hadn't been able to find him when she'd first awakened, feeling slightly shamefaced but rested. She assumed he was out running fence and went about her own work, determined to speak with him sometime that day.

It was evening before she got the chance. They sat down to the meal in silence, neither feeling able to start a conversation. The events of the day before, and that morning, were still too close to the surface in their minds.

When they both reached for the same biscuit, Caitlin drew her fingers back hastily, silently berating herself. This was ridiculous; they were acting like strangers. Couldn't they even look at each other without feeling this wariness and tension?

When she handed Nick the bowl of mashed potatoes, their fingers touched, and she let go too quickly. He nearly dropped the bowl. Trying to hide her embarrassment she broke into speech, saying the first thing that came to mind.

"We've been officially invited to the Fourth of July celebration at the Carrington ranch."

Nick eyed her flushed face but didn't say anything.

"Megan called this afternoon," she continued. "It seems Logan—Logan Carrington—he's our local celebrity, you might say, invited us." At Nick's raised brow she added, "Not a real celebrity, of course. I mean, he isn't a movie star or something."

She was nervous, and she knew she sounded stupid. She jumped to her feet, hurried across the room to the refrigerator and picked up a butter dish, then closed the door and stood looking down at it as if she'd never seen butter before in her life.

Nick reached around from behind, took the dish from her nerveless fingers and set it by the sink. Turning her slowly to face him, a finger beneath her wobbly chin, he raised her face to his. But her eyes refused to move higher than the dark hair she could see curling at the open neck of his blue work shirt.

"Caity, look at me." Warm coffee-scented breath stirred the hair at her temple.

"No," she answered in a tiny voice, straining against his hold.

"Why?"

"I can't. I'm too embarrassed about yesterday and this morning. I—" She shook her head, his shirt blurring before her misty eyes.

"You have nothing to be embarrassed about. I'm the one who's sorry." Framing her face with both hands, he leaned forward, lightly touching his lips to her mouth. Her eyes jerked to his. "I knew that would make you look at me." He smiled sweetly, and Caity's heart melted.

"You don't think I'm a s-shrew? Or a lush?"

Laughing lightly, he shook his head. "If I told you what I really think about you, you would probably slap my face."

Caitlin's blush deepened, her green eyes aglow.

"You're a beautiful, sexy, warmhearted, delightful woman," he told her in deep, throaty tones.

"All that?" she asked, bemused.

"And more," he whispered, bending closer. "So much more." He drew out the words against her mouth. Holding himself in check, he kept the kiss light, soothing. "You're also a great cook," he added, drawing back a little. "And I've had nothing to eat since yesterday morning." Dark eyes locked with hers. "You make me weak with hunger," he whispered.

Caitlin would have dissolved at his feet if he hadn't held her up where she stood. At that moment she would have given him anything—everything—all he had to do was to ask. Somewhere in the back of her mind, a part of her realized that he was different, not only more confident, taking the initiative, but something else—something she couldn't quite define.

Nick let his hands drop slowly from her face and, taking her hand in his, led her back to the table. After seating her like royalty, he reseated himself.

"Now, tell me all about Logan Carrington and the July Fourth celebration." He smiled into her eyes.

They talked companionably while they ate, Caitlin explaining about Megan's long-standing interest in Logan, without giving away any secrets that had been told to her in confidence. When the meal was finished, Nick helped with the dishes as he had in the past while they arranged the next day's work.

The room lay in shadow, the only sound a whisper of air from the open window causing the curtains to sway gently. They played hide and seek with a shaft of moonlight slanting across the floor and onto the bed, spearing the restless figure lying prone across it, tangled in the sheet.

Sweat dotted his upper lip, and the hair across his brow lay clumped together in damp rats' tails. The moisture-touched muscles of his arms and chest gleamed dully as his body twitched in agitation.

His teeth were chattering, his body shuddering in the throes of a bone-numbing chill, his eyelids twitching, as his head jerked back and forth across the pillow. His taut fingers gripped the sheet, the muscles of his shoulders and neck standing out. Head back, chest straining, he tried to breathe against the weightless, smothering object pushing against his chest, closing over his head.

"No-o-o!" Jerking upright, eyes wide, Nick stared tensely about the room. Sweat dripped form his chin, matting the dark pelt of hair on his heaving chest. "Oh, God," he whispered softly. "Oh, God."

It was the dream, back again and more vivid than ever. He had thought, hoped, that after talking to Matt, piecing it together in his own mind, he'd seen the last of it.

Moving from the bed like a tired old man, limbs shaking, he reached automatically toward the bedside table, searching for something. His hand hovered there, his brain identifying the need—a cigarette. He was reaching for a cigarette. Dropping back onto the covers, hands between his knees, he stared across the room to the open window.

So, Drew was beginning to make himself known in little ways. That scared him as much as the dream. He didn't know this other person, this phantom who lay buried deep within his subconscious. And he wasn't sure he wanted to. Nothing he'd learned so far about this other personage endeared him to Nick. Drew, the man from his past, the man he was becoming once again.

As far as he was concerned, he was Nick, a person he was coming to know and be comfortable with. Drew was the unknown factor, the enigma—a frightening shadow from a dreamlike life he couldn't totally recall. A figure he was beginning to resent as if he were another person entirely, and not another facet of his own personality.

"Nick! Is anything wrong?" Caitlin's voice drifted up the stairs.

Not now, please. He couldn't let her see him like this. Holding out trembling hands, clenching them, he slammed them suddenly against his thighs.

"N-nothing," he croaked in a whisper that didn't travel beyond the room. "Nothing's wrong." He tried in a louder, steadier voice. "Just a bad dream. I'm fine—go on back to bed. Sorry I disturbed you."

"Are you sure you're okay?" Her voice sounded nearer.

Panicking, he jumped to his feet and nearly tumbled to the floor when his unsteady limbs refused to support him.

"I'm okay," he whispered desperately, trying to believe it himself. Then, louder, "I'm okay, Caitlin. Please, go back to bed."

"Can I get you anything?" Her voice came from the other side of the door. She wanted to take care of him as he had taken care of her earlier that morning.

"No. Please, go away." Fists clenched, eyes closed, he waited, hoping . . .

"I can't just go away, Nick. Not when I know something is bothering you. Can't you tell me about it? Sometimes, if you talk about something—like a nightmare, for instance—it takes the fear out of it." Cheek pressed against the door, she waited.

That was what he'd thought once upon a time, but he knew better now. "It's just a dream I have about . . . drowning." Maybe if he humored her a bit she would go away, let him work this out for himself. Clenching his jaw to keep his teeth from chattering, he crossed his arms over his chest.

"Is this the first time you've had the dream?"

"N-no," he answered truthfully.

"Can I come in, Nick?"

"No!" he almost shouted, and then more softly, calmly, he added, "No, I'm not dressed." That didn't sound right, either. "I mean, I'm dressed for bed."

"Is it from before we met—the dream, I mean? Did you really come close to drowning?"

"Y-yes, I think so. I'm not really sure," he hedged.

"Nick, could you be suffering from amnesia?" she asked boldly. "Could the amnesia be caused by a near-drowning accident?" Her voice wobbled from pent-up excitement.

Damn! How could she have hit it so perfectly right on the mark? Even with the nightmare to spur his memory, it had taken Matt's idle remark to bring it into focus. He hesitated in answering, not wanting to lie to her about this. "I . . . don't know, but I suppose it could be," he admitted reluctantly.

"You remember the day we went to town to get your booster shots?"

"Yeah, I remember."

"I tried to tell you then, but you—well, anyway, I talked with the doctor about people who have amnesia—"

"You told the doctor I had amnesia?" Who else in town, or outside it, knew?

There was something in his voice that caused the hair to stand up on the back of her neck.

"N-no, not exactly. He just guessed it was you I was talking about, and I didn't exactly say it was amnesia," she stressed somewhat fearfully.

"And?" He was standing now, moving toward the door, his weakness, his nightmare, forgotten for the moment.

"He said trauma, an accident, could cause it. Or sometimes it's just something our mind doesn't want to, or can't, deal with on a conscious level, and we bury it—forget it."

"What did he say the chances were for total recall?"

She could almost feel the quiet desperation underlying the question. "He said most of the time it returns a little at a time," she answered softly.

Leaning his hot forehead against the cool wooden panel, Nick spoke. "I see."

"Are you angry with me?" she asked when the silence had stretched too long.

"What?"

"Are you angry because I talked to the doctor without first discussing it with you?"

Maybe he should be. If the doctor talked to the wrong people... "No," he answered huskily. "I'm not angry with you." Hands against the door, palms flat, he could feel her on the other side.

"I'm glad. I'm glad you aren't angry. I... care about you Nick." Her voice so low he could barely hear her, she pressed closer to the door.

"Don't, Cat. Don't care about me. I don't deserve it." He was lying to her, was living a lie each day he left her in the dark about his true identity, and yet he couldn't tell her... "I don't want to hurt you—but I will," he finished, his voice hardly above a whisper. He didn't know if she heard him or not.

"Good night, Nick," she murmured softly.

"Good night." The words sounded so final, almost as if they were saying goodbye. A chill of premonition slid down his spine.

Moving to the window, he stared out into the darkness. How many eyes, he wondered, were watching him right now?

His body was already in motion when the shot rang out, and that was what saved his life. Because he'd turned, the bullet missed his heart and lungs and embedded itself in the muscle of his left shoulder.

At first he didn't know what was happening; there was no pain, only a jerk as the bullet impacted with flesh and bone. The pain came later, when he dropped to the floor, jarring his arm against the wall, sending fingers of white-hot agony shooting into his chest.

The door banged back against the wall as Caitlin flew into the room, calling his name. She reached automatically for the light switch, flooding the room with brightness. Nick blinked, staggered to his feet and threw himself across the distance in a reflex move, knocking Caitlin to the floor an instant before his fingers found the light switch.

"My God, what are you doing? That was a gunshot—was that a gunshot? What's happening?" Struggling to breathe beneath his weight, Caitlin hurled questions at him, fear and disbelief warring with each other in her voice. "Answer me! What's happening? Do you know what's happening?" Finally managing to get her hands free, she gripped his shoulders tightly.

Nick gave a little shudder, groaned deep in his throat and went limp, his face flopping against her neck.

"Nick?" Fear fluttered in Caitlin's throat as her right hand stuck damply to his bare shoulder. There was an odor she couldn't immediately identify, and then it hit her. Blood! The substance oozing between her fingers, dampening the gown across her chest, was blood—Nick's blood.

"Oh, no! Oh, God! Nick!" She didn't know what to do. Her right hand, fingers extended, hovered near his shoulder, but she was afraid to touch him. She didn't want to hurt him—but that was silly; he was already hurt and bleeding. Dear God! She couldn't let him bleed to death all over her.

Cautiously she began to disentangle herself from him, rolling him onto his right side. His head hit the floor with a thump, and Caitlin winced.

"I'm sorry," she whispered, knowing he couldn't hear. On her hands and knees beside him, she glanced desperately around the darkened room. What should she do now? Why didn't he wake up and tell her what to do? Pressing a finger on the side of his neck, she felt the pulse there, weak and thready.

"God, please, don't let him die—don't let him die," she whispered brokenly.

She crawled to the bathroom and grabbed a towel, then crawled back to him. As she tied a makeshift bandage around his upper arm, she prayed it would help. Maybe it would at least slow the bleeding until she could get help. Tears blurring her vision, he was only a shadow lying motionless beside her; she could hardly distinguish the rise and fall of his chest. Caitlin tensed suddenly, turning toward the window, senses alert. Had she heard something?

"Caity! Caity!"

On hands and knees, she moved to the window, then peered over the sill, down into a yard bathed in silvery moonlight. A dark figure stood beneath a mimosa tree, one hand cupped to his mouth, the other wrapped around a long dark object.

"Caity!" The voice, a loud, raspy whisper, called again, "Caity, damnit, answer me!"

"W-what do you want?" Then, "Why?" she asked, tears streaming down her face, clogging her throat so she could hardly get the words out. "Why did you shoot him? David, why did you shoot Nick?"

"What? I didn't shoot him! Come downstairs and let me in."

"N-no!" Dropping back to the floor, Caitlin began to crawl back toward Nick.

"Caity, listen to me, I didn't shoot him. Please, let me in. Caity, come on, it's me. You know me, I couldn't shoot anyone."

That stopped her for a minute. David—the David she had grown up with—could never have cold-bloodedly shot a man. But the man standing below, holding a rifle, wasn't the David she'd grown up with. She couldn't believe him, no matter how badly she wanted to; she couldn't trust him with Nick's life. Pressing her hands over her ears, she tried to block out the sound of his continued pleas.

Kneeling once more beside Nick, she touched his cold face and began to worry about shock. After dragging the sheet and blanket from the bed to cover him, she tucked them firmly around his prone figure.

"What should I do now?" she asked the man lying quiet beneath her hands. The doctor! Of course, how stupid, she needed to call the doctor—and the sheriff. The numbness slowly left her mind, letting her practical self once more take over her actions.

Checking his pulse, tenderly smoothing the tangled hair back from his forehead, she pressed a light kiss on his unconscious brow.

"I won't be long," she promised. "Hang in there, please."

Careful to stay low, Caitlin moved silently from the room into the hallway and down the stairs, listening alertly for the sounds of an intruder in the house. In the living room, still in darkness, she found the phone and dialed hurriedly.

"D-Dr. Shepherd?"

"No, this is his wife."

"I need the doctor," she whispered, the words tumbling together in her mind. "I need him to come out here as fast as possible. There's been an accident—someone's been shot." She paused to take a quick breath.

"Who is this, please?"

"Caity—Caitlin Barratt. I'm at home."

The doctor's wife assured her that her husband would be on his way immediately. "Have you notified the sheriff?" she asked, hoping to take Caitlin's mind off the shooting.

"N-not yet," Caitlin sniffed into the receiver, wiping the back of one hand across her watery eyes and runny nose.

"Would you like me to call him for you?" Marilee Shepherd asked gently. Caitlin agreed, then heard low murmuring in the background before the doctor's wife asked, "Have you applied pressure to stop the bleeding? And it's important to keep the patient warm—shock, you know."

"Yes, I've done that."

"Good. The doctor will be with you shortly."

"I want to get back to Nick. Thank you for your help. Goodbye."

Someone was pounding furiously at the front door. Caitlin hesitated. It was too soon for the doctor or the sheriff. Moving cautiously toward the door, she called out, "Who is it?"

"It's me, Caity, David. Honey, let me in. You know I'd never hurt you. Please."

Suddenly she believed him; despite the evidence to the contrary, she knew he wouldn't hurt her, and she didn't believe he'd shot Nick. She needed someone, someone she knew and trusted . . . Unlocking the door, she stood back to let him in.

"Oh, honey." Pulling her into his arms, David held her trembling body close to his. "What happened?" he asked after a moment, holding her away to look into her eyes.

"I don't know," she answered brokenly. "It happened so fast. We were talking—"

"Where?" he asked abruptly, his hands tightening on her arms.

"Upstairs. I was in the hall—he'd had a nightmare." She paused. "I went upstairs to see if he was all right and then we . . . talked a little." Looking back over her shoulder, toward the stairs, she said, "I need to get back to him—he's bleeding."

Pulling away, she hurried to the stairs. David followed more slowly.

"Dr. Shepherd is on his way," she threw back over her shoulder. "And the sheriff."

"Sheriff!" David echoed.

Caitlin paused and looked back at him, hearing the strange note in his voice. "Yes, the sheriff—a man's been shot here, David."

"It was probably hunters—a stray shot."

"At night?" she asked skeptically.

David, one step below her, touched her arm, and she realized that the rifle he had been carrying earlier was nowhere to be seen.

"Caity, listen to me." Something urgent in his voice, his touch, transmitted itself to her. "Whatever happens, I didn't shoot Nick. You have to believe that." Blue eyes locked with hers, he asked, "Do you believe me?"

She had to; something inside her knew he was telling the truth. "Yes," she answered slowly. "I believe you."

"Thank you." A smile twisted his ruined face. "Now I'm going to ask you to do something you may find strange, but just keep trusting me, okay?" Caitlin nodded. "I'm going to leave in a minute—" She started to protest, but he silenced her with a slight shake of his head. "I can't be here when the doctor or the sheriff arrive, especially the sheriff."

Caitlin supposed she understood that. David's reputation for odd behavior was a good basis for steering clear of the law, even when the law was a man he'd known all his life.

"There's one other thing. You can't tell anyone—not anyone," he emphasized, "that I was here tonight."

"B-but—"

"No one, Caity—you understand?" He glanced nervously over his shoulder toward the front door. "I've got to go. Can I trust you?" he asked. His eyes begged her to agree.

"But why? Can't you tell me why?"

"I can't tell you—not now. All I can do is trust you—just like you have to trust me. Swear!" He shook her arms, and Caitlin, feeling his fingers like ice against her skin, could only nod. In the silence the sound of tires on gravel could be heard.

"I have to go."

His sense of urgency fired her own. "Out the back door," she instructed. "Hurry!" she whispered, the sound of a car door being slammed sounding loud in the still night.

Thirty minutes, five trips up the stairs to see if the doctor needed any help, and a pot of coffee later, Caitlin sat at the kitchen table across from the doctor and the sheriff and told her story. With two omissions: Nick's nightmare and David's presence.

"What makes you think it was a stray shot from a hunter's rifle?" the sheriff asked Caitlin when she offered David's explanation of the accident.

"I don't know, but I can't think of any other logical reason for his being shot, can you?"

"That's probably the right of it, sheriff," the doctor said. "That was a rifle shell I dug out of his shoulder."

"He's going to be all right, isn't he?" Caitlin asked anxiously.

"Yes, he'll be fine. He was lucky. That shot could have been fatal, but it missed everything vital, cut a ridge across the left side of his chest and landed in the fleshy part of his shoulder. Hitting the bone is what slowed it down, and that's why it didn't exit." Dr. Shepherd rolled down his shirtsleeves while he talked and buttoned his cuffs.

"Should he be in a hospital?" Caitlin asked.

"No." The doctor shook his graying blond head. "He was conscious for a short time, and he made his thoughts on that subject quite clear. And after a look at his right hip and thigh, I can understand why."

The other two occupants of the room were suddenly very attentive. "Hip? What's wrong with his hip?" the sheriff inquired, not sounding as casual as he would have liked.

"Some kind of an accident, I would guess. He must have been cut rather severely. Probably spent a long time recuperating in a hospital, and that explains his present attitude. I suppose I shouldn't say this, ethics and all, but they could have done a better job of it. The scarring is pretty bad."

Caitlin and the sheriff glanced at each other and then away. A tension had entered the room; the doctor seemed to be the only one who was unaware of it.

"Well, one last look at the patient and I think I'll head on home." Dr. Shepherd stood, gathered his things and motioned for Caitlin to follow. At the foot of the stairs, he stopped, lightly touched her on the shoulder and smiled.

"Cheer up, he's going to be fine. You'll need to check the bandage for bleeding a couple of times during the night. Bring him in sometime, oh, say tomorrow afternoon, so I can change it.

"I left some antibiotics for you to give him. Just follow the directions on the bottle. I've given him a shot for pain, so he should be comfortable the rest of the night. However, I left some painkillers, too, in case he needs them later. Other than that, keep him quiet and let him heal. Okay?"

Caitlin nodded.

"Oh, by the way..." He hesitated. "Have you determined if his problem is memory loss or not? I must say, he didn't appear at all retarded to me a little while ago when he told me in no uncertain terms what he thought of hospitals—and doctors, too," he confessed with a slight grin.

"Yes, I think that is what happened to him, and..." She hesitated, recalling Nick's strange reaction to the doctor's knowledge of his amnesia. "I think it was possibly caused by a near-drowning accident."

The doctor nodded. "That could easily happen. When he's feeling better, if he wants to talk to me, I'd be glad to see if there's any way I can help him. You might mention that to him a little later."

Caitlin nodded again, then waited for him at the foot of the stairs. After she saw him out, she found Sheriff Raymond still sitting at the kitchen table, showing no sign of leaving. She felt so weary she just wanted to lie down somewhere and not have to move for the next eight or ten hours.

"I looked around outside, but it's too dark to see anything tonight. I'll come back in the morning and take another look."

Caitlin stood quietly, her eyes on her hands, which were locked together before her.

"He tell you anything about that other accident?" Was it her imagination, or was there a particular emphasis on the last word?

"Dr. Shepherd?"

"Rivers."

"No," she answered.

Standing abruptly, the sheriff picked up his hat, looked her directly in the eye and asked, "You want me to send someone out to stay the night with you?"

"No." She shook her head. "I'll be fine. I'm just dog tired."

She looked it; her eyes were ringed with dark circles and seemed like green bottle glass in a dead white face. It was on unsteady legs that she followed him to the front door.

"Stay away from the windows in case that hunter comes back. And lock this door behind me—oh, I took the liberty of locking the back door for you earlier."

His glance caught and held hers, neither one giving anything away in the look. And then he was gone.

He knew. He knew someone else had been there. And he knew she wasn't telling the truth, not the whole truth about what she'd seen that night. Why had David been carrying a rifle—and where had it been when he'd entered the house?

He was wet and cold and mad at himself. He should have suspected something when the man began hanging around town. Of course, he'd had no way of knowing who he was then; his partner hadn't told him about finding out there was an informer in the area, or that he'd taken care of—*thought* he'd taken care of—the man who'd been sent to infiltrate the group.

Well, he knew now, and he'd missed the opportunity to get rid of him. That shot should have killed him, and instead it had only wounded him. He'd bungled it, just like his partner had.

He should have taken care of Rivers and Frazier when he'd stumbled across them and their conversation at the old stone house. But he'd been so panicked at the little he heard that instead he'd run to his partner. He'd had to threaten to beat the story about the informant out of him. The fool should have told him about it before now, but no, he'd wanted to exact a little vengeance on the informant for personal reasons.

Damn! How had this whole thing gotten so out of hand? It was time to get out. He'd told his partner that tonight, right after he'd learned who Rivers really was.

The next time he tried to get rid of him, he'd make damn certain the job was thorough. When *he* killed Nick Rivers, the man would stay dead. And then he'd take care of Frazier and the loudmouth responsible for bringing them here.

It was thanks to that survivalist garbage that the Feds were on to them, but he'd be damned if he was going to take a fall. He wasn't spending the rest of his life behind bars, and he'd told his partner that tonight. Let him take the rap if he was too greedy to know when to quit. One more shipment—that was all the fool could think of—the big one that would set him up for life on some small island in the South Pacific.

Before now he'd suspected the man of using some of the drugs they were smuggling over the border, and now he was sure of it.

Well, he was getting out as soon as he could take care of a few loose ends.

His only regret was Caity Barratt. He wished she hadn't become involved in all this. If there was any way possible, he would see that she didn't get hurt. He owed her that.

Chapter 10

Good morning.''

Nick turned his head slowly toward the sound. The simple movement sent shafts of pain darting across his chest and down his left arm. Closing his eyes, he swallowed, mouth tasting like a dirty sock.

"Water," he croaked.

Caitlin held a glass to his dry lips, supporting the back of his head with one hand. He drank thirstily, turning his head aside when he'd had his fill. After gently easing him back, she set the glass on the nightstand and clasped her hands nervously before her.

"Nick?" she asked hopefully. Eyes closed, he made no answer, not so much as a twitch of an eyelid. "Nick?" she tried again, her heart sinking with every passing moment. Didn't he know her any longer? Had the shock of the accident made him regain his memory? All night long, as she sat awake in the room beside his bed, forgoing sleep, she had worried about it. Would he awaken a stranger? Remembering nothing about the past few weeks, not even her?

"Nick?"

"What?" he finally asked.

"Aren't you going to ask what happened?"

"No."

"But, don't you want to know—"

"I was shot. It's happened before."

Caitlin caught her breath. "You remember being shot before?"

"No, but I remember waking up feeling like I feel now."

Nonplussed, she stared down at him, his beard a dark mask covering the lower half of his face. Opening his eyes abruptly he stared back at her, a mutinous expression evident in the set of his jaw and his glittering dark eyes.

Caitlin laughed, dispelling the tension that had crept into the room with her spoken greeting. "Oh, Nick, you're going to be a terrible patient, aren't you?"

"I'm getting up. There's work to be done, animals to feed, eggs to collect—"

"All done," she informed him with a satisfied grin.

Nick scowled at her, not happy about it in the least. "You must have been up since daybreak to have everything done by now."

"I didn't do it—at least, I helped, but young Fred Taylor came around this morning. He said the sheriff had called him and told him I needed some help for the next few days." She spread her hands and shrugged.

"Great!" he muttered bad-humoredly.

"How are you feeling?" she asked, changing the subject.

"Like I've been shot," he grumbled.

"Are you hungry?" He started to shake his head, winced, then muttered a negative answer. "Do you need to go to the bathroom?" she asked tentatively, her cheeks turning pink.

"I can get to the bathroom myself," he informed her indignantly.

Sighing, Caitlin stuck her hands in the pockets of her jeans and turned away.

"Where are you going?" he asked quickly.

"Well, if you don't need me, I have things to do downstairs."

"I need you." Caitlin halted in her tracks, the deep timbre of his voice going through her like a jolt of electricity, lending new meaning to those three little words. Her back to him, she hesitated, then turned to face him.

"You do?" she breathed softly, a glow starting deep in the eyes locked with his. Tension was back in the room, but different this time. The flame-colored hair lying loose about her shoulders fairly crackled with it.

Nick felt himself drowning in her sea-green eyes, going down for the third time, when a growling noise invaded the air. His right hand clutched at his lean stomach. Looking startled, his ears turning a bright pink, he grinned sheepishly.

"I guess I'm hungry after all," he murmured reluctantly.

Caitlin shook her head, unable to make the transition so easily from the intense feelings building between them to the mundane.

"Right." She nodded, backing toward the door. "I'll just go make you something." Outside, she leaned back against the door for a moment, feeling giddy.

Later, after he had eaten, Nick lay back against the snowy pillows, watching her gather the used dishes to take downstairs.

"I haven't seen any sign of the sheriff this morning. You did call him last night?"

"Yes, he was here earlier, looking around outside."

"Looking for what?"

"Tracks." She avoided his eyes. "He—we—think it must have been a stray shot from a hunter that did . . . that." Cup in hand, she motioned toward his shoulder.

"A hunter, huh?"

"Y-yes, it happens sometimes. People . . . get shot . . . accidentally."

"Is he coming back? The sheriff," he explained at her blank look. "He'll probably want to ask me some questions."

"Oh, no, I'm supposed to take you in to the doctor's office this afternoon so he can change your dressing. Bart asked us to stop by then."

"Oh," was his only comment.

Noticing his pale face, Caitlin suggested, "Why don't you take a nap while I do these?" She gestured to the stack of dishes on the tray.

"Just for a few minutes," he agreed readily, surprising her.

"What about . . ." She nodded in the direction of the closed bathroom door.

"I went while you were downstairs."

"Nick," she protested softly. No wonder he looked so drained. She was sure he shouldn't have tried it on his own this soon.

"It's only a flesh wound, Caity," he informed her tiredly. "You rest now. I'll check on you later."

"Right." He closed his eyes, listening to the small sounds in the room, crockery and utensils clinking together, the whisper of movement Caitlin's body made as she crossed the floor, the soft click of the door opening and closing. He found comfort in the normal everyday sounds, and he drew on it, keeping other less comfortable sights and sounds at bay.

He tried to sleep, allowing his mind to drift, his consciousness to float away. But reality intruded, and he began to think about last night. The shock of the bullet, the stunned surprise when he realized he'd been shot, and the pain.

Where was Matt? Did he know of the shooting? And when would he contact him again? Questions chased each other around inside his head until his mind closed down and exhaustion took over. He slept.

Downstairs, Caitlin finished the dishes, then paced the floor fretfully. Had she done the right thing by not telling the sheriff about David's presence last night? All morning, every time she'd seen Nick, she had thought about David and the disappearing rifle. Round and round her thoughts had gone. Nick had been shot with a rifle; David had been holding a rifle before he came into the house. What had he done with it? Where had he gotten it? Was it his, or had he found it where it had been left by whoever shot Nick?

They were questions only David could answer.

She had to talk with him; she had to know the truth. Her eyes settled on the phone. No, she couldn't call from here; Nick might somehow overhear, and she didn't want to have to explain. She would have to go to the Jones house.

After ascending the stairs, Caitlin opened the door carefully, making no sound, and peered inside. Nick lay as she had left him, eyes closed, breathing gently, his mouth slightly open.

"Nick," she whispered softly. She could detect no change in the rhythm of his breathing, and his eyes remained tightly closed. Backing out the door, pulling it closed, she breathed a sigh of satisfaction. She could be there and back in an hour, long before he woke up.

* * *

Nick awakened gradually, becoming aware of his body in stages. Both his heels ached with a burning sensation, a cramp knotted the muscles of his right thigh, and his left shoulder and his chest throbbed like a toothache. There was a nasty metallic taste in his mouth, and he needed to go to the bathroom.

He expected to find Caitlin somewhere in the room and was disappointed when he didn't. Sliding onto his side, gritting his teeth against the pain, he negotiated his way to his feet, across the soft carpet and through the narrow bathroom door. A few minutes later, when he came back into the room, he gave no sign of seeing the figure lurking in the shadows. Climbing gingerly onto the bed, sweat beading his brow, he lay back with a sigh of relief.

"Hello, Matt."

"You knew I was here?"

"Yeah, I smelled tobacco as soon as I opened the bathroom door. You might as well enter a room with a naked soprano belting out an aria."

"I was going to ask how you feel, but I can see you're sharp as a tack," Matt muttered, crossing the room to stand at the side of the bed.

"You shouldn't be here. Caitlin—"

"Is not at home. I watched her drive away."

"How did you get in?"

Matt grinned.

"Right, so what happened to you last night? Did you see who fired the shot?" Nick barked the questions, oblivious of his own weakness.

"I didn't see anything. There's a lump the size of a golf ball on the back of my head. I came to just in time to avoid being found by your friend the sheriff."

"Who do you think put your lights out?"

"I don't know—it could have been anyone. Whoever it was, I didn't hear a damn thing."

"You think it could have been Jones?"

"Maybe. He can move without a sound in the dark."

"I'd like to know what he's afraid of."

"Losing his life sounds about right."

"No." Nick shook his head. "There's more to it than that. I think he stopped worrying about that a long time ago."

"What, then? His sister, the librarian?"

Devil in Disguise 167

"Maybe," Nick replied thoughtfully.

"So what do we do now?" Matt eased himself down in the big easy chair pulled up alongside the bed. "I don't suppose you've remembered anything?"

"No—nothing. But I have developed an interesting urge." Matt raised his heavy blond brows suggestively. "For a cigarette," Nick informed him in disgust.

"All right!" Matt grinned wider, fishing for one in his pocket.

"Don't." Nick stopped him. "Caitlin doesn't smoke. She'll smell it, and she thinks I don't smoke, either."

Matt dropped his hand onto the chair, tapping his fingers rhythmically against the arm.

"What can you tell me about Logan Carrington?" Nick asked.

"Carrington?" Matt whistled softly. "Big bucks. Family name steeped in history. One of his ancestors fought at the Alamo, one was a hero during World War One, and this particular Carrington is being strongly urged to throw his own hat in the political ring. He's resisted so far."

"Wonder why? Where did he get the big bucks?"

"Old family money made from oil, cattle, farming, property, investments—you name it, he's got a hand in it."

"Could he have a hand in a little gunrunning and drug trafficking, as well?" Nick wondered out loud.

"The man's lily white."

"Yeah, well, dig deeper, find out everything you can. What about women?" He looked questioningly in Matt's direction. The other man was eyeing him oddly.

"What?" Nick asked.

Matt shrugged, rubbed a hand down the side of his face introspectively, then shrugged again. "This all seems so familiar," he answered slowly.

"Familiar? Me lying in bed with a bullet hole in me? I must lead one hell of a life."

"Yeah—and demanding information like just now. It's hard to believe sometimes that you can't remember most of your past. Your actions are like an echo of it."

"Not to me they're not. It's weird having no memory beyond a few months ago—no childhood, no family. Nothing. It's as though I dropped into the world a few weeks ago, full grown, from outer space. I walk around feeling like a freak most of the time.

"If it hadn't been for Caitlin, I'd probably still be wandering around eating out of garbage cans, or taking handouts whenever I could get them. I'd never have gotten this far without her help. She's amazing." Nick shook his head, smiling at the time she had put into helping him regain his memory when she wasn't even sure if that was really his problem.

"She works hard all day, right alongside me, doing men's work. I know she's exhausted at the end of the day, but at night, after supper, when the dishes are done, she gets out the books and works with me, pouring the facts down my throat, forcing me to learn—or remember. It's been as hard for her as it has for me. She borrowed books from the library to help me piece things together. And finally, though at first I didn't realize that was what was happening, things began to come back little by little."

"She sounds like quite a bro—lady," Matt agreed before returning to the more immediate problem at hand. "So, who do you suppose fired that shot at you? You still think Jones isn't involved in this?"

"Oh, I think he's involved, all right, but I don't think he's the one who shot me."

"Who, then? Carrington? Is that where your suspicions lie?"

"I don't know his name, and I can't see his face clearly, but I think the man responsible is the man we've been looking for. Apparently word of who I really am has gotten out to the wrong—or, depending on how you look at it, the right—people."

The two men had become so involved in their conversation that they didn't hear the footsteps on the stairs, nor the door opening softly. But the startled gasp drew their attention.

Matt jumped to his feet, while Nick swore softly beneath his breath. Caitlin stared from one to the other, a hand gripping the door handle. It was like a tableau, a painting, as the seconds ticked by and no one moved or spoke.

"You!" Caitlin broke the tense silence. "You were on the porch that night—talking with Nick." Her eyes grew large, her face stark white as the buried memory surfaced. "My God, you said you were going to k-kill me." She was out of the room in a flash, leaving the two men wearing identical stunned expressions, staring at the empty doorway.

"Go after her, man," Nick barked. "Bring her back."

Matt caught her at the front door, subdued her with difficulty, then hauled her kicking and screaming up the stairs and into the room.

Nick was sitting up in bed, a fierce scowl darkening his handsome features. Matt swore loudly as Caitlin kicked him hard on the shin, twisting and turning furiously. Teeth bared, lips parted to bite Matt's arm, she drew back when Nick spoke.

"That's enough, Caitlin—Matt." His voice rang with quiet authority.

Caitlin looked at him in surprise. Matt dropped his hands from her and moved out of range with the air of one falsely accused.

"Where," Nick asked slowly, "did you get the asinine idea Matt wanted to kill you?"

"You aren't fooling me anymore, N-Nick, or whoever you are." She had recovered from her surprise with a vengeance. She watched his face tighten at her words. "This is all a farce." She rubbed her sore wrists. "Y-you," she pointed a finger at him, "are a farce. This w-whole ploy, the amnesia—everything—it was all—you-you are just setting me up for the—k-kill—" Eyes swimming in tears, breathing in uneven gasps, she faltered.

"What?" he asked only the one word.

"L-last night—th-that shot was meant for me—"

"You!" The two men spoke as one.

"Y-yes. This is my old room—"

"Caity, Caity, what you're saying doesn't make sense. If Matt and I wanted you dead, and if Matt were the one doing the shooting, he would know I was in this room and not you."

"B-but I heard him—"

"You heard something," Nick agreed, "but not a plan to murder you."

"Then it was you they were after? But why?"

"I thought it was a wayward hunter who shot me," he answered laconically, one dark brow arched high.

"Do you believe that?" Caitlin asked.

"Do you?" Nick countered, watching her face closely. Her gaze met his briefly, then slid away, and suddenly, painfully, he knew she was hiding something. She knew more about the shooting than she was telling—maybe even who had fired the shot?

"I think you have more questions to answer than I do," she answered obliquely. "Who's the giant?" She jerked her head in Matt's direction.

"Oh, hey now," Matt protested, but Nick silenced him with a look.

"I don't know much about him," Nick started out truthfully, improvising along the way. "He came by one day, when you were gone, looking for work." He shrugged, grimaced, then continued. "We struck up a conversation after I told him you weren't hiring. He's been by a few times since, just to talk."

Caitlin eyed him in silence. He sounded sincere, and the story was plausible, because she remembered Shay asking if a big blond had come by looking for work. She wanted to believe him, because even now, weak and injured, with a two-day growth of beard, suspicious of him as she was, the sight of him made her heart go wild and her knees go weak.

"How did he happen to be here, in this room, today?"

"I guess we better tell her the whole truth." Matt spoke suddenly from behind her. Startled, Nick's eyes flew to his face. "I've been camping out in that abandoned house out back on your property." Caitlin turned angrily to face him. "I ran out of cash—couldn't find any work." Somehow he managed, big as he was, to appear small and pathetic-looking. "Nick's been giving me a handout now and then."

Don't overdo it buddy, Nick tried to caution him with his eyes. She isn't going to buy the hard-luck story, anyway. A more unlikely looking undernourished specimen he'd never seen. Matt's six-foot four-inch frame was packed with enough solid muscle for two, maybe three, people.

"Oh." Caitlin backed to the chair Matt had recently vacated, looking uncertain now, and flopped down. "Oh," she murmured again, feeling sorry for him, almost against her will. Fiery-tempered she might be, but she could never turn away a stray dog or cat, or a human being in need. "But what about the conversation I overheard," she asked suddenly, remembering, a glint of distrust in the look she turned on him.

Red-faced—Nick wondered how he managed that—Matt mumbled something, cleared his throat nervously, and spoke more clearly. "It was man talk—you know, not fit for mixed company." Matt's eyes darted to the floor in feigned embarrassment, while he peeked impishly at Nick from under his lowered lids.

Swallowing dryly, Caitlin looked down at her hands in embarrassment. She understood now. Man talk. She'd interrupted a conversation of the kind men have with other men in locker rooms about women.

Give me a break, Nick thought in disgust. Any fool could see through that act, and Caity, he knew, was nobody's fool.

"I'm sorry," Caitlin said contritely. "I guess I misunderstood." Nick jerked his head in her direction. "The accident—it was upsetting—I guess I owe you both an apology—"

"No!" Suddenly Nick wanted to be done with the lies. Caitlin looked at him in surprise.

Matt interceded by stepping closer to the chair and taking up the conversation once more. "What Nick means," he began, shooting a quick glance in his partner's direction, "is that it was just a misunderstanding, a natural mistake. You don't owe us an apology. We owe you one for not being straight with you in the beginning about my staying on your property."

That's an understatement, Nick thought unhappily. If—when—she finds out the truth about all this, she'll never forgive me, never want to see my lying face again. And he couldn't blame her.

Caitlin smiled, and both men had to catch their breath at the beauty of it. "Let's forget it." She was relieved to have it explained so satisfactorily. Her nature wouldn't allow her to hold a grudge. Her temper flared like a match to tinder, but fizzled out just as quickly when dampened. She wanted to believe them, so she did. Consulting her watch, she spoke to the room in general.

"It's about time Nick got dressed for his visit to the doctor." She stood and headed for the door. "And since he doesn't care for assistance from me," she glanced back over her shoulder, reminding him of his earlier refusal, "Matt—is it?" At his quick nod, she continued, "Matt, you can help him get dressed. When you finish, Matt, come downstairs. I'd like a few words with you."

After she left the room, the two men looked at each other warily.

"Did you have to be so hokey?"

"Do you have to be so grouchy?"

They had Nick dressed in record time, and did it all in total silence.

* * *

Caitlin and Nick were on their way home from town. The trip to the doctor, and the added bonus of a dressing change by Hildy, had left Nick feeling weak and shaky. The doctor had said he was coming along fine, whatever that meant, and that he wouldn't need to see him again for a week. Hildy had demonstrated the proper way to change the dressing for Caitlin and loaded her down with enough material to bandage a whole army.

Sheriff Raymond had been his usual charming self, saying little but insinuating plenty. He had found nothing, he told him, during his investigation of the ranch and the surrounding terrain.

When Nick asked about footprints there was an interesting glint in the sheriff's eye, but he only stated that there were no clear prints. The conclusion being that Nick had caught a stray shot from a hunter who probably didn't even realize he'd hit anything.

It was hard to swallow, now that he knew who he really was. Hard to believe in such a convenient accident, but it suited his purpose to accept the verdict.

Sheriff Raymond promised, tongue in cheek, to crack down on trespassers in the area. And Nick made a mental note to tell Matt not to be too quick with his visit to the sheriff.

"What made you ask Matt to stay on at the ranch?" Nick asked now, out of the blue.

"I need the help, since you're going to be out of commission for a while." She captured his glance with a smile. "And since the two of you have become friends, I thought you'd be pleased."

"I see." It made him feel strange inside, knowing she was doing it even partly for him. If she knew the truth, if she ever learned the real purpose for Matt's being there—and his . . .

"You need a haircut." Her glance taking in the black hair well below his shirt collar, Caitlin instinctively slowed the Jeep as they passed a barber shop at the edge of town.

"I don't feel much like sitting in a barber chair right now. Maybe you could trim it a bit in a day or two," he suggested tiredly.

"Me!"

"Sure." He glanced at her. "Haven't you ever cut anyone's hair?"

"No. That is, once I cut Megan's. And Aunt Letty nearly had a stroke. Meg's hair was down past her hips. Both of us could sit on our hair back then. Meg hated it. She's so small, she said it made her look like a hairy gnome. So one day we were playing beauty shop, and I cut off her braids. She's worn her hair short ever since."

"What about you? When did you decide to cut your hair?"

"In college. It was the fad at the time. The girls all wore short hair, and the guys wore theirs long."

"Was there a particular guy—one you cut your hair for?"

"No, not really." His voice sent shivers down her spine. Feeling uncomfortable, she changed the subject, and they discussed the upcoming Fourth of July celebration at the Carrington ranch. It was only a couple weeks off and, Caitlin reasoned, his arm would be well on its way to being healed by then, so he could go with her and have a good time.

The next few days passed slowly. If Nick had thought he would see more of Caitlin, he was sadly mistaken. She changed his dressing and brought him his meals. They would have a brief, unsatisfying conversation, and then she would leave.

After insisting that Matt move his things from the stone house and into the room next to Nick's, Caitlin removed all her father's possessions, taking what she wanted to keep downstairs and sending the rest to a church charity. Nick seemed to be the only one not altogether happy about the new arrangement.

He began to experience his first twinges of jealousy as the days passed slowly by, with Caitlin and Matt spending more and more time in each other's company. They ate their meals together in the kitchen, and Nick imagined Matt sitting at his place, an arm's reach from Caitlin. In the evenings they watched TV together.

A small set had been moved into his room, but Nick couldn't get interested in it. Sometimes he could hear them laughing, or discussing a particular program before saying good-night at the foot of the stairs, and it was all he could do not to throw open his door to make sure that was all they were doing.

Slowly it ate at him. Matt was good-looking, undoubtedly attractive to women, and didn't have the stigma of a past he couldn't remember. Matt knew exactly who he was, where he'd been and where he was going. And he knew, from remembered experience, how to treat a woman.

Nick couldn't help imagining them alone in the intimacy of the night. Their glances meeting, eyes locking, an awareness springing up between them, leading to... Jumping from the bed, he paced restlessly within the confines of the room, trying to drive the disturbing pictures from his mind. He had no right to feel possessive toward Caitlin. He could offer her nothing—only half a man. But he did feel possessive, damnit! He felt like a nervous virgin with his first girlfriend, scared and confused.

Throwing himself across the bed, groaning at the ensuing pain, he cursed himself for a fool. Matt wasn't interested in Caitlin, nor she in him. They worked together; that was all. She spent time with Matt because he was learning the workings of the ranch, just as he himself had had to do.

Images of Caitlin standing close to demonstrate something, her hair blowing across his lips, her scent filling his nostrils, the heat of her body suffusing his, drove him from the bed once more. "I'll kill him," he muttered dangerously, remembering. "If he touches her, I'll kill him with my bare hands."

Hot, tired and short of temper, Caitlin muttered an imprecation beneath her breath. The windmill serving the chicken yard and horse trough was acting up. That was why she was standing twenty feet off the ground, a wrench in her hand, rubbing the sweat from her brow. She'd promised to cut Nick's hair later that day, and the thought added to her problems by making her hands shake. Not a good condition for working any distance above the ground with heavy tools.

The cause of her nervousness could be summed up in one word: Nick. He was different. She wasn't sure if it was because of Matt's presence, or if he was still angry because of her suspicions the day she had found Matt in his room. She had wanted to discuss his amnesia for days now, but she'd felt too constrained by his manner to broach the subject.

He never once met her eyes now when they were together; his voice was always harsh, his answers terse. Hurt and confused by the changes in him, she spent more time with Matt and less with Nick. That was why his reminder about cutting his hair had surprised her.

Thinking about it now, her palms became sweaty, and she fumbled, then dropped the wrench. Calling, "Look out!" to Matt standing below, his eyes on something in the distance, Caitlin moaned in horror. Too late, Matt looked up and saw the object hurtling toward him.

The heavy metal tool struck him across the right side of his face, the blow stunning him for an instant. He staggered, throwing out his hands to catch at the tower, holding on.

"Matt! I'm sorry! Are you all right?" Agitated, hurrying to climb down to his assistance, Caitlin missed her footing, wavered, then fell with a scream.

Matt caught her in midair.

Caitlin, concerned only with the bloody welt and bruise rapidly forming across his cheekbone, touched him tentatively, her eyes dark with guilt.

"Oh, Matt, I'm so sorry," she apologized again. "I don't know how I could be so clumsy."

"It's okay," he assured her gruffly. "I'm not hurt." He held her for a moment, hardly registering the feather weight of her in his brawny arms.

"Yes, you are," she protested. "Let me down. I'll get some ice."

He let her slide slowly from his arms before leaning down and splashing cool water from the tank over his hot face, stinging the cut below his right eye.

"No need. See, all better." He looked up at her from his bent position, a grin softening the hard features.

Shaking her own head, she leaned over with a grin and planted a quick kiss on his rough cheek below the bruise. Neither had noticed the tall figure watching from his upstairs window.

"You're a nice man, Matthew Frazier. I hope I can still count on you to be my friend after this. Nick and I are lucky to have you."

"Yeah, you are," he laughed.

"I'm sorry about your cheek. But at least the windmill's fixed. You sure you don't want some ice, some antiseptic?" she asked anxiously, continuing to eye the growing bruise with self-condemnation.

"Naw, I'm fine."

"I'll bet you're going to have a beaut of a shiner."

"It won't be the first—maybe the first from a gorgeous red-head, though."

"Oh, sure. And I'll bet you've used that line a million times before." But she laughed and felt her cheeks grow warm. What woman didn't appreciate a compliment from a good-looking man?

"I guess now that Nick's better you won't be needing me." He didn't much like the idea of going back to camping out every night. And the canned food he'd been existing on before moving into the ranch house didn't come close to Caitlin's fried chicken.

"Whoa, wait a minute. He's better, not well. If you'll settle for room and board and," she named a modest amount, "I can still use you. There's plenty of work around here, as you well know by now. And the food's not bad." His appetite was enormous, she'd noticed.

"It's a deal," he answered, sticking out his hand. He didn't want to take money from her, but he knew she wouldn't let him stay otherwise. The money could be returned after the job was over.

Caitlin laughed as they shook hands. "Well, if you'll put the tools away and excuse me, I'll go fix lunch. I have to play barber this afternoon." Turning quickly away to hide her nervousness at the idea, she moved toward the house.

Caitlin assembled the items she thought she would need on a small round table beside the straight-backed chair she had placed beside the window.

"I heard the truck leave." Nick spoke for the first time since she'd brought him lunch.

"Matt's hauling feed to the critters." Her smile fluttered; he hadn't taken his eyes off her since she'd entered the room.

"Should I take my shirt off?"

"I don't have a cape like the barber uses, so I thought I'd use this." She held up a violently purple towel for his inspection. "But maybe you'd better take the shirt off, too. Hair down the collar itches like crazy."

Standing beside the bed, his eyes on her face, Nick began to unbutton his shirt, one button at a time. Caitlin, mesmerized by the slow, deliberate movement of his long, tapered fingers, watched with bated breath as the naked expanse of hair-roughened skin grew. When his fingers reached the waistband of his jeans, she forced her glance away, needlessly rearranging the scissors and comb on the table.

"I—I think it's best if your hair is wet, so if you come into the bathroom, I'll wash it first." She struggled to get a hold on her wayward emotions.

Standing in the doorway, waiting for him to join her, she kept her eyes strictly away from his chest. Nick was beside her before she could move, the solid wall of his chest grazing the tips of her breasts as he squeezed past.

"Sorry," he murmured deeply, while she wished he hadn't spoken at all. She ignored deliberately the tingling sensation starting where he'd touched her and spreading in all directions. Her pointed nipples rubbing against the rough cloth of her shirt made her mouth go dry and her knees quake.

"How do we go about this?" Nick asked, standing before the sink. "I've never had anyone wash my hair—to my knowledge," he added wryly.

"A second first for me today." She spoke without thinking.

"I don't understand." He frowned at her.

"I think I gave Matt a black eye a little while ago. A tool I was using fell and hit him . . ." Her voice died out at the tight expression on his face.

"Is that all you gave him?"

"Now *I* don't understand." She looked puzzled.

"Can we get on with this?"

"Y-you need to bend over," she directed in confusion. The bathroom, which seemed to have shrunk with his entrance, shrank even more in the next few seconds in the face of his unexplained anger. Because that was exactly what she saw in his dark eyes—anger.

"Like this?" he asked in a strained voice. Knees bent, face toward the sink, he stooped awkwardly.

"Oh, look, this isn't going to work. You can't stay in that position for the time it will take to wash your hair."

"I'm okay," he answered shortly. "Just get on with it."

Indignant at his tone, growing angrier by the minute herself, she turned the faucet handle too hard, spraying them both with cold water. Nick yelped and jumped back as cold water hit his bare chest and splattered the front of his jeans. He moved, as though to straighten from his crouched position, but she forestalled him by pushing his head down firmly. "Hold still," she snapped.

Adjusting the water temperature with one hand, she grabbed the green plastic shampoo bottle with the other and managed to drop it in the sink. Silently thanking the manufacturer for having the foresight to make it unbreakable, she scooped up the gooey mess that had spilled and plopped it on his hair.

"Aren't you supposed to wet it first?" Nick asked, his voice coming from somewhere near her waist.

Giving him a dirty look that he couldn't see, Caitlin shoved his head under the faucet and, with both hands, began to work up a rich, bubbly lather. Over and over she scraped her nails against his scalp, rubbing, massaging, then rubbing some more.

After the final rinse she wrapped a towel around his head and stood back. Her fingers and hands throbbed all the way back to her shoulders, but she felt sure his scalp was tingling even more. Nick rubbed his hair with the towel, looking at her strangely from beneath its folds.

"If that's what you go through every time you wash your own hair, I'm surprised you have any left," was his passing comment as he sidled out the door.

Caitlin stuck her tongue out at his back, then clamped her mouth shut, feeling foolish, but oddly satisfied, too.

Chapter 11

Nick sat waiting for her with his back to the window, the light creating a halo around his motionless form. The sable hair, finger-combed back from his high forehead, stood up in spikes at the top and sides of his well-shaped head. Water dripped from the ends and was absorbed by the purple towel draped around his shoulders.

With his face in shadow, Nick studied her with unfathomable eyes. He saw the signs of her recent labors on his behalf in the damp patches down the front of her beige and cream blouse, and the short hair pulled loose from her topknot, a curl stuck to one glowing cheek.

The long-fingered hands lying loose between his slightly spread knees tightened fractionally at the remembered feel of that silky hair and the intoxicating fragrance of her woman's scent.

Caitlin stood in the center of the room, silence looming between them like a heavy mist. She licked her dry lips nervously, and though she couldn't see it, she knew he followed the movement with his eyes. Clenching the hands dangling at her sides, nails biting into her palms, she swallowed with difficulty and found her voice.

"Maybe this isn't such a good idea after all. I told you, I've never done this before. What if I make a mess of it—cut one side shorter than the other?"

"It'll grow back. It needs to be cut—I trust you," he answered in a deep-timbred voice.

Guilt speared her. Would he still trust her if he knew the secret she had kept about David's presence the night he was shot?

"P-perhaps you shouldn't," she answered, watching as his left brow reached toward the raven's wing of wet hair arching determinedly across his forehead.

He made no comment, only kept his eyes on her face, waiting with that peculiar stillness that seemed to be bred into him. Caitlin crossed the room unwillingly and moved up behind him, glad at least to be out of his range of vision.

She picked up the scissors with unsteady hands and contemplated the silky dark strands before grasping a swatch between two fingers and beginning to cut it at an angle, as she had seen stylists do. When the first dark strands fell before the scissors, she closed her eyes briefly, praying this would soon be over.

The herbal fragrance wafting from his hair, combined with the purely masculine scent he exuded, interfered with her breathing, making it virtually impossible to remain detached, as she had promised herself she would.

While the tufts of severed hair lying on the floor grew, the strong contours of his head and neck became more apparent. Caitlin hesitated, feeling her pulse lurch at her first clear view of his profile.

The skin pulled taut across his elegant cheekbones had lost its sun-bronzed hue during his confinement. The fine lines radiating from his eyes and mouth were more evident. She could admire the beauty of his sensually carved mouth with its full lower lip held uncompromisingly straight. The firm square jaw thrust pugnaciously forward. The dusky shadow of his beard, showing through the skin of jaw and chin, giving him an even more virile aura.

Her fingers itched to trace the rugged planes of his forehead, to follow the path of the thin white scar still visible from his tangle with the barbed wire.

"You like Matt, don't you?" he asked abruptly, startling her from her erotic fantasy.

"I—yes—don't you?" She was puzzled by an indefinable something in his voice.

"He's a good man."

"Yes," she agreed, nodding, continuing to snip at his hair, wishing she dared to lean forward and lay her mouth against the vulnerable-looking space between his neck and shoulder.

"He's hardworking and likable." Again Caitlin agreed with a slightly raised brow. He didn't need to sell Matt to her; she already liked him.

"Attractive, too—blond hair, blue eyes, muscles and all. The kind of man a woman could go for."

"Gray," Caitlin corrected absently.

"What?"

"Gray," she repeated. "Matt's eyes are gray, not blue. Almost the exact shade of an ice cube."

"You sound as though you've studied them rather closely."

"No, but they are an unusual color—rather unforgettable." Personally, she preferred huge dark eyes, black as midnight, ringed with thick curling lashes.

Body rigid, he agreed with her. "Yes, they are unforgettable."

Thankfully, Caitlin saw that she was nearly finished with his hair. All that remained was the front. Stepping around his jean-clad knee, she stood between his sinewy thighs, her jutting breasts on a level with his eyes.

The move sent alarm bells ringing sharply inside Nick's head. He was finding it increasingly difficult with each passing day to remain objective where she and Matt were concerned, not to mention remaining detached regarding Caitlin herself. He had deliberately brought the subject of Matt between them, probing her feelings as if he were testing a sore spot, looking for the pain, hoping to keep his own feelings at bay.

Struggling to hide his undue interest, Nick couldn't resist one quick glance at her breasts and the shadowy hollow between. He looked hastily away, but he couldn't stop his mind from filling in what the shadows hid. He moved restlessly in the chair.

It took no stretch of the imagination to recall those lush globes with pale mauve circles and budlike nipples in the center. He could feel them against the palms of his hands, or rubbing insistently against the hair on his chest.

He stared hard at the middle button of her blouse in an effort to find neutral ground. But his eyes refused to obey his pleading command to stay there. Instead they began a down-

ward journey over a narrow cinched-in waist to slightly flared
hips, where they were stopped short by the creases created by
the fit of jeans stretched tight over her hips and belly to the
juncture of her legs.

Caitlin, too, was aware of the provocative nature of their
proximity. Everything became exaggerated to her supersensi-
tized nerves. His hair took on a life of its own, wrapping
around and clinging stubbornly to her fingers. Her breasts
heaved with the escalated rhythm of her breathing.

The silence of the room, broken only by the metallic snip of
the scissors, added to the feeling of intimacy like a fine web
drawing them closer. Gooseflesh rippled along both arms and
down the backs of both legs. Her clothing became uncomfortable, chafing roughly against her tender skin. The air in the
room felt stifling hot, then cold. Caitlin's fingers became icy,
and her palms began to sweat.

She was almost finished; she couldn't lose her cool now. Just
a few more snips . . .

"Matt and I discussed his staying on for a while," she said.
Maybe if she talked she wouldn't be so aware of Nick's powerful attraction.

"I saw your *talk* from the window." Nick was suddenly reminded of the kiss he'd seen earlier, and he couldn't keep the
jealous anger from his voice.

The odd tone caused Caitlin to take a step back and eye him
curiously. "Are you angry with Matt about something?"

She'd noticed that the two had spent very little time together in the past few days, but had assumed it was because of
Nick's injury and the time she'd needed to teach Matt the
workings of the ranch.

Pulling the towel from his neck, bits of black hair flying,
Nick jerked to his feet, paced to the window and stood with his
back to the room—and Caitlin.

"From this window I have an excellent view of the chicken
house, the barn—and the windmill."

So that was it. He'd seen Matt catch her when she fell, she
thought, having already forgotten the light kiss she'd planted
on his injured cheek. What was the matter with him? Did he
want his friend to stand by and let her hit the ground?

"If that's so, then you know Matt kept me from a nasty fall.
I'm very grateful to him for that, and for the way he's worked
so hard since he's been here."

"Is that why you kissed him? In gratitude? Or has all the time you've spent in his company the last few days made you realize you feel more than gratitude for him?"

"That's none of your business," she answered tightly. He was acting as though he owned her. And it hadn't been that long ago that he'd rejected her out of hand. Was this just a dog-in-the manger attitude—or was he truly jealous?

"You're right, it isn't any of my business who you choose to give your favors to. Just don't spread any in my direction from now on," he snarled.

"You jerk! If you weren't hurt, I'd slap your face for that." She slammed the comb and scissors down onto the bedside table and stood glaring at him with her hands on her hips.

"Try it," he whispered dangerously, in a tone Matt would have recognized as boding no good for the one on the receiving end of it. Without seeming to move, he stood so close to her that she could feel the air fairly crackle with his anger.

It was too much of a challenge for her to resist. The tension between them had been building since his first day at the ranch. Anger was a good cover for sexual awareness, and they both needed a release.

Caitlin drew her hand back in sudden blinding fury at the audacity of his thinking he could tell her how to behave—who she could kiss. He didn't want her kisses; he'd already proved that. She let fly, but Nick captured her wrist before her hand could do more than fan the air before his face.

Her eyes like polished jade, she stared stonily at him. His grip on her wrist hurt, but she wouldn't give him the satisfaction of admitting it. With twin flags of anger flying in her cheeks, she defied him with her eyes to do his worst.

Black eyes blazed down into green. He would be damned if he would give an inch. She'd started this by admitting she wanted to hit him. No, she'd started it by kissing his best friend. He looked at her in confusion. He was fighting himself, and her, too. How could he be angry with her for turning to another, when he'd pushed her away? But he hadn't wanted to! It was because he felt unworthy of her that he . . .

His eyes searched her face for a clue to her true feelings and lingered on the slight quivering in her full bottom lip. His faltering glance tried to move away, but his eyes clung determinedly to her mouth.

His anger died suddenly, an indefinable emotion taking its place. He didn't want to fight with her—he wanted to hold her.

All of a sudden, Caitlin couldn't seem to breathe. The hand at her wrist had loosened; she could have drawn away easily if she'd tried. But the air around them began to feel almost solid, pressing the two of them together. Her nipples hardened as they drew to within an inch of his bare, muscled chest.

"I'm sorry," he whispered. "I didn't mean what I said. I don't think you flirted with Matt. I don't want to fight with you."

"What *do* you want to do with me?"

"This . . ." he murmured as his mouth descended slowly toward her upraised lips.

Caitlin felt his warm breath stroke her face, and then his touch as his tongue caressed first her bottom lip and then the top one before drawing away.

She opened her eyes slowly and was held enthralled by the smoldering fires in the depths of his glance. She could hear the uneven tenor of his breathing. See the quick bunching of muscles in his jaw and throat as he swallowed. He had one hand on either side of her face, his fingers laced in the fire of her hair, and she felt the roughness of his callused hands as he drew her inexorably nearer.

His lips recaptured hers, more demanding this time. Mouths hot and hungry, they devoured each other. He forced her lips open with his thrusting tongue, and, tentatively at first, she met his challenge.

Nick explored the sweet moist recesses of her mouth, sending shivers of ecstasy racing down her spine. Caitlin answered his passion with her own. Their mouths touched, tasted, fused; their tongues met, explored, and dueled, driving each other wild.

Nick pulled her tightly between his legs, fitting her into the cradle of his hips, while kissing her lips, eyes, cheek. Caitlin's hands moved to his thighs, rubbing up and down the rough material sheathing the powerful muscles beneath, feeling him tense with restrained excitement. The same excitement surged within her, drowning her in hot liquid desire.

She wanted him, wanted to feel his hands, his lips, on the most secret and intimate places of her body. She wanted him to lay her down, strip the clothing from both their bodies and make wild, passionate love to her.

Nick's lips left hers to plant a tantalizing kiss in the hollow of her throat, causing her to whimper softly into the short hair at the side of his neck. Head reeling at her impassioned cries, his lips seared a path from neck to shoulder. One hand left her face to draw back the collar of her blouse, baring a creamy shoulder to his hot, questing mouth. Caitlin gasped and quivered at the delicious sensations coursing through her, then breathed a kiss against the rough pulse at his throat.

"Oh, Caity, Caity," he moaned, his lips against her hair. "I tried—I really tried—not—to—let—this—happen—" His mouth recaptured hers, the last words smothered on her lips.

Caitlin's hands slid from his waist toward his hips, causing his body to tighten even more in excitement, then moved to his back, probing the hollow of his spine, feeling the light film of sweat, kneading the muscles of his back and shoulders. Aroused beyond thought, she drew herself closer, pressing her breasts flat against his chest, feeling the hard muscles beneath the surface. Her fingers traveled over the strong tendons along the back of his neck and explored the hard ridge of his spine.

Nick slid his hands under her blouse, rubbing the bare skin of her back and shoulders, raising goose bumps wherever he touched. She wasn't wearing a bra, and he allowed his hands to roam unrestrainedly, bringing them both to the edge.

In one fluid movement he slid to the floor, taking her with him, and eased her back gently to lie on the soft carpet. His burning gaze locked on hers, one hand on either side of her, he leaned over her.

Supported by his right arm, he ignored the pain in his healing shoulder. Another, far stronger pain took precedence over everything else. Thrusting one leg between hers, he covered her.

"It's still your decision," he rasped out, his meaning clear. "Yes—or no."

Her answer was to lift her head and press warm lips to his. Burying her hands in his hair, she drew his body slowly down to hers until his weight, a welcome burden, crushed her breasts flat between them.

He allowed her to take control, enjoying the feel of the hot, moist kisses she planted along his face and chin between long satisfying trips to his mouth. Her hands roamed his back and shoulders restlessly, her body writhing beneath his.

He was fast reaching the point of no return, his desire for her a raging fever in his blood. But his experience was limited, despite what Matt had said about the many women in his past, and he wasn't sure he knew how to satisfy the woman beneath him. The mounting fear that he would be unable to hold on to his own passion long enough to satisfy hers held him back. What he would give to be able to call on some of Drew's experience now . . .

With his left hand he covered her stomach, his palm flat against the material of her jeans. He could feel the quiver of her muscles dancing in anticipation. Caitlin snuggled against him as their legs entwined. She made no protest when his hands sought the buttons of her blouse, fingers icy, but the palm fiery hot against the quivering skin at her waist.

Drawing away, Nick slid the blouse back inch by inch, the material dragging abrasively against her taut nipples, sending new spirals of ecstasy crashing through her.

As her body was slowly bared, Nick gazed at her shapely beauty, heart kicking in his chest. Eyes dark with desire, he held her gaze while his hand moved magically over each breast. He fondled one small globe between finger and thumb, rolling it gently, its nipple becoming marble hard.

Dipping his head, eyes still locked with hers, his lips brushed both nipples; then, turning his head slightly, he rubbed a raspy cheek against the sensitive nubs. Caitlin gasped, panting, and the rosy peaks grew to a new pebble hardness.

Caressing her flat stomach, one hand paused long enough to unsnap and unzip her jeans, the fingers tracing an inch or so below the opening, then sliding upward across her narrow rib cage to her breasts. Caitlin arched her body, half-ice, half-flame, into him, her fingers trailing restlessly up and down his spine, her throat emitting soft moans of pleasure and delight.

Nick moved his lips to her waist, across her stomach to the open edge of her jeans. His hands began slowly to skim the jeans from her body, revealing a sharp pelvis and long, tapering thighs. He knelt at her feet, his eyes traveling the length of her body, scorching her with their heat. A pair of white lace and silk bikini panties hid nothing from his view.

When he made no move to come back to her, Caitlin raised herself on one elbow, a questioning look in her glowing green eyes. "What is it?"

"You're beautiful," he whispered.

"So are you." She moved closer.

"No—I—my—hip—m-my—leg—"

"The scars? Are you worried about the scars?"

"You know?"

"Yes, Dr. Shepherd saw them when he treated your shoulder."

"They're ugly."

Caitlin shook her head, touching a finger to his lips. "No part of you could possibly be ugly. I think you're beautiful inside and out."

Turning his head aside, he whispered, "You don't know me."

"I know I . . . care about you."

Nick closed his eyes, his face twisted in a mask of warring emotions. He resisted her as long as he could before his eyes were irresistibly drawn to her face. Then, with a cry of triumph—and defeat—he could resist her no longer. Pressing her back into the carpet, bare chest against bare chest, he covered her with his body.

They discarded their clothes quickly, if clumsily, helping each other with eager, fumbling fingers. Caitlin's breasts tingled beneath the wiry hair on his chest as he tucked her curves into his own more angular contours. It was flesh against flesh, man against woman.

Instinctively Caitlin arched against him, feeling his arousal hard against her belly, causing ripples of delightful anticipation to go skidding through her body.

Nick's hand seared a path down her abdomen and hip, exploring her thigh, moving up along the inside, over tight curls and silken skin to her belly. Breath hot against her skin, his tongue made a path down her ribs to her stomach, while his hands searched for pleasure points. Caitlin's senses reeled as if short-circuited, pleasure radiating outward from every touch, every kiss.

Passion pounded through her heart, body and soul.

Sliding his legs along the length of hers, his mouth at her breasts, his fingers nestled against her soft wiry curls, he gently probed a deeper inner softness. Caitlin whimpered against his mouth, arching her body to accommodate his ardent fingers. Tearing his lips from hers, he buried his face in her sweet-smelling hair, feeling the silky mass cling to his rough chin.

"I can't wait," he groaned.

"It's all right—it's all right," she gentled him, her lips gliding against his shoulder, tasting salt on his sweat-slickened skin.

Yielding to the driving need that had been building between them for weeks, Caitlin welcomed him into her body. Melded against him, her world encompassed only Nick and his need. Their bodies flowed together like warm honey, and though she hadn't expected it, she caught fire from him, and they soared together.

Nick had never dreamed skin could be so soft, or lips so sweet. He rode the tide of their passion till his soul splintered, shattering into a million pieces, never to be the same, and he took her with him. Heads thrown back, their mingled cries of joy filled the air as he filled her with life. And Caitlin returned his passion, borne along on the tide of his loving.

At the peak of their pleasure, Caitlin's eyes flew open and, their glances locking, they watched the flames of passion burn out of control in each other's eyes. The naked emotions laid bare for each to see added a whole new deeper dimension to the act, and the tide of fulfillment raging through both of them.

Breath rasping in his throat, his body still joined with hers, Nick raised himself to look at her. His heart clenched at the sight of the serene glow on her face, the radiant light shining from her eyes. With an unsteady finger, he traced the line of her smiling lips.

"It's never been like that for me," he whispered in awe.

"How would you know?" she asked softly, only meaning to tease him a bit.

Eyes darkening, body going stiff, he levered himself away from her.

"Nick, I didn't mean that the way it sounded. I'm sorry—I didn't mean to hurt you."

"It doesn't matter. What you said is true." His back to her, he retrieved his jeans, clutching them to him, embarrassed now by his nakedness. Once more he became aware of the imperfections of body—and mind.

"Nick, please." She touched his shoulder in contrition, crying inside when he flinched from her. "I didn't mean it the way it sounded. Aren't we ever going to be able to talk about your past?"

"Past? You've just reminded me that I have none—none that I can talk about." He felt driven by what he did know, what he was hiding from her. It was guilt, not her unthinking remark, causing him to turn away. But he couldn't tell her that; perhaps it would be best to let her think—no, he couldn't do that to her. He couldn't let her think he'd used her.

"I can't discuss my past," he admitted bleakly, knowing she thought he meant he didn't know his past when instead he meant exactly what he'd said: he couldn't discuss it with her—not yet.

"It isn't your yesterdays I'm interested in," she told him honestly. Her hand sought his, buried in the crush of clothing he held protectively against him. Stroking the back of his taut hand, she leaned forward, lightly touching her lips to his bare shoulder.

He quivered at the touch, his head swinging in her direction, meeting her imploring glance. He watched her glide with fluid grace to her feet, standing proudly naked before him, one hand extended—waiting. He looked at that hand for a long moment, as if memorizing its structure. Then her fingers moved slightly, beckoning to him.

He didn't know he was moving until he felt his large hand taken by her smaller one. He followed her to the bed. Halting beside it, raising her face to his, she drew him to her with her eyes. Hands in her hair, he held her, kissing her as they fell back onto the bed. No more words were necessary; their bodies spoke the same language.

Someone was in the room; stealthy sounds moved nearer to the bed. Senses alert, body tense, Nick awaited the right moment to spring. He knew it wasn't Caitlin, because she'd reluctantly left him hours ago.

A dark shadow, darker than the rest, loomed nearer, looking huge in the eerie moonlight. Nick held his breath and moved swiftly, surely. One hand at the shadow's throat, the other curved for what could be a fatal blow if delivered with enough force, he hesitated, hearing his name choked out in familiar tones.

"Drew—it's—me—"

"Matt?" he asked in surprise. "What the hell are you doing?" Dropping his hands, the adrenaline still pumping, he took several deep breaths and sat down on the bed.

"N-nearly getting myself killed," Matt croaked in answer. One large hand rubbed at his sore throat; the other hunted for the chair somewhere behind.

Nick reached for the lamp on the bedside table. Matt's quick words stopped him.

"Don't. The house is being watched."

"Watched? By whom?"

"That's a good question. There seem to be one or two interested parties wandering around outside tonight."

"What's here to interest so many people?"

"Not what," Matt corrected. "Who. You haven't forgotten your little accident?"

"No, of course I haven't. It's just ... I was willing to subscribe to the popular theory of the careless hunter."

"Don't you believe it for a minute. Our hunter knew exactly what quarry he was after. The two-legged variety."

"Yeah," Nick agreed dejectedly. Things had been so much simpler when he was only a slightly retarded hired hand. "I've been trying to get a word alone with you for days. What brought you here tonight?"

"I saw our friend Jones earlier today."

"So?"

"He was skulking around the stone house, and for once he didn't see me first," Matt told him with satisfaction. "He was removing something from the fireplace."

Reaching for the ever-present cigarette, he flipped open a book of matches, struck one and held it to the tip.

Nick glanced at the ash tray that had miraculously appeared with Matt's advent to the house.

"I followed him back to his place," Matt continued between drags on the cigarette. "Unless he stashed the package along the way, that's where it is now.

"He's a hard man to track, especially on his home turf. I'd wager he knows every tree and rabbit hole by sight." Matt shook his head in admiration. The man was good; one leg shorter than the other or not, he moved like a wraith through the night.

"Any idea what the package contained?"

"Nope. I couldn't get a close enough look, but it was about the size and shape of a large manila envelope. Flat like one, too."

"Envelope? Maybe it's old love letters he doesn't want anyone else to read."

"Sure, and he was feeling lonely and unloved, so he decided to dig them up and take them home to read, right?" Matt asked sarcastically.

Nick shrugged. "I suppose stranger things have happened."

"We both know Jones had something more exciting to hide in that fireplace than old love letters." Matt puffed on his cigarette for a few moments in silence. "I wonder what he really did have in that envelope."

"Beats me." Nick sighed tiredly. With one thing and another, his whole body was one massive, throbbing ache, his mind fuzzy with fatigue. "Did you see what he did with the package?"

"Naw. I couldn't get to a window fast enough." Matt ground out the cigarette in the ashtray.

"You know," Nick spoke suddenly, feeling the weight of his precarious position, "this sounds like one of those dark comedies you read about. Everybody knows who and what I am—except me." There was no humor in the forced laugh.

Matt leaned over to lay a comforting hand on his shoulder. "In the old days, a situation like this would have had you champing at the bit, ready to take all the risks, gung ho for action," Matt remarked reflectively.

"Maybe I'm getting old—or maybe the accident knocked some sense into my head." He didn't acknowledge it, but he welcomed the man's gesture of friendship.

"I like the change," Matt said gruffly, his grip tightening for a moment before his hand fell away.

Chapter 12

Caitlin awakened slowly, face turned toward the early morning sunshine filtering into the room. Birds in the trees outside the window sang a chorale to the sunrise. Raising languid arms above her head, she stretched tired, aching muscles. Her lips curving at the pictures brought to mind by a slight twinge here, an unfamiliar ache there, she recalled, vividly, the smoldering passion of Nick's loving.

Nick. The name wafted through her memory, accompanying images of him holding her close during and after their lovemaking, his face soft, dark eyes dreamy, a slow smile on his sensuous lips. Caitlin shivered at the remembered thrill of those lips, hearing the echo of his deep-timbred voice whispering soft words of love.

She wanted to throw off the covers, leap from the bed and dash up the stairs to him. However, in the next instant, reality struck like the blow from a powerful fist, and she knew she wouldn't go to him. Though they had lived in the same house for weeks, had been as intimately close as two people could be, she felt—still felt—as though he were holding himself apart from her.

Last night, after their lovemaking, they had parted reluctantly, but a sense of strain had entered their manner with each other and, in the end, the night had ended badly.

Caitlin understood that he felt embarrassed about his lack of memory, haunted by his past. But it was driving a wedge between them, and she was afraid that unless he somehow regained his memory, they would never have the chance to build any kind of a future together.

The phone on the bedside table rang, piercing her unhappy fog, and she reached for it thankfully.

"Hi, it's Megan. I know it's early, but I wanted to catch you before I had to leave for work."

"It's okay. I'm awake."

"Good. How're you doing? I haven't heard much from you in a while. I know with the accident and all you've been busy, so I thought I'd give you a call."

"I'm glad you did. I wanted to invite you over for dinner tonight, if you can make it. What do you say? I know it's short notice."

Megan laughed. "It's not like I have to consult my engagement calendar to see if I'm free. Sure, I'd love to come. But are you going to have the time to prepare a meal for guests? I know it can't be easy with Nick laid up—"

"You're forgetting about Matt, Nick's friend. He's been a real help. He was a bit awkward around the horses at first, just like Nick was, but he's picked things up real fast. I don't know what I'd have done without him."

"He sounds a real paragon," Megan replied tartly.

"Is something wrong? You sound . . . put out."

"Nothing's wrong—not really. I'm just kind of irked at men in general. David's still acting so secretive, and then there's Logan. He's been calling almost daily. I gave in about the Fourth of July picnic, because practically everyone in town will be there. But I don't want to set David off again."

"Why does he dislike him so? They used to be friends."

"It has to do with something that happened a few years ago, when you were back East."

"Is it the reason you and Logan broke up?" Caitlin asked tentatively.

"Yes."

"I'm not prying, Meg. . . ."

"I know. I've never spoken about it to anyone, except David—and your father.

"There was a girl, a Mexican girl, about sixteen. She worked as a maid for Logan's mother. She used to come into the library all the time. She told me she wanted to learn English so she could read all the books on the shelves. Then she'd laugh like it was a big joke, but I knew she meant it.

"It seems she had a boyfriend, a lover, who was a gringo. That's all she'd say about him. I could tell she was crazy about him and wanted to please him.

"Late one evening at the library, she fainted and narrowly missed hitting her head on the corner of a shelf. I wanted to call the ranch and have Logan send someone for her, but she wouldn't let me.

"Anyway, to make a long story short, she rode a bicycle and was in an accident on the way home. It was hit and run. She died, and it turned out she was pregnant. They never found out who hit her."

"But what does all that—sad as it is—have to do with you and Logan?"

"David believes Logan was the father of Maria's child—and that he killed her."

"Oh, Meg! Why in the world does he think Logan would be capable of murder? Logan Carrington?"

"I don't know, Caity. He never explained. But apparently your father agreed with him. I felt so badly about that poor girl—I'd gotten to know her, and everything—so I let them convince me not to see Logan again."

"Dad never mentioned it to me," Caitlin murmured thoughtfully. But if her father had had something against Logan, it was good enough for her. Maybe it wasn't such a good idea for Meg to see the man again. "What are you going to do?"

"I'm not sure. I think I'll wait till the picnic. That's only two weeks away, and I can see how we both feel after that. How are you and Nick getting along?" she asked, changing the subject.

"I think I've fallen in love with him, Meg." The spontaneous revelation came as more of a surprise to her than to her friend; she hadn't realized she'd given up the battle against loving him.

"Caity! That's wonderful! I'm so happy for you. What about him? Does he feel the same?"

"It's complicated. There's a lot neither one of us is saying right now."

"Is it because of his past?"

"It's because he doesn't have a past—that he can remember." She sounded agitated. "I swear, sometimes I almost want to hit him over the head with something just to see if, when he wakes up he remembers. Only then I'm scared he will, and that he'll forget all about me."

"Oh, Caity. It'll work out—I know it will. I'll tell you what, we'll have a double wedding. You and Nick, and me and the first guy who comes along and sweeps me off my feet. Deal?"

"You idiot." Caitlin laughed, feeling better. "Go to work. I've got to get up and cook breakfast for two hungry men."

"Lucky you," Megan cooed derisively as she hung up.

The men came down for breakfast together, both looking as though they'd spent a restless night. Caitlin hadn't been sure what to expect from Nick, but the impersonal looks and polite rejoinders to her attempts at conversation hurt her beyond belief. Matt eyed them both furtively, feeling the building tension, and decided to make a hasty exit. Excusing himself as soon as possible, he carried his dishes to the sink and quietly left the house.

Nick sat toying with his food. He knew he should say something. But every time he looked at her, he saw her in his bed, tangled red hair spread wildly over his pillows, face soft and rosy from his lovemaking. And he couldn't get the words past his throat.

Caitlin sipped at her steaming coffee, eyeing with nausea the untouched mass of congealing food on her plate. He regretted making love to her. He didn't have to say it; she could read it in his averted eyes.

"Caitlin."

No, please, don't say it, she pleaded silently. Don't say anything. If you do, I'll break into a thousand tiny pieces and disappear.

His hand touched hers where it lay on the table, his fingers hot next to her icy flesh. "Yesterday... it was beautiful...."

Her startled eyes darted to his face, only to have her worse fears confirmed. There was sadness in his dark eyes, and another emotion, farther back, that she couldn't interpret.

"But?"

"But I have nothing to offer you."

"Have I asked you for anything?"

"No, not yet, but I'd want to give you things. Things like a name. One I knew was mine." Because even though he knew his real name, she didn't. And he couldn't tell her—not yet.

Her heart leaped at the words. A name? His name? And then she realized what he was really saying, and her spirits plummeted. He wasn't talking about marrying her, only about telling her who he really was. But she had to make him understand that her only concern was for him, not a nebulous past he might never remember.

"Nick, things don't matter, names don't matter, only people matter."

"They matter to me." He watched the light die out of her eyes. "I—I'm sorry." He wanted to tell her the truth, if only he knew it.

Caitlin pulled her hand from beneath his and stood. "I understand." Holding herself stiffly, she quietly left the room. She didn't see him clench his fist or hear the fervently whispered, "I wish to God *I* did!"

Caitlin made it to her room, shutting the door softly behind her, before completely breaking down. Oh, God, what was she going to do? She had fallen in love, really in love, and he didn't want her. He didn't care about a future with her; he cared only about the past. A past that didn't include her.

Throwing herself across the bed, she buried her face in the pillow in an attempt to stifle the harsh sounds of her weeping. It was happening again—all her life it had been the same. Every time she loved someone, one way or another they deserted her.

The loud bang of the outer door being slammed echoed throughout the house. The sound seemed to release the floodgate of her emotions, and Caitlin yielded to the compulsive sobs, harsh, racking sobs that tore her apart, letting them fill the room with her sorrow.

Nick stomped into the barn, curses falling from his lips, anger in every rigid line of his body. Matt, spreading fresh hay in the horse stalls, stopped to eye him warily.

"Trouble?" he asked.

Giving his friend a fulminating look, Nick picked up a shovel and began shoveling manure into the wheelbarrow. After a few minutes, sweat streaming down his face, a spear of pain stabbing his left shoulder, he stopped to lean dizzily against the shovel.

"Are you trying to kill yourself?" Matt asked in disgust.

"Just—butt out—Matt," Nick panted. "This—doesn't—concern you."

"Right!" Matt turned away. When he looked over his shoulder a few minutes later, he was alone.

Dinner was a disastrous meal. Caitlin, Nick, Matt and Megan sat around the kitchen table, avoiding each other's eyes, pretending to enjoy the simple, hearty food and ignoring all except the briefest of polite dinner conversation. Caitlin was astonished to see Megan and Matt take an apparently instant dislike to each other. When they addressed each other at all, there was veiled hostility in the simplest words.

Caitlin and Nick each pretended the other wasn't there, casting sidelong looks at each other when they thought no one was looking. If asked what they were eating, no one could have answered without checking first.

Later, as the women cleared the table, the two men waiting in the living room, Megan inquired softly, "What's wrong with you and Nick? I thought you were getting along so well."

"He has a conscience," Caitlin answered obscurely.

Since conversation appeared to be out, they tried a game or two of cards later. That didn't work, either. Megan accused Matt of cheating, and Matt accused her of being a paranoid female.

Nick paid no attention to anyone—except Caitlin. He was tempestuously aware of every breath she took. And when her knee accidentally brushed his under the table, it was like a jolt of high-powered electricity passing through his body. He almost leaped off his chair. Megan and Matt looked at him curiously, and Caitlin blushed in embarrassment. He'd recoiled as if her very touch repelled him.

The evening went steadily downhill from there. Fearing that her best friend and her newest hired hand might actually come to blows, Caitlin was thankful to see Megan falsely claim to have enjoyed the evening and make preparations to leave. Nick excused himself, saying he was tired, and went upstairs as soon as Megan was out the door. Matt stayed behind, despite Caitlin's protests, to help straighten up.

"It was a terrible dinner," she said, abruptly breaking the long silence.

"It was a great dinner," Matt contradicted.

"No." Emptying an ash tray, Caitlin shook her head. "It was awful—" Her voice broke, and she gulped hard, unable to stem the hot flow of tears sliding down her cheeks.

Somehow she was in his arms crying all over his broad chest. With uncertain hands, Matt patted her heaving shoulders awkwardly. He wasn't adept at holding distraught women while they cried, and especially not while they cried over another man. And that, he was sure, was what this was all about.

"Don't cry," he murmured. Mouthing comforting words he hadn't realized he'd known, he stroked her soft hair.

"I don't k-know what's w-wrong with m-me. I'm n-not normally a c-cry-baby," Caitlin hiccuped.

"Of course you're not." Matt rubbed her shoulders, wondering uneasily what he would do if she needed a handkerchief. He didn't carry one.

"I'm just so c-confused and m-miserable—"

"And tired," Matt added. "You've been on your feet all day working, cleaning and cooking. There's been a lot of excitement around here lately. I think you're not used to so much all at once. What you need is a good night's sleep."

"You think so?" Caitlin snuffled, raising her head to look up at him with eyes like rain-misted emeralds. Matt's arms tightened fractionally. Drew, you lucky devil, he thought, wondering what it would be like to have this woman crying over him. Just for a moment, he considered hauling his friend downstairs to show him his handiwork.

"I'm sure of it," he answered and, turning her out of his arms, led her toward the door. "Come on, there's nothing more to do in here. It's time you were in bed." He left her at her door after lightly touching one soft shoulder reassuringly.

Then he strolled thoughtfully into the living room, where he sat staring out the window, a cigarette dangling forgotten in his hand. After a time, he crushed it out in an ashtray and headed for the stairs.

* * *

The next day Nick decided to pay David Jones a visit once he finished his chores.

There was very little around the ranch that Matt or Caitlin would allow him to do until his shoulder was completely healed. Gathering the eggs from the boxlike nests in the long chicken house was one of them. And he enjoyed doing it. In the past, he'd always thought, if he thought about it at all, that eggs came from blue, pink or yellow Styrofoam cartons and were available only in the dairy section of the local grocery store. Now, bending down to a cluster of brown eggs, looking snug against the hay, Nick almost toppled over in surprise.

Where had that thought—that memory—come from? He could see pictures in his head. Long lines of groceries, a checkout stand, even the girl who worked the night shift at the twenty-four hour grocery he frequented, chewing her gum and studying her books in between customers.

She was working her way through college, she'd told him once when he'd asked, flirting with her a little, and that was why she worked nights. He always shopped at night because he hated the daytime crowds.

What else? his mind screamed. What else? But that was all; the pictures were gone. When he probed his memory, it was like feeling blindly along a blank wall in the dark. Just for a moment he'd found the door, opened it a crack, spilling light into the darkness, and then it had closed with a snap.

In frustration he drew the basket back in his hands, prepared to hurl it from him, then glanced up. Caitlin was watching him curiously from the doorway. Feeling like a fool, Nick lowered the basket.

"I was just gathering the eggs," he told her unnecessarily. The recent memory fading from his mind, he gazed at her with unconscious longing. In holey jeans and a faded T-shirt, the sun behind her creating a halo of fire around her head, she was the most alluring creature he'd ever seen.

"I didn't know you were here." She felt the need to explain that she hadn't been following him.

"I'm almost finished."

"Good." Their conversation had nothing to do with what their eyes were saying to each other.

"Nick," she murmured, catching her breath. Her skin tingled from the electrified feel of the air around them.

Nick took a step toward her, drawn by the sudden blaze in her eyes. He wanted her; the night they'd made love had only whetted his appetite for her. The past and all its connotations be damned, he wanted her. Wanted to pull the pins from her glorious hair, bury his face in its fire and let it bring warmth and light to his darkened soul.

He wanted her—and then he remembered. Caitlin could see it in his eyes as they became flat, hard, expressionless. He looked away.

"Here." Thrusting the basket into her nerveless fingers, he brushed past her and hurried outside, leaving her to stare after him with despairing eyes.

He needed to get away for a while. Needed some time alone to figure out what loving Caitlin would mean in his life. What if he never totally regained his memory? Would he—could he—give her up? And even if he did regain his memory, what about the life he led? Could he make a total commitment to her under the circumstances? How would she feel about him when she learned he was something totally different from what he appeared? Those were the things he considered on his way to take a look at what David Jones had in his possession, something so secret he'd had to hide it on someone else's property.

Exhausted by the time he reached the Jones house, trembling, gasping for air, he hid behind a boulder, leaning weakly against it to catch his breath. A sudden sound close by alerted him that he wasn't alone. Sinking down against the cover of the rock, he peered cautiously over its edge. It was Jones, carrying some strange looking gear, headed toward the boundary between his land and Caitlin's.

For a moment Nick was torn between following him and searching the house for the package Matt had seen. But the mystery of the hidden envelope intrigued him, and he was exhausted, so the decision was made before David disappeared completely from view.

After waiting until he was sure David wasn't coming back, he slid slowly from cover. The simplest form of entry turned out to be a window and, judging from the feminine decor, he knew he must be in Megan's room.

Once inside, he scanned the room with guilty curiosity, taking in the canopied bed and skirted vanity. He wasn't happy about sneaking into her home or prying into her personal belongings. But he couldn't help the curiosity he felt about the people who were closest to Caitlin.

He found David's room easily enough. It was at the back of the house, facing away from the drive to the road. Pushing the door open, he looked guardedly around. The room was sparsely furnished, almost stark in its simplicity.

There was no place to search, unless he looked under the bed, rifled the drawers or felt between the mattresses. And anything David felt the need to hide so carefully wouldn't be in such an obvious place. Besides, the idea of rifling the man's sock drawer was distasteful. For the first time the realization of what his life as an agent must have been like really hit him. Poking into other people's possessions, prying into their lives, plotting, pretending, winning their confidence, perhaps even their friendship and loyalty, and then using it for your own ends. Using it to betray and possibly destroy them. He felt sick to his stomach.

The justification, of course, was in the knowledge that these people were criminals, drug peddlers, gunrunners—murderers—people who trafficked in human misery. But standing here, staring at David Jones's private sanctum, the knowledge didn't make him feel any better. He couldn't get past the fact that the people living in this house were vulnerable, had lived through their own personal tragedies—and they were the closest thing to a family Caitlin had.

He had almost convinced himself to leave the room, and the house, when his eyes settled on a door. It was set back almost in the corner of the room, beside the six-drawer chest, and at first glance he had dismissed it as a bathroom. But something forced him to cross the room and open the door.

A string dangling from the middle of the ceiling brushed his face as he stepped through the narrow aperture. Nick pulled it, flooding the small windowless room with bright yellow light.

"Well I'll be damned." He whistled shortly. David Jones was an enigma. Gun collector, war hero, expert tracker—photographer? And now he realized what he had seen David hauling with him minutes earlier. Photography equipment.

The small darkroom was about the size of a walk-in closet and was set up with everything necessary to develop pictures. As in the other room, everything appeared neat and orderly.

Three large, rectangular plastic trays sat on the long counter lining one wall. Each was labeled differently: developer, stop, hypo. Nick didn't know a lot about photography, but he recognized some of the equipment from his recent studies. The gray metal thing that reminded him of a microscope was an enlarger. The small red light over the double stainless steel sink was called a safelight, and would provide the only light while David was printing the pictures.

Opening the cabinets overhead, he found a film storage area, and in the cabinets below were large white plastic jugs of chemicals. Wire was strung across one side of the room, with clothespins attached to it. He figured that was where David hung the prints to dry. The wires were currently bare.

It was strange; the setup here looked professional, as though David really knew what he was doing. Why, he asked himself, hadn't Caitlin mentioned such an obviously well-developed interest? Perhaps it just hadn't occurred to her, or perhaps it was an interest she knew nothing about.

A tall metal filing cabinet sitting by itself in the corner of the room drew his attention. There were no pictures, no negatives in evidence; this was the obvious place for them to be stored.

The first three drawers opened easily. The negatives, inserted in clear paper envelopes, had been placed in labeled folders according to category. Some were only dated; others had names as well as dates. Mostly they were pictures of wildlife, probably taken on David's own property. Then Nick began to notice something they all had in common. All the pictures had been taken at night with an infrared lens. The negatives showed a lot of white and very little dark. The printed pictures would be just the opposite. It seemed David Jones only practiced his hobby, if that was what it was, after dark.

Nick squatted down before the last drawer. This one was locked. He searched for the key, but it was nowhere to be found. What he did find was a small pointed paper knife, and with a little jiggling, he managed to open the drawer.

At first he thought it was empty and wondered why Jones found it necessary to lock an empty drawer. Then his nimble fingers located a loose panel and a false bottom. And, taped to the bottom, a large square manila envelope. All thumbs, thoughts buzzing around like angry bees in his head, he lifted the envelope and bent back the metal clasp, spilling three eight-by-ten glossies into his shaking hand.

"So that's it," he muttered. There was no need for an explanation. The pictures were clearly labeled with dates, times,

names and brief captions. He stared at a picture of two men.
He recognized one, and although the face of the other was unfamiliar, he knew the name. Almost before he could compre-
hend what he was seeing, a voice jerked him around.

"So, we meet again."

As he twisted around, Nick's eyes swerved automatically to
the snub-nosed .38 special pointed at his gut.

"There's no need for that, unless you're the one who tried to
kill me a few months back. But then, you wouldn't have sent
for the FBI if that was the case, now would you?"

David Jones relaxed his rigid stance and dropped the barrel
of the gun toward the floor.

"So it was you they sent."

"Yeah," Nick answered, relieved to see the gun move away.

"How come you didn't let me know who you were before
now?" David asked curiously.

"I didn't know who I was until a little while ago myself.
Somebody tried to kill me, and in the process I lost my memory."

David shook his head. "We're both in deep trouble." He
took the pictures from Nick and looked at them for a moment. Then he nodded toward the one with the two men, "They
know I informed on them, and they know you're back.
That—" he nodded to Nick's injured shoulder "—is a mistake they won't make again. I figured it was you the night that
happened.

"I was there, at Caity's house. I spoke to her just afterward. She accused me of doing the shooting, but I finally convinced her I hadn't. I didn't see who fired the shot, but I saw the
flash where it came from—the area where the old ranch house
stands."

She hadn't mentioned David's presence; such loyalty to her
friends only made him admire her more.

"What I want to know is, why you didn't speak up the other
day when Matt and I came to your house?"

"Scared," David mumbled. Then, louder, "I was scared. For
all I knew then, you could have been one of them. And that FBI
badge could have been fake, or taken off the real agent—after
his death.

"I been expecting them to make a move against me every day
the last few months. I don't know how, but they know I'm the
one who spilled the beans.

"I'd have kept my mouth shut till hell freezes over if it were only their little war games. But drugs . . ." He shook his curly dark head. "I saw what drugs did to the GIs in Vietnam. The people who sell that garbage are scum."

"So what happened to you? Did we meet or not?" Nick asked curiously, referring to the rendezvous they were supposed to have had months ago.

"I arrived early. Something told me it was going to be bad. When I got there, the place was already staked out. I hid and waited for you to arrive, but you never showed—I figured you'd been expecting to find the place crawling with men anxious to get me in their rifle sights.

"But it was quiet here—too quiet. The next day I started finding dead animals, their bodies mutilated, all over my property. I didn't have to wonder why. They were letting me know what was in store for me—soon, but not just yet. They wanted to make me sweat a little first, let me worry about Caity.

"That's why I've been keeping an eye on Caity's place at night. I been doing that for a long time now, since just after her father died. He knew about the survivalists and their leader, and he didn't trust the man an inch."

David laid the gun down and revealing picture on the top of the dresser and motioned for Nick to precede him out of the room. "Come on, I'll make us some coffee."

David took up his story as he ran water into a glass pot and then poured it into the top of a coffee maker. "I don't sleep much at night. I haven't been able to since coming home from Vietnam. So at night I began to go out under cover of darkness and take pictures. There was a doctor at the VA hospital who got me interested in photography.

"It was during one of those nights I stumbled across the two men you saw in the photos checking out their cache of guns and drugs. You've met one, the other is the leader. Until then, I'd figured as long as the survivalists let me alone, I wouldn't bother them. But I overheard a conversation that night that made me curious, and when everyone had gone, I crept down to the storage shed where I'd seen the two men and had a look. That's when I called Washington."

"Can you show me where this storage shed is?"

"Sure, but it won't do any good. The stuff is gone. A few days after that night we were supposed to meet, I took a chance and made my way back there. I don't know what I had in mind—burning the stuff, maybe.'' He shrugged. ''It doesn't matter, because it was all gone.''

''Damn!'' Nick slapped his hand against the table.

''Yeah, and I haven't been able to find the stuff since. Sometimes I still search, but I have to take it real careful—and I don't like leaving Caity alone too long.''

Nick took a sip of his coffee and nodded. ''Maybe we could get you some help. Maybe if we had a couple dozen men searching, we could come up with something. If we don't find it, we've got no case.''

''Maybe not,'' David answered, narrowing his eyes on his cup before looking up at Nick from under hooded lids. ''I overheard a couple of interesting facts on my nightly trips. There's a large shipment coming over the border soon—guns and drugs. But I'm not sure when, or where the hiding place will be.''

Caitlin and Matt were clipping chicken wings when Sheriff Raymond arrived early that afternoon. Matt had balked at the idea until Caitlin had explained that if they didn't clip the feathers in the hens' wings, they would fly over the fence and lay their eggs where she would never be able to find them. Even then, it was necessary to reassure him frequently that though the chickens squawked and generally put up quite a fuss, they were not in fact being hurt.

''Afternoon, Caity.'' The sheriff spoke to her, but eyed the man.

''Sheriff,'' she replied, continuing to work.

''You're new around here, ain't you?'' he asked Matt.

''Yeah, I am. Been looking for work in this area for a while.''

''That right? How'd you happen to find work here? I thought Caity already had a hired hand.''

''Bart, you know Nick can't do much right now,'' Caitlin put in. ''Matt's a big help. So don't try to run him off with your tough guy act.''

''Now, honey, you know I'm only concerned for your welfare.''

''It's for my welfare he's here, otherwise I'd have all this work to do alone,'' she told him in exasperation.

''But two strange men, Caity, and you all alone—''

"Damnit! I can take care of myself!" She nearly resorted to childishly stomping her feet.

"How'd you know she needed help? You just...happen along?" Bart persisted, once more directing his attention to the man.

"No, sir. I happened along before she needed help."

The sheriff cocked one dark brow, stuck his booted foot on the first rung of the gate and rested his elbow in a relaxed pose on his thigh. "How's that again?" he asked with interest.

"Matt came by looking for work and met Nick. Nick explained the situation at the time, and they became friends. He happened to come by just after Nick got hurt. That's the whole story. Now, anymore questions, Sheriff? Or can we get back to work?" Caitlin asked impertinently. You would think he was her guardian or something, the way he acted.

"Well, that sure sounds lucky for you, honey. Here I was thinking old Fred's boy was out here every day and feelin' guilty 'cause I'd sent him, when his dad needs help real bad right now." His piercing gaze bored into Matt's gray eyes.

"Then I guess it's lucky you came by, Bart, 'cause you can rest easy now, knowing I have help and young Fred is on his dad's place where he belongs," Caitlin told him too sweetly.

"Where you from?" Bart ignored Caitlin.

"Down around Austin," Matt replied, wondering if Raymond gave everybody new around town the third degree.

"Austin, huh? I know a few people around Austin—what did you say your name was?"

"I didn't. It's Matt—Matt Frazier."

"Uh-huh. You know this Rivers character before he showed up around here?"

"No, no, I didn't," Matt lied blithely without batting an eyelash.

"Where were you about a week ago?"

Feeling uncomfortable, Matt wasn't sure just how much he should say; he looked toward Caitlin before answering.

"He was staying in the old ranch house. Why? Do you suspect him of something, Sheriff?" It wasn't only her hair that was blazing at the moment.

"Now, Caity, there's no need to go gettin' all hostile on me. It's my job to ask questions. That's what you all pay me for."

Caitlin stared into his guileless eyes and backed down, the rigidity slowly leaving her body. He was right; she was getting upset over nothing.

"I'm sorry, Bart. You're right, it *is* your job, and I know Matt has nothing to hide." She didn't see the ironic light in the gray eyes he turned on her. "Maybe it's the heat getting to me." Wiping an arm across her face, dislodging a few stray feathers stuck to her cheek, she asked, "How about a glass of iced tea? Matt and I could use the break."

"That's real thoughtful of you, honey. I sure could use a cold glass about now."

"Come on, then. You all sit on the porch and get acquainted while I fix the tea." Caitlin led the way to the house.

"Where's Rivers?" the sheriff was asking, as Caitlin backed out the screen door carrying a tray with a pitcher and three tall frosty glasses.

"He went for a walk," Caitlin said, forestalling any answer Matt might make. The truth was, neither of them knew where he'd gone. They hadn't seen him since before lunch, when he'd left Caitlin in the chicken house.

"M-m-m, good tea." Bart smacked his lips, wiping the moisture from them with the back of one beefy hand.

"Thank you," Caitlin acknowledged politely, if a little dryly, while Matt murmured his quiet agreement. "You ever find out anything about the shooting, Sheriff?"

"Naw, not really." Bart relaxed back against the lawn chair, crossing one ankle over the other as if prepared to sit a while and pass the time. "I did get over and talk to Megan and David though."

"Oh?" She hoped she was hiding her nervousness at the mention of David's name. Even though she hadn't managed to find David at home and get the chance to discuss that night with him, she was confident of his innocence.

"Seems neither one of 'em can really alibi the other. They were both in their own room all evening, didn't see each other the whole time."

"You can't tell me you suspect Megan—that's ridiculous!"

Matt swung his gaze to Caitlin's flushed, indignant face. Did she realize how conspicuous the lack of David's name was in her protest?

"Now, I ain't accusin' anybody, honey. I just got to ask the questions. Besides, I thought we'd pretty well established it was a stray bullet from a hunter's rifle that found your man," he added consolingly.

The man was good, all right, Matt conceded. He asked just the right questions and made insinuations right and left without actually accusing anybody of anything. But unless he was way off mark, the man hadn't missed Caitlin's glaring omission. Just what, he speculated, did that omission signify?

And what was the real purpose behind the sheriff's visit?

Nick had plenty to tell Matt that evening as he walked through the chores at his friend's side.

"So it was Jones. I guess we'd better get some men out here to help us find the stuff," Matt said, unknowingly repeating Nick's own idea.

Stopping to light a cigarette, he looked up at the night sky in a way reminiscent of how Nick had the first night he spent on the ranch.

"It seems like old times," he said.

Nick stopped beside him, hands in his pockets, shoulders back, face turned upward as he contemplated the big and little dippers. He recognized their familiar pattern with a tiny thrill. His memory was coming back a little at a time, just as Caitlin had said the doctor in town had predicted. He wished he could tell her, could share the excitement with her. But it was too soon. For her safety, he had to keep his silence a while longer.

A few minutes later, Matt dropped the cigarette butt and ground it under his heel.

"Let's keep Caity out of this as much as possible. It's going to be a rude shock when she learns people she knows are involved in smuggling and murder," Nick said. "You'd better go over to Jones's later tonight and call about getting some field agents out here, otherwise Caity might hear."

Matt nodded and followed him up to the porch, where they could smell the mouth-watering aroma of freshly baked bread and pot roast coming from the open back door.

Chapter 13

This summer was going to be another scorcher. Though it was only the end of June, the temperatures hadn't dropped below the hundred-degree mark for the past seven days. If the weather didn't break soon, Caitlin was afraid she would.

It didn't help that for the past couple days the two men had seemed to shut her out, disappearing frequently without a word of explanation. It wasn't that they shirked their work, only that she felt so isolated from them. Their heads were together constantly, and if she entered a room the conversation stopped, or one would immediately start up about some innocuous topic. It was driving her quietly insane.

The really strange part was that, despite their predilection for disappearing, if she decided to go someplace, one of them would pop up seemingly from out of nowhere to accompany her. And invariably it was Matt. Nick continued to maintain the aloofness he'd worn since the day they made love.

And that, too, was driving her around the bend. But somehow she knew that if she was patient she would break through his protective shield and reach the caring man she'd found once before.

Matt had gone off on one of his mysterious trips after asking to borrow the truck, and Nick was somewhere upstairs. The air crackled with a tense, waiting quality, as though any minute something would happen. It hadn't rained in a while, and Caitlin knew the unnatural stillness in the air around her meant a storm was imminent.

Wandering around the living room, the afternoon heat too intense to do any real work, she switched on the TV.

Time sped by unnoticed, and the room darkened while she stared at the set, not really seeing the program. A resounding crash jerked her back to an awareness of her surroundings. Thunder? The sound came again, accompanied immediately by a low rumbling noise and the soft irregular patter of rain on the roof.

She jumped from the chair and hurried to the door. It was indeed raining, the soft sporadic sounds giving over to a strident deluge. Smiling, she opened the door and stepped out onto the porch, her nostrils filling with the scent of rain. Lightning fluttered in the distance, and wind whipped at the trees, swirling through the branches and causing the leaves to dance madly.

Moving off the porch, down the steps and into the yard, Caitlin held her face aloft, eyes closed, allowing the rain to partially soothe away her unhappiness. She had always loved the rain, and she had walked and played in it often as a child.

From his upstairs window, Nick looked on in disbelief. Was she crazy? Didn't she realize thunderstorms were dangerous? A jagged streak of lightning split the sky, followed immediately by a booming clap of thunder. Nick's gut twisted with fear for her. There was enough danger in their lives; Caitlin didn't need to go looking for more.

Events were quickly coming to a head, and each day the danger drew nearer. He and Matt had agreed that the one vulnerable link in their chain was Caitlin, so they kept a guard on her at all times.

He'd put her life in jeopardy, albeit unknowingly at first, just by staying on the ranch. And if that wasn't enough, he'd somehow managed to ensnare her emotions, as well. She had given him more than a job and shelter, and he was repaying her with danger and deceit.

If the time ever came when they could again be together in the most intimate sense of the word, it would have to be a time when he was able to come to her as a whole person, a time after she was apprised of his real identity and his deceit—or not at all.

Lightning darted across the sky again, and the house shook, windows rattling with the resulting thunder. His introspection diverted, Nick's glance sharpened on the woman cavorting like a wood nymph through the storm. Pounding on the glass, he yelled at her, telling her to get inside and out of danger. But she couldn't hear him above the voice of the storm. Exasperated, frightened for her, he bolted from the room, down the stairs and out into the yard. When he caught her, he promised himself, he would shake her till her teeth rattled.

Drenched to the skin, feeling more alive than she had for days, Caitlin reveled in the rain, blissfully unaware of the wrath about to descend upon her head. Lifting her arms above her head, she whirled around and around, laughing in sheer delight.

"What the hell do you think you're doing?" His words reached her only seconds before hard hands grasped her rain-slick shoulders, shaking her into a gasping silence. The sudden shock of his angry presence held her spellbound for an instant before she yielded quickly to fury.

"Take your hands off me," she spat at him, jerking in his hold.

"Do you know what you're doing? Don't you realize how dangerous an electrical storm can be?" His curt voice lashed at her, his face a glowering mask of rage.

"I don't need you to tell me what I can or cannot do." She flashed him a cold look of disdain. All her carefully hidden hurt and resentment came out in the look.

"Well, somebody needs to, since you obviously don't know enough to get in out of the rain." His dark gaze swept over her in contempt. The unrestrained wrath of the storm seeped into his veins, the thunder and lightning becoming a part of his fury. Wind whipped at their wet clothing, pulled the pins from Caitlin's hair, wrapped the trailing wet strands around her neck, slapping them across his angry face.

Caitlin shivered, aware of how her clothes clung revealingly to her body. Shaking the rain-plastered hair from her forehead, she pulled away from his unresisting hands and crossed her arms protectively over her body. Involuntarily, her eyes traveled down the wet shirt hugging his broad chest like a second skin to the threadbare jeans delineating every muscle of his lower body.

A slow flush started low, quickly spreading to her face. Closing her eyes to block out the provocative sight of him, she turned her head away, embarrassed by her thoughts.

Nick, hands resting on her shoulders, felt her tremble. He slid his hands down over her arms, still crossed against her breasts, and applied gentle pressure to draw them from her body. His thought was to take her hand and lead her from the storm. He tried hard to keep his eyes from lowering to the front of her wet T-shirt, but it was like trying to take food from a starving man. Her taut nipples stood erect, inviting his glance, the dusky aureola plain against the loving drape of her shirt. He wondered if she had deliberately left off wearing a bra recently to taunt him with her beauty.

The hands at her wrists tightened, thumbs moving in slow caressing circles. Caitlin's eyes shot open, her glance slamming into his. What had happened to his anger? Her heart in her mouth, her whole being filled with a waiting stillness, she watched his simmering glance glide slowly down her body. Pulse hammering, senses spinning, she endured the purely sensual appraisal.

Voice quivering, he whispered her name. As the rain soaked his ebony hair, running like tears down his lean cheeks, dripping off his nose and chin, Caitlin felt the urge to stand on her toes and touch her tongue to the moisture, tasting him through the rain.

His face drew nearer, hovered for a brief span of time, then descended, but Caitlin's hands went swiftly to his shirtfront, bunching the material in her grasp, holding him off.

"Don't do this to me, Nick, not again, not unless you mean it—really mean it. I can't take your blowing first hot and then cold."

"I mean it, Caity." His warm breath fanned her lips. "I always meant it." All his noble thoughts about keeping them apart were swept away by his longing to have her again in his arms.

As though his words were a key releasing her bonds, she flung herself against him. He hauled her, weightless, into his arms.

Heart skyrocketing, Caitlin buried her face against the pulse throbbing in his throat. Blood coursed through her veins like a runaway train. Only in his embrace did she feel this exhilaration.

Stepping carefully, ankle deep in black mud, her arms wound tightly around his neck, Nick carried her toward the house.

The loud report was audible even above the sounds of the storm. Nick jerked to a standstill, his head held alertly erect, eyes searching the surrounding area.

"What is it?" Caitlin asked quickly in alarm.

Setting her on her feet, Nick grabbed her hand, cautioned her to stay low and darted swiftly across the field, puffs of mud and grass kicking up along their path. The closest building was the barn. Nick veered toward it, pulling Caitlin along in his wake. A bullet whizzed past his head so close that he swore silently; he had felt the heat of its passing.

"What's happening? Is someone shooting at us?" Caitlin asked between gasps. The barn seemed to her eyes to be getting farther away.

"Later—I'll explain later—just run—"

A bullet splintered the red-painted wood inches above Nick's hand as he shoved the door open and pulled Caitlin to safety. He slammed the heavy door and barred it behind them.

"My God! Someone really is shooting at us. Why?"

"It's a long story. Get over there in one of the empty stalls." He pointed behind her right shoulder while he moved quickly toward the back of the barn. Caitlin, ignoring his directive, followed on hands and knees, watching as he barred that door, as well.

"Explain! Tell me what this is all about! I have a right to know," she whispered, nose to nose with him as he swung away from the door.

"Be still! How the hell can I protect you when you won't do as I tell you? And I can't hear anyone outside if you're going to screech in my ear."

"Screech?" she screeched. "I don't screech!" Whirling around, still on hands and knees, she scrambled away.

Huddling in a corner, cold and frightened and angry, Caitlin peered into the shadowy depths. Unable to judge time, she had no idea how long she sat. Long enough for her limbs to stiffen and her wet clothes to chill her clammy skin, long enough for her anger to blot out anything but their narrow escape and to speculate about the person behind the attack.

"Caity." Nick's voice reached her in a loud whisper. "Where are you?"

"Here," she called to him. "I'm here."

His big frame blocked out what little light there was in the doorway, and then he crawled over to join her.

"Are they gone?" she asked. The noise he made scrabbling around for a comfortable spot sounded loud in the stillness.

"Maybe. What I'm really worried about is Matt. We're safe enough here for now, unless they come barreling in with a tractor or a truck. It's too wet to burn the barn. But Matt could walk right into an ambush," he added darkly.

Caitlin gasped at the idea, at the cold matter-of-fact tone of his voice. This was a Nick totally unlike the man she'd come to know and deeply care for.

"A-ambush?" she echoed. "You mean like on TV and in the movies kind of ambush?"

"Yes, Caity," he answered slowly. "That kind exactly." There was a new tone in his voice that she didn't recognize, a hardness she'd never heard before.

"Who? Why? This is no stray bullet from a hunter's rifle now." At his lack of an answer, she drew herself up on her knees, peering at him through the gloom. An indefinable tension had taken sudden hold of her body. But it was nothing like the sexual tension she experienced whenever Nick was in close proximity.

"Th-there *was* no hunter—was there?" Thrusting her face toward his, she demanded, "Answer me. Was there a hunter or not? Was your shooting an accident?"

"No."

The soft murmur only confirmed what she already suspected. Like a puppet whose strings had been abruptly severed, she dropped back, huddling once more in her corner.

"Who are you?" she asked in a small voice.

"My name is Andrew Rivers. I'm a special agent with the FBI." His tones were as devoid of feeling as he could make them. Unpalatable revelations would sound just as unpalatable couched in any terms.

"FBI? You mean I've had an FBI agent living in my home, eating at my table, sleeping in my be—" Horrified, her voice broke off.

"It isn't what you think."

"No? And you know what I'm thinking? Along, of course, with what's good for me—like not standing in the rain—" Her voice rose alarmingly. "It isn't healthy to stand in a thunderstorm, but it's perfectly all right to be a target for someone with a rifle. I'm afraid I fail to see your logic.''

"Caity, please, listen to me—let me explain. Matt and I have been protecting you—"

"Protecting me," she interrupted. "This is how you protect someone? By getting them shot at? I've never needed protection until now—not until I had the misfortune to meet you.

"What a fool I am." She laughed without humor. "I was actually taken in by your performance—first you were a retarded bum, and then a poor unfortunate with a case of amnesia. You're good, very good. You deserve an Oscar. I've never seen a performance to rival yours—" She gulped down a sob and asked abruptly, "Are you married—or anything?" She had to know.

"No."

She gave a small sigh and sagged a little farther into her corner. She wasn't a highly religious person, but it relieved her to know she hadn't been making love to another woman's husband. She'd thought she could handle that guilt if it ever became necessary, but she was glad she wouldn't have to.

"You don't understand . . ." Nick continued his explanation after a slight pause.

"No, I don't, but you're going to explain it to me," she told him coldly. "Starting with why you're here and who Matt is."

"Matt's another agent. We're partners—"

"You mean that was an act, too? You knew him before you met—or whatever—here?"

"Yes, apparently we've known each other since college. We were assigned this operation together."

"Operation?"

"Yeah, I guess there isn't any reason to keep you in the dark any longer."

"No, I don't suppose so. It's rather hard to hide the fact that someone wants to kill me," she agreed sarcastically.

"It wasn't you they were after, or only indirectly."

"Well, now that makes me feel better already."

"Be quiet! Damnit, you wanted to know it all, so just shut up and listen." Hands clenched, jaw set, he turned his head away from her. It was killing him; she was never going to believe he hadn't been using her from the start. Why did this have to happen just when he'd decided nothing was more important than their being together?

Caitlin breathed slowly in the sudden silence, holding herself tightly in check. If she let go, just the least bit, she knew she would lose it completely.

"I was sent here to make contact with a person who had information about a man heading the largest survivalist group in the United States."

"Survivalists?"

"Yes. People who believe that eventually Russia and the U.S. will go to war. They intend to pick up the pieces when it's all over. They're trained in all kinds of survival techniques. They store food, guns, medicine, equipment—anything and everything they think they'll need when the end comes. They also learn to survive on what will be left afterward."

Caitlin shivered. "They sound paranoid."

"Perhaps. Who knows what motivates people like that? Maybe the majority truly believe in what they're doing. Of course, as with most things, there are the fanatics, the crooks, the users, who believe in one thing and one thing only—money, plenty of it, any way they can get it.

"The group we're after has a less pure motive than survival. Their motivation is greed. They get money from the sale of illegal drugs and guns."

"And you really think a group like that could be around here?" she asked incredulously. "That's impossible. We'd all know about it. They couldn't possibly hide an organization of that size without the people around here finding out."

"Their existence has been known for quite some time. We didn't pinpoint the town of Fate until recently, but the company has been keeping an eye on North Texas for a long time. We just never knew who the leader was—until now."

A long silence followed his revelations. Eventually she asked in a hollow voice, "How do you know all this?"

"David Jones has known about the survivalists since he was in high school. Logan Carrington and his father started the group. After his father's death, Logan carried on without him. But he's more interested in money than in ideals.

"One night, while he was taking wildlife pictures, Jones stumbled across Carrington and his partner unloading a shipment of guns and drugs. He got pictures, and when he was sure of what was happening, he got hold of the FBI. That's how I came to be in Fate. Unfortunately, somehow Carrington or his partner discovered my real identity and tried to kill me. The result was what showed up that first day on your ranch. Apparently I'd been wandering around for the past few months not knowing who I was or anything else until you found me and eventually figured out what was wrong. I guess Carrington must have eventually worked out for himself who I was, and that shot I took in the shoulder was the result."

They both heard it at the same time, the sound of a vehicle coming to a stop, then the slam of a door. Nick was up like a shot, slipping on the hay, falling to his knees, regaining his feet all in one continuous move, while bellowing at the top of his voice, "Matt! Ambush! Stay down, man—take cover!"

Crawling slowly from her hiding place, Caitlin peeked around the edge of a stall. Nick had the barn door open a few inches, his face pressed to the crack. Nick? That wasn't his real name. Andrew. Could she ever get used to calling him that? No, he'd become Nick to her, and Nick he would always be.

A loud report from close by caused the hair to stand up on Caitlin's arms and the back of her neck. Someone was shooting at Matt. God, this was real. There was someone outside who wanted to shoot them—kill them.

Matt stumbled from the truck and ran in a serpentine fashion toward Nick. "So they've finally come out into the open, partner? Looks like we've got a fight on our hands," Matt said, panting as he slid inside the barn.

The next two hours were the most terrifying and nerve-racking of Caitlin's entire life. She would never forget crawling on hands and knees through the mud, knowing that at any moment a shot could ring out, tearing through cloth and flesh, shattering bone and sinew, bringing pain and death.

They left the barn single file, under cover of darkness, with Matt in the lead. Not a sound was heard from the man, or men, who had shot at them. If anyone was still hiding in the wet blackness, they managed to sneak past them without mishap.

Knees bruised and stinging, hands scraped raw, feeling like a pincushion from the burrs and nettles she'd picked up, head reeling, certain half her hair had been torn out by the roots and left hanging on tree branches, she arrived at the Jones ranch, their only hope for shelter. Here, too, Caitlin crouched in the mud, waiting while the men scouted out the house and decided it was safe.

Megan met her at the door and pulled her inside. David had told her what was going on two days earlier, when strange men, agents, had begun showing up at their house under cover of darkness. Words tumbling over each other, she had asked questions without waiting for answers. Now, offering comfort, she led Caitlin toward her bedroom.

Caitlin's last sight of Nick was over her shoulder, his gaze meeting hers with an unreadable light before he turned away.

"You think our sniper will have guessed where we've gone?" Nick asked Matt while they changed into dry clothing provided by David.

Caitlin and Megan were somewhere in another part of the house. In an attempt to protect them from needless alarm, the men had silently agreed to discuss this night's events alone.

"He might. He's wily enough. What worries me is if he decides to follow us here. He has access to enough firepower to blow this house off the face of the earth," Matt answered.

"He won't do that. Too many questions to be answered if he did. He may have friends in high places, but some things can't be covered up without involving a whole lot more people than is safe. You've heard the old adage 'Loose lips sink ships.' Too many people mean too big a chance of the wrong thing slipping out."

David entered the room with three mugs of steaming coffee. He and Matt had met several times in the past several days while working out strategic ways of searching Logan Carrington's numerous holdings in the area without arousing his suspicion or getting caught by any of his survivalist lieutenants.

"It's too bad Carrington moved his stash. If we could have gone in and gotten it right away, all we would have had to do was get one of his men to talk a little. Then we could have been waiting when the big shipment he's expecting comes in," Matt said.

"I think he moved it when he got word that Rivers was back. Even if he knew about the amnesia, he couldn't take the chance of him waking up one morning and suddenly remembering everything.

"I think he's biding his time, waiting for this latest shipment. Once it arrives and his deal is made, he'll be beyond our reach.

"From what I saw, with the stuff in that shed alone, he could outfit a small army. I think he moved everything so no one—

and I mean no one—knows where the stuff is but him," David finished meaningfully.

"You mean in case his partner gets any ideas of his own?" Matt clarified.

"That too. But remember, no evidence, no crime," David continued. "Even if Logan knew about the pictures I took, pictures have been doctored before. I think his only worry at the moment is keeping his merchandise out of anyone else's hands. He'll have time to dispose of Rivers or anyone else, after he's made his deal." He looked significantly at the other two men.

"What you're saying doesn't bode well for his partner," Nick said.

David shrugged. "They deserve each other. What I don't understand is why he came after you and involved Caity—unless it was to get back at her father. In all the time I've been watching her house, expecting something like this, he's never made a move in her direction."

"I guess he couldn't be sure what I might have told her. Maybe he wanted to scare me a little—see if I was faking the amnesia. See if I'd come after him."

"When did you say the big shipment is due out of Mexico?" Matt asked David.

"From what I overheard, any day now."

The same thought struck all three simultaneously.

"The Fourth of July," Matt said. "The perfect time to load the trucks and move everything to its final destination without anyone noticing. From what I understand, the whole town turns out for Carrington's big bash."

"That's right," David confirmed. "The picnic lasts most of the day. Then there's the carnival, set up especially for the occasion, that gets going about midafternoon. The barbecue and the fireworks finish the day off after dark."

"So we have two days to find the stuff," Matt said, spelling out what all three of them knew.

Hiding a yawn behind his hand, listening to the other two theorize, Nick wondered what Caitlin was doing. She was probably in bed asleep after her ordeal. He had to admire her spirit. Confused and angry as she had been, not once had she complained during the trek from her house, a trip that made him shudder when he recalled their vulnerability.

He'd had one heck of a lucky stroke the day he stumbled onto her ranch looking for a drink. He hoped he had the opportunity to tell her how proud he was of her. Right now she didn't trust him, wasn't talking to him, thought he had played her for a fool. She didn't believe the amnesia was for real, and maybe he should just let her continue believing he was a bastard. That might make it easier if he had to leave her.

Caitlin lay snugly in bed, trying to forget the last few hours. Naturally, the more she tried to ignore them, the clearer the pictures became in her head.

Rolling onto her side, Caitlin wondered what Nick—or should she call him Andrew?—was doing. She couldn't, no matter how she tried, picture him as an FBI agent. The idea seemed ludicrous. Those men were hard, unfeeling, gun-toting robots, their feelings and beliefs a reflection of company policy, with no room for individualism—or humanity.

Nick wasn't like that. His feelings were real, human. He was gentle, caring—how could he shoot someone?

It was no use. She couldn't sleep. Throwing aside the covers, she climbed from the bed. What she needed was a drink of water.

On tiptoe, she crept from the bedroom. Treading softly, she moved into the living room. A light was burning in the room across the hall from Megan's bedroom. It was the den. Uncertain of what possessed her to do it, she crept closer and, with gentle fingers, pushed the door open and tiptoed inside, shutting the door quietly behind her. A blanketed figure lay on the divan, feet hanging over the edge, face turned toward the wall.

"Matt, is that you?" she whispered softly, moving closer. The soft light from the desk lamp that had been left on didn't reach across the room where the figure lay enshrouded in gloom.

In a flash the covers were thrown aside and her wrist was captured in a punishing hold.

"Do you usually creep around half-naked in the middle of the night looking for Matt?" Nick's voice grated harshly on her ears.

"I wasn't looking for anyone," she answered indignantly, pulling at her wrist. "And I'm not half-naked," she added after a moment. The blue cotton nightie belonged to Megan, who was half a head shorter, but it still struck the top of her thighs, decently covering her, she reasoned.

His eyes traveled the length of her, bringing a flush of color to her pale cheeks. When their glances met once more, the spark in his had reached blazing proportions. But it was desire she read there now, not anger.

"Are you still angry with me?"

"Shouldn't I be? You've had ample opportunity to tell me the truth, explain what happened to you. You could at least have told me you were regaining your memory," she finished in a thin voice.

"I'm sorry." When she moved to turn away, obviously not accepting his apology, his temper sparked again. It was frustration, he knew, making him so short-tempered, and fear for her. They still weren't out of the woods, not by a long shot.

"I'm trying to explain, if you'll stay and listen." He grabbed at the hem of her gown.

Goose bumps rippled down the backs of both legs at the touch of his warm fingers on her skin. She wanted to give in; she wanted to let him hold her. She wanted to hold him, to reassure herself that he was all right, that everything would be all right in the future. A future they would share together? He hadn't mentioned any long-term arrangements, except maybe, she allowed herself to hope, that one time when he'd mentioned sharing a name—his name—with her.

She shivered again, but this time it was with a chill brought on by the realization that he had probably known his name at that time and lied to her.

"I'm going back to bed—"

Her words were cut off beneath his mouth, as, with a jerk and a deft move, he had her flat on the couch, lying partially beneath his nearly naked body. She tried to resist him—was determined to. She held her lips tightly closed, her head stiff. Her arms, though trapped between them, pushed against his hair-matted chest. She chose to ignore the tide of feeling his hard hand generated as it moved under her gown, skimming her hips and thighs.

"No!" She managed to wrench her throbbing lips from his, her eyes sparking green fire.

"Yes," he whispered deeply. As he nuzzled her soft cheek and smooth neck, his hands moved seductively on her body. "Yes," he breathed against her cheek before gently covering her mouth.

Caitlin was shocked at the instant flaring of her senses, the eager desire to respond to his hands and lips. He'd lied to her. He'd put her life in danger—but oh, could he kiss. Excitement sang through her veins, stole the breath from her lungs, painted pictures in her mind. Slowly, reluctantly, she parted her lips, allowed him entry, succumbed to the powerful seduction of his mouth and hands.

Caitlin quivered, moving restlessly as sensations bombarded her. His hair-roughened legs slid along the length of hers, the weight of his pelvis pressed into hers, while his delicate-rough fingers kneaded her breasts beneath the thin gown. The silky texture of his hair tickled across her face as he slanted his hungry lips over hers.

She was lost.

With complete abandon, she gave herself over to his sensual demands, exulting in his male strength. With his hands, lips and body he made love to her, arousing her needs one by one and then fulfilling them—totally.

Her body sizzled with fire, a fire of his making, one only he could extinguish. Slowly, tenderly, he joined his body with hers, and the fire burned brighter, out of control, consuming them both, exploding, leaving them bathed in a warm afterglow.

"I didn't intend for that to happen." Breath coming in soft gasps, he kissed the moist hair at her temples, smoothing it back with delicate fingers.

"Are you sorry?" she asked throatily.

"Never," he breathed against her kiss-swollen lips.

"Oh, Nick, I love you so much," she whispered tremulously.

His body stilled, and he drew slowly away, a curious trembling to his beautiful mouth.

"Nick, what is it?"

He shook his head, eyes lifting to hers. Caitlin caught her breath, hardly able to sustain the look in their extraordinary depths. Hands at either side of her face, he drew her to him and worshipped her with his lips.

He hadn't said the words, but the message in his eyes was enough for her for now.

Tucking her into the curve of his body, he settled her against him. "You're tired. You need to sleep now."

"I don't want to leave you," she protested quickly.

"I wouldn't let you if you tried. I want to sleep tonight knowing you're safe beside me."

Settling them both against the couch, he listened to the reassuring sound of her even breathing and held her close as he lay staring into the night. Little by little he was remembering more and more of his past, but there were still large gaps in his memory. He'd wanted to say the words for her sake, to tell her that he loved her, but he couldn't, not yet. He still didn't know what the future might bring, and he still wasn't sure if he could live with her without knowing exactly who he was and where he was going in this life.

Chapter 14

The next morning Caitlin was introduced to the men who had been working on her behalf for the past few days, though she'd had no idea of the fact. Every time she looked into a pair of cool, polite eyes she tried to equate Nick with these men's quiet, zestful, almost arrogant attitude. It was impossible; Nick wasn't like these men. A new drive and determination were obvious in him, but he also had a warmth, a caring, the others lacked. Matt was the only exception; he, too, had become an intensely involved part of what was happening in her life and with her feelings.

An early-morning scouting expedition by David and Matt had turned up no surveillance teams. For the moment, at least, it appeared they were safe from Carrington and his band of survivalists.

It had been decided that Megan would call home as soon as she reached the library, and again before leaving in the evening. Now that Carrington had shown his hand, her safety was in question, too, but it would have given too much away if she'd stayed home from work.

Finally Caitlin and Nick had their first few moments alone since dawn.

"Will she be all right?" Caitlin asked.

"She'll be fine. We'll keep a close watch on her. Don't worry," he reassured her, touching a gentle hand to her cheek.

"Are you going with them?" she asked, referring to Matt, David and the others.

"Yes, but you'll be safe here. Someone will be close by at all times. I won't let anything happen to you, I promise." His fingers moved to stroke her neck, his thumb rubbing gently across her delicate cheekbones.

"I'm not worried about me. It's you they shot, you they want out of the way." She was unable to say *dead*, but the word loomed darkly in both their minds.

"They've tried three times, and I'm still here. I'm not so easy to get rid of—you'll find that out," he ended softly. Was that a vow she read in his liquid black eyes? she wondered.

"I don't want to get rid of you—ever." Eyes locked, their faces drew closer....

"Oh, sorry." Megan turned hurriedly to step out of the room and walked full tilt into Matt's brawny chest. Caitlin and Nick sprang apart, then grinned at the short woman, her nose almost buried against the big man's shirtfront.

With a red face and a mumbled, "Excuse me," Megan left for work.

Matt watched her diminutive figure hurry out of sight with a slight grin on his rough features before turning back to the couple standing close together, watching him.

"All set?" he asked. "We've got a lot of ground to cover and, if our theory is correct, not much time to do it in."

"Yeah," Nick answered with a quick glance at Matt, "I'm ready. Who's staying with Caity?"

"Tom Spencer. He's a good man. We've worked with him before, and he'll take good care of her."

No one had commented on the fact that Nick hadn't recognized the man, nor any of the others, though several had worked with him in the past. With a long last look at Caitlin, Nick joined the others and left.

Tom Spencer came in, explained that he would keep watch from outside, then left again. Caitlin stood in the middle of the kitchen floor and stared at the chaos the men had left behind.

Grabbing a dishcloth and some spray cleaner, Caitlin set to work. By the time she had the dishes done, Megan had called to let her know she had arrived safely at work.

With the house once more restored to its usual order, Caitlin strolled to Megan's room and looked for a good book, anything that would take her mind off worry about Nick and her present situation. Selecting a mystery with an intriguing cover, she settled on the bed and began to read.

Caitlin awakened slowly, the book she had been reading lying open across her chest. Something had roused her, but she couldn't place what it was. Like a dream she couldn't quite remember, a sound distanced itself in her memory. Wondering whether Tom Spencer had been accidentally locked out and was trying to get in, she climbed from the bed and hurried to the kitchen door.

The door was unlocked, and there was no sign of Tom. Glancing at the clock on the wall beside the stove, she saw with a slight shock that it was late afternoon. She'd slept the day away.

An empty feeling in her stomach reminded her that she hadn't eaten, except for a quick cup of coffee and a slice of toast that morning. Wondering if Tom was hungry, too, she put water on for coffee and went to the door to call him.

When there was no answer, she stepped outside and looked around, a slight uneasiness gripping her. He should have answered. Where could he be? Surely he wouldn't go so far away that he couldn't hear her if she called to him—called for help?

She hurried back inside, stopping long enough to lock the door, then rushed to the telephone on the kitchen wall. She would call Megan at the library and tell *her* about the missing agent, since she had no way to get hold of Nick or Matt.

Lifting the receiver to her ear, she began to dial the familiar number, then realized there was no dial tone. No dial tone! Laying the receiver on the table, she moved the phone back and forth to make certain it had not somehow come loose from its connection. But when she held the receiver to her ear once more, the phone remained dead. It was too much of a coincidence. Everything that had happened the last few days, Tom being missing, and now a dead phone.

What should she do?

A slight sound from the door caused her to turn quickly around. She looked at the door handle. It was turning, first one way and then the other. Someone was out there, and something told her it was definitely not Tom.

What should she do? She didn't have a car, so couldn't get away, and the phone didn't work. But there were a Jeep and a truck and a phone in working order at her own ranch. Was it a crazy idea? Trying to get to her place without whoever was outside catching her? Maybe, but she didn't know what else to do.

The door rattled again, louder this time. She just caught herself from calling out to ask who was there. Maybe they would think she was asleep, or that no one was home. But what if they didn't take the silence as proof of that? What if they came in?

With one last desperate glance at the turning knob, Caitlin hurried to the front door. Opening it with trepidation, she glanced stealthily through a small crack. She couldn't see anyone, but that didn't necessarily mean someone wasn't hiding, waiting for her to bolt from the house.

There was nothing for it; she would have to take the chance and move into view. The sounds from the back door had become louder now. Either the person on the other side of it thought she was asleep, or he didn't care if she heard him.

Caitlin slid through the narrow opening and stood for an instant crouched in front of the house. So far, so good; no one had taken a shot at her, and no one intent on capturing her had moved into view. As she made a mad dash toward an outcropping of rock, she gave one last hurried glance behind her toward the house, then pelted hell for leather down the path that would eventually lead to her own house.

Hiding, she looked down on her farmhouse and outbuildings in the distance. Finally, satisfied that she was alone, she moved into the open, prepared to run for cover at the first sign of trouble.

The first order of business was to try the phone inside. But when she entered the house, she saw from the smashed phone lying on the floor that she was out of luck. Without stopping, Caitlin ran to her room, grabbed her purse with her keys inside and hurried outside to the truck, which was parked where Matt had left it the day before.

The truck wouldn't start. Lifting the hood, she saw at a glance why. Wires had been ripped loose and hung like broken fingers from the engine.

"Damn!" Not even bothering to close the hood, she hurried to the Jeep parked behind the barn, but she pulled up short before she had even reached it. From the way it sat so close to the ground, there was no question it had four flat tires, and all she had was one spare.

What now? No phone and no transportation—wait a minute! The horses! She could saddle one of the horses and ride into town.

In seconds Caitlin stood crooning softly to Flame. Caesar, in the next stall, danced nervously about.

"It's okay, boy, it's okay," she said. "I'll have to leave you here, but you'll be all right. We'll get some help and then I'll see you—"

A prickling sensation began at the back of Caitlin's neck, standing the short hairs on end. Breath suspended, knowing she was no longer alone, she turned slowly to face the intruder.

An imposing figure stood in the shadows, backlit by the glare from the open door, features unrecognizable. A tremor of fear rippled down Caitlin's spine. The figure moved abruptly, and then she recognized him.

"Oh, Bart, it's you." Hand at her breast, she flashed him a smile of relief.

The sun was well on its way down when Nick, every joint and muscle aching, came within sight of the Jones house. So far they had turned up nothing, not a sign of anything that even hinted at irregularity. Carrington employed numerous Mexican workers and Nick was willing to wager that every one of them was a green-card carrying legal. The man was as wily as a fox. Even the setup for the survival games, which David had seen many times, had been dismantled, and every trace of it had disappeared.

The agents all carried two-way radios and searched in pairs. Avoiding Carrington's laborers had not been easy with the coming of darkness. Carrington's men were familiar with the terrain; Nick thought it would be no mean feat to elude detection.

Three times in the last couple hours Nick had tried to reach Tom Spencer by radio, and each attempt had met with failure. There were logical reasons why Tom might not have received one, or possibly two, of the signals, but not all three. Both Nick and Matt began to feel alarmed, especially after they compared notes and realized that in their desire to bring things to a head as quickly as possible, they had neglected to tell Caitlin the identity of Carrington's partner. And when, shortly after the fourth attempt to contact Tom failed and the agent assigned to keep Carrington's partner under surveillance called and said he'd lost him, that was all Nick needed to be on his way to Caitlin.

Leaving Matt to control things in the field, Nick headed swiftly to the Jones ranch. He couldn't rest easy until he knew for a fact she was safe.

As he approached the house, a feeling of unease increased with each step. Spencer should have acknowledged his presence by now. Moving cautiously, he skirted the house, looking for evidence of forced entry. It was there. The back door hung loose from its hinges, shattered by repeated heavy blows.

Drawing the gun Matt had given him, his heart in his mouth, fear tying his gut in knots, he began a systematic search of the house.

He checked under beds and inside closets, behind furniture, any place he could think of where a person might hide—or hide a body. And as each place turned up empty, the hand squeezing his heart in his chest squeezed a little harder. A cold sweat broke out over his body, sticking the shirt to his broad shoulders and making the .357 Magnum slide against his palm.

Leaving the vacant house, he began an equally systematic investigation of every hollow and thicket, starting close to the house and working his way out in an ever-widening circle. All the while panic grew as his mind flashed pictures of Caitlin in captivity—or worse—freezing his heart, turning the blood to ice in his veins.

Nick found Spencer about two hundred yards from the back of the house, at the bottom of a steep ravine. He had been hastily buried in a shallow grave.

"Damn!" On his knees, he pawed the dead leaves and twigs aside, cursing under his breath at the shattered side of the man's head.

"Damn!" he repeated. "Damn you, Carrington—damn you
to hell. What have you done with Caity? I'll find her," he
promised, lifting the slighter man's lifeless body in his arms and
vowing, "If you've hurt a hair on her head, I'll send you to hell
where you belong."

Caitlin sat, as she had so many times in the past, at her own
kitchen table across from the sheriff, each holding a cup of
coffee. Only this time it was different. Her eyes slid toward the
pistol held loosely in his right hand, the barrel pointed at her
chest.

"Why, Bart?"

"For the money, of course." His usual good-ole-boy drawl
was missing.

"You'd shoot me for money?"

Even in the near dark—he wouldn't let her turn on a light—
she saw his glance shift away as she spoke.

"There won't be any need to harm you—if you just relax and
do as I tell you."

"Did you follow me from the house, or have you been waiting here all along?" she asked calmly.

"I followed you. I wasn't sure you were in the house, but
after I took care of your bodyguard," he ignored her startled
gasp, "I had a look. When I found the front door open, I figured you must have headed here."

"You shot Nick, and you're the sniper from yesterday."

"How astute you are, my dear. Your father always said you
were a bright child." He commended her almost proudly.

"You leave my father out of this," she began angrily, thinking of all the times her father had had the man to the ranch.
How he had taken time to campaign for his good friend's elec-
tion. "You're a criminal, a murdering liar and worse. Drugs,
Bart, how could you get mixed up in drugs?"

"That wasn't my idea. The guns were enough. They brought
plenty of money for everybody. Carrington's the one who
added drugs to the pot."

When she made no comment, he referred back to the past.
"I was always straight with your father. My, ah, association
with Carrington didn't begin until just before your father . . . died." Something in his tone made her uneasy, but this
wasn't the time to press the issue, she knew.

"How exactly did your, ah, association," she mocked him, "with Logan begin?"

A strange mixture of guilt and relief prompted him to answer. "Carrington got that little Mexican girl working for his mother pregnant. That was about the same time he asked Megan to marry him. Somehow your father found out about the maid. Now, a lot of men would have shrugged their shoulders and figured Carrington was sowing a few last-minute wild oats, paid the girl off and forgotten it. Bill wasn't one of them."

There was something strange in being held at gunpoint by a man who at the same time spoke admiringly of your father, she thought.

The sheriff went on. "Bill felt responsible for Megan and David, and he took his responsibilities hard. He told Carrington he'd have to break it off with Megan, take care of the Mex girl and the baby." He paused.

"So Logan did—he took care of the little Mexican and her baby." Caitlin gasped at the cold, expressionless statement. "Your father knew about the survivalists, had known since the beginning, and he suspected Carrington had killed her not just because she was pregnant but because she'd found out something he didn't want her to know. He pushed me to find proof—" His words came to an abrupt halt.

"And you did, didn't you?"

"Yeah," he answered after a moment, coming back from wherever he'd gone. "I found proof, all right, and I went to Carrington with it. And he offered me more money than I could ever dream of making in a lifetime—ten lifetimes."

"And you took it." Cold contempt rang in her voice as she glared at him from green eyes, eyes the exact shade of her father's.

"Bill looked at me just like that when he realized what I'd done—"

"Dad knew?" Caitlin broke across his words.

"Yeah, he confronted me with it, the day he had the stroke—"

"Oh God!" Bile rose in her throat. "You killed my father!"

"No! I loved that man as if he were my own flesh and blood—my brother—I'd never have harmed him—"

"But you did. He believed in you, stood behind you, trusted you—and you betrayed him. You murdered him the same as if you put a bullet from that gun you're holding in his brain."

She was only repeating what his subconscious had accused him of since that day almost three years ago when her father had stood, face contorted with anger and contempt, and accused him. But it was Bill's eyes he remembered the clearest, eyes filled with pain and bitter disappointment.

"It's over now. I can't change it. I have to go on with what I started."

They didn't speak again, but sat silently waiting for the cover of darkness.

"Are you the one who tried to kill Nick before I met him?" Caitlin broke the long uncomfortable silence.

"No, Logan did that. I didn't even know the Feds were on to us until after it was all over. Thanks to that damned surviva crap Carrington's father started, the whole operation is ir jeopardy.

"But the Carringtons have contacts in Washington. Hi money greases a whole lot more palms than mine." He sounded as though he were trying to justify his actions to her. "He thought he could take care of the problem without me know ing about it. He bungled the job, of course."

Bart stared through the gloom at her. "It seems, according to Carrington, that Jones got wind of our operation and turned us in. Logan intercepted the agent they sent—your Nick—and tried to drown him, even ran over him with his boat."

Caitlin shuddered, thinking how close Nick had been to death. "How did you fit Nick in with this supposedly d-dead agent?"

"I didn't, not at first—I was just concerned about you having a strange man out here, especially one who wasn't quit right in the head. At first I only came out to check on you— make sure you were okay. I owed your father that."

Caitlin made a disbelieving sound in her throat and glance pointedly at the gun.

"It's true," Bart insisted. "But when I saw him again, really looked at him, something clicked in my brain. I didn't know what it was at the time. I thought maybe I'd seen his face on wanted poster.

"So I made some inquiries and got a veiled warning via friend in Austin to keep out. That only made me more susp cious, and I began to suspect 'Nick' wasn't what he seemed. I decided to keep an eye on you and him and keep delving till I found what I was looking for.

"I should have put two and two together and known he was a Fed, but right about then Carrington's crazies started leaving dead animals as a warning to the general public to stay off his land. And they started playing their war games, scaring some kids on a camp-out into believing men from outer space had landed in their pasture."

He sounded as though he expected her to sympathize with his problems. Shaking his head, sipping at the cold bitter coffee, he continued. "In the meantime, Mabel Henderson got gossiping with Carrington's mother about you and this Nick character, complete with before and after description. It didn't take long for him to become suspicious."

Mabel Henderson, Caitlin thought with angry dismay, you have a lot to answer for.

"Logan called me that same day, and I made a visit to the doctor—"

"Dr. Shepherd!"

"The same. He told me about your interest in amnesia."

"So to make a long story short, you decided to get rid of Nick—and me."

"It isn't like I want to, honey."

"Don't call me that!"

They sat mutely after that, in ever-increasing darkness, until Caitlin asked to light a candle and Bart reluctantly agreed. Then they sat avoiding each other's eyes.

Where are you Nick? she called to him mentally. Surely by now you know I'm missing. Please—please come and find me.

"What happens now?" she finally found the courage to ask.

"I'm getting out. I have plenty of money stashed, so while everyone, including Carrington, is busy tomorrow at the Fourth of July celebration, I'm making my move."

"What about me?"

He made no answer, only stared at her hands, gripping each other tightly on the table.

"What are we doing here?" Caitlin stood on the porch of the stone house, holding a flashlight, the sheriff's gun prodding her in the back.

"You'll see." He ushered her inside, directed her to the stone fireplace and made her sit on the floor beside it.

Kneeling, laying the gun on the floor beside him, well out of her reach, he told her to direct the light into the black gaping mouth of the flue. Pulling with both hands, grunting, he removed a large piece of stone. Inserting a hand, he pulled an object from the opening, then another and another. Three grimy bags lay on the hearth in the glow of the flashlight.

"Money," Caitlin stated dully. "When did you put that in there?" She knew before he answered.

"I was hiding some of it here the day your daddy discovered what I'd done."

"He saw the money—"

"And guessed it was a payoff," Bart confirmed.

It was too much. All of this—Nick—her father—the unhappy years since his death, trying to keep the ranch he had loved from being swallowed up in taxes and mortgages—all for money, this man's greed. Blinding anger choked her. With seething rage she raised the flashlight and brought it down on the sheriff's head. The aim was somewhat deflected by his hat, causing only a glancing blow. But it was enough to knock him off balance and allow her time to lurch to her feet and dive out the door.

Bart was a big man, but the years of police work had made him quick on his feet. He was after her in a flash, his hands narrowly missing the tail of her T-shirt as she fell down the steps.

He was quick, but she was quicker, and she had the advantage of having grown up on the ranch. She knew it better than the back of her hand. Darting around rocks and bushes, under low-hanging branches, bent almost double, she remembered Nick telling her to stay low. What she wouldn't give to have him beside her right now.

After what seemed like hours but was in reality only minutes, she stopped, pressing against the smooth face of a jutting rock. She held her breath against the gasps that threatened to split her body apart, cupping both hands over her mouth to smother the sounds. All she could hear was the thunder of her pulse pounding out of control against her eardrums.

Slowly getting her bearings, Caitlin began to walk quickly, noiselessly, in the direction of the Jones ranch. Unable to keep her pace slow, she gave in to her fear and began to run. In moments her breath was coming in soft gasps as a painful stitch ripped at her right side. The terror in her mind was too real to be ignored.

Glancing back over her shoulder, fearful of seeing a large form in close pursuit, she ran full tilt into an immovable object. Before she could come to her senses, hard hands wound around her, imprisoning her against a solid wall.

Jerking her head, twisting her body, kicking and yelling, she tried to get loose.

"It's all right, Caity, it's all right. You're safe. Easy now...easy...easy..." The deep soothing tones eventually penetrated the barrier of her fear. Hesitantly at first, she relaxed into the comfort offered by his warm embrace. Feeling her acceptance, eyes closed, cheek against her hair, his arms tightened protectively while she sobbed against his chest.

"Caity, Caity, it's all right, sweetheart. I've got you now, and I'll never let you go." Whispering endearments against her wet cheeks and the curve of her neck, hands roving her body frantically in an attempt to reassure himself that she was really there and unharmed, he held her tightly. Eventually her crying lessened until all that remained was a soft intermittent hiccuping sound.

"N-Nick—oh, N-Nick I—w-was—so s-scared—"

"I know, baby, I know. So was I." Hands at either side of her face, he planted soft kisses on forehead, eyes and cheek. "Can you tell me what happened?"

"B-Bart—I couldn't f-find the man—Tom—and then someone tried to get in—the phone wouldn't work—I was so s-scared—"

"Sh-sh-sh, take your time." Smoothing the hair from her damp face, he crushed her suddenly in his arms, holding her bone-crackingly tight, his body trembling against hers. After a moment, his emotions once more under control, he released her and slowly drew away.

"Okay?" he asked softly.

"Y-yes, I'm fine."

"Can you tell me where the sheriff is?"

"The stone house. He'll have gone back for the m-money."

"Is he armed?"

"Y-yes."

"Matt." He turned to the man stepping silently from the shadows. "Take Caity to the house. I'll go after Raymond."

"No!" Caitlin all but shouted. "No, I'm not going to leave you. I can show you the q-quickest way to get there."

Time was of the essence if they wanted to intercept the man before he got away. Against their better judgment, one protectively placed on either side of her, the two men escorted her back the way she'd come.

After all the drama, all the fear, it was pathetically easy. Bart Raymond was sitting on the porch waiting for them, a cigarette in one hand, the flashlight she'd bashed him over the head with lying on the porch beside him.

"I knew you'd bring them here," he told her quietly.

"Why didn't you run?" she couldn't help but ask.

"Run? Where to? I realized the truth while I was chasing you a little while ago. You knew exactly where to run—where to find safety. I have no place to go. And running is all I have left. I'm too old for that kind of life. Fate, Texas, is my home. These are my people.

"I don't belong in some foreign country where I don't speak the language, with people who are strangers." Squashing the cigarette out on the steps, he looked up at Matt. "The money's all there in the house by the fireplace." Eyes on Caitlin he added, "I never spent a penny of it, not even the money your father caught me with. Every penny I ever took from Carrington is in there."

Against her will she felt sympathy for him. Once big and powerful, a man to to be reckoned with, now he looked pathetically small and defeated.

Matt gathered the bags of money, marveling at the irony of the sheriff's hiding his ill-gotten gains in the same place where David had hidden the evidence that had led to his capture. Using the man's own handcuffs, Matt cuffed his wrists together while reciting him his rights by rote. Bart smiled dryly, not bothering to protest the act, though he, too, knew the words by heart. As Matt led him away, Bart stopped to look back over his shoulder at Caitlin.

"I never would have harmed you, Caity. Just like I never would have harmed your daddy. I'd have given every penny of that money back, but by then it was too late. Your daddy was gone, and it didn't matter anymore."

Then the darkness swallowed him.

"I think he really meant that." She sounded astonished. "If Dad hadn't had a stroke that day, maybe none of this would have happened."

"I don't understand." Nick stood close to her, listening with a puzzled frown.

"I'll explain on the way to the house," she told him, taking his big hand warmly into her own.

Chapter 15

The sheriff was sequestered at Caitlin's in the hope that Carrington wouldn't learn of his arrest. Bart had immediately become voluble, telling Matt and Nick everything he knew about Logan's operation. He couldn't, however, tell them when or by what route the shipment of arms and drugs would be arriving the next day. Logan kept such details to himself, telling his men things strictly on a need-to-know basis.

Plans were made and discarded about how to confiscate the arms and drugs and accomplish Logan's ultimate capture without alerting the man or putting any of the townspeople in danger. As the discussion continued, Matt and David came up with a workable plan.

The night was spent in working out the details. Megan and Caitlin kept the men supplied with hot coffee and sandwiches.

Caitlin and Nick had no opportunity for private conversation, but a warm look passed between them each time their eyes met across the room. And just before she went to bed, as she filled the coffee cups one last time, his arm came around her to squeeze her waist as she bent near him.

* * *

The Fourth of July fell on a Saturday, a day that dawned bright and clear, with temperatures in the 90s before the clock struck noon.

Megan and Caitlin, after a long argument with Nick and David about their safety, arrived at the Carrington ranch at one o'clock, just as the festivities were getting under way. Driving between the tall stone pillars marking the entrance to the winding drive, Megan gave Caitlin a narrow look.

"Are you nervous?" she asked. In the beginning, when she had first learned of Logan's criminal activity, she'd been upset. But she'd had years of doubt to prepare herself for the blow, so she had accepted her brother's revelations with equanimity.

"Like a sinner at the gates of heaven," was Caitlin's instant reply.

"Me too. I hope I can pull this off. The idea of pretending to enjoy Logan's company, knowing all I know, makes me feel nauseous." Megan looked pale.

"I know the feeling."

"It's going to come off all right, isn't it?" Megan begged for reassurance. She was thinking more of the men—David, Matt and Nick, along with the other men assisting them—who were in hiding, waiting for the important shipment. The one that would tie Logan unquestioningly to the illegal activities and lead to his suppliers across the border.

Caitlin squeezed her friend's cold fingers where they rested on the seat between them.

"It's going to be fine. We've got three great guys orchestrating this thing. They're three winners, Meg—I know it."

Megan nodded, maneuvering the car toward the roped-off field to one side of the huge house. The field at the other side was already swarming with people enjoying the many delights offered by the carnival. The aroma of cotton candy, fresh hot popcorn and corn dogs assaulted their noses.

"Do you see Logan?" Caitlin asked, peering through the crowds.

"Not yet, but there's his mother—oh no, look who she has in tow. Mabel Henderson."

"Come on." Grabbing Megan's arm, Caitlin sidestepped into a tent promising "A Sight to Rival the Seven Wonders of the World."

By three o'clock neither of them had caught a glimpse of Logan, even though they had split up for a while and gone in opposite directions, then met later in front of the fortune teller's tent.

As the day wore on, they finally gave in to nature's needs and sought out a tent offering food and drink and a place to rest their aching feet. That was where *Logan* found *them*.

"So, my eyes don't deceive me. Here, seated before me, are the two most beautiful women in town," a deep baritone said from behind them.

Megan turned slowly. "Logan." The sight of his masculine blond beauty would never fail to stir a woman's senses, even one who knew him for the evil creature he really was. "I was beginning to think you had invited me and then decided not to attend yourself," she teased.

Squeezing onto the bench next to her, his hard muscular thigh pressing hers, he smiled dazzlingly down into her eyes.

"It's taken me too long to get you here for me to pass up the opportunity of spending every minute I can in your charming company." Teal blue eyes devoured her face.

Caitlin moved her hand under cover of the table to touch Megan's thigh, a signal that she was about to leave.

"Oh, look, there's Shay." Caitlin glanced up and spotted the woman coming through the tent's opening. "I'll see you later, Meg, Logan."

Caitlin caught Shay at the entrance and pulled her back outside.

"What's going on? I'm starving," Shay said, resisting Caitlin's tugging.

"So am I, but it's too crowded in there. Let's get some lemonade and a corn dog," she suggested. Caitlin had no idea where she would put more food, since she was already stuffed with hamburgers and chili.

They parted company after a while, and Caitlin was finally able to slip away to use the two-way radio in her purse. Following the instructions Matt had carefully given her, she managed to contact him where he waited close by.

"Matt? He's here. We've been looking for him since we arrived, but we couldn't find him. Then he found us. Meg is with him now. She'll stick like glue till I signal her otherwise."

"Right, good work, Caity."

"Caity." Another voice, one she recognized instantly with a little thrill, came over the radio.

"I'm here, Nick."

"Did he say anything odd to you, or seem surprised to see you? Did he mention the sheriff?"

"No, no he didn't. He only had eyes for Meg," she answered honestly.

"Well, keep away from him and stay within plain sight of several people at all times," he cautioned earnestly. "And remember, I'm close by."

"I'll remember," she answered softly.

The evening dragged after that. Caitlin spent it talking with several acquaintances she hadn't seen since the last Fourth of July celebration and in dodging the Henderson menace.

Just before dark, with the barbecue in full swing and Logan acting as master of ceremonies with Megan at his side, Caitlin slipped away unobserved in the dark.

In the shadows at the edge of the crowd, Matt and Nick stood in a prearranged spot, waiting for her. Nick wanted a look at the man who had tried to kill him. He still wasn't sure whether he wanted the man's face to jog his memory or not. A whole lot of questions would be answered, but the answers no longer held much importance for him.

Working their way through the throng of people, careful to keep out of Logan's sight, Caitlin led Nick to within a few yards of the man. Matt had remained behind to keep in touch with David.

"That's him—do you recognize him?" Caitlin pointed out Logan Carrington, an underlying note of nervous dread in her voice. She wanted him to remember—didn't she?

Nick heard her anxiety and couldn't help responding to it with an equal amount of apprehension. It was a moment before he could bring himself to look in the direction she indicated.

Nick stared at the tall blond Adonis smiling and shaking hands like a politician. The man certainly didn't look the part of a cold-blooded killer. Dredging the forbidden dream from the far reaches of his memory, he tried to equate the blurred, terrifying images with the aristocratic man standing before him.

He wanted to remember—he strained to remember. He reached into the far depths of his mind and drew forth every bit of detail, every sound, every sensation, from that night in an attempt at discovering something, anything, that would forge the link between past and present.

Caitlin, standing with bated breath at his side, felt him tremble beneath the hand she laid on his arm. She wanted to look at his face, wanted to see for herself if his memory had returned with his first look at the flesh and blood figure of Logan Carrington. But she couldn't—she was afraid of what she would find written there.

Nick continued to watch the man standing before him with an arm wrapped around Megan Jones. It was no use; the face was no more familiar to him now than when it had stared back at him from the picture he'd found in Jones's darkroom.

He wanted desperately to be able to turn to the woman at his side and tell her with a clear conscience that, yes, he recognized the man—his would-be killer. But in all honesty he couldn't.

He could feel her tension in the slight hand gripping his arm, the breathless waiting quality in the air around them. What would she say if he told her the truth? Told her that part of his past, the personal, intimate details of who he was, continued to be a mystery? Could she accept him as he was? Or would she feel, as he did, that he was only half a man? What would that mean to their relationship?

Was the memory of his past as important as the time he'd spent with Caitlin? Could he live from day to day, waiting, wondering if there was something in his past he *shouldn't* remember, something that would keep them apart if he did? He couldn't imagine any such thing, but the uncertainty was there—would it always be?

God! What should he do? Tell her the truth? Or lie?

Caitlin moved her cold fingers against the muscle bunched beneath her hand. What would his answer mean to her? Could she accept it if he told her that his past was still a dark and murky blur? Could she live with the unsettled question of his amnesia? Would she one day awaken to find herself tied to a man she didn't recognize? One who couldn't remember her? Was the return of his memory even now putting distance between them?

"Yes," he answered suddenly, making his choice, though whether it was good or bad, only the future would tell. "Yes, that's the man. I remember . . . everything."

Caitlin gasped softly at his side, dropped her hand from his arm and drew slightly away. "Y-you do? It's come back? All of it?"

"All of it." There would be legal bumps; he couldn't stand up in a court of law and point the finger of guilt at Logan Carrington, but those were hurdles he and Matt could handle.

"Nick! That's wonderful—isn't it?" She sounded happy for him, but also confused at his lack of emotion. Why wasn't he more excited? Why wouldn't he look at her? Had he already discovered, along with his memory, that now she wouldn't fit into his life? How could there be room in the life of a man like him—Andrew Rivers, special agent with the FBI—for an unsophisticated, small-town rancher like herself?

"Yes." He wished he could put some real enthusiasm into the word. "It's great," he answered coldly. Already the lie, along with the others he'd told her, ate at him. He wanted there to be no more lies between them, and yet he'd just told her the biggest lie of all.

"Nick?" she asked again. "What's wrong? Can't we discuss it?"

"There's no time. I have a job to do. We'll discuss it later." He would have to tell her the truth, he realized suddenly; he couldn't go on lying to her. Because after all the doubts had been taken out and thoroughly examined, one fact remained: he loved her. He couldn't tell her now—or maybe ever—but it was true, and he wanted there to be nothing but the truth between them.

But until the job here was finished there could be no question of telling her how he felt. Whether it was the *real* truth or not, what was between them had to wait. And besides, who knew? before the night was over, the question of his memory might be academic anyway. He might be dead.

Darkness had fallen. The sounds of the carnival had died down, and people were getting ready for the fireworks display. Adults spread blankets on the ground and called to their children. The carnies were closing down for the night, preparing to enjoy the show that was about to begin.

A hand descended heavily on Nick's shoulder, causing him to jerk swiftly around,.

"It's time," Matt stated quietly.

Nick nodded without comment and touched Caitlin reassuringly on the arm. Then he and Matt drifted back, melting into the darkness. Caitlin looked for a child, a young boy, to deliver a message and instead found her path blocked by Mabel Henderson.

"Well, well, I thought that was you I saw earlier, but just when I thought to come over and have a nice little chat, you disappeared." The tiny woman crouched unmoving in Caitlin's way.

"Excuse me, Miz Henderson, I—"

"Now don't run off, dearie. We're due for a chat. I want to hear all about that handsome mystery man you got stayin' at your place and how he come to be shot—"

The woman's beady little eyes and beaklike nose were beginning to make her look like a vulture to Caitlin's anxious eyes. "Miz Henderson, really, I haven't got the time—"

"Nonsense. Who's that blond giant I just saw you with?"

Alarm coursed through Caitlin; if this woman got any louder... They were already drawing attention.

"I don't know." She cut quickly across the woman's incessant chatter, surprising herself as well as the hovering woman with her next words. "He said he was looking for Logan—he had an urgent message for him. Something to do with business that couldn't wait."

"My, my." Close-set eyes snapping, she listened avidly, then retorted, "That poor boy, always working. Never any rest—like I was telling his poor mama this mornin'. The boy's going to kill hisself, just like his daddy did, poor man. Never any rest. Why, the boy's been packin' all day long. Gettin' ready for a big trip to Europe. Something to do with one of his companies over there."

The piping voice went on and on, but Caitlin had stopped listening. Logan was getting ready to run, and unless they caught him tonight, he would get away scot-free to peddle his filthy brand of business elsewhere.

"If you'll excuse me, Miz Henderson, I need to deliver that message." Her eyes scanned the crowd.

"No need. I'll be happy to deliver it for you, dearie. I got to give him a message from his mama, anyway."

It would have to do, Caitlin decided; time was a-wasting. She told the woman what to say, then watched her mince away before turning to blend back into the crowd.

* * *

"It's nearly over." Nick found her half an hour later in the darkness. "They've got the goods."

"David?"

"He's fine. They didn't have to fire a shot. All we have to do now is get Carrington and it's in the bag."

"Where's Matt?" she asked nervously.

"He wanted to keep a closer eye on the man." Sensing her disquiet, he asked, "What's wrong?"

"I—nothing. Mabel Henderson said Logan has been packing all day."

"And what else did that old busybody tell you, Caity?" Logan asked smoothly from behind.

She froze, a tremor of fear sliding down her spine. Nick reached toward the bulge beneath his shirt at his waist.

"No, I don't think so, Mr. Rivers," Logan said dangerously, nudging him with a muzzle of a gun. "Turn around, both of you." His arm around Megan's neck, he held a small snub-nosed pistol to her head.

"Meg! Are you okay?" Caitlin took an involuntary step forward. Logan pushed Megan away and grabbed Caitlin, twisting her arm behind her back.

Caitlin moaned and fell against the man, her eyes jerking to Nick. He caught Megan to keep her from falling and cursed beneath his breath when he saw that Logan had Caitlin, and pain was darkening her eyes.

The bastard could shoot him, but he couldn't stand by and allow Logan to hurt her. He might end up with a bullet, or in hell, but he'd take that son of a bitch with him.

"Nick, no!" Caitlin read the intent in his eyes.

"Stay where you are!" Logan jerked Caitlin's arm an inch higher, and she bit her lip in pain, afraid to cry out in case it incited Nick to do something crazy. "The four of us are going to take a little ride. You'll drive, Rivers, but first, remove the gun in your belt and drop it on the ground."

"It isn't going to work, Carrington." Nick stalled for time, wondering where Matt had gotten to. "You'll never make it."

"That's your considered opinion, is it?" Logan laughed contemptuously. "It was easy enough to dispose of you once, though I'll be the first to admit I didn't do a thorough job of it. This time there won't be any resurrection, I can assure you. Now quit stalling and drop the gun. Now!" He jammed the barrel hard against Caitlin's temple, forcing her to smother a whimper of pain.

Swearing softly beneath his breath, Nick did as he was told, his gaze a threat in itself, never leaving the face of the other man.

"All right, around back." Logan nodded toward the drive that wound around to the back of the house. They moved like zombies, stiff and unnatural, Nick leading the way, with an arm around Megan's shaking shoulders.

On the drive behind the house, a silver Mercedes sedan awaited them. Logan directed Megan into the passenger seat and Nick toward the driver's side.

Matt sprang suddenly from out of nowhere, but Logan was quick. Jerking Caitlin even closer, he whirled out of the man's reach.

"You'll have to do better than that," he told Matt with a sneer of contempt. "I wondered when you'd join us, but you're a bit late—we're nearly finished here. Just a small matter of a trip down the road to meet a man with some money for me and I'll be gone."

"I'm afraid you're going to be disappointed, Carrington. The man with your money is on his way to jail about now." Matt spoke in a conversational voice while cautiously inching his way to the right.

He was hoping to draw Logan's attention so completely that Nick would be able to jump him. It was a ploy they'd used many times in the past. With Matt being the bigger of the two, most people expected him to do the strong-arming, but it was usually the other way around.

Knowing better than to even glance in Nick's direction for fear of giving the game away, Matt prayed that somewhere a spark of memory would ignite Nick to action.

He didn't have long to wait. Before the thought had left Matt's mind, Nick moved. Grabbing Carrington's gun hand, he jerked it upward at the same time that he swept Caitlin aside and wrapped his other arm around the man's throat. The gun discharged toward the sky simultaneously with a loud burst of rockets from the fireworks display being enjoyed by the crowd.

The two men struggled for possession of the gun, with Logan trying to wrench it from Nick's grasp. Nick bent Logan's wrist back as far as he could, at the same time sidestepping the man's flailing feet.

The gun dropped to the ground from out of Logan's numbed hand, and Matt dived for it. Then Logan and Nick fell to the ground, Logan on top. They continued to struggle, throwing wild punches.

Megan and Caitlin held each other on the edge of the action, cringing every time a punch connected. The sound of fists hitting flesh and bone made them both feel ill.

"Matt, please, can't you stop them?" Caitlin pleaded as one particularly nasty punch landed against the side of Nick's head and slammed it back onto the concrete drive. But Matt realized what Caitlin couldn't: Nick needed this physical release for all the pain the man he fought had brought him.

Nick shook his head in a dazed fashion, narrowed his eyes on the sadistic smile of the man above him and threw a punch that snapped Logan's head back. Almost in slow motion, Logan was lifted by the force of the blow and thrown back to land, spread-eagled on the ground at Matt's feet.

"Good punch." Matt grinned as he looked down admiringly at the unconscious face of Logan Carrington.

Caitlin was on her knees beside Nick, wiping at the blood on his face, while Matt called for assistance on his radio and Megan helped him handcuff Logan.

"Are you hurt?" Caitlin asked anxiously, her eyes roaming his bruised and battered face.

"Hell no." Nick grinned, wiped a smear of blood from his mouth and pulled her into his arms.

Surprised, Caitlin relaxed against him, her cheek against the reassuringly steady beat of his heart. It was finally over. The nightmare that had begun three years ago with the death of her father was over.

Logan and his cohorts had been taken away. The people of Fate continued with their Fourth of July celebration, in ignorance for a while longer of the evil that had touched their lives. Megan and Matt had joined David at the Jones ranch, while Caitlin and Nick had returned to her house.

"Nick?" Caitlin knocked on his bedroom door. "May I come in?"

The door swung open, and a shirtless Nick stood confronting her, a washcloth held to a particularly bad bruise on his right cheekbone.

"You look like you've been in a fight," she commented dryly, moving into the room and following him to the bed, where he sat down, still holding the cloth against his face.

Grinning around the washcloth, he eyed the bundle of supplies in her hand, recognizing them from his trip to the doctor's office not so long ago.

"How's your shoulder? Did you do any damage to it during the fight?" She was being so matter-of-fact that she surprised even herself. What she really wanted to do was to fall on his neck, tell him that she loved him and that she wanted to spend the rest of her life with him.

"It's a bit stiff," he answered, flexing the muscle, "but I'll live." God, she looked so good. She must have taken a quick shower when they returned. She smelled like the woods just after a rain. Her hair was piled on the top of her head, curling around her face and neck the way he liked it. What he wanted to do was lie back on the bed, pull her into his arms and stay there for a long, long time.

"Are you just going to sit there holding that cloth to your face, or are you going to let me put some of this antiseptic on your cuts and bruises?" Why did he keep looking at her like that? Like the cat who'd swallowed the canary?

Laying the offending washcloth on the bedside table, he lifted his face toward her hand. At the first stinging touch of the medication, he drew his breath in sharply and pulled away.

"I think you like doing that," he accused, dark eyes on her flushed cheeks. "Every chance you get, you paint me up with some bad-smelling, fire-stinging ointment."

Unaccountably hurt by his words, Caitlin turned swiftly away before he could see the rush of tears to her eyes. "I'll just leave you to do it yourself, then—what are you doing?"

Nick had sprung from the bed, crossed the floor to the door, slammed it shut and locked it, and now stood leaning back against it with his arms crossed over his deep chest.

"I'm not letting you run away again, that's what I'm doing. We have a few things to get straight between us, and I don't want you to run off before we do."

What had come over the man? Certainly she had come to expect him to act more forcefully since his memory had begun to come back, but this was an altogether different Nick from the one she was used to. A small dart of pain pierced her heart.

His memory had returned tonight, and already he was changing, becoming a person she didn't recognize.

"I have something important to tell you, Caitlin. Something I hope will make you as happy as it's made me. I have my memory back." He practically beamed at her.

"Of course you have. You told me earlier."

Nick moved forward, grasping her shoulders with unsteady hands, and shook her slightly. "No," he bellowed. "I mean, it's *really* come back. When Carrington slammed my head against the concrete, suddenly I was in the water and he was hitting me across the head and shoulders with an oar—and—" He shrugged. "It was just there—my memory was suddenly just there."

"You mean you'd lied to me earlier?" There was no answering joy on her face. "You'd lied to me again?" she asked stiffly, drawing away from his hands.

She was supposed to be joyous, not angry. She was supposed to smile at him and snuggle into his arms, not frown and pull away as though his touch repelled her.

"I—I don't know what to say. I lied to you—yes. But I didn't know what else to do. I wanted to tell you the truth, but I was afraid," he admitted.

"Let me out of this room, please," Caitlin said stonily. He'd lied once too often; she couldn't forgive him so easily this time. Her own fears and worries about his memory were forgotten in her hurt and anger. She was being unfair to him, but she couldn't see it through her pain.

"Caity, please, you have to understand. I felt like half a man, floundering around with no clear knowledge of who I was—where I was from—whether I liked baked potatoes or French fries. I know that sounds dumb, but you don't know what it's like to be lost—so lost you can't find yourself—so lost you don't know your mother and father's names, or if you even have a mother and father like everyone else."

Caitlin stood with her back to him, facing the door. He'd moved out of her way as she shouldered past, determined to leave the room—and him.

He was right; she didn't know what it would be like, and she wouldn't like to find out.

"I love you, Caity."

Her fingers froze on the doorknob. The words—he'd said the words!

Like someone in a trance, she turned toward him, her eyes going immediately to his. Yes, the glow, that special glow, was there. She'd seen it in his eyes before, and she'd wanted to hear the words on his lips then.

"I love you, Caity," he repeated, his hands cupping her face gently. "I love you," he breathed against her waiting lips.

Without hesitation, Caitlin opened her lips to him, tasted him, melted into him. The question of his lies could be settled later, along with all the other mundane problems they would have to face. At that moment all she wanted was to feel him, completely whole, mind and body, in her arms.

Bending, he lifted her unresisting body into his strong arms. "I love you, too," she breathed against his neck as he laid her on the bed.

Caitlin stood looking at the Christmas tree decorated with red satin balls and green plaid ribbons. Packages were piled beneath it in colorful disarray. It was a beautiful tree, all the more so because it was the first she and Nick had decorated together as man and wife.

So many changes had taken place in the past six months. A new sheriff had been appointed to take Bart's place, a young man with a family who had been on a large city police force before coming to Fate. He and his wife and child fit well into the small town and were already well-liked. He'd asked Nick to be a deputy, and Nick was thinking it over.

Madeleine Carrington, as much a victim of her son's dishonesty as the town, had sold the big mansion and moved to California to live with a widowed sister.

Shay had been shocked to learn of Bart's part in Logan's schemes, but she hid her feelings and, shrugging her shoulders philosophically, went on with her life. Life was too short, she told Caitlin, to mourn things you couldn't change.

The most noticeable change was in David. He hadn't become gregarious, by any means, but there was a crack in his shell. Megan hoped he would continue with his photography, something he appeared to enjoy, and which he was good at.

They were coming over for Christmas dinner later that afternoon, in fact. And Megan? Well, she always looked for the bright side and the good in most people. She would forget her part in Logan's insanity and go on with her life.

The town was finally recuperating from its shock; people were beginning to talk about it after months of almost compulsive silence. Even Mrs. Henderson, who had been conspicuously absent, was once more making her rounds, finding the new sheriff and his family food for many a long gossip.

Logan and Bart were awaiting trial in a federal court in Austin. Bart was going to turn State's evidence, but with the murder of the agent Tom Spencer, that would more than likely bring him a life sentence, at best. Logan would also be tried for murder, as well as several counts of smuggling and the sale of illegal arms and substances.

Old Fred Taylor had even discovered what had happened to his missing cows. They had found a way to get onto the adjoining property and mixed in with with his neighbor's larger herd.

Caitlin and Nick had been married in September in a small church ceremony attended by Megan and David, Shay and Matt. Caitlin was officially Mrs. Andrew Jonathon Rivers, but she still called her husband Nick. Matt had gone back to Washington, promising to visit whenever he could.

"M-m-m, something smells good." Nick, coming up silently behind her, buried his face in her neck and sniffed appreciatively.

"Me or the turkey?" Caitlin laughed, shivering at the touch of his warm mouth on her cool skin.

In the months since their marriage, his touch had never failed to set her senses aflame. Turning around in his arms, sliding her hands up his chest, she laid a kiss at the open collar of his shirt.

"How long before dinner?" he asked, swallowing tightly as she nuzzled the springy hair on his chest. Kisses from Caitlin were more precious than anything he could name.

She slid one hand beneath the waistband of his jeans, and he caught his breath sharply. His hands, which had been still until now, caressed her back and waist, cupped her bottom and drew her hard against the cradle of his hips and the results of her questing hand.

"How long did you say it was till dinner?" he asked again.

"A couple of hours, but—oh . . ." she moaned as he kissed the side of her neck, caressing it with his lips. "Megan and David are coming . . . over . . . soon. . . ."

Slipping his hands up her hips and under her sweater, he rubbed his palms against her breasts, feeling them swell against his hands.

Drawing her down onto the rug before the hearth, he quickly slipped her sweater over her head.

"Nick! We can't—" Speaking from the woolen folds, Caitlin tried to make herself heard while pulling the sweater back down. "Nick, stop it." She batted at his hands as he tried once more to pull the fluffy garment over her head. "Megan and David will be here soon."

"How soon?"

"Half an hour or so—what are you doing?"

"That's time enough to give you my Christmas present." He laid her back against the rug, minus her sweater, and grinned down at her. "And collect mine from you."

Caitlin smiled up into his wicked black eyes and began to pull his shirt from his pants. Everything else could wait—everything but Nick.

* * * * *

Silhouette Sensation

COMING NEXT MONTH

TRAVELLING MAN
Elizabeth Lowell

For as long as Shelley Wilde could remember, she had wanted a home of her own, a place where she was understood, where she was safe. Now she had what she'd wanted and she didn't want to lose it.

On the other hand Cain Remington was a travelling man. His work took him all over the world. He had learned that home was a state of mind, not a place. Could he persuade Shelley?

IMAGINE
Anne McAllister

He was a dream come true. She'd picked him out of a hundred other men. Jack Neillands was Frances's perfect man. Inch-for-masculine-inch Jack embodied her fantasy lover.

More than that, Jack was clearly interested in turning fantasy into reality! In fact, he really couldn't take a firm 'No' for an answer — he even made being 'just friends' a dangerous proposition.

Silhouette Sensation

COMING NEXT MONTH

THE VOW
Dallas Schulze

Brittany was alone, frightened and pregnant. Dan's death had shattered her dreams: her parents offered no support. There was only Michael Sinclair, so kind and so strong, who wanted to take care of her and the baby. How could she *not* accept his offer of a marriage?

Michael first appeared in *Donovan's Promise*, his parents' story, but now he's very much an adult and we were all glad to see him have a romance of his own. Donovan was a big hit with you all; like father, like son?

CODE OF SILENCE
Linda Randall Wisdom

Anne had been running from the law for three years; she'd changed her name, her looks and her address whenever anyone came too close. Then she and her daughter found a small town in Montana they liked. A quiet, friendly town.

Nikki made friends and Anne made a home for them both. But Sheriff Travis Hunter made his interest in them clear and, if there was one thing Anne didn't need, it was the local lawman taking an interest ...

TAKE 4 NEW SILHOUETTE SENSATIONS FREE!

Silhouette Sensation is a thrilling Silhouette series for th woman of today. Each tale is a full 256 pages long - a beautifu blend of sensitivity and sensuality. When you've enjoyed your FREE Sensations there's an extra treat in store!

You could go on to enjoy four more exciting new Sensations, delivered to your door each month - at just £1.65 each (we pay postage and packing). Plus a FREE newsletter and lots more!

No strings attached - you ca stop receiving books at any time.

EXTRA FREE GIFT
If you reply within 10 days

Post the coupon NOW and we'll send you this cuddly teddy plus a surprise mystery gift!

FREE BOOKS CERTIFICATE

To: Silhouette Reader Service, FREEPOST,
PO Box 236, Croydon, Surrey CR9 9EL.

NO STAMP NEED

Please send me, free and without obligation, four specially selected Silhouette Sensations, together with my FREE cuddly teddy and mystery gift - and reserve a Reader Service Subscription for me. If I decide to subscribe I shall receive 4 new Silhouette Sensation titles every month for £6.60 post and packing free. If I decide not to subscribe, shall write to you within 10 days. The free books and gifts are mine to keep in any case. I understand that I may cancel or suspend my subscription at any time simply by writing to you. I am over 18 years of age. *Please write in BLOCK CAPITA*

Mrs/Miss/Ms/Mr _____ EP08

Address _____

_____

_____ Postcode _____

Signature _____

The right is reserved to refuse an application and change the terms of this offer. Offer expires December 31st 1991. Readers in Southern Africa please write to P.O. Box 2125, Randburg, South Africa. Other Overseas and Eire, send for details. You may be mailed with other offers from Mills & Boon and other reputable companies as a result of this application. If you would prefer not to share in this opportunity, please tick box. ☐

mps
MAILING
PREFERENCE
SERVICE